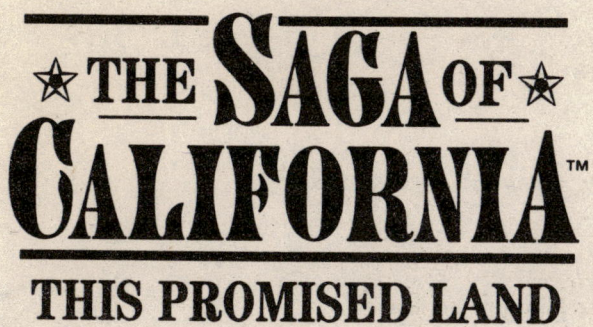

THIS PROMISED LAND

Robert Easton

LEISURE BOOKS   **NEW YORK CITY**

A LEISURE BOOK®

May 1996

Published by special arrangement with Golden West
Literary Agency.

Dorchester Publishing Co., Inc.
276 Fifth Avenue
New York, NY 10001

If you purchased this book without a cover you should be aware that this book is stolen property. It was reported as "unsold and destroyed" to the publisher and neither the author nor the publisher has received any payment for this "stripped book."

Copyright © 1982 by Robert Easton

All rights reserved. No part of this book may be reproduced or transmitted in any form or by any electronic or mechanical means, including photocopying, recording or by any information storage and retrieval system, without the written permission of the Publisher, except where permitted by law.

The name "Leisure Books" and the stylized "L" with design are trademarks of Dorchester Publishing Co., Inc.

Printed in the United States of America.

*To those who came first to this promised land
and also for
Louise and Jack, Travis and Dick and, once more,
for Jane.*

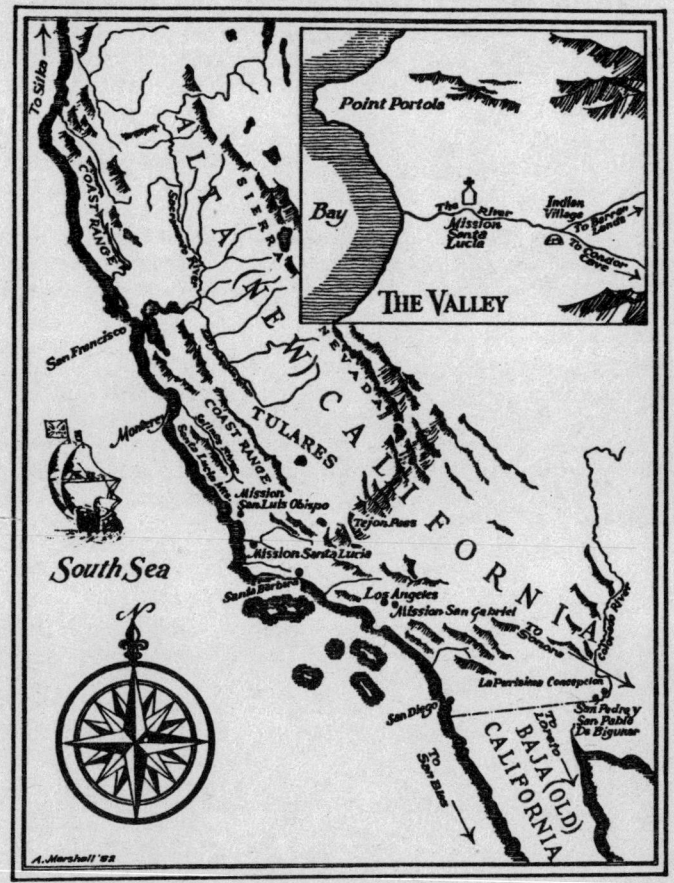

Prologue:
LOSPE AND ANTONIO

They represented the collision of two very different cultures. Their love was a spark thrown off at the moment of impact.

Lospe's people were there first. No one knows where they came from, how they reached that fabled coast where Antonio found them. Probably they were descended from a band of Asiatic nomads who entered North America over a land bridge connecting the two continents at Bering Strait.

Following an ice-free corridor along the Mackenzie River, these first Americans moved southward into our Midwestern plains where they scattered in many directions. One group gradually made its way westward until it reached that stretch of California shoreline lying between present day Malibu at the northern outskirts of Los Angeles and Morro Bay some two hundred miles farther north. And when one tribelet of this migrating group of hunters and gatherers came to a gracious v-shaped valley which no human eyes had seen before, descending from brush-covered pine-crested mountains through rolling grassy hills to the sea, its leaders decided to settle.

Antonio had much the same feeling they must have had when he first saw the valley some thousands of years later. Here was evidence of that tacit understanding between land and man existing perhaps since human life first appeared upon earth. Here was a good place to live.

Exactly what Lospe's ancestors called their place we do not know. But their descendants or successors, perhaps deriving the word from earlier tradition, called it "Olomosoug" meaning the place of new beginnings.

Our certain knowledge of it begins with Lospe herself. She was born in a village at the head of the valley in 1760 and was still living at the site alert in mind and body, mistress of a spacious hacienda and eleven leagues of land, when starry-eyed young Father Michael O'Hara, sole occupant and custodian of crumbling Mission Santa Lucia, interviewed her nearly a century later and made extensive notes of their conversations. He found her language and perception remarkable.

As a baptized Christian, Lospe had the double vision of an experience extending from the Stone Age almost into our own time, and the intellect to encompass it. Similarly moving from an old world into a new, her lover Antonio, an educated Spaniard, was born in a small town in Catalonia on the slopes of the Pyrenees not far from Barcelona, and came to California with the first overland expedition under Gaspar de Portola y de Rovira. Antonio, later known as the blond ranchero, wrote an unfinished memoir of his experiences which provides the basis for much of this book.

As for the legendary Father Rubio whose diary was recently discovered hidden, perhaps deliberately, in the centuries-old archive at Mission Santa Lucia, gentle Rubio was a native of the island of Majorca, a boyhood friend of the renowned Father Junipero Serra, whose steps he followed to the New World and up the coast to New California. Rubio's dictionary of the native language shows it to have been remarkably direct and to the point, not unlike our own, yet capable of extraordinarily sophisticated shades of meaning.

I have translated freely from the original documents in hopes of capturing spirit as well as substance and making my narrative easily understandable to modern readers, interpolating comments and adding footnotes where they seemed helpful.

In this fashion we come to a day in September 1769.

I
First Contacts

Chapter One

Lospe woke feeling it was going to be the most important day of her life. Yet it began in the usual way. She and her cousin Kachuku rose with other members of the household from their sleeping mats before sunrise and went down to the river to bathe. Squealing with excitement they plunged into the cool water that ran from the side of Iwihinmu, the sacred mountain, far away eastward at the center of their world. The river represented the Stream of Life. Immersing themselves in it, they felt one with the forces that flow through the universe and find form in all created things.

Upstream beyond a bend, screened by willows and tall cottonwoods, boys and men were doing likewise and their shouts floated down to Lospe and Kachuku. With customary openness regarding such matters, the girls joked about how cold the exposed genitals of the males must feel in that chilly water.

They were just nine years old. Koyo, Lospe's mother, and Lehlele, her aunt, Kachuku's mother, bathed with them freely in the first light of Sacred Sun, which was rising over the dark peak at the valley's head. Coming from the other world of supernatural power, it added to the momentous feeling of anticipation which stirred in them all.

"Do the A-alowow have children with them, I wonder?" Kachuku whispered, continuing a conversation begun when the two had gotten up.

Lospe shook her head. "Didn't you hear, stupid? They don't even have any women!"

Approaching along the coast from the south the A-alowow, the White Ones, had camped near the mouth of the valley where the river entered the sea. Although none of the People of the Place Called Olomosoug had ever seen a white person, they had heard much about them. Far to the south and east they lived in large towns and rode upon the backs of four-legged beasts as large as elk. They carried magic sticks which emitted fire and killed at great distance. From time to time they sailed past the mouth of the valley in enormous canoes with huge white wings. Seafaring neighbors of the Olomosoug had paddled close enough to see the color of their faces; and there was a legend, often repeated at firesides, that some day the white men would come among them and be their benefactors.

After rubbing their bodies dry with polished sticks, the girls put on their deerskin skirts, consisting of a rather narrow apron in front and a larger back piece extending below the hips, both stained bright red, and started back up the path toward the village. Its cluster of oval-shaped thatched houses lay in shadow at the foot of the steep hillside surmounted by the chalky bluff, where the river emerged from its mountain wilderness. The dwellings were grouped in irregular fashion along three lanes, and near the center was a plaza or ceremonial meeting place. There was a cemetery at the western edge, some of its graves marked with red-painted stones, some with multicolored poles hung with baskets and bowls, if the deceased were female, bows and arrows if male, and on the level land by the river lay the playing field they were walking beside. The boys and young men played shinny, an early form of hockey, there and Lospe played with them when they would let her.

"The A-alowow must have women somewhere or they couldn't be born!" Kachuku insisted.

"Not necessarily. As Grandmother says, if they are Sky People they didn't need to be born!"

"Grandmother doesn't know everything!"

"Daughter, what are you girls discussing so secretly?" Koyo called from behind them.

"I was telling Cousin she hadn't rubbed my back quite dry!" Lospe replied innocently.

"Why not ask her again?" Kachuku whispered. The procession to welcome the strangers was scheduled to begin soon after breakfast. The girls already had asked half a dozen times if they could take part and been put off each time.

"Let's wait till after breakfast. People always feel better after food!" Lospe replied.

A hunting hawk, passing close over their heads made her think she had decided rightly because, as she reflected, a hawk knows

This Promised Land

its own mind, and she knew in her deepest heart she would succeed in her plan.

Their grandmother was crouched by the fire smoldering in a ring of stones of the earthen floor at the center of the house. Because of her great age old Seneq no longer went to the river to bathe. She was tending the large stone bowl that held the porridge, while at the same time moulding cakes of acorn meal and toasting them on a stone slab, making extras to be carried as gifts to the A-alowow; and she was keeping an eye on Kahip, her daughter-in-law, who crouched in the shadows near the wooden bedsteads, too despondent even to try to run away.

Seeing the poor creature Lospe thought again how terrible it was anyone so young and beautiful as Kahip should have to die. But Kahip knew the penalty for her misconduct was death. The fact she was a Tulamni from the Great Valley Beyond the Mountains made no difference, nor did the fact she was married to foolish Uncle Tinaquaic. Custom was custom. Yet the idea of executioners' arrows piercing that young body, not many years older than her own, so emaciated now from anxiety and refusal to eat, was almost more than Lospe could bear. She had never seen an execution, scarcely heard of one, until Koyo explained they were necessary at rare times as a last resort to preserve order in the world and the good will of the Sky People. Lospe knew that as chieftainess her mother must make hard decisions but wished she hadn't made this one.

Kahip looked up hopefully as the girls entered but neither dared show sympathy for her.

"Come and eat!" old Seneq ordered gruffly with the impatience of one who has prepared food that is waiting. "There's much to be done today! Don't dawdle!"

The entire family gathered around the fireplace under the smoke hole. There was Lospe's brother Asuskwa, twelve, as reserved as she was outgoing. There was Kachuku's brother, Alul, thirteen, wordy, boastful. There was Kachuku's father Ta-apu, who'd been a father to Lospe since her own father's death. There was his wife, Lehlele, her mother's beautiful younger sister. And there was her obese and foolish Uncle Tinaquaic.

Ladling porridge into their eating bowls with an abalone shell, Seneq saw each one justly served. While she was engaged in this, two old widows entered by the eastern door each carrying a stick of wood. They were too feeble to forage readily and like other poor and needy often came to the house of their chieftainess for food. Wood was all they could offer in return. "Come, Old Sisters, and be welcome!" Koyo greeted them graciously, and they advanced and placed their sticks on the pile by the fire before taking their places in the family circle. Seneq doled out porridge to them grudgingly, suspecting them of malingering, yet knowing that custom demanded that members of a chieftain's household share their food with the needy. For several moments all ate in silence, enriching their mush with pine nuts or dried grubs or a pinch of honeydew* from bowls that stood handy. The family's pet condor, tall as a small child, waddled out from the shadows, arching its red head in hopes of being fed, and their gray coyote-like dogs with similar hopes whined and wagged their tails.

Lospe was on the point of asking if she and Kachuku could join the procession to greet the A-alowow when the curtain of the western door was thrust aside and Cousin He-ap entered. He wore a red skirt like a woman in contrast to the nakedness of the other men and the two boys. His dark hair was banged in front like a woman's, gathered at the back into a long braid wrapped with a woven leather belt decorated with tiny white sea shells. He-ap was an a-aki, a homosexual prostitute, a skilled dancer and entertainer, admired for his many talents, but little loved, and he was also layer-out of the dead. It was he who would take charge of Kahip's body after her execution. Glancing at her he taunted: "I'm waiting, Kahip!" Using her given name was a greater insult than if he'd actually called her "whore," and he giggled when she lowered her head and made no answer.

Coming to the fire he crouched beside her husband, foolish Tinaquaic, and gave Tinaquaic's bare rump a suggestive slap; then he helped himself to porridge. No one said a word though Lospe quietly despised He-ap for his cruelty to Kahip. Motioning in Kahip's direction, he inquired sarcastically of Koyo: "Why not make a present of her to the A-alowow? Since they haven't any women, they must be starved for it!" He looked around smiling with satisfaction at this witticism. "Yes, indeed! They'd give her a ride she'd never forget! A far better one than a certain person I could name!" And he nudged Tinaquaic who blushed as usual when people turned their attention to him. The other grownups chuckled.

"Hush your nonsense and eat your breakfast!" old Seneq scolded mildly.

*exuded from carrizo grass

This Promised Land

"Nonsense! Why nonsense, Grandmother?" He-ap helped himself to one of her cakes and chewed with satisfaction. "I know you think these strangers are going to be our benefactors. Everything is going to be just lovely now they've arrived! I doubt it. Before long they'll be raping our women, stealing our food. You'll see! You don't know men as I do!" Glancing around again, he winked one blued eyelid and sniggered suggestively. "It's their peckers and bellies they'll be thinking about!"

Although He-ap was allowed great freedom of behavior, this seemed to Koyo to be going too far. "Now is not the time for such talk, Cousin!" she reproved him gently. "We should be planning how best to welcome our visitors. Are you prepared to dance and sing?"

"No, Mother, let him speak on!" Asuskwa, Lospe's brother put in. Until now he and Alul had been gobbling in the manner of hungry boys but now he spoke up forcefully: "I think Cousin is right. Why should we trust these strangers? Why are they coming into our land? Not just for their health, I bet you!"

Old Seneq turned on him irately. "And let our neighbors beat us to them and receive their friendship and gifts, perhaps win their support against us? A fine chief you'll make some day! Can't you get it through your impertinent head that this event was foretold? Why, before I was half your age *my* grandmother was telling *me* about it! What's more I listened, I didn't take it upon myself to express half-fledged thoughts! The coming of the A-alowow was ordained by the Sky People ages ago and you're not going to argue with them I hope?"

Seeing how the wind was blowing, Alul joined in. He was jealous of his cousin who bested him with bow, hockey stick, and in most other ways. "I'm going to invite the Sutupaps"—literally "those who are carried on the back"—"to visit our house!" he boasted. "And if they'll let me, I'll ride one of their four-legged beasts!"

"Hear that?" Seneq grunted proudly. "That's the way to talk!"

Asuskwa subsided sullenly. He seldom spoke at fireside. But when he did it was usually to the point. While disagreeing with him in this instance, Lospe admired the way he'd spoken up like a man and she noticed her mother and Uncle Ta-apu exchange glances. Ta-apu added quietly: "There may be truth in what Younger Brother says. We must be on our guard. But we must also be glad the A-alowow have come at last. They are beyond doubt a people of great power from whom we can learn much." And then Koyo announced: "Up, now, everyone! As Grandmother reminds us, there's much to be done! We must paint! We must dress! We must prepare gift trays!" Wiping her eating bowl with her little finger, she licked the finger, farting and belching to show satisfaction and gratitude for her meal. "Sister, shall we begin with our hair?"

Lehlele reached for the piece of pine bark that lay by the fire among the eating utensils. Heating it in the coals, she began to singe Koyo's chestnut bangs into a neat line, a hair at a time, reenforcing the evenness of the line skillfully with red ochre and brushing frequently with a dried thistle burr fastened on the end of a stick. Koyo wasn't beautiful and no amount of effort by Lehlele could have made her so, nor did the charcoal she wore on her face in mourning for her husband help matters. The People of the Place Called Olomosoug tended to be tall and well formed. Koyo was rather short and plump. But her gorgeous auburn hair and large intelligent brown eyes gave her distinction and she had a serenity and dignity which lent grace and authority to everything she did.

Lospe decided the moment for her question had come. "Mother," she began with all the innocent persuasiveness she could muster, "shall Beloved Cousin and I begin painting too? Aren't we going with you to greet the A-alowow?"

But Koyo was ready for her. "Tidy your beds and pick up your things! Don't I see grass dolls scattered right and left and even something that looks like a charmstone? If you've been into my charmstones again, young lady, you won't be going anywhere, I promise! I've warned you they can kill you!" Koyo, as was the habit of her people, never disciplined Lospe except by deprivation of privilege when necessary, never struck or punished her or her brother physically in any way, but lovingly yet firmly built that confidence which is so essential to a child's stability and self-esteem.

Obediently the two girls went toward their bedsteads of smooth willow poles interlaced with milkweed cord and curtained like the grownups' with reeds for privacy.

While straightening her sleeping mat, Lospe slipped the dangerous charmstone under it for returning to its proper place when no one was watching. It was shaped like a flying condor and had in fact come from Koyo's private storage basket where sacred implements and regalia were kept. Then she replaced her doll with

This Promised Land

the dried grass hair and white shell bead eyes in the treasure chest under her bed. Wima, the village carpenter and master craftsman, had fashioned the chest for her as part of his annual donation to the family. It was made of redwood that had come drifting down the coast from the north where the tall trees grew. Using a sharp stone, Wima had adzed the boards smooth, bored holes at their ends with an awl made from the little bone next to the shinbone of a deer, sewn them together with fiber cord, painted the outside a rich deep blue like the sky, and decorated it with a red border and iridescent fragments of abalone shell that shone like little stars.

As Lospe replaced the doll among her two precious dried hummingbirds and a sanddollar, her most prized possession caught her eye and she felt compelled to take it up and feel it again. It was an ancient silver belt buckle, battered, tongueless. A ridiculous thing, you might think, but not to her. Her father had acquired it while on a trading journey to the great southern capital of Muwu* by the sea where the Island People came ashore in their bright red canoes bringing sea otter skins and flint points, and foreigners came from the east across the desert trails bringing red ochre and beautiful black and white blankets of wool.

Her father was an eccentric man, not invariably successful despite his high social standing but always delightful. In return for four red fox skins and four large abalone shells and a piece of green serpentine, he acquired ownership of the broken buckle. He got it from a Mojave, who had it from a Yuma, who had it from a Pima, who had it from a Navajo, and so on eastward from hand to hand back to the land of the Sutupaps, or in other words New Mexico. When Koyo complained about its costliness and uselessness, Koxsho replied curtly it was a thing of beauty which pleased him. "Who knows what secret power it holds?" he added; and when Lospe admired it, he told her that men in that distant land had white skins and wore clothes with ornaments such as this at the middle of their bellies. "Someday perhaps they will come here and you will see them!"

She made up her mind then and there that they would come and she would see them. After her father's sudden death she begged the buckle from Koyo and kept it brightly polished. It was a chief reason she was determined to join the procession that day.

---

*Mugu near present day Ventura

Chapter Two

A few weeks earlier, some 300 miles to the south, the Spaniards left their base camp on San Diego Bay and began their march northward into a mythic land. Despite the scurvy he was suffering from like most of the others, Antonio felt his excitement rise at the prospect. "Weren't we going to find the legendary Port of Monterey?" he wrote later. "Establish a presidio and mission there to forestall the Russians advancing from the north and those villainous English pirates who roamed the South Sea* and waylaid the King's galleons? And who knew what treasure and adventure lay ahead of us in this land which had captivated men's imagination for centuries?"

If it hadn't been for the unpleasant incident that morning with Juan Lopez who borrowed his reata and failed to return it, Antonio could almost have forgotten his aching joints and bleeding gums. He considered confiding his problem with Lopez to Jose Ortega, the veteran chief of scouts who rode beside him guiding the long column, but wishing to make a good impression on his mentor decided not to. Instead he gave vent to rising spirits.

"Jose, I was thinking of Columbus just now. He was a Catalan like me, you know. Colon was his real name. That's pure Catalan. A wise old Jew of Barcelona financed him long before he knelt before Queen Isabel at Granada. The leading soldiers and missionaries he brought to the New World were mostly Catalans!"

"Expect me to believe that?" Ortega gave a slight shake of his reins, a signal to his buckskin to walk a little faster, and to the boy that he was talking too much. But Antonio went on, oblivious.

"It's part of our Catalan heritage, Jose. Up in our corner of

---

*the Pacific

what you call Spain, we remember how our Catalonian Empire once included Majorca and Minorca, Sicily and Naples and even Greece, and our merchants and statesmen were welcome in Egypt and Constantinople. Yes, Columbus stands for all of us: a frugal, persistent, ridiculously independent-minded fellow. Dreaming and daring he found a new world. That's the ambition of every Catalan!"

"I think your animal's left hind shoe is loose," Ortega replied dryly. "Even through all you say I can hear it rattle!"

Though fond of Antonio, Ortega was at times annoyed by his coltishness. A first rule of the trail is to keep your mouth shut. When talking you may miss what's going on around you and also give warning of your approach, which can prove hazardous to health, and although Antonio had learned much since leaving Loreto on the Gulf of Cortes sixteen weeks earlier, there were times when he relapsed. Now he fell silent to listen. There it was: the telltale clink of iron against hoof. "I'll fix it after we make camp. Can we reach that hollow before dark?"

"It all depends on the pack train. You know how slowly Rivera moves."

"He and the Governor are going to have trouble, I predict!"

In response Ortega simply raised a finger to his lips as if brushing away an itch.

A few yards behind them rode Governor Portola, commander-in-chief of the Sacred Expedition whose purpose was to extend the frontier of New Spain hundreds of miles northward and westward from Old or Lower California while bringing a multitude of heathen to a knowledge of the true God. Gaspar de Portola y de Rovira, Antonio's distant cousin, was a typically stocky Catalan fifty-three years of age, face richly lined by experience and fully bearded to conceal the effects of smallpox. This was his moment in history, though the bloody dysentery he was suffering from as a result of scurvy made him feel anything but great. He wore black traveling cape over dark blue dragoon's uniform, and a red cockade on the upturned brim of his tricorne proclaimed his captain's rank. At his right rode his second in command, fiery little Lieutenant Pedro Fages, another Catalan, and at his left—as if substantiating Antonio's claim about Columbus and his leaders—was still another Catalan, Sublieutenant of Dragoons Miguel Costanso of Barcelona, the brilliant young engineer and cartographer, a close friend of Antonio's. Like him and Fages, Costanso was cleanshaven in the new French style.

"Immediately behind the officers rode Domingo Malaret, our standard bearer," Antonio noted, "also a Catalan volunteer, muleback, the royal banner bearing its arms of Castile and Leon with golden fleece on a white field waving gallantly above him in the afternoon breeze. Portola had added the acorn emblem of Catalonia in each corner of the flag." Then came five more volunteers from the Free Company of Catalonia, all who were well enough to travel of the twenty-five who'd arrived by ship at San Diego, and then the gray-robed Franciscan fathers Juan Crespi, a Majorcan, and Francisco Gomez, a Castilian, also riding mules.

Behind them trudged fifteen Christianized Indians from Old California. "Like Portola, Ortega, and me, they'd traveled up to San Diego from Loreto on a trail of cactus and heat." Unnamed in everyone's record except Antonio's, these nearly anonymous Indian pioneers did the expedition's dirty work. "Their feet were bare. They wore coarse woolen loincloths and shirts and carried axes, mattocks, spades, and crowbars for constructing trail where necessary."

But here the going was easy. In the warm sunshine the first division crossed the level land that lies north of the present mission and old presidio of San Diego, skirted the shore of the false or enclosed bay much as the freeway does today, and ascended a small grassy valley.

Close behind followed the second division. Its hundred loaded mules were led by an old gray bell mare, tended by muleteers, guarded by colonial "leather jacket" cavalrymen like Ortega. These veterans weren't wearing the garment which gave them their name. "It was a sleeveless coat made of several layers of buckskin that could turn an arrow at any but close range. But it weighed nearly twenty pounds and was carried behind our high-cantled saddles until danger threatened." On their left forearms, however, the Leather Jackets wore circular shields of multilayered bullhide, also arrow resistant. Armas, heavy pieces of leather for protecting their legs, forerunners of modern chaparejos, hung from each side of their saddlehorns, while on their breasts rosary crosses, clearly visible against blue shirts, sheathed them in the invisible armor of God. "Steadied in their right hands were seven-foot lances, vestiges of the days of chivalry, points glinting in the sun, butts resting in stirrup cups." Short-bladed broadswords and short-barreled muskets completed their armament. Seasoned by years of frontier duty, they were probably as tough and well suited to their job as any cavalry in the world at the time.

The third and last division consisted of extra horses and mules, the caballada, herded by more Leather Jackets. "Like those of the pack train they were under command of fussy old Fernando Rivera, captain of provincial troops," Antonio continued. "Friction between Rivera's native criollos and mestizos* and the Spanish born Catalans was increasing, as the incident between me and Juan Lopez that morning made clear, and the march barely begun."

Because of balky mules and loosening loads the pack train fell behind, which in turn held up the caballada and rear guard and encouraged a tendency among the loose horses and mules to run away and rejoin those left at the San Diego camp. Tempers began to fray, shouts grew shrill. Meanwhile Antonio and Ortega reached the first Indian village of the new march, and as its inhabitants came streaming joyfully from their thatch huts—similar in design though not in size and refinements to those of the Place Called Olomosoug—to greet the wonderful strangers, the scouts reined aside allowing Portola to ride forward. Two naked chieftains were advancing with attendants bearing gifts.

As gravely as if he were about to negotiate with two Austrian generals on the field at Madonna del Olmo, Portola dismounted and went to greet them. Portola was not an explorer at heart and would have preferred an assignment with less risk and hardship but he was a responsible man and prepared to do his duty. He had served with distinction in Italy during the War of the Austrian Succession and later in the abortive invasion of Portugal during the Seven Years War. Steady, likable, he'd been selected as commander-in-chief because of his experience and dependability, also because by birth he was a member of those minority groups—Catalan, Basque, Majorcan, even Sicilian, Neapolitan, and French—which reform-minded King Carlos III, himself of French blood, was placing in positions of responsibility, finding them abler and more trustworthy than the Castilians who'd dominated the Spanish bureaucracy for centuries.

At the invitation of the chiefs, Portola sat upon the ground, Lieutenant Fages beside him, and accepted their gifts of grass seeds, acorn meal, and a dozen small fish, also two nets cleverly woven of grass, offering in return red and blue glass beads and

---

*criollos were Spaniards born in New Spain, mestizos of mixed Spanish-Amerindian blood

bits of red ribbon while half-naked women and girls and totally naked men and boys crowded around in noisy delight.

According to Antonio: "Portola's view of Indians was on the whole the one generally accepted among us: they were like children, deficient in reason, but could with firmness be taught and redeemed. His differed in that it included a larger respect than usual, augmented now during a march into strange territory by the necessity of friendly relations with people who greatly outnumbered us." But there was no doubt in Portola's mind as to the supremacy of the white race, or the Roman Catholic Church, or the imperial majesty of Spain in North and South America and other remote regions. Thus for a combination of reasons he listened tolerantly to a long harangue from one of the chiefs of which he didn't understand a word, yet caught the friendly sense, while naked youngsters and grownups, pressing close, attempted to touch his fascinating clothing, sword, and spurs.

"What have we here?" The low voice of Miguel Costanso, his friend the brilliant young engineer, sounded confidentially in Antonio's ear. "Nature's innocents as envisioned by Rousseau?"

Like Antonio, Costanso had attended the University of Barcelona before enlisting and had been exposed to the liberal ideas of the new French Enlightenment, and these were the first previously uncontacted Indians he'd seen since arriving by ship at San Diego. "They seem utterly uncorrupted by civilization," Costanso went on sotto voce, adding skeptically: "but I suppose, given a few weeks contact with us, they'd become as corrupt as those we've left behind!" reminding Antonio how the Diegueños, after a first enthusiastic welcome, became thievish and insolent, even boasting how their bows were more powerful than muskets, until Fages ordered a clod of earth which he likened to a man placed on a log and had Malaret fire at it from a distance of thirty paces and demolish it. Yet Antonio suspected that the covetous attitude of certain Spaniards toward the Indians' baskets and feathered headdresses and women might have been reflected in the Diegueños' behavior.

"Why so negative?" he replied to Costanso with some warmth. "You're as familiar as I with the belief that somewhere in the New World a new kind of man will be found. Why not in New California? Why not by us? Wouldn't it be in keeping with the reason you admire so much? Now look there!"

Encouraged by the friendly attentions of the Indians who crowded close and touched their gray robes with admiration and pointed with awe to their rosaries and crucifixes, Fathers Crespi and Gomez had begun explaining with the help of signs the meaning of the cross, of Jesus, and the importance of venerating the symbol on which the Savior died, and their audience was listening with such rapt interest it seemed a miraculous conversion was about to take place which would substantiate Antonio's positive views. But when the friars overzealously raised their crucifixes and asked their new friends to kiss the cross as a sign of devotion, the Indians pushed them away and shook their heads, while a noticeable flagging of warmth permeated the crowd. Noticing it Portola, after a punctilious farewell, rose and prepared to resume the march.

"See what I mean?" Costanso continued as they rode along. "If these are Rousseau's innocent savages, they won't stay innocent long!"

"But this is just one instance. Why jump to conclusions?" Antonio retorted.

"Why not? Are these poor creatures, happy now in their ignorance, to be better off subject to a Christian god than free under their pagan ones? No, when the Church becomes their taskmaster here as elsewhere in New Spain, their souls may be saved, but their faces will be a good deal longer!"

They were careful to keep such remarks from the ears of the two fathers. Though much reduced by their Bourbon king, the Inquisition was still powerful and Rousseau's novel *Emile* had recently been burned in Madrid. Nevertheless in Madrid as in Mexico City the ruling clique was greatly influenced by French fashion and discussed not only Rousseau but such other revolutionary thinkers as Voltaire quite openly. Catalonia had long been a hotbed of independent thought as it sought to regain its lost autonomy. Books could easily be smuggled across the border from adjacent France. While at the university Antonio joined an underground group and read *The Social Contract* secretly, dreaming of the day when personal and political freedom might return to his native land, which enjoyed its bill of rights even before England's Magna Carta. Similarly he and Costanso had been exposed to Freemasonry, the secret weapon of those revolutionary times. The American Revolution was less than ten years ahead, the French less than twenty. So the two young agents of a new day carried the seeds of subversion into a promised land. They had no specific program. They simply represented a new state of mind.

Chapter Three

As Lospe watched her mother and her Aunt Lehlele singe their bangs and paint their faces, preparatory to greeting the white strangers, her expectancy rose to overflowing.

"Don't you girls want to join us in the procession?" Koyo teased. "Why aren't you freshening your paint?"

Squealing with delight, they hastened to do so. "Make me as pretty as you can!" Lospe whispered to her cousin, wishing Kachuku could apply the white lines representative of the sun's rays which would have decorated her cheeks and chin had she not been in mourning for her father and her face blackened with charcoal. Even so she would be allowed to wear the village colors of alternating red and blue stripes around her chest. Men and boys were trimming their beards, plucking out superfluous hair with clamshell tweezers, painting their bodies in a manner similar to the women, while He-ap was putting on his best skirt fringed with seashells, giggling: "I wonder what a white man's i-ikpik looks like? They must be ashamed of it or they wouldn't keep it hidden by clothes!" Everyone laughed at this bawdy joke, though Seneq scolded him mildly, while continuing to arrange the seed cakes she had baked before breakfast on the basketry trays the girls would carry to present to the A-alowow, and keeping an eye on Kahip who watched mournfully from a corner as if the executioners' arrows were about to pierce her tender young body.

When the girls finished painting, Kachuku brushed Lospe's straight red hair with a brush made from the stiff brown fibers of the soaproot and Lospe did likewise to her dark tresses and then they put on their best otterskin skirts fringed with beads and tiny balls of asphaltum, then their long, polished bone hairpins with abalone shell ornaments and small feathered decorations.

"What are you doing with that trinket, silly child?" Seneq

This Promised Land

shrilled, as her sharp eye caught Lospe surreptitiously removing the brightly polished silver buckle from her treasure chest.

"I'm taking it as my gift to the Sutupaps!"

Her grandmother broke into a loud cackle. "What makes you believe they'll like anything so nonsensical as that? They might think you stole it from them and become angry at all of us!"

She was moving to take the buckle away when Koyo intervened. "Let be! Why shouldn't she carry it if it reminds her of her father?" Koyo's eyes were shining proudly. Seneq subsided grumbling: "Nobody treats me with respect any more! But let me tell you it's *I* who should be going to see these white ones! I always maintained they would come, when you doubters laughed at me. But now my legs are too old to carry me!"

Koyo had sent out messengers as customary to tell people when and where to meet and to prepare gifts but still some insisted on coming to the house to ask questions and make complaints. Payanit, the master bowmaker, appeared with a complaint against Shamik, the wealthy trader. Payanit claimed he'd made a fine bow for Shamik, skillfully backed with deer tendon, with the understanding he would receive three beaver skins and a handsome new serpentine bowl, but Shamik was now saying the agreement called for only two skins. It was Koyo's duty to arbitrate such disputes, and she said she would take the matter under advisement. Payanit left satisfied.

When at last all were ready, they started toward the meeting place. Lospe thought her mother stunning in the long ceremonial cloak made from the skin of the grizzly bear her grandfather had killed. Koyo's chestnut hair gleamed in the sun and though her face was still blackened in mourning for Koxsho she bore herself serenely. Men and boys looked handsome too in fresh paint, hair up in topknots, flint knives thrust through it, strings of bead money and necklaces of shell beads and eagle claws forming concentric circles about their necks; and in the pierced septums of their noses shone shiny mollusk shell pins. In their waistnets, which did not conceal but rather set off their earth colored skins, they carried red ochre, wild tobacco, flints, plus various trinkets they might give or trade the A-alowow as opportunity afforded.

As agreed by the Council of Twenty, bowstrings were left unstrung. Proper conduct had of course been much debated. Some like Lospe's brother Asuskwa believed the Spaniards were coming into their land for no good purpose. Others thought them merely traveling through to some distant destination as their ships had done by sea for many years. Others like Seneq regarded them as deities fulfilling ancient prophecy. Still others believed them reincarnations of ancestors, pale ghosts returned from the Land of the Dead, and were reluctant to have anything to do with them. Most agreed, however, they should be warmly welcomed and the source of their great power studied and if possible acquired. At the urging of Owotoponus, newly become chief astrologer and head shaman, the council decided that a special ceremony should be held before going to meet the strangers, so that communal strength would be at its height and the tribelet protected against evil supernatural power.

As they approached the meeting place, Lospe saw the enclosure of fragrant freshly cut sage and willow boughs, also the tall hateful figure of Owotoponus adorned with plumes and paint and wearing a skirt of condor feathers. He accosted her mother with shameless familiarity, pointing to his skirt where the tip of his huge erection was emerging through the black feathers. "Look, here comes the red-headed stranger!" he cried, playing on the double meaning. "He's glad to see you! Very glad to see you!"

Though such conduct was totally out of keeping with a sacred occasion, everyone within hearing laughed, as did Koyo, though not very heartily. She tolerated this unseemly behavior because she too was newly come to power and hesitated to assert herself against Owotoponus whose magic she feared.

Lospe frowned and burned inwardly with anger and shame. Everyone knew of course that Owotoponus had the largest penis in the village. Such things were common knowledge in a community where men and boys went naked and in a culture which placed emphasis on openness. Gossiping daily in the sweathouse by the river, or while gathering seeds and acorns, or over their grinding stones, Lospe discussed them naturally with the other girls and women, and there was nothing particularly salacious in their talk. Sex was regarded as simply one more natural function of the body and frequently engaged in despite rules to the contrary, penis size being a factor in social standing along with heredity, wealth, and talent.

As the life force moved in Lospe when she squirmed at her naming ceremony under the tedious words of old Quati, Owotoponus' father, then astrologer-priest, so it was believed to move in the penis, and the larger that organ the more important its owner in community eyes, if he were acceptable in other ways.

Even before succeeding his father as paha, Owotoponus could

This Promised Land

have taken almost any woman he wanted except Koyo whom he desired above all others, yet who detested him; and now that he held nearly absolute power, only her mourning for Koxsho protected her, as old Quati's interpretation of her dream protected Lospe; and Lospe with a powerful surge of emotion remembered her dream.

That day, less than a year ago, had dawned warm and clear. Before leading his group of newly adolescent girls up the sacred hill, old Quati stopped at a momoy bush* that grew in the sandy river bottom.

He said gravely to the bush with its broad green leaves and large white bell-shaped blossoms: "Grandmother, I am going to take one of your roots! Do not be angry with me since this will enable your children to see you more clearly!" Momoy was truth, was all the world seen with absolute clarity, past, present, future. But she was also death and must be treated with utmost respect. Only experienced practitioners like Quati were allowed to administer her to young people.

Lospe watched with awe while he dug a little hole with his knife at one side of the bush. Selecting a piece of root which suited him, he clipped it off with his black obsidian blade and replaced the soil with great care. "Thank you, Grandmother!" he said even more gravely, bowing to the bush. "I hope I have not hurt you!" Though frightened Lospe trusted old Quati, as did the others. He had been paha longer than most of their parents could remember and his wisdom was very great.

Filling his tightly woven water basket at the edge of the river, he began to climb the grassy round hill—she could see it clearly now across the valley as she stood at the ceremonial meeting place, easily distinguished by the single live oak at its rounded summit—where they would experience their dreams. When he reached the top, panting, moving slowly because of his great age and weight, Quati explained: "This hilltop symbolizes our Middle World. If your spirits are pure, you may see truly in all directions!" and they could indeed see a marvelous sight: valley below with its winding river, sky above, mountain tops all around, and Lospe was glad she had dieted and meditated for three long weeks in preparation for this moment, the climax of the puberty ceremony, thinking of the dream she wanted to have.

*jimson weed

Robert Easton

With deliberation Quati mashed the piece of momoy root in his green serpentine bowl, steeped it in the water of the river which flowed from the Heart of the World, then tasted the mixture to be sure it was correct.

Turning to her he said: "Little Sister, you will be first." Her heart dropped and rose with excitement. "You will have a beautiful dream. Do not be afraid. Ask questions of your guardian spirit when he appears. Pay close attention. Remember everything he says and be sure to listen for the song he may give you!"

With mingled fear and joy she took a sip of the bittersweet liquid, then lay down on her mat on the young grass. "In a few moments you will feel sleepy," she heard Quati saying kindly. "Do not fear. I shall be beside you when you wake!" His voice was already sounding strange, as if reaching her from a great distance, echoing down a long canyon.

Next she seemed to be falling off the hilltop into an abyss of darkness. Soon she began to see many dazzling colors as when you close your eyes tightly. These assumed fantastic shapes of creatures never encountered in real life, serpents with forked tails, winged monsters with many heads, all breathing fire. Then for a long time she seemed to be floating in space. Suddenly the sun was setting. Before falling asleep she felt sure she would see a Sacred Condor in her dream as her brother had done four years earlier. Flying toward him out of the setting sun, Asuskwa had seen a giant bird approaching at great speed. Passing close above him, the condor crooked its bald red head and looked down as if about to tell him something but passed swiftly on leaving only the sound of its whistling wings. That sound transformed itself magically into the very song one should hear from one's dream helper:

> Out of the sun I come,
> Out of the sun I come,
> With magic wings I sing,
> With magic wings I sing,
> Flying where no one knows,
> Flying where no one knows!

Then Asuskwa knew that Sacred Condor had given him a message and in future he could turn to him for help in time of need. Lospe had prayed repeatedly to Sun and Morning Star to send her such a vision. But now instead of a condor coming toward

This Promised Land

her out of the west she saw a tall yellow-haired man sitting astride a large four-legged animal the color of her own hair. His skin was white. He wore a long knife and carried a firestick, and shining at the middle of his belly—for he wore clothes—was a silver buckle like the one her father brought from Muwu and which now belonged to her. She listened intently for what his apparition might say but he merely looked down at her with surprise as if he could not quite believe his eyes. She listened for the song he might give her but he gave her no song, just that astonished look. Then the look changed to one of amusement as he began to laugh and his laugh was merry as a bird song. "Why are you laughing?" she inquired, piqued by his gaiety. "Because you will not marry until you are fourteen!" he replied even more gaily. Then she woke. The sun was rising. It seemed she had been asleep only a few minutes. Actually all day and all night had passed. She felt dizzy and sick at her stomach. "Do not be alarmed!" Quati's voice was saying soothingly. "All will be well. Here, have some broth. Then we will talk!"

He had made a fire and prepared broth from the seeds of the chia sage. Her head cleared rapidly after she sat up and drank. Roundabout, the other girls were still asleep, and the sun struck Quati sitting in the center of them and made him shine like a polished stone.

"What did you see in your dream, Little Sister?" he inquired gently. She told him. He looked surprised. For a while he said nothing. Then: "Your dream is unlike any I ever heard of. But momoy does not deceive. She means the Sutupaps are coming and they will be your helpers, and she means you must not marry until you are fourteen!"

"When will they come?" she asked breathlessly. Quati shook his head. "That I do not know. But they will come! Evening Star will lead you to them."

"But I thought Evening Star was an emblem of death?"

"That is as it may be!"

Chapter Four

Another hour and the expeditions's first division stopped to make camp in the grassy hollow which Ortega and Antonio had selected. The other divisions still lagged, and thus the nagging problem of what he should do about Juan Lopez' insolent treatment of him that morning had not materialized for Antonio, but he felt sure it would soon.

As the sun went down, the tinkle of the lead mare's bell could be heard at the lower end of the little valley and by degrees the loaded mules and the caballada came straggling in behind her, to the accompaniment of exasperated blows and oaths and shrill whinnies of recognition from reunited animals. The packs were placed in a circle on the ground, each pair of rawhide bags or wooden water barrels and other gear standing more or less upright to form a kind of low breastwork. The officers' and padres' tents were pitched at the center of this circle, while the men threw down their saddles around the perimeter as they chose. Lieutenant Fages' regular army Catalans kept to themselves, Captain Rivera's colonial Leather Jackets formed another group, the half-caste muleteers a third, Christianized Indian laborers a fourth.

Antonio was chatting with Fages outside Portola's tent when Rivera came to explain the delay of his two divisions. It was a commonplace matter but Rivera's touchiness made it seem large. He felt himself the outsider and was bitterly jealous of Portola. At fifty-nine Old Fussbudget, as Fages termed him, was much the oldest of the officers, his full dark beard well streaked with gray. He'd governed Old California until Portola replaced him and felt convinced, not without justification, that thirty years' experience on the frontier made him better qualified to command the expedition in search of the Port of Monterey than an officer recently arrived from Spain.

This Promised Land

Rivera had been a great favorite with the Jesuit fathers who first missionized lower California, after earlier attempts at colonization failed, and held nearly absolute sway there. They made the desert bloom. Their lonely missions became oases of life and faith in a desolate land, and Rivera and his Leather Jackets became in effect their private army.

"Why, the Black Robes even had their own ships, their own navy, mind you! and plenty of gold, silver, and pearls if we can believe half what we hear!" as Fages put it to Antonio. True, gold and silver bullion to the amount of over 5,000 pesos was found after the expulsion but most of the charges were never fully substantiated. They were, however, a chief reason King Carlos replaced Jesuits with Franciscans and Rivera with Portola.

So Rivera's feathers were badly ruffled. But what irked him viscerally was the fact that Portola was a peninsular, that is, born in Spain, a gachupin, which is to say a gentleman and member of the noble class, and a regular army man while he was a criollo, a commander of provincial troops, a member of the ignoble class as his service record plainly stated, and therefore of inferior social and professional standing no matter what he might do.

Portola greeted him with easy courtesy. "How goes it, Don Fernando? Usual delays?"

Rivera took this to imply he was habitually tardy. Haughtily he began to explain. Then realizing he was boring everyone, he grew red-faced and embarrassed. Antonio turned away out of delicacy. Fages, never one for niceties, could not restrain a smile. He disliked Rivera and vice versa. That he, Fages, should one day be governor of California or that Rivera should supplant him, or he in turn succeed Rivera, was beyond anyone's wildest imaginings. Thus the first three governors of the new land stood within arm's length never guessing what lay in store.

Portola listened patiently to Rivera's gaucherie, at last observing casually: "The animals will be well guarded tonight, I suppose?"

This seemed to Rivera a final affront. "Of course!" he snapped, and was stamping away toward his tent as Portola's Genoese servant appeared bearing a tray with glasses and a brandy bottle.

"My, our Country Cousin has a thick skin!" Fages murmured, helping himself to a glass at Portola's request. Fages would have dressed his man down then and there but that was not Portola's way. He shrugged and raised his glass. "We all serve the King!"

Robert Easton

* * *

Antonio threw his saddle and blankets down among his fellow Catalans intending to bivouac with them. As Portola's protégé he was free to come and go though nominally a Leather Jacket under Rivera's command. "I'd enlisted initially in Portola's dragoons regiment then at Cadiz preparing to embark for New Spain," he confided to his memoir. "There was little to keep me at home. My father's death when I was eleven left ownership of the family farm—grapes, apples, wheat, in the green Segre Valley near our house in the town of Balaguer in the Pyrenees foothills—in the hands of my oldest brother. Francesch provided as best he could with my mother's help for the rest of us, and this included sending me, with the bishop's approval, to the university for those two stimulating years in the study of law." But when he got into difficulties with the authorities because of clandestine activities in the liberal cause, his brother's willingness to support Antonio, not to mention the bishop's, took an abrupt decline. "Thus the idea of adventure in the New World under protection of a powerful and well-to-do relative suddenly gained strong appeal. We prided ourselves, rather fatuously perhaps, on a family tradition which said that an ancestor fought with the Romans against the invading Visigoths, and another with the Visigoths against the Moors, never giving up their Catalan identity, you understand, while a third, our most illustrious Jordi, had been with Pere the Great who conquered Sicily and became king there, making possible the extension of our empire into Naples and Greece."

Landing at Vera Cruz in the viceroyalty of New Spain, Antonio's dragoons proceeded to the northwest frontier in Sonora where there was fighting against Seris and Apaches, and it was in the Cerro Prieto or Dark Mountains that Antonio first heard the music of a war arrow and learned the frustration of combat with an enemy who cleverly kept just out of musket range, while devastating the countryside with murderous raids. "I saw the naked body of my captured comrade, Mateo Sal, scalped, split open from neck to crotch, castrated, spread-eagled face upward on the stony earth in the form of a cross, and left staring at the sky."

Accompanying Portola on detached assignment to Lower California to prepare for the Sacred Expedition, he came under tutelage of Jose Ortega, second in command to aging Rivera, and with him led the way northward as scout.

This Promised Land

Now as he walked toward the bivouac of the Catalans, it was that moment of respite before the evening meal, camp had been pitched, fires lit, most of the animals turned out to graze under guard, and Ortega called to him good humoredly from a group of lounging bearded Leather jackets: "Blondie, come here a minute!"

Turning and starting toward them, Antonio felt a sudden constriction in his throat, for among the weathered veterans crouched around Ortega he noted the sturdy figure of Juan Lopez, and the recollection of Juan's treatment of him that morning flooded over him. A strict rule of the trail, where a man's welfare not to mention his life depends directly on his belongings and replacements are often impossible to come by, is the sacredness of personal property. To borrow a reata was questionable conduct at best, to fail to return it unforgivable if deliberate. Antonio felt certain from Juan's manner that it had been deliberate. Crouching at ease, the mestizo held his cigarette cupped between thumb and forefinger, smiling his impudent gap-toothed grin. Yet Antonio had never knowingly given him offense and could not understand why the veteran should pick on him.

"What were they raking our Old Man over the coals for?" Ortega inquired in lowered tone as Antonio drew near. Before the boy was half through answering, Juan interrupted caustically: "You gachupins think you're too good for us ordinary people. That's the heart of the matter!"

Lopez had been a mere drifter, one step ahead of starvation, when Rivera during a visit to the mainland recruited him for the California Company based at Loreto. Thanks to Rivera he now had a place in the scheme of things—a uniform, a horse, a mule, thirty pesos a month though payment was usually in goods, a cabin by the shore of the Gulf near the old presidio with a wife and three children, also a small garden, six goats and two pigs. Juan was fiercely loyal to his benefactor and resented gachupins like Portola and Antonio who in his jealous view ruled what he regarded as his own land, the one we now call Mexico, and lorded it over him and Rivera. By putting Antonio down, he put down a whole structure he resented and hated. Like Rivera he remembered better days among the Jesuits when there had been no Catalans at the head of columns, and also he was envious of Antonio's blond hair and exceptional height, being no more than average size himself and quite dark.

Robert Easton

If he let Juan's insult pass, worse would follow, Antonio knew. The time had come to bring things to a head.

"Which reminds me, friend," he replied with elaborate politeness, "you borrowed my reata this morning to make, or so you said, a corral for catching the riding animals, promising to return it. You haven't." He could see that Juan was sitting on it.

"Must have left it behind!" Juan retorted with a shrug and a wink at the others.

"Then you'd better start making tracks for San Diego!"

"Says who?"

"Says I!"

Juan spit and stood up. Ortega leaped between them. "Fellows, you know the Governor's orders! Juan," he turned to Lopez, "where's Antonio's reata?"

Juan laughed derisively as if it were all a fuss over nothing. "I was just going to give it to him!"

He tossed the coiled leather rope toward Antonio who let it fall without attempting to catch it, giving the other his eye until Juan dropped his. Then he bent and picked up the reata. Ortega tried to close the matter with a stern warning: "No more of this, you men hear me?" But Antonio did not think it would end there.

When moments later he joined his Catalan countrymen, Antonio found them busily cleaning their muskets, polishing belts and cartridge cases, grumbling as usual, breaking off to joke him: "Your mestizo buddy give you a bad time?"

They were scornful of the mixed blood colonials, though their own blood was itself like a bouillabaisse, being a mixture of Iberian, Roman, Visigoth, Moorish, French, and Jewish, among others.

"Had to straighten out a matter," Antonio replied noncommittally, recoiling his reata so that his touch would be on it. Though he prided himself on belonging to the Spanish noble class, in reality no great distinction since it numbered several hundred thousand, most of them impoverished, Antonio did not share his fellow Catalans' scorn of the colonials, since he was serving by Portola's design as one of them. "What's going on here? Why the spit and polish?"

"Orders! Our little lieutenant wants to be a general!"

Unbelievable as it sounded, Fages was going to make them stand inspection while on the march. "And you so weak from

This Promised Land

scurvy you can hardly stand? He must be out of his mind!''

"We're Regular Army!" Bumbau explained sarcastically. "We've got to show you Leather Jackets—and Governor Portola—how good we are!"

"Show Portola how Fages lost the war against Portugal, you mean?" Bonnel continued in similar vein.

"The Governor's too easy on him!" Bumbau rejoined.

"They're both Catalan, that's why!" Molas put in. "Perdre el seny!"*

They were speaking Catalan which resembled old Provençal. Only the officers, with the exception of Rivera, could have understood it, and they were too far away to overhear.

"Polish my gun barrel!" Bumbau grumbled on, "so it'll shine in the moonlight while I'm standing guard and an Apache get a better shot at me!"

Any ferociously hostile Indian was considered an Apache and in truth they didn't know what to expect in an unknown land, perhaps even Apaches with guns obtained from French or English traders or captured from Spaniards as had happened in the Sonora fighting. The California Indians were supposed to be friendly but nobody had fully tested that supposition.

"I'll make a ten times better target riding around the caballada on my mule than you standing guard at camp!" Antonio rejoined.

"Quiet, here he comes!" Corporal Yorba warned.

Yorba lined his six men up as though they were a regiment and held them at "inspection arms" while Fages inspected their tattered blue coats and red waistcoats and examined every weapon. The little lieutenant strutted along the line like a gamecock while Antonio watched the proceedings from a respectful distance. Finding a speck of dirt in Miguel Pengues' powder pan Fages snapped at Yorba: "Give this man extra duty!" And to Miguel: "See this doesn't happen again, my man! Once the arrows are flying, it's too late to put your weapon in working order!"

Antonio knew the Leather Jackets would be snickering contemptuously at these proceedings but had to admit he was impressed. There was something rather wonderful in little Fages' challenging the chaotic unknown which surrounded them, insisting on his bit of order. It was common knowledge that he re-

---

*He's lost his good sense

garded himself as a conquistador in the tradition of Cortes and Pizarro almost two-and-a-half centuries earlier—undaunted by any circumstance, adding whole nations to the royal domain. Antonio wondered how Portola would handle such grandiose dreams along with Rivera's impudence.

He was dreaming himself some hours later wrapped in his poncho, using his leather jacket as mattress, head pillowed on his saddle, when he felt a sharp kick in his rear end.

"Up, Blondie, and put your skinny ass in that saddle!" It was Mariano Carrillo, his companion on many a night watch. Unwrapping himself with a grunt in response to Mariano's toe, Antonio saw the corporal's lean figure moving off through the moonlight to rouse others of their watch. Groping sleepily he found his low-crowned, wide-brimmed leather hat, the one item of clothing he habitually removed before going to bed. With it on, he was fully dressed and awake.

Rising he picked up saddle, saddle blanket, and bridle and stepped carefully among sleeping bodies toward the patch of grass where he'd picketed his mule. He'd been so involved in the scene between Rivera and Portola, and the confrontation with Lopez, then Fages' incredible inspection, that he'd forgotten about replacing his horse's loose shoe until not enough daylight remained. Intending to do it first thing in the morning, he turned the sorrel out to graze with the caballada and caught up black Diablo for the night's work.

The mule at the end of sixty feet of reata snorted at his approach but quieted at his word of reassurance. Diablo was in fact gentle and reliable, belying his name, and very speedy. Bridle and saddle were soon slipped on and Antonio was riding with the others, dark silhouettes in the moonlight, toward the hollow in the little valley where the caballada of nearly two hundred animals grazed.

Exchanging greetings with their predecessors, they in their turn began circling the herd, each riding in an opposite direction, guided by the indistinct mass of grazing bodies and the tinkle of the gray mare's bell somewhere near its constantly shifting center. There were eight of them including, as Antonio saw with a start, Lopez. One of the last things he'd heard before falling asleep was Lopez impudently playing a jig on his fiddle to his comrades' approving cheers. As they passed each other now

This Promised Land

they did not speak, but Antonio could feel animosity radiating toward him through the dark. "I put Juan to shame publicly," he thought. "A man can never forgive that. I must be on my guard!"

As usual during a first night on the trail the caballada was restless and inclined to run away. The riders spoke to one another and to the animals from time to time and occasionally sang in low tones to let their charges know they were under guard, and occasionally the light of the half moon glinted on spur or bit, giving that lurking Apache, if he were indeed there, an ideal target. All went well until about two o'clock.

Then fog came rolling in from the nearby sea shrouding everything in mist, creating a strange new reality in which shapes, sounds, even thoughts, grew distorted. Visibility decreased to a few feet. As contact between them and the riders diminished, the grazing animals became more restless, while the men increased their talk in an effort to retain control. The ever present unknown, sensed by all of them more keenly now, challenged by Fages at his absurd inspection of the evening before, seemed to be rising to engulf them. Antonio was half expecting what followed.

Echoing from every side of the hollow at once, rose a savage wild yell. Apaches! was his first terrified thought as he reached for his gun stock. But as the yell rose and echoed again he recognized the voice of a coyote distorted by fog, darkness, and his apprehensions into something quite appalling. He guessed its consequences. As if using one set of feet the caballada departed full speed for San Diego and the base camp.

It was a mad chase through foggy darkness laced by patches of moonlight. Dangerous as a stampede of cattle can be, a stampede of horses and mules can be worse—faster, more crazed, harder to handle. Diablo had been swept up in a torrent of bodies, Antonio realized with dismay, and was running almost out of control. Wild neighs rang around them, pounding hooves deafened him. The thought of gullies, cliffs, or falling under those trampling hooves flashed through his mind. He shouted, screamed, tried to stop the flood by waving his hat, a pitifully ineffective act, then saw with alarm that Diablo was racing along the edge of a deep barranca, straining desperately to keep from being forced into it. He remembered seeing it the day before, an ugly gash in the valley floor that could swallow and cripple or kill a horse and man. The fear-crazed animals around them had pressed Diablo to its brink when Antonio became aware that the shape crowding him most closely bore a rider on its back. Lopez. Just as he was about to be forced over the edge, Antonio drew rein hard, slowing Diablo for an instant, and Lopez and his roan slid by and almost went into the barranca themselves.

It happened in a second and was lost in the onward rush of the stampede. It might even have been accidental. Antonio felt sure it was deliberate. Through all the turmoil and confusion he'd sensed a deadly intent, and something hard and cold which had never been there before rose in him and remained fixed.

At dawn they overtook the herd feeding in rich grass on the shore of the false bay, almost within sight of the masts of the *San Carlos* riding at anchor in the true one, and flogged them back toward camp. On the way they met Ortega, Rivera, and a party of Leather Jackets come looking for them. Mariano Carrillo explained what happened. Rivera was furious, Ortega philosophical. After all, no animals had been hurt or lost. Neither Antonio nor Juan said a word about what occurred between them. No one else knew. It became for the time their private secret.

Back at camp, tortillas and hot chocolate were gulped down and preparations for the march begun. Antonio's chestnut sorrel had lost its loose shoe during the stampede, and when he asked Ortega if he should replace it before the march resumed, since time would be required to load the mules, the sergeant inquired somewhat testily why he hadn't done so the evening before, then told him to go ahead.

Antonio got the shoeing rack from his pack, hobbled Babieca's forelegs, and attempted to raise the left hind one and crouch under it in farrier style to replace the shoe, but Babieca, still agitated by the stampede, kept sidling out of his grasp with a snort of protest. Under ordinary circumstances someone might have lent a hand but in the urgency of a delayed departure, no one did, and since Antonio was too proud to ask, he might have been a long time at his task had not a gruff voice suggested: "Why don't you put a sideline on him?"

It was Pablo, the muleteer. Pablo was a zambo, that is to say part Indian, part black. His skin was dark as jet, his curly hair prematurely gray, his strength herculean, his temper often fierce, but Antonio placated it more than once with a little tobacco and listened to lore of camp and trail such as only old Pablo knew. Pablo's mules were loaded. Noting the boy's difficulty, he'd left them in custody of his partner and stepped over to see if he could help.

They fashioned a non-slip loop of Antonio's reata around the neck at Babieca's shoulders with a second much larger running loop passing through it to the hind foot and back again so the foot could be drawn off the ground and the horse immobilized on three legs. Pablo was holding the sideline in place, talking soothingly to Babieca, and Antonio had finished rasping the surface of the foot smooth and was crouched under it, mouth full of nails, beginning to pound them one by one into the new shoe, when Rivera came storming up. The captain was still smarting from his embarrassment of the evening before and the stampede of his caballada hadn't improved his temper.

"What's going on?" he demanded. "You're delaying everything!"

"But," protested Antonio, "this horse is limping already! Were he to go lame..."

"Are you disputing my judgment?"

"But Sergeant Ortega told me..." Rivera had already turned to Pablo.

"Load your mules, lobo!* Don't stand there!"

"They are loaded," Pablo replied with dignity, continuing to hold Babieca who balanced precariously on three legs above the crouched Antonio.

By now the whole camp was watching. Portola strolled over. "Captain," he remarked quietly, "it's true we have no time to waste. The season is well advanced and we must cross the passes before the snows. The Port of Monterey lies far ahead. But a lame horse might hold us back. I expect normal delays. I make allowances for them."

He wished to establish his leadership and to show that when circumstances warranted he could be concerned about the smallest detail of the expedition. Having made his point, he turned away without waiting for a reply as Rivera had done to him the evening before.

They marched onward into the marvelous land, the sea at their left, hills of grass rolling inland toward distant dark mountains at their right, wreaths of fog withdrawing as the sun rose higher,

---

*like zambo, a pejorative term denoting a person part Indian, part black

everywhere a sense of mellowness and well being. "It drew us onward," Antonio wrote later, "as if we were magnetized by its beauty, each alluring vista suggesting another." Antonio thought he'd never seen any landscape more beguiling unless it was his own Catalonian coast. "Even here were similar inviting canyons with sweet streams, ferns, willows, similar oaks, alders, sycamores, even pinkish petaled roses with golden hearts—even blackberries and other familiar plants and trees common throughout our northern Spain so that I seemed to be coming into my own country again; and yet it was all wild, strange, familiar yet new, like a wonderful memory or dream being re-experienced."

As he rode he felt a sense of release and rejuvenation. The night before with its fear and hatred became momentarily a thing of the past. Here lay a whole new life, a chance to begin again, and he recalled Montalvo's romantic fable of a land of surpassing beauty called California that was supposed to be an island lying somewhere near the Indies. Its only metal was gold, its only inhabitants women. The fabulous island's ruler was lovely Queen Calafia of dusky hue. Quite possible, it all seemed.

Antonio's lightheartedness increased daily, Lopez notwithstanding. Partly this was due to better health in which the others shared. The purple splotches disappeared from Costanso's legs. Portola's bloody flux left him. Fages' teeth became firm in his gums, while Antonio's joints stopped aching—much as his friend Doctor Prat had predicted before they said good-bye at San Diego. The fact that scurvy was related to diet was just beginning to be understood. Captain Cook, then in the Pacific on his first famous voyage of discovery, would return his crews to England without losing a man to scurvy, thanks to a ration including fresh foods and citrus; and Prat, a Catalan with an inquiring mind like Antonio's and Costanso's, was similarly ahead of his time. He'd repeatedly urged all who would listen: "Eat the wild asparagus, watercress, rose hips, berries!" which grew near the San Diego camp. But while some like Antonio followed his advice, most considered it beneath a white man's dignity to eat grass and roots like animals or Indians, or zambos such as old Pablo.

Even the well-informed Father President Serra thought the "loanda," so named because it was prevalent aboard slave ships touching at Loanda* on the west African coast, a contagious dis-

---

*now Luanda, capital of Angola

This Promised Land

ease related to sea travel. As evidence Serra cited Fages' Catalans who'd reached San Diego by ship and were suffering from it most. But Prat who'd himself come up from San Blas on that terrible wandering voyage of one hundred and ten days—longer than it took to cross the Atlantic—replied: "Nonsense, my dear father! Ship diet was mostly wormy biscuit and rotten bullybeef, while you who traveled overland from Loreto had plenty of activity in unconfined surroundings as well as the benefit of occasional wild herbs and fresh meat—and initially the vegetables and fruits of the old Jesuit missions! Look at the Indians," was Prat's crowning point, "wild or Christianized, they don't have the loanda! Neither do our zambo and mulatto muleteers, so poorly rationed they must supplement their diet with herbs and roots! They're better off than we who eat civilized food!"

Now all on the march were unknowingly curing themselves by exercise in sunlight and fresh air and, more importantly, the fresh foods given them by Indians. "Thus the generous savages made possible their own conquest!" Antonio noted.

Against his adventurous will, Prat had remained at the San Diego base camp. There with Father Serra and a handful of others he would tend the sick and help establish a mission and presidio.

North of the present town of San Clemente the promontory of Dana Point descending abruptly into the sea forced the explorers to turn inland, as the highway turns today, and soon they came to the pleasantest place yet seen, the valley of the Santa Ana River in what is now a center of Southern California's urban sprawl. No photochemical smog obscured their view of the distant San Gabriel Mountains. No housing developments marred the natural outline of grassy hills and valley. Bordered by lovely groves, the river ran cold and clear toward the sea. Here, too, the Indians were especially friendly and in addition to the usual gifts offered to share their land with them and build houses for them to live in if they would stay, offering their women as wives or companions for the night according to their custom. But the soldiers remembered Portola's stern warning: "We shall be a mere handful amid thousands of potential enemies. To survive we must win their friendship by kind treatment. Suppose they were to unite against us? Some of you served with me in the Cerro Prieto.

Suppose we were to be attacked by a thousand Apaches? Besides, how can we win their souls to God if we mistreat their bodies? For him who touches a woman fifty lashes will be waiting." Not that Antonio didn't dream often of touching a woman. At nineteen his sexual powers were nearing maximum and he'd exercised them fully for the first time with a waterfront beauty named Nina, "a passionate creature part Berber, part Gypsy, quite unrestrained," at Cadiz and enjoyed the process so much he was quite ready to try it again, unaware that Nina in return for his virginity had given him a tiny dark spirochete which was living in his blood, a surprise present he was carrying to his promised land. But mindful of Portola's warning he restrained his natural inclinations toward the Gabrielino charmers, though his exceptional height and blond hair made him a target for their smiles. Instead he helped Costanso estimate the flow of the river at one-and-a-half square yards. Fages inquired about the existence of gold and silver but the Gabrielinos seemed not to understand his meaning. Their ornaments were simple shells, feathers, bones. Then an extraordinary thing did happen.

About one o'clock while Portola, Fages, and Rivera were conferring with three chiefs under a live oak, the earth began to tremble violently. Simultaneously there was a subterranean rumbling as if a huge monster were growling beneath the earth's surface. Several loaded mules were knocked to their knees. Trees gave off a hissing sound as their branches tossed and swayed. The Gabrielinos' numerous dogs ran away howling, tails between legs, while the people prostrated themselves in supplication to the dread forces and began to moan and wail.

The quake lasted for the duration of an Ave Maria, as Antonio noted, and was repeated three times at brief intervals. The terrified Indians believed it was caused by the writhings of huge serpents on whose backs the earth rested and their shamans blew smoke from clay pipes to the four directions to placate these monsters, while Crespi and Gomez offered prayers to Saint Joseph, patron of the expedition, foster father of Jesus.

Recalling his experiences campaigning in Italy, Portola surmised the tremors were caused by volcanoes in the mountains ahead. Rivera agreed, citing volcanoes near the City of Mexico where earthquakes often occurred. But Fages, independent as usual, offered the example of Lisbon: "All but destroyed a few years ago though no volcanoes exist anywhere near it!" Costanso, when asked his opinion as a man of science, coolly answered that the causes of earthquakes were not adequately understood. "But like the similarity of flora and fauna we find here, including redtailed hawks and oak trees, to those of Spain the explanation probably lies in natural causes such as climate, soil condition, and earth structure."

The alarming experience drew them together, Catalan and Leather Jacket, and that night for the first time in a week Antonio slept with less fear of a knife between his ribs. Had he only known, Lopez was feeling much the same. "The crazy fool tried to ride me into a barranca during the confusion of that stampede!" Juan complained to Ortega. "And I never meant anything but to have a little fun with him about his reata!"

"Don't let your sense of fun get the better of you, Juanito," Ortega cautioned. Between Rivera and his protégé and Portola and his, Ortega wanted to hold neutral ground. He could tell Antonio was keeping something to himself and guessed it concerned Lopez, for the boy uncharacteristically said little during their long scouting rides. With the others, they rose each day before dawn, saddled and breakfasted, then led the march, which was usually only about ten miles because the mules were heavy laden and sometimes trail had to be constructed, and then after camp was pitched about three, they scouted forward into the afternoon to determine the next day's route, returning to camp by dark. In fact, despite his rising spirits, Antonio was uncertain what to do about Lopez. He was not even sure he should confide in Ortega, as formerly, and it was not the sort of thing he could discuss with Costanso.

As for Rivera, he was biding his time, confident the inexperienced Portola would make a serious mistake, indeed believing, as he confided to Mariano Carrillo, that the haughty gachupin had already done so by bringing too few provisions for so long a march.

From the Santa Ana River the mile-long column wound its way over low hills to the valley of the San Gabriel where a mission would stand, and here they found the land blackened by fire in the method used by the Indians throughout California to encourage new shoots and remove excessive growth. Here too an earthquake struck, and the men began to grumble that Saint Joseph must have forgotten them. "Knowing how action can dispel apprehension, Portola ordered the march resumed," Antonio recalled, "and our Christian Indian laborers built a bridge of logs over a deep arroyo and under Costanso's supervision cut a trail upward across a brushy ridge." Thus they continued westward by stages until one afternoon they looked down upon a broad plain, the site of present Los Angeles, stretching before them toward the sea.

Almost as they laid eyes on it another earthquake struck them. "Gracious Mother of God!" exclaimed black Pablo, crossing himself and touching the sprig of sage he wore on his hat for good luck. And Luigi, Portola's Genoese servant, made the sign against the Evil Eye with the first and fourth fingers. Nevertheless they descended toward a river that flowed through the plain and camped in a beautiful grove of oaks not far from the present Los Angeles Civic Center. "What an ideal place for a settlement!" Father Crespi exclaimed. But for Antonio there was a doubt. Something dangerous lurked about the place, something akin to the chaos he'd felt so powerfully that night of the stampede. He could not have said what it was and finally dismissed it as imaginary.

Bearing strings of shell beads, also baskets of meal ground from acorns and grass seeds, the inhabitants of a nearby village came to greet them, and old men smoking wild tobacco in clay pipes shaped like tubes, blew mouthfuls of smoke at them as a sign of peace. Portola and Rivera made presents of Cuban tobacco and glass beads in return.

Next morning being August first, feast day of Our Lady of Los Angeles de Porciuncula, the expedition rested and proper solemnities were observed, Crespi and Gomez officiating. In honor of the occasion and to impress the Indians who were watching, the fathers wore their best vestments—fine white amices, albs, stoles, cinctures, chasubles, maniples—as if in a cathedral instead of under open sky. On this day plenary indulgences could be obtained if one were in a state of grace, yet Antonio knew he was not insofar as Lopez was concerned, gladly wishing the wretch dead at times, at others regarding him as no more than a nuisance who must be lived with. Still, now as he knelt with his fellows upon the sun-warmed earth and thought how isolated they all were in an unknown land, beyond the edge of Christendom, a feeling of brotherhood came to him which was encouraged by the words of Crespi and Gomez. Crespi, the indefatigable had, he knew, been up since dawn laboring with a big tong-like bake iron over a bed of coals to make enough altar breads so each communicant might

This Promised Land

have one. Yet the industrious father's memory was so poor he was obliged to read from his missal. Nevertheless his words permeated the boy's receptive mind, which in true Catalan tradition was doubtful yet full of faith.

> Our Holy Lady,
> your gift of water

(It had been carried from the nearby stream in a silver basin and placed before the golden cross on an improvised altar of brushwood.)

> brings life and freshness to the earth,
> washes away our sins and brings us eternal life.
> We ask you now to bless this water,
> and to give us your protection this day
> which you have made your own.
> Renew the living spring of your life within us and protect us
> in spirit and body,
> that we may be free from sin and come into your presence
> to receive our gift of salvation.

Gomez, less vigorous than Crespi but gifted with eloquence, spoke to them about the significance of this feast day of Our Lady of Porciuncula. "Near Assisi there existed in Saint Francis' time a small chapel. Though the building had been allowed to fall into ruin, the spot seemed to young Francis ideal for a retreat and so he built a hut there and called the place his 'little portion' or 'porciuncula,' or as we today might say with all humility 'that piece of the earth's surface which Our Lord has allotted us for our work.' " Antonio, listening intently, could not help but wonder what place might be allotted him in due course, by God's will, and if it might resemble his home place in the winding green valley of the Segre with its orchards, vineyards, and grain fields looking up to the slopes of the high Pyrenees. "At Porciuncula," Gomez continued, "Francis received a revelation concerning remission of sins which might be obtained by those visiting the chapel he restored in honor of Our Lady of Los Angeles, and so I propose," he concluded, "that we name the lovely spot where we have prayed this morning, 'the Valley of Our Lady of the Angels.' "

Robert Easton

Rising to his feet, Antonio could have forgiven Lopez, taken him by the hand and embraced the man with true brotherly love, but when he saw the other's backside walking obstinately away, the divine inspiration disappeared.

Chapter Five

With anger Lospe watched the tall hateful figure of Owotoponus escorting her mother toward the shallow ravine that led to the entrance of the ceremonial enclosure, with its fragrant freshly cut sage boughs. Waiting in the ravine hidden from view, Lospe knew, were the shamans and prominent laymen who composed the Council of Twenty. Twelve were Owotoponus' ritual assistants. All were members of the prestigious A-antap Society, the secret religious organization which held supreme power among her people.

All prominent citizens belonged to A-antap from childhood. She had been a member since the age of seven and already knew some of its secret words but nothing could have induced her to reveal them, for the penalty for doing so was death. Yet for no reason she could at the moment have named, she rebelled at thought of the secrecy and exclusivity of A-antap. It did not seem right, open, loving, and it was dominated by Owotoponus.

Still hidden from view, the council filed along the ravine until all were opposite and directly eastward of the enclosure of fragrant boughs which stood on the level of the meeting place slightly above the ravine. Then as if by common consent they emerged and entered the enclosure in solemn silence, Owotoponus and her mother leading.

"Where did they come from?" Lospe heard a surprised child ask as the crowd fell silent. "Hush!" its mother answered in an awed voice. "From beyond the peaks!" and Lospe remembered her own first childish questions

"How did we humans get here in the first place?" she'd asked old Seneq, who was peeling willow stems for weaving into a basket. Scratching herself—the fleas were very bad that summer—her grandmother replied: "Little Daughter, it wasn't easy. And we must always be grateful to the First People, for they made us, and also to Lizard, who intervened at the proper moment. After the Flood which occurred longer ago than anyone can remember, when death was created and the Middle World destroyed, the First People were transformed into the plants and animals we know today, while others ascended into the sky to escape death and become celestial beings. One day up there in their crystal palace, Sky Coyote, Sun, Moon, Evening and Morning Star were discussing how to make man. Coyote wanted man to look like him because, he said, 'I have the finest hands!' The others disagreed. Lizard sat listening quietly in the background as Lizard usually does. Finally the others gave in and agreed that man should have hands like Coyote's. So they gathered around the Great Flat Rock of Creation, which as I have told you is at the very summit of Iwihinmu at the Center of the World, and just as Coyote was about to put his hand down firmly upon it and thus create man, Lizard slipped forward and placed his handprint on the rock first, and that is why we must be grateful to Lizard. Otherwise we should all have paws like Coyote!" Seneq explained there were three worlds. In the Upper World lived the all-powerful Sky People such as Sun, Moon, Morning Star, Polaris, and Condor. The Lower World was inhabited by monsters and evil spirits who emerged at night and caused trouble. "We of the Middle World must be very careful not to offend the supernatural forces above and below us, my child, or that might be the end of us. That is why we need Sacred Condor to mediate for us and guide us." That was the summer before the Spaniards came, the summer when all things seemed beautiful as they would forever be. After the Bear Dance designed to placate the grizzly bears who were numerous and dangerous and competed for the same food as the People of Olomosoug—nuts, grapes, berries, fish—the family, with the exception of old Seneq and her husband, Lospe's grandfather, Masapaqsi, who were too old to travel so far, made its annual journey into the back country.

First consulting Quati, her father learned there were no stars near the moon to indicate danger to humans, also that *Masiqloka-i-ivilike* or Orion's Belt, "the three steady persons," would be visible in the east, and in return Koxsho gave Quati a beaver skin. They went straight eastward toward the rising sun to those mountains, which before long would be hemming Antonio, Ortega, and the other invading Spaniards against the shoreline, a

This Promised Land

source of irritation to them as well as of mystery and wonder. Koxsho led, followed by Uncle Ta-apu, then Lospe's blood uncle Tinaquaic not yet married but foolish as the day he was born, then her brother Asuskwa and cousin Alul the boastful, then Koyo and Lehlele, finally Kachuku and herself. Kachuku brought her doll but Lospe left hers at home, feeling all at once too grown up for it.

Since they were going to be gone more than a month they carried sleeping mats, food, cooking bowls, sharp digging sticks for extracting bulbs and roots, and large cone-shaped baskets for gathering the pine nuts, berries, and cherries of the back country, and around their necks suspended on thongs the women wore a short cane whistle which they would use to give warning if they met a bear. To protect themselves from sunburn they rubbed their bodies with red ochre, cherishing that lightness of skin which was a mark of distinction and beauty, along with thin lips and graceful figures.

Following the river they entered the dark mountains. The hillsides around them became steeper, harsher, and yet more fragrant with new kinds of shrubs and flowers, the air drier, wilder. It seemed they were entering another world and in a way they were. Leaving behind grassy valley and oak woodland, they were moving into the upper Sonoran life zone with its scrub oak, junipers, digger and pinon pine, mule deer, lion, grizzly, brush rabbit, and dusky-footed woodrat. Ahead lay the transition zone with sugar and yellow pine, mountain chicadee, and acorn woodpecker. It was the interfacing of these various zones and their multitude of life forms which helped give the atmosphere its excitement. Meanwhile the tough leathery-leaved chaparral consisting of many aromatic components, chamise, wild lilac, bear brush, ash, quinine bush grew down the slopes around them like a dense fur covering the earth's back.

Though their people had been following this trail for centuries, Koxsho was careful before starting to show gratitude to Earth for the privilege of passing over her. Taking a handful of soil, he let it fall reverently through his fingers, while singing a song improvised for the occasion:

> Earth upon which we step,
> Earth upon which we step,
> Be forgiving toward us,
> Be forgiving toward us,

Robert Easton

With grateful hearts we thank you,
With grateful hearts we thank
you!

It seemed a good song and they all felt they would have a successful trip. There would be no hurry. They would stop to gather, rest, swim, hunt, as the spirit moved. Everything around them—the plants, trees, rocks as well as the dust under their feet—would be alive with meaning and would know of their presence, and thus they would be surrounded by a silent company of living things whose kinship to themselves they must respect.

As the trail wound from side to side of the river wherever the going was best, now under the shade of giant cottonwoods, now across burning hot flats of purple mint and acrid vinegar weed, then through beds of ferns and roses, always following the rushing living water, something new and exciting seemed about to happen. Perhaps the condors knew what it was. Already they were soaring overhead craning their red heads down curiously.

"They are looking to see if you are worthy of visiting the Heart of the World," her father joked in response to Lospe's question. Though she'd seen condors many times, the question of what they might be thinking had never occurred to her before. "The Nesting Place of the Condor is close to the Heart of the World," Koxsho went on. "It is a place of very great power, so we never go there unless purified first. That is why they are coming to look us over—to see if you have been a good girl!" She was pleased by everything he said but not by his manner, which made her seem still a child.

"And will we see the Dance of the Condors?" she asked gravely.

He looked at her no longer with amusement. "Perhaps," he said, adopting something of her tone, "who knows?"

Looking up she wondered if the condors knew of her new maturity. The birds' huge dark wings, each with a triangular patch of white underfeathers, remained motionless, never flapping while they sailed the pathways of the sky in majesty and beauty. These were the days when condors ranged North America from British Columbia to the Florida Everglades, dramatizing the sky and captivating the imaginations of many aboriginal peoples. They were worshipped in a variety of ways, as thunderbird, as bringer of rain, as dread emblem of an almighty sky power, a power linked perhaps through some mysterious gene memory to their remote

This Promised Land

predecessor, the largest bird ever to fly, the gigantic vulture *Teratornis incredibilis*. With its wingspread of eighteen feet, *Teratornis* soared over Southern California twenty million years earlier when the outline of an almost tropical land, dense with palms and tree ferns, was much as it is today though many coastal valleys such as that occupied by Lospe's people were bays and inlets and the emerging Los Angeles basin erupted with numerous volcanoes spouting smoke, hot ash and lava. Far back in the Pleistocene Epoch a hundred thousand years or more ago, modern condor evolved, and *Gymnogyps californianus,* as he would be called, had been looking down with his blood-red eye upon the life beneath him ever since—upon saber-toothed cat, giant lion, upon mammoth and giant ground sloth, mastodon, prehistoric horse, and camel and, for the last thirty or forty thousand years, men and women.

Although most neighboring tribelets held the eagle especially sacred, Lospe's people felt a special affinity for the condor because their territory included its secret nesting places.

"And will we go to the Heart of the World, my father?" she asked.

Koxsho looked down gravely, then shook his head. "No one goes to the Heart of the World—no one but holy men!"

"Why?"

He fell silent, searching her eyes with his, then, darkening with a strange look, shook his head again, and she knew she'd asked a question she shouldn't have asked, but was not sorry. She was already thinking she would go to the Heart of the World somehow and see there the Great Rock of Creation, which Seneq had described with Lizard's handprint on it.

They camped that night where a grove of tall sycamores arched their white arms over the river. The water ran swiftly between banks lined with alders and maples, and vines offering ripe blackberries. There was a nice clean sandbar too, free from ants and ticks, on which to sleep, and nearby on the bank in a ledge of mother rock were six smoothly rounded grinding holes or mortars, where seeds had been ground for centuries. Some were as deep as her arm was long, and it thrilled Lospe to reach into them as if she were reaching back into time. While women and girls ground seeds for supper in these ancient mortars, the men and boys caught fish, first stupefying the trout by mashing a narcotic soapweed root in the water, then catching them by hand. They were added to the rabbit Ta-apu killed earlier with his throwing stick. After the meal Tinaquaic made music with his elderberry flute, or panpipe, while cigarettes of hollow cane stuffed with wild tobacco were smoked and stories told.

Playing together by the light of the moon while the grownups talked, Lospe and Kachuku pretended they were The Ancients who first ground seeds in the nearby mortars when those holes were no deeper than the length of your finger. Nobody knew much about The Ancients except that they lived long ago. Occasionally a charred stone tool of a style no longer in fashion was found in company with huge bones of animals which no longer existed, and some of those bones and flint points would eventually be dated back more than thirty-thousand years, leading experts to conclude that mankind inhabited the New World much longer than previously believed.

As Kachuku and Lospe constructed their imaginary village in the sand with sticks and stones, leaves, bits of moss, the moonlight helped transform it into a reality in which The Ancients lived, married, bore children, built houses, died, and were buried. Finally their mothers called them to bed. Night Wind, the breath of darkness, was beginning to come down the canyon rustling the leaves above their heads.

"If you can stay awake and listen," her father said solemnly, "Night Wind may tell you whether we shall see the Dance of the Condors!"

"I'll stay awake!" she vowed. Next she knew she woke suddenly. The fire was burning low. Everyone else was asleep and something was stirring in the bushes behind her. Was it the bear Quati warned them against? Glancing fearfully around, Lospe saw nothing to be afraid of. Kachuku lay motionless beside her, clutching her doll. Beyond Kachuku, Coyote Boy was curled into a grayish brown ball. Not even he heard the thing in the bushes. Whatever it was, it steadily approached. Lospe was about to cry out when she thought, No, that's childish! Wait! And immediately she heard Night Wind say something in the leaves above her. She strained to hear what he said but could not make out. But as she turned back toward the fire, her father's leg casually stretched and nudged a log deeper into the coals. Flames shot up. The rustling in the bushes stopped and she saw her father open one eye, look at her, and wink. Then she knew they would see the Dance of the Condors and learn the Secrets of the World.

* * *

This Promised Land

Many days later toward evening, Koxsho said: "Look up!" Ahead through an opening in the trees rose an enormous dark mountain. It seemed to Lospe like the back of a huge beast. Lofty pines stood up like a mane on its summit. Huge ledges of white rock were like ribs in its sides. Grandeur, awe, mystery exuded from it, and an air so wild it was almost terrifying. "That is the Heart of the World," her father said, "and that is the Nesting Place of the Condors!"

When they reached the foot of the mountain next morning, dozens of condors were sunning themselves with outspread wings in a grand array hundreds of feet above them on the edge of a white cliff over which the river poured in a giant waterfall.

"They are making their morning prayer as we make ours," Koxsho said in hushed voice.

The birds were turning this way and that, like dancers, extending their enormous wings so the sun could touch their feathers with its life-giving rays.

"That is the Dance of the Condors!" Koxsho whispered. "We must always remember that Sacred Condor is from the beginning. He is indivisible. But also he is many. Each day he travels around the world and sees what cannot be seen by human eyes. And each morning he dances here in honor of Sun Our Ruler."

The condors nested on the face of the waterfall cliff in caves marked by whitened droppings. Since their nests were impossible to reach from below, men and boys clambered up through the growth of the surrounding hillside and descended from above. Lospe watched anxiously while Koxsho, secured by a yucca fiber rope, descended toward the first nest. Huge condors were swooping near. She was afraid they would tear him with their sharp beaks or brush him off the face of the rock with their mighty wings, but her mother said not to fear, he was acting with reverence and would be safe. "He will take only one, a young bird, the one allowed by custom!"

All the nests in the area belonged to her family, Lospe knew. No one else was entitled to remove birds, collect feathers, egg shells, or sacred down from them. Sometimes old Seneq would berate her grandfather, urging him to exploit their rights more fully. "Forebear, woman!" Masapaqsi would reply sternly. "Are you never satisfied? You have food. You have clothing. You have a roof over your head. What more do you want?" Still she kept urging.

There was no young bird in the first nest but Koxsho collected feathers and a plentiful supply of down. Uncle Ta-apu descended to the second nest. It contained a dead chick, which he did not touch. Tinaquaic, timid and awkward, did not descend but her brother Asuskwa climbed down fearlessly and found a young bird which they brought back with them to the women waiting at the base of the cliff. It was covered with soft down like gray fur and hissed like a snake when Lospe stretched out her hand to it but soon became quite tame. They kept the chick in a large basket and fed it entrails and eyes of fish caught in the Great Pool. Because hidden at the foot of the waterfall was the largest pool in all their world. The river plunged thundering and foaming into its depths, while on its surface floated feathers of the condors who bathed far above, and in its green recesses huge trout eddied back and forth like dark logs. With condors, trees, rocks, mountains, they were ancestors, prototypes who inhabited this source place so close to the Heart of the World.

As Lospe watched the chick with her brother at her side, she felt the touch of Asuskwa's hand. Pledging her to secrecy he opened the hand and showed her a small gray oval stone. "What is it?" she whispered. "It's a magic condor stone," he whispered back. "I found it in the nest. Promise you'll never tell anyone?" She promised, her heart full of excitement and admiration at her brother's daring. The stone might enable him to see what was hidden and acquire anything he desired.

And then suddenly a shower of ladybugs fell upon the family like orange snow and clotted on logs and boulders roundabout. Koyo was inclined to see in them a bad omen but Koxsho exclaimed: "No, they bring good luck. They've ridden up from the valley on the wind and will sleep here under the snow all winter, returning to us in the spring like the sun itself!" In his roamings Koxsho had learned many things, for he was an independent spirit unusual among his people in that it was new ways, rather than accepted ones, which appealed to him most, and it was from him that Lospe and Asuskwa had inherited their unconventional attitudes.

"Far above us ages ago," Koxsho continued addressing her in the new serious way, "the side of Iwihinmu was pierced by a lightning bolt hurled from the sun, which caused the river to gush down. We call its water the Tears of the Sun because it was shed for the benefit of all living things. Just as Sun brings us drought and death, he also brings us water and life!"

His words inspired her to ask if he would take her with him to

This Promised Land

the summit of Iwihinmu and show her the Rock of Creation about which Seneq had spoken. He looked startled, then dubious. "Please!" she begged. Still he made no answer. His eyes seemed strange and far away. She knew her request was audacious. No one went to the Heart of the World except old Quati and his fellow astrologer-priests, and they jealously guarded their special privileges. She was aware of her mother's anxious look. Ta-apu, too, looked solemn. "Nobody goes to the top of Iwihinmu but holy men!" she heard him say, as if speaking on behalf of her father to extricate him from a difficulty. "Yes, holy men!" Koxsho echoed thoughtfully. Her father had three enormous clawmark scars on his right cheek because once when impersonating a deer too cleverly in the stalk disguised under neck-skin and antlers, a lion had leaped upon him and clawed him, but he killed the lion and made its tail into a quiver for his arrows; yet whenever he was disturbed inwardly as now, the scars darkened too as if reflecting his troubled thoughts. Then suddenly he burst out: "But why not a holy woman?" catching her up in his arms, laughing as she had never heard him laugh, squeezing her tight. "Yes, why not?"

Once Koxsho's mind was made up nothing could stop him. "You may meet the monsters who emerge from the Lower World!" Koyo objected fearfully.

"You sound like old Quati trying to frighten us!"

Koyo looked aghast at such blasphemy. "You may meet the sorcerers themselves!" she argued in a small fearful voice.

"Then we shall meet them!"

Asuskwa wanted to go but Koxsho said no, this would be a brave girl's turn. So he and Lospe climbed alone through the dark forest, the great trees silent around them, the stream rushing beside them, her hand in his. "If you hear strange sounds, do not be afraid," her father counseled in a tone of cheerful audacity, squeezing her hand. "It will only be the bullroarers of the sorcerers trying to frighten us!" And then he explained that the sorcerers and astrologers, Quati and the others who dominated their lives, coming from all the regions occupied by the People of the Land and the Sea, met in secret upon the slopes of Iwihinmu at this time each summer to conduct magic rites and renew the understanding by which they kept everyone else in subservience. "And if you see strange lights," he added not quite so gaily, "it will only be old Quati and his friends waving firebrands!" She understood the risk they were taking. She knew the penalty could be death.

By now the air was thin and cold, and quite dark. Koxsho scooped a hollow in the leaves to make a bed and they crawled in and covered themselves with earth and leaves, curling close together for warmth, and as she felt his strong male body embracing her, her blood beat faster, thinking of the man who would embrace her in love some day, for such things were known to the village children from an early age.

In the grayness of dawn they emerged upon the crest. Alone on a level space three mighty pines stood like sentinels. At their feet lay the huge flat rock, which she knew at a glance must be the Rock of Creation about which Seneq had spoken. Silence and mystery reigned everywhere. Yet all around, too, snowflowers thrust up their red thumbs in gestures of joy through the carpet of brown pine needles. As she was about to climb upon the rock and see if Lizard's handprint was there, her father said gently: "No, we had better not do that! Let's look instead at what was created!"

She followed him to the eastern edge and saw what the rising sun was revealing. As it came up out of the desert beyond the horizon, it struck them fully, nothing intervening, as if creating them too along with that day, and they were silent because there was nothing to say in the presence of such beauty. After watching a moment they went reverently to the northern edge to see what would be revealed from there. At their feet lay the Great Valley like a bowl of shadows containing many nations, and along its right side rose the Snowy Mountains stretching in a dazzling vision until lost from view, and along the left side the Earthquake Mountains extended similarly though grassy and without snow—perhaps because they had shaken it all off, Lospe thought. Westward toward the sea their own dear land unfolded in familiar contours like a beautiful offering, and southward over intervening ranges the channel islands rose from the sea like foreign countries, and Lospe imagined the Princess of the Islands, Luhui, cruising among them in her red canoe. Luhui's canoe was painted bright red and spangled with abalone shells and at its center, as well as a compass stone, there was the vertebra of a whale cushioned with sea otter skins on which Luhui sat in regal splendor while three strong rowers sped her swiftly over the sea.

As the sun rose higher and showed them all this, the night drained away from every side like sorrow and evil departing from

This Promised Land

them, leaving the land shining with joy as if newly made in the first moment of creation.

"What we are seeing is holier than all holy men!" her father muttered softly, and following his example, she knelt and prayed while facing the rising sun.

But in the distance she heard the bullroarers and shrill deerbone whistles of the sorcerers and was afraid, as she was afraid now, remembering, as she stood at the meeting place and thought of Owotoponus and his power, and heard the music of the sacred whistles rising from inside the ceremonial enclosure.

Chapter Six

An hour after Mass, Antonio, Lopez, and all the rest received what Antonio suspected might be a divine rebuke. Once again the earth shuddered violently making a total of fourteen shocks so far. Perhaps Saint Joseph had indeed forsaken them! Perhaps Our Lady of Porciuncula had turned a deaf ear to their recent prayer!

Sensing a general uneasiness Portola encouraged a hunt by way of diversion, and Ortega suggested to Antonio with casual heartiness as if to make up for past testiness: "Shall we see if Our Lady will grant us an antelope?" He wanted to draw the boy out of his unaccustomed silence.

After putting fresh flints in their gunlocks, they rode off across the plain that stretches from the site of downtown Los Angeles westward through Hollywood toward Santa Monica and the ocean. The chaparral-covered Hollywood Hills rose dark at their right. Ahead lay brownish green meadows dotted with many clumps of dark green berry and grape vines, all watered by invisible springs. It was an inviting prospect and the day one of those lovely August ones, balmy yet cool, the air still alive with spring vitality before the dull heat of autumn begins.

Fresh expectancy rose in Antonio. He felt he was about to unburden himself, say and do things heretofore impossible. Just ahead, beyond the next rise in the gently billowing sunlit meadowland, something marvelous seemed to be waiting, and he imagined a beautiful brown and white buck with high-pronged horns who would appear as if by magic and stand still to be shot. But the numerous bands of antelope bounded away as they approached. Growing impatient he suggested: "Jose, maybe we'll have better luck if we separate?"

After a moment's thought Ortega replied: "Very well, but let's stay within sight of each other, eh?" His tone implied it might

This Promised Land

be a bit risky to go off alone in strange terrain but Antonio could see nothing to fear in such an expanse of lush beauty. He was becoming a little restless under Ortega's supervision, yet he loved the man dearly and respected his knowledge and leadership, which was why he wished to appear strong in his eyes in the matter of Lopez.

At thirty-five Ortega was tending toward corpulence though extremely tough and durable as many rounded objects are. As chief of scouts he traveled three times farther than nearly anyone else—reconnoitering next day's route, returning to camp, leading the way the next day—and though others including Antonio might accompany him depending on circumstances, he alone always covered the ground three times. Alone among the enlisted men, Ortega could talk to officers or fathers and be listened to respectfully as an equal, indeed often as a superior in experience and judgment. He'd been born, as he told Antonio, on the mainland not far from the City of Mexico, the son of small shopkeepers, and could have followed their footsteps. But hankering for adventure, he crossed to Lower California and enlisted under Rivera in the Leather Jacket Company, where he rose rapidly to sergeant, a much more important and better paid rank than nowadays. Marrying Antonio Carrillo, Mariano's cousin, he became supervisor at the San Antonio mining camp near the tip of the peninsula and it was there that Portola, making an inspection tour as new governor, met him.

Don Gaspar was so favorably impressed he persuaded Jose to reenter the service, appointing him paymaster and superintendent of supplies at the Loreto presidio, a highly responsible position, with an understanding he would be made lieutenant after serving with the expedition planned for New California. "Meanwhile, can you take this young dragoon," indicating Antonio, "and turn him into a frontier cavalryman?" A magnificent chestnut sorrel stood tied to the rail at the edge of the parade ground nearby. Pointing toward the animal Ortega said casually: "There's your horse, my boy, if you can ride him!" His tone implied no great difficulty. Feeling confident Antonio mounted. The sorrel bucked murderously. But with Portola and Ortega watching, he had no choice but to stick, though his teeth were nearly jarred out of him. Then Ortega saw him properly outfitted as a Leather Jacket and took him under his tutelage. Not till long afterward did Antonio discover the sorrel was Ortega's favorite. Indeed with uncharacteristic sentiment Jose had named him Babieca after the legendary charger of El Cid, Spain's national hero, and like his namesake, this Babieca too was a dark chestnut with cream-colored mane and tail.

In those early days they rode shoulder-to-shoulder in confidence. Now Antonio had deliberately dropped from Ortega's sight behind a slight rise when he heard someone cry out directly ahead. Spurring Babieca he breasted the rise and saw a lovely pond of fresh water surrounded by lush grass, and at its edge Lopez and his roan floundering side by side—and a few yards away, similarly floundering, a beautiful antelope buck such as he'd imagined.

Galloping toward them he became aware of an unpleasant odor, and that first intuitive uneasiness he'd felt about the region returned like a twinge from an old hurt, while at the same instant Babieca's feet sank suddenly into what Antonio at first thought smelly black mud, then realized with a shock was sticky black tar. Underlying the inviting pond and pleasant meadow was a layer of black stuff as dangerous as quicksand.

Lopez, horse, antelope were all mired in it. The more they struggled, the more they sank. Lopez, Antonio realized as he managed to find a bit of firm ground on which to halt Babieca, had lost his head and was thrashing wildly: "Help me, man!" he screamed, "I'm going under!"

I ought to let you sink, Antonio thought grimly, but I could never hope to obtain an indulgence from Our Lady of Porciuncula if I did. "Stop thrashing!" he yelled back. "Lie flat! You'll sink more slowly!"

But Lopez continued to thrash and scream. Loosening his reata, the same Juan had borrowed, Antonio threw him the running loop, calling to him to knot it around his waist. Wrapping his end around his saddlehorn, he whirled Babieca and set spurs, and after a hard struggle Lopez came out of the mire and onto the firm ground where he lay gasping like a smelly black fish.

"And what happened to you, my friend?" Antonio inquired sarcastically, riding back to him, recoiling his rope as he came. "Whew, you stink!"

"That damned antelope misled me!"

"No, you misled yourself! You were in such a greedy guts hurry you paid no attention where you were going!"

Ortega galloped up, attracted by the shouting. After nearly being sucked under themselves, he and Antonio finally got ropes onto Lopez's roan and, with their horses pulling side by side and

This Promised Land

Juan helping, extricated the animal. But the beautiful antelope remained beyond their reach, hopelessly bogged. "I'm going to shoot it!" Antonio announced, watching its futile struggles. Nearby were carcasses and bones of creatures who'd become similarly mired: deer, coyote, antelope, even a lion and a huge vulture following their prey too greedily.

"Don't waste powder and lead!" Ortega advised. "It will die eventually!"

"That's what I mean!"

Antonio put a ball through the antelope's noble head, and as he watched its expiring convulsions, he thought that perhaps there but for the grace of the Lady of Porciuncula he might have been fatally trapped himself. He did not guess that ages before him, indeed ever since the time of *Teratornis incredibilis,* the treacherous brea* had trapped prehistoric saber-toothed tiger, giant wolf, sloth, horse, and mammoth. But he understood why so many vultures were wheeling overhead, some of them huge red-headed ones larger than eagles, with patches of white feathers under their wings.

That night by the campfire Lopez played his fiddle impudently as usual and complained for all to hear: "After I'd risked my neck trying to reach that bogged antelope and provide us with meat," and it was true no one had been successful in the hunt that day, "this prankster," indicating Antonio, "deliberately delayed helping me and taunted me until Jose arrived and shamed him into doing something!"

Antonio decided not to dignify this lie with a reply. Yet he admitted there was plausibility in the words. Suppose Juan actually believed them, was actually telling the truth as he saw it? A first painful comprehension of what might be another's legitimate point of view, one which seemed wholly irreconcilable with his own, broke in upon his mind. He turned for help to Jose. But Ortega remained neutral. He'd not said a word about Antonio's going off alone against his advice. Now he simply stated what he'd seen at the tar bog, and suggested the matter be dropped. He wanted no further quarreling. It might endanger his promotion. Above all he didn't want trouble between two of his men to become a cause célèbre between Catalans and Leather Jackets, which it was becoming, and he hoped Antonio had learned a lesson.

*tar

Antonio never forgot the antelope or the lesson. Years later he wrote: "It represents the beautiful illusion which lives in this land and can lead a man to destruction."

Next day he and Ortega in company with Martin Reyes, Jose Verdugo, and Juan Olivera reached the sea at the Santa Monica bluffs. Finding their way north blocked by the mountains that descend abruptly to the water in the direction of Malibu, they turned back and, discovering a low pass, the one taken now by Sepulveda Boulevard and the San Diego Freeway, emerged into the San Fernando Valley. The entire expedition camped that night near the present community of Encino. Guided by friendly Indians they crossed the valley without difficulty, ascended Fernando Pass, and entered the Santa Clara Valley of Southern California near the present site of Newhall, where they turned westward and descended the broad valley toward the sea.

Soon they met Indians of a distinctly different type: taller, handsomer, livelier, living in larger, better organized villages. These were of the same ethnic family as Lospe and her people, the group we now call Chumash, and shared with them common customs, religion, and related languages. They were mostly dark haired though some were fair, and though the men went naked, some of the women wore woven rabbit skin capes above stained-red deerskin skirts like those of Lospe and Kachuku, and the men too wore such capes in cold weather. All were if possible friendlier than any yet encountered, and finding them created a general sense of elation among the Spaniards and there were renewed jokes about meeting before long the fabulous dusky hued Queen Calafia herself.

Approaching the sea near present Ventura, the scouts and Costanso who accompanied them that day saw a line of mountainous islands beginning some fifteen miles off shore and running westerly parallel to the mainland, and they knew this must be the Channel of Santa Barbara mentioned in their two guidebooks: Cabrera Bueno's sailors' manual and Miguel Venegas' *Natural and Civil History of California.* Two authors could hardly have differed more widely in their treatment of a common subject, Antonio decided, when he read these guidelines to his promised land. Cabrera Bueno, a veteran captain of galleons such as sailed annually from Manila* across the Pacific to Acapulco, New

---

*following the Japanese current northward and eastward they usually made land near the California-Oregon line

Spain's chief western port, gave a workmanlike description of the coast as a sailor might see it, including the latitudes of such major landmarks as Cape Mendocino and Point Pinos which forms the southern arm of Monterey Bay. Venegas' *Natural and Civil History* by contrast was an at times fantastically flowery compendium, by a Jesuit scholar, of observations and surmises by early explorers and was based largely on the Franciscan Juan de Torquemada's famous *Monarquia Indiana* first published at Seville in 1615. The *Monarquia* described California as a marvelous land of extraordinary fertility and natural wonders, whose inhabitants were very partial to Spaniards and where there was even "a strongly fortified city inhabited by a polite and well governed population." Torquemada omitted the dusky queen but linked California with the legendary Straight of Anian, the direct passage to India, supposed to lie north of the North American land mass, a concept fascinating the European mind for centuries. Perhaps California was an island. Perhaps it contained the long-sought golden city of El Dorado.

Approaching the water the explorers saw upon it three of those large canoes Torquemada described as being maneuvered by the natives with incredible speed and skill. The graceful craft flew like gleaming red birds over the calm blue sea, and on a promontory nearby stood the most impressive settlement so far discovered. It contained more than thirty well thatched houses shaped like half oranges arranged along lanes, and some proved to be as large as sixty feet in diameter. "The people who streamed from them in joyous welcome numbered about four hundred and were of the same superior type recently met with," Antonio recorded. "They gave us enough fish to load the entire pack train, mostly bonita; also many seeds, nuts, and small cakes of meal; also many exquisite bowls of wood and stone as symmetrical as if turned on a lathe; as well as baskets of a design and quality far superior to any yet seen. But most remarkable were their canoes."

Several were drawn up on the beach. Examining one, he and Costanso found it about twenty-five feet long made of planks of varying widths sewn together by stout fiber cord, gracefully pointed and raked at both ends, sealed with tar and painted bright red. "And look there!" Costanso exclaimed with unusual emotion. Imbedded in its central thwart was a flat stone, painted red with black lines radiating from its center over half its diameter, and at its center, standing upright from a small hole, was a stick eight inches long. "That must be their combination sundial and compass! The stick casts a time shadow and the central ray of that circle of lines must always mark true north or true south, depending on which way they are going!"

So it proved. The captain or owner of the craft, a large friendly man with a beard wearing a distinctive cape of bear skin, demonstrated how the compass stone could be rotated in its socket as Costanso surmised, so that its markings faced north or south. "Could they have come originally from across the sea in these?" Antonio speculated. "You know how the Philippine Islanders are said to be experts with canoes, often traveling great distances from one island to another. And if our ships can cross the South Sea on the northern current, why could not they?"

"It is not impossible," Costanso agreed, "though it strains my sense of reason. More likely they developed them simply to go back and forth between mainland and islands. Wouldn't you have done the same, sitting here and wondering about that mysterious line of purple mountains that rises from the sea?"

The canoe belonged to islanders come to the mainland on a visit. They were referred to as Michumash which Antonio rendered simply "Chumash." "We inquired about the hazards of a voyage over open water," he noted, "which had now become quite rough, and were told they usually made it early in the day when the sea was calm. Several more canoes approaching now, we saw how their crews, kneeling, dipped their double-bladed paddles in unison now on this side, now on that, singing together a wild sea chanty, making the craft fairly fly! Reaching the breaker line, they rode a great comber in with amazing skill, then leaped from their craft and bore it on their shoulders, still singing, to its appointed resting place."

While at the beach Costanso calculated the latitude with the help of his English octant, a forerunner of the modern sextant. When held to his eye its reflecting mirrors enabled him to see sun and horizon simultaneously and measure the angle between. Then using tables keyed to the Peak of Tenerife on the Canary Islands,[*] he computed the latitude of the Village of the Canoes and compared his results to those in Cabrera Bueno's nautical manual. Costanso's figures were thirty-four degrees, thirteen minutes; Cabrera's thirty-five degrees, three minutes; while Father Crespi, using his old-fashioned astrolabe, came out at thirty-four degrees, thirty-six minutes. "And thus began the first of many controver-

---

[*] a reference point similar to modern day Greenwich, England

This Promised Land

sies over our exact position," Antonio recalled. "Costanso sure of his superior knowledge and more modern equipment, Crespi, while acknowledging this, unable to rid himself of a lurking suspicion he was dealing with a godless young skeptic whose conclusions might in some degree be influenced by the Devil!" Like Portola, Crespi and Costanso were keeping diaries because the Viceroy and Inspector General in Mexico City were expecting a detailed account of the journey, as was Father President Serra at San Diego. Every statement would be carefully scrutinized by official eyes and questions asked.

Chapter Seven

The music coming from inside the ceremonial enclosure was made, she knew, by two old men Tup and Quolog who had removed their deer tibia whistles from the watertight basket where the instruments were kept moist and vibrant. The sound of the whistles was eternal, as old Quati had said more than once, but it was now also the voice of Owotoponus and his new power, and thus hateful to Lospe.

After a few moments the Council of Twenty filed out of the enclosure and formed a semicircle on the dancing ground facing her and the other people of the village. Her mother and Owotoponus stood at its center. Owotoponus held in both hands the sacrosanct redwood box decorated with fragments of abalone shell. His twelve assistants, decked with feathers, each representing a month of the year and a ray of the sun, stepped forward, six on each side, and formed a smaller semicircle, likewise facing her and the audience. While the sacred whistles continued to sound, Owotoponus advanced a few steps more carrying his precious box and stood at the heart of this new circle; and while his assistants placed offertory baskets in front of the crowd, he waited, and then when all, even Lospe despite herself, were holding their breath with suspense he opened his box and removed the Sunstick from its bed of sacred down. But then her deeper feeling broke through and she remembered her bitter animosity toward him, which dated from that day she visited the summit of Iwihinmu with her father.

As they descended the sacred mountain in the light of the early morning, Koxsho said quietly: "Certain things need not be spoken of to others!" And when they arrived back at the foot of the waterfall where the rest of the family was waiting eagerly to hear

This Promised Land

all they had seen and done, they said only that they had been to the Heart of the World. No amount of persuasion could extract more. She read wonder and envy in their eyes and felt fiercely elated, quietly proud deep at heart, and not even her brother's private urging could move Lospe. "I am keeping your secret," she replied, referring to the stone he'd taken from the condor nest. "You keep mine! Tell no one where I've been!"

Returning down the river they stopped at the venerable Cave of the Condors to make offerings and give thanks for their successful journey.

While climbing the hillside toward it—it was in an outcropping of rock some distance above the trail—they saw a large figure standing at its mouth with back toward them and easily recognized Owotoponus, unmistakable by size and authoritative manner. He was painting something on the rock at the upper lip of the cave mouth, apparently wholly engrossed in his work, and paid them no attention as they approached. Her father leading, they halted at a short distance and watched as Owotoponus dipped his yucca fiber brushes first into one tiny bowl of pigment—red made from hematite, white from diatomaceous clay, blue and green from fuchsite and serpentine—then into another and applied the color to the rock with swift firm strokes. He was painting something which looked like a bird in flight. Back through time as everyone knew, his predecessors had painted figures on the interior walls of the cave depicting the forces that governed the Three Worlds. Sun was represented by a fiery circle, Moon by a crescent, Milky Way by flecks of white on a dark background. Water Skater, the mythic messenger, took the form of a huge bug. And at the far end of the cave, alone upon that entire wall, was the large, very dim, very old, very sacred painting of Condor which had been done in simple black outline ages ago by some unknown hand. Despite its enormous significance, it was a crude figure rather like the scarecrow Lospe and Kachuku had helped erect in Seneq's garden. It was not a real condor. Nor were any of the other paintings in the cave real. It was a symbol. But what Owotoponus was doing was the real thing. His bird had life, was actually flying. And when with a touch he completed its red head, she saw, amazed, that it was not only Sacred Condor but actual condor soaring miraculously out of the living rock. She was a little afraid, too, for Owotoponus even at this earlier time was acquiring great power and might be painting to magically kill someone and might harm them should they disturb him.

At last her father inquired in a polite and friendly way: "Cousin, what are you doing?"

Koxsho never disparaged Owotoponus' eccentric behavior, finding it akin to his own. While still a youth Owotoponus had begun going off alone like this, meditating, fasting, seeking power, taking momoy, and painting on cave walls what he saw while under its influence. Returning to the village, he claimed special connection with the Sky People. Everyone thought him absurd at first. Lospe recalled hearing how he flushed and bit his lip and how tears of rage and vexation came to his eyes when they scoffed at him. But when he accurately predicted events, cured illness, gave wise counsel, people began to seek him out. And as he felt his power grow he became increasingly ambitious to succeed his aging father. But Quati would not step aside. So Owotoponus was like a smouldering fire which cannot take flame.

After a long moment he replied to Koxsho almost inaudibly while continuing to work, as if her father were not worth noticing: "Ask the rock!" He clearly wanted to disparage but Koxsho refused to be offended and replied good humoredly: "Cousin, what do you mean?"

"I mean this rock is like a beautiful woman and I am making love to her, so you should ask her what I am doing!" Owotoponus snapped out as if annoyed by stupid questions. Turning, he looked fully at Koyo. He had adored her since they were children but she would have nothing to do with him, being wholly taken up with Koxsho. Now she was very angry but controlled herself.

"Let us leave this joker to make love to his rock," she replied while serenely meeting his eye, "since there is no woman who will love him!" Though Owotoponus' power might already be great, Koyo still held personal power over him.

Owotoponus laughed softly, sardonically, but Lospe could sense his pain and bitterness and it troubled her.

"Not until we have made our offerings will we leave!" her father insisted, still good humoredly, believing Owotoponus under the influence of momoy and not quite himself. Taking Koyo by the hand, he led her on into the cave and the others followed, filing past Owotoponus who without a word resumed his painting. They scattered seeds as customary at the back wall before the painting of Sacred Condor, Lospe wondering if Condor would know of the stone her brother had secretly taken from the nest on the face of the cliff, and as they made their offering the rays of the sun came in at the little window called The Eye of the Sun,

This Promised Land

bored long ago in the eastern wall where the rock was thin, and shone directly on the ancient painting but Lospe noticed a moment later that it did not touch the new one Owotoponus was doing.

"We shall see!" she heard him mutter grimly as her father and mother emerged ahead of her, and her father echoed calmly: "We shall see!"

Thinking these thoughts Lospe now watched Owotoponus remove the Sacred Sunstick from the down-filled box as a sound like the sigh of the wind passed through the crowd around her. Because this was the most powerful instrument in their Middle World. It looked like a mushroom at the end of a long wood stem. Its head was a stone disc with red and white rays radiating from its center to symbolize the sun. Bits of seashell embedded in the knob of dark tar at the point of radiation represented stars. Its shaft, which penetrated up into the knob, was polished cedar. Bending down, Owotoponus stuck it into the earth so that the shadow of the disc fell at his feet, and thus he brought the power of the sun under his control. It was a moment of deepest solemnity. For all his shortcomings, during it Owotoponus became their intermediary with the forces that govern the universe.

With an authoritative motion he struck the stone with his magic scepter. This was a shorter stick with a quartz crystal fastened to its end, and the crystal, flashing brilliantly as he struck, transformed the sunlight into all the colors of the rainbow, while Owotoponus muttered phrases in the secret language of A-antap. Then he spoke aloud so everyone could understand: "Great Sun, author of life and death, is with us!" pointing to the shadow of the disc at his feet. The atmosphere became so charged with suspense that people's stomachs could be heard rumbling with nervousness. "This is another of those moments of profound change revealed to me by the Celestial Ones. Take courage. Sun is with us. Let us go to meet the A-alowow with confidence. Sun is with us. Praise the Sun Our Ruler! Praise the Sun Our Ruler!" His voice rolled it out across the valley, strong and deep, and Lospe felt a tingling she could not suppress, evil though she knew Owotoponus to be. She glanced at Kachuku who stood beside her. Kachuku's eyes were starting right out of her head. "Praise the Sun Our Ruler!" Owotoponus continued, and as if entranced the people answered with one voice: "Praise the Sun Our Ruler!" But Lospe's thoughts were again lost in fierce hatred and dread as she remembered his first public pronouncement after succeeding his father and becoming chief shaman and astrologer-priest.

It was on the third day of June, the month when all paths are open, that the criers at Owotoponus' order summoned everyone to the meeting place to witness the prodigy he predicted, the mating of Sun and Evening Star in broad daylight. Lospe remembered how she trembled with expectancy, also with hatred because she felt sure Owotoponus had caused her father's death and was preparing a powerful move against her mother. During the night a fog had drifted in and shrouded everything in mystery and silence. Now it began to clear. Painted and adorned with plumes, Owotoponus stood beside the Wisdom Stone, that circular block of unknown origin, with the hollow at its center said to be the opening to Upper and Lower Worlds, a seat of judgment on all matters of highest importance. In his right hand he held the magic scepter with the crystal at its end. Intoning, he waved it slowly back and forth and it sparkled in the sunlight beginning to break through the fog. "Prepare to observe the Sun Our Ruler directly!" Ocean and Earth have sent us a mist so that we may behold a miracle without being blinded. Watch!"

The sun rose higher as they watched. Suddenly a black dot appeared moving at steady speed across its face. "That is Evening Star!" Owotoponus' voice rang out triumphantly and Lospe remembered how she had trembled. Even the courageous figure of her mother seemed to shrink a little, newly bereaved and now having to face this. "Yes, that tiny black dot is Evening Star," Owotoponus continued exultantly as if speaking directly to Koyo, as if *she* were Evening Star. "She's the wife of Sun, as we all know since they bed together at evening. But when she wanders from her path like this and they mate in broad daylight before all the Sky People and all of us of the Middle World, we can be sure something very unusual is about to occur!" Again everyone trembled, and Lospe's heart turned icy cold. What was she seeing? What was about to occur? How could Owotoponus know? What enormous power he had!

What she was seeing was the famous Transit of Venus of that year of 1769. Father Rubio explained it to her years later when she was a neophyte at Mission Santa Lucia. Learned men of Europe had journeyed to various parts of the earth to observe it. Captain Cook watched it from Tahiti and a group of French astronomers even went from Paris to the tip of Lower California to do likewise, in hopes of determining accurately the distance between sun and earth. Wherever they were these eager scientists measured the time it took Venus to cross the sun's face, and later compared their measurements, and by triangulation, using the distance between their observation points as base, determined the distance to the sun more precisely than ever before. But Lospe and her people believed Owotoponus had foreseen the whole matter and revealed it to them by his magic power, which indeed he had, just as by his brilliant painting of the condor on the rock of the cave lip he had caught and made available for them and succeeding generations down to our own time, the condor spirit as well as the bird itself in awesome mystic yet living flight.

By use of star maps painted on stone tablets or cave walls, bead markers placed at established points on a Sacred Condor's wing to count lunations, from the accumulated esoteric lore of hundreds of years, from his own observations and those of his fellow astrologer-priests, Owotoponus knew that Evening Star passes between earth and sun at regular intervals, that the last transit had occurred in the Month of New Directions, or June, eight years before and the next could be expected in the Month When the Sun's Brilliance Begins, or December, 1874. It was this extraordinary knowledge and the ability to use it which set him and his brethren apart and gave them such unique power. And as for the great change he predicted, the Spaniards were at that moment assembling at San Diego Bay preparing to begin their northward march.

In businesslike tones Owotoponus was calling for more donations. "Do we want the white men to think us stingy? Do you suppose they will share their precious knowledge if we treat them like casual passers-by?" It was the kind of extortion he knew so well how to employ. "Nor do I work for nothing! I too am hungry!" People dared not hold back. They came forward with strings of shell money, seeds, beads, cakes, feathers, bits of crystal, and placed them in the baskets which had been set before them. A portion was carried away by his assistants, while the remainder was arranged on trays such as Lospe and Kachuku already carried.

Then Koyo stepped forward. In firm clear voice she announced: "Let us go now to greet the strangers with friendship and gifts.

Courage! Let us be worthy!" Lospe was very proud of her. She saw all the generations of their family of leaders standing erect in her mother's firm straight body and marveled at how bravely she bore her many burdens.

Chapter Eight

As for the Spaniards, mountains descending abruptly to the sea had once again blocked their way northward. Reconnaissance inland up the Ventura River nearly as far as present Ojai revealed no promising interior route. Rivera, ever cautious, argued for further scouting rather than risk advancing along the beach at low tide "where we shall be at the mercy not only of the sea but of these numerous people and their allies should they decide to fall upon us!" but Portola, feeling pressed by time, preferred the shoreline route. "It is nearly September. We must place our trust in God and the hospitality of our new friends!" And so they struck out along the beach at a point they named and is still called The Rincon or Hazardous Corner, where attacks did occur later and blood was shed as Rivera feared.

Strung out along the sand for nearly a mile at the foot of steep bluffs they would have been at great disadvantage if attacked, but Antonio, Ortega, and other scouts fanning out ahead and searching the ravines along the bluffs could find no hostile signs. Each settlement—and they were increasingly numerous—welcomed them lavishly as if attempting to outdo the one before and soon they came to another large town where workmen were engaged in constructing canoes, laying out designs with fiber strings, smoothing planks with rough pieces of sharkskin. They named it Carpinteria or the carpenter shop. Here the people were speaking a different dialect from that spoken at Ventura. Here too the mountains receded and the expedition was able to travel somewhat inland across fertile mesas with tall grass and magnificent oaks, watered by cool canyons with good streams. On their right, rugged mountains ascended steeply through slopes of gray-green chaparral to rocky brown summits. On their left the placid channel lay like a dark blue lake with a purple line of mountainous islands beyond it. And now the shoreline curved and ran almost due west so that they seemed to be traveling with the sun along a marvelous corridor formed by earth, sea, and sky, through air so balmy it seemed to bathe them with pleasure.

"We must build a mission here!" Father Crespi exclaimed from the back of his red mule Sonora Girl. Setting and climate reminded him of his native Majorca, the legendary golden island of the Mediterranean. Costanso thought it resembled his native Barcelona coast, while Portola recalled the Italian littoral near Genoa, said to be the world's most beautiful. "I find it too perfect," Antonio disagreed. "There's an old Catalan saying: 'Beware of that which has no flaw.'" The others scoffed at him as a killjoy, but he was remembering the tar bog.

Forewarned by runners and smoke signals, people were coming to greet them and accompanying them joyously from town to town in what amounted to a triumphal progress. At the present site of Santa Barbara five hundred appeared, bringing more fish than the visitors could hope to eat, beside acorn meal and a variety of seeds and nuts, and a tall handsome chief, as noble a savage as even Rousseau might have envisioned, Antonio noted, painted from head to foot and decked with feathers, welcomed them with a long and friendly harangue, to which Portola replied graciously, giving in return presents of beads and red and blue ribbons. They camped that night by a gushing spring on the shore of a lagoon near the later presidio and present city hall, and the friendly Indians stayed at camp so late making so much noise with their singing and dancing, flutes and whistles that the officers finally had to ask them courteously to leave so that men and animals could rest. 'A-alapsyuxtun," or "People of the Village of Syuxtun,"* the people called themselves, and gave the Spaniards to understand that still larger populations lay ahead. And so it proved, for after resting a day they continued, "and soon," as Antonio wrote later, "discovered a large estuary in the center of which was an island, and on the island a very large village and on the shore of the estuary five more, so that the total people who came to greet us bearing all manner of gifts and food must have exceeded two thousand. They could have crushed us by sheer weight of numbers, but instead welcomed us as if we were gods!"

Officers and fathers speculated as to the reason for so dense a population—"greater than anywhere in New Spain except the

*a Chumash tribelet

This Promised Land

Valley of Mexico!" Costanso contended—and they agreed that only an extraordinary bounty of land and sea could support so many people who made no attempt to till the soil. Since leaving the Village of the Canoes they had encountered ten thousand, they estimated, and now California seemed to be living up to its legendary promise and they asked themselves what other wonders lay in store.

For several days they'd been seeing ahead of them a long finger of land pointing far into the sea, its bluffs shining white in the morning sun. From their guidebooks they knew this must be Point Conception, landmark for Philippine ships, point of treacherous currents and violent winds, and as they climbed the bleak and windswept finger, a new and sharper air bit into them. They saw that all surrounding growth had been compressed close to the earth by the prevailing winds and on the hills inland stunted trees looked like hunchbacks fleeing this desolate place.

From a high rock at the end of the point they looked down hundreds of feet into surging foam. Somewhere out there lay Asia. They felt they'd reached the end of the world and Portola likened it to the westernmost projection of the Old World, Cape Finesterre in northwest Spain, visited as a youth during a pilgrimage to the sacred city of Santiago de Compostela nearby, and as if to substantiate the similarity, close by they found an important town where the Indians explained that this was indeed a holy region known as their "western gate" where souls entered The Land of the Dead. "Typical of the misdirected faith we must correct," Father Gomez commented, "though it shows us they have the capacity for true spiritual development."

Costanso and Antonio exchanged glances. Mass had been held before the morning march as usual. At times, depending on his mood, the expedition's sacred purpose seemed uppermost, rising to captivate Antonio's imagination with an idea so much larger than himself, so much greater than even the King, that he felt enlarged and supremely confident to be part of it, Lopez aside. At other times as now he seemed to be an invader violating virgin natural beauty and innocent states of mind, as Costanso had said and the earthquakes warned.

At Point Conception the Santa Barbara channel ended. Its accompanying row of islands sank away into the sea, and the coastline turned abruptly northward. Now it seemed they were indeed entering another world, less illusory, a colder, harsher, much less luxuriant one. Two days and the mountain wall upon their right which had hemmed them against the sea nearly all the way from San Diego suddenly opened, in late afternoon, and they beheld an incredibly beautiful v-shaped valley penetrating like an avenue far inland; but the fog which had hung offshore all day moved in and enveloped them so they could not be sure exactly where they were.

That evening, inspired by what must have been premonition, Antonio sought out old Pablo and found him hunched under his poncho over a solitary fire in the lee of a sand dune. Ostracized by the other muleteers because of his color and fierce temper, he often bivouacked alone, and Antonio was never sure what mood he would find him in, but felt encouraged when at sight of him Pablo began to sing in mock derision:

> In the lee of a sand dune
> A black man warbles, fervently:
> "Dear Mother of Jesus, I'd like to be white
> Even if I was only a Catalan!"

"Why so hard on me, old friend?"
"How do I know I'm your friend?"
"I did as you told me today."
"How was that?" Curiosity mollified Pablo's tone somewhat.
"I didn't eat those mussels like the others did, remembering what you'd told me about red tides."
"Yes, I warned them but no one listened!" Pablo resumed with disgust.

Marching along the beach they'd come to some rocks encrusted with mussels and the others had stopped to help themselves, delighted at prospect of a free feast, but remembering Pablo's warning never to eat seafood when there was a red tide and noting a tinge in the breaking waves, Antonio abstained and now was very glad he'd done so, for most of the others including Ortega and the officers were complaining of stomach cramps and headache.

"So they have cramps, eh? and diarrhea, eh?" Pablo snorted derisively when Antonio informed him. "What do you expect me to do, cry?"

"What's a red tide, Pablo?"

"I don't know. But I know the Indians say you should never eat fish or shellfish when you see one!" Actually Pablo was referring to the red-pigmented Protozoa which periodically occur

This Promised Land

and render seafood poisonous to humans. He grew irritable again and his voice rose sarcastically. "You say you listen to me, but I listen to everyone! I have to!" His father, "a piece of black ivory," as he put it sardonically, had come from Loanda in a Portugese slaver with chained-down hatches to Cuba where Pablo had been born a bastard slave on a great plantation. His mother was a Siboney Indian from that remnant of native Cubans which still exists in the mountains not far from Havana. They were and are a gentle people, given to singing and making hammocks. Pablo had inherited his mother's short fleshy body, and deep at heart her sweetness, elsewhere his father's ferocity and strength. As a rule he was quiet, cheerful, performing his duties willingly, never remiss. Pablo's packs never came undone, his mules were never laid up with sore backs or feet. But when roused he became murderously ferocious. As a boy he'd stowed away on a ship bound for Vera Cruz, made his way inland to the Northwest frontier where there was fighting gainst Apaches and Seris, tried to enlist in the provincial forces, been rejected because of his blackness, gone on across the Gulf to Loreto, that last jumping-off place where the hardiest and hungriest assembled and there Rivera gave him his chance. "How do you think I escape the lash?" he continued, spitting into the fire, which hissed back at him, "the calaboose? starvation? death? By listening! Like the black pinacate* I keep my head to the ground. So I hear what's going on! I know what the worms say to the roots! If a white-skinned gentleman like you had warned them against those mussels, they'd have listened. No, let them shit their insides out for all I care! Let them ache their heads off!"

"We Catalans also know what it is to be oppressed," Antonio reminded him gently. "We've been under the boot for centuries. The Governor has declared tomorrow a day of rest because so many are ill. Why don't we go exploring, you and I?"

"Because that would upset the order of things. Young gachupins and old zambos aren't supposed to go exploring together!"

"If I arrange it will you go?"

Pablo chuckled as the irony of the idea began to appeal to him. He drew his poncho up a bit around his broad shoulders as the wind blew the fog in across the dunes. "That would be a joke, wouldn't it? You and this old Indian putting the laugh on the grandees?"

*stink bug

Chapter Nine

Their misfortunes began the previous spring, Lospe reflected, when the snakes first emerged and were sluggish after their long sleep.

Her father led the family up the deceptive North Fork to the asphaltum seepage to get fresh tar for sealing water jugs and fastening arrow points to shafts, decorating skirts, trading to neighbors. Already Koyo had several times expressed fears for his safety, now that Owotoponus was paha and held supreme power as astrologer-priest. But Koxsho belittled her apprehensions.

"Would you have us hide and not go about our affairs as usual? Besides, your father is still active as chief! We cannot shame ourselves before him!"

She replied: "The Cult," by which she meant the association of A-antap sorcerers, "have never forgiven you for going to the summit of Iwihinmu. Now that The One I Fear is a member you will be in danger doubly!"

"Nevertheless I have my way to go!" Koxsho answered with the stubbornness of a man who cherishes his freedom of action, "and I trust you will go with me."

The tar seepage flowed into the nearby creek discoloring the water. They set up camp on a fresh sandbar as usual. All seemed peaceful and secure, and Lospe remembered the tranquility of that moment. They lit a fire, prepared the evening meal. Tinaquaic played his four-holed elderberry flute charmingly while she worked beside Koyo. Taking a few steps upstream where the creek was clear of tar, her father knelt to drink beneath an overhanging limb, not noticing what lay along it dark and motionless as its bark. "Rattlesnakes almost never go into trees. They usually rattle when approached," she explained long afterward. "They

This Promised Land

almost never strike without coiling." But this was no ordinary snake. Excluded during his early years from the cult of the sorcerers such as met upon the slope of Iwihinmu, Owotoponus roamed the wilderness like a wild creature, aware of his inborn talent but having no standing except his belief in himself and his determination to succeed. "He painted magnificently and he learned the language of wild creatures, of birds, snakes, bears and deer—that lost language animals and humans once shared—and even, everyone believed, how to transform himself into them."

As her father raised his head from drinking, the sensation at the right side of his neck was like that of a wasp's sting, as the fangs deftly touched. His muffled cry drew her and the others. He died at their feet, writhing in terrible agony, neck, head, upper body swelling and turning black, all of them watching helplessly, despairingly. There was absolutely nothing they could do.

When it was over they heaped up a funeral pyre of dry limbs and laid Koxsho's body on it. "Beside him we placed his beautiful sinew-backed bow, his arrows, throwing stick, pipe, net, knife, shell bead necklaces, all his most precious belongings except the silver buckle which he kept at home in his treasure chest." The flames rose high. "Moved by sudden impulse I cut off a lock of my hair and threw it on the fire." The smoke carried its acrid odor through the hills he had roamed and loved, while his spirit traveled westward toward the Land of the Dead. "I did not cry. I was too deeply moved." Neither did her mother shed a tear. Both covered their faces with charcoal from his pyre, and both were sure, as was all the family, indeed everyone in the village, that Owotoponus had caused Koxsho's death. He was in the snake or his magic motivated the snake. "If a rattlesnake bit you and you didn't die," Lospe explained to Father Rubio and later to Father O'Hara, "it was a warning. If you died, it was because you'd offended the supernatural, perhaps the Sun, or perhaps some powerful person who sent the snake to kill you. Everything had a cause. Nothing occurred by chance. An eye, the Sun, watched all things by day, and an eye, Polaris, all things at night. Everything was known. Ravens were spies, toads informers. In such a world we were constantly in danger, constantly in need of protective power."

Lying awake that night she imagined her father's spirit passing through the air like a musical sound toward Kumqaq, or Point Conception. There it would bathe in the sacred pool of fresh water at the foot of the white bluff. From there taking the form of a shooting star it would fly westward and people ashore would say they heard a sound like distant thunder which in reality would be the Gates of the Dead closing behind her father. Before arrival at the Gates he would have passed through the Deep Canyon where the Two Rocks continually clashed together, and farther on the Two Ravens would have pecked out his eyes and he would have replaced them with two beautiful poppies from the many growing nearby. Passing on he would have met the Old Woman With a Sting in Her Tail who killed all mortals who came her way, though souls passed her by unscathed. Until at last her father's spirit would reach the Dark River which circled the Land of the Dead and come to the fateful Bridge of Poles which all must cross who would enter Paradise. The bridge represented those very same poles erected in cemeteries and sacred sites in the mortal world. Standing upon them, the soul was judged. Evildoers were turned to stone. Or frightened by the horrible monsters who appeared at either side, they fell off and were transformed into fish, frogs, or snakes living on in the dark slime for all eternity. Likewise with nonbelievers. But beyond the bridge lies the Bright Land where good souls go and abide forever, Lospe thought, with abundant food. There it is always summer. There my father lives!

While old Quati lived, her grandfather Masapaqsi had been well if feeble and continued to act as chief effectively because of his great prestige, but then he began to decline. The curing shamans disagreed how to treat him, as doctors usually do, though they were skilled practitioners and could splint broken bones and perform trepanning and other delicate operations. The truth was that each feared being blamed for Masapaqsi's death.

It was at this point that Owotoponus came forward and announced that the cause of the old chief's decline was the mustache of a lion magically introduced into his body by the wicked sorcerer at Hequep, their neighboring village. Perhaps he could save the life of their beloved leader although it was probably too late. He danced all day and all night around the dying man's bed, shaking his magic cocoon rattle softly, while Seneq was bathing Masapaqsi regularly in chamise water to ease his pain and feeding him chamomile tea and cascara sagrada imported from the north and balsam root as well.

When Owotoponus finished his dance, he offered prayers, then blew smoke to the four winds over the old withered body so that, to everyone's speechless astonishment, Masapaqsi sat up and sneezed, demanding to know where he was.

Owotoponus nodded confidently. "This is the crucial moment!" Opening the little bag he wore attached to his upper leg, he drew out a pinch of golden dust. The bag was made of the scrotum of a deer with the hair still on. The dust came from the fine yellowish moss which coats the undersides of sycamore leaves. Hummingbirds use it to line their nest. He had ground it up with the dry yoke of a quail's egg. "Who knows what else he added?" Lospe said. "Perhaps the death camas* all poisoners used, perhaps the deadly a-ayip made from ground rattlesnake bones. Whatever, it quieted my grandfather. Owotoponus wanted him out of the way, you see, since he stood between himself and my mother, yet wanted to manage his going for his own advantage!"

Just as old Masapaqsi expired, Owotoponus made a mark with his forefinger on the center of his chest, applied his sucking tube to it vigorously, and extracted the mustache of a mountain lion. "Look there, we are indeed victims of the evil magic of our neighbors!" he exclaimed, holding it up as evidence his diagnosis had been correct. "Of course he'd previously concealed the mustache inside the tube," Lospe went on. "Some suspected the hoax. But few wanted to believe it. Most wanted to be fooled. They wanted to believe that the hair represented evil power. It was the accepted way. It had always been so."

The death of Masapaqsi was followed by what Koyo dreaded: controversy over who should succeed her father and be to Owotoponus as Masapaqsi had been to Quati, partner in ruling. In the normal course of events, it would have been Lospe's foolish Uncle Tinaquaic but Tinaquaic had discredited himself irrevocably in public opinion, and public opinion was very important no matter how readily it might be swayed by those who knew how to do so.

Seeing Masapaqsi's feebleness, Old Seneq had more than once upbraided him: "You grow old but you do nothing to insure the succession of your only son!" Masapaqsi retorted: "I could have taken a second wife who might have given me an heir I could be proud of but I remained loyal to a scold. See what she's given me! An idiot who sits tootling his flute and playing with his i-ikpik on street corners inviting the girls to look!" She rejoined: "You brought this upon us by your blindness in never allowing

---

*Zigadenus venenosas

the boy a chance to become a man but always belittling and chiding him because he was timid and spindly legged. No wonder he plays with himself! There is nothing else he feels able to do—though it is true as you say that he manages the flute beautifully! Now listen to me: The Great Fair will soon take place at the Painted Rock in the Plain of the Carrizo Grass where all borders meet. Would it not be a fine thing if your son were to lead a party there and by conducting negotiations at such an important occasion demonstrate his fitness to succeed you?"

"The boy is a failure and always will be!" Masapaqsi shouted at her. "He is lazy and dirty and lies asleep after sunrise! Why should we pamper him further? Let him prove himself!"

Nevertheless she persisted and at last had her way. Tinaquaic did not wish to make the trip. The mere thought frightened him. But he could not resist Seneq's insistence. It was her idea that he go alone. "Then when you return you can claim full credit for your achievements! People will look up to you! And when time comes for you to succeed your father, they will follow you gladly!"

So Tinaquaic set off alone. With his mother's encouragement he had put on showy moccasins. They were made of unsoled single pieces of deerskin rising to his ankles, their fringes decorated with shell beads. The large carrying net which he wore on his back, resting on his hips, suspended from his forehead by a long loop of woven fiber, was full of fox and beaver skins, serpentine, asphaltum, abalone shells, and condors' down and feathers to be exchanged for the tobacco, honeydew, obsidian, and chewing gum of the interior.

He took the easy route up the North Fork that led to the Barren Lands where the Painted Rock stood as a natural wonder in the middle of the plain of the Carrizo Grass. It was sacred ground. No violence was permitted there. People of all nations could gather there to trade in peace. The rock was considered a mystic entrance to Earth herself. It was shaped like a huge open womb and could be entered at ground level from the grassy plain surrounding. In its oval hollow two hundred people could sit to trade or five hundred stand for a ceremony, while hundreds more looked down from the rim above. Around the walls of the hollow were paintings which surpassed all others in the known world in beauty and extent, and when ceremonial fires were lit their colors blazed with the power and the glory of the Sky People who inspired them.

This Promised Land

Tinaquaic found many arrived before him. When they learned that he'd traveled such a great distance alone and was the son of a chief, it turned out as Seneq predicted: they looked at him with respect as someone important and he began to regard himself that way too. Rich men made much of him. Chiefs greeted him. Girls smiled at him whereas back home they had laughed. Travel creates such illusions. Tinaquaic became so puffed with false pride he felt able to pick and choose. But when Kahip gave him a glance he fell headlong. She was a Tulamni from the Great Valley Beyond the Mountains, graceful and seductive. When her father, a shrewd trader, saw what was up he raised the bride price sky high, so that when all arrangements were concluded, Tinaquaic had given away everything he had. The usual ceremonies followed, and Kahip was glad enough to accompany him home, fondly imagining she would be the wife of a chief some day.

Masapaqsi grumbled about the high price. But Seneq hailed the whole affair as a triumph. Her beloved son had shown himself a man at last. Kahip was beautiful, no one could deny, and at first she was modest, helpful, full of fun.

"See, what did I tell you?" Seneq crowed.

"Just wait!" Masapaqsi replied turning his face to the wall.

For a few days the illusion lasted. Tinaquaic strutted. Kahip bloomed. Then the temporary power accruing from his journey began to wane and Tinaquaic went limp in body and spirit. "I don't know what's the matter with me!" he complained pathetically to passers-by. "What do you think I should do?" But they responded with cruel laughter or a wisecrack. Soon he was sitting on streetcorners grinning idiotically, masturbating as before in abject self-abasement, while Kahip hung her head in shame. It was a terrible disgrace for all the family. They kept the news from Masapaqsi, who was sinking fast, but the Council of Twenty could not overlook it when they met to select his successor.

A deputation led by Owotoponus—adorned with plumes and ceremonial paint—arrived at sunrise, the traditional hour, and offered the chieftaincy to Koyo. Owotoponus explained he'd taken momoy to foresee the future, sought the advice of the Sky Powers, and all indications relating to her assumption of leadership were favorable, "even though your apostate husband dared trespass on the forbidden Heart of the World!" he added under his breath, wishing to make her feel uncertain and submissive to him.

She treated him coolly, thanked the others graciously, and

asked for three days to consider the matter. Koyo had never wanted public office, knew its heavy responsibilities and thanklessness, was by nature gentle, retiring, and loathed the idea of being associated with Owotoponus in exercise of power. But for the honor of the family, to compensate for Tinaquaic's disgrace, and more particularly for Asuskwa's and Lospe's sake, she finally accepted. Unless she did so, her children would never have the chance to succeed her.

Even then the matter was far from settled. There were those who opposed her because she was a woman, notwithstanding the famous Princess Luhui who ruled over seven cities and four islands. They pointed out that Luhui came to power only after long and bloody civil war and that within memory no woman had ever led the People of Olomosoug. Koyo's adversaries also argued that for her to do so would be interpreted as a sign of weakness, would lead to insults and sorceries such as practiced upon Masapaqsi, to incursions upon their territories and eventually war. Also there were those who held her suspect by association because Koxsho had dared to go to the forbidden Heart of the World.

The matter was finally settled in the traditional way: the game we now call "peon" in which you conceal a stick behind your back with one hand and your opponent guesses which hand the stick is in. It reflected the celestial guessing game which took place nightly, all believed, between Sun, ruler of the universe, and Sky Coyote, benefactor of mankind. At the end of the year their score was totaled. If Sky Coyote won, the year to come would be good, with plenty of rain and much to eat. If Sun won it would be bad with much suffering and death.

Shamik, Koyo's opponent, the wealthy trader who would later try and defraud Payanit the bowmaker, was shrewd but Koyo was fortunate, and for good fortune there is no substitute everyone had to admit. It meant her power was greater than Shamik's.

All neighboring villages were informed as was the province chief at U-upop near Point Conception. All authorities confirmed Koyo as chief. There were visitations, ceremonies, festivals. Red banners were erected and Koyo and Lospe walked in triumph through the streets of the capital by the shining sea. Chiefs from as far away as modern day Santa Barbara and San Luis Obispo attended, and even Luhui came skimming across the water in her canoe and made Koyo a gift of twenty beautiful sea otter skins.

Still the new leader's troubles were not over. Saddled with a mate like Tinaquaic, Kahip was not one to resign herself. When

This Promised Land

He-ap met her out gathering and they "made the creature that has two backs," as Lospe expressed it, "many did not blame her." Nobody blamed He-ap. His role was to service female as well as male. But Shamik and his friends raised a new outcry. In theory if not in practice, adultery was a crime punishable by death. Complicating the matter, Koyo was newly come to power and Kahip a foreigner. For Koyo to appear lax in a matter of public morals, especially where a foreigner was involved who was also her sister-in-law, could be very harmful to her politically. Her position became quite precarious. Shamik and his friends made a great fuss, demanding the death penalty for Kahip. But to execute a foreigner for any cause was bound to create grave intertribal problems. And sure enough, when the Tulamni heard of the business they sent word that if their daughter were executed they would declare war. With the approval of the Council of Twenty, Koyo referred the matter to the provincial council and was still waiting to hear their decision when word of the white men's coming reached her.

For her, their approach represented among other things a welcome diversion. It might allow her time to find a way out of her dilemma. She also believed with all her heart that the Spaniards would be a great benefit to her people.

At last the procession to greet the A-alowow was ready to begin. Preceded by He-ap whirling, leaping, clowning and by Tup and Quolog playing their deerbone whistles, accompanied by other musicians with split cane and turtleshell rattles and bullroarers whirling frightfully, Koyo at their head, they began to move as one people down the valley toward the sea. The herds of elk and antelope gazed at them curiously. Lospe had never felt so excited. "Above us condors and eagles wheeled, infusing us with their noble spirits, and spontaneously we began to sing, Mother and Owotoponus leading:

> We are the People of the Land and the Sea,
> We are the People of the Land and the Sea,
> We bathe in the River of Dawn,
> We bathe in the River of Dawn!

Then Koyo led the traditional question-and-answer, her voice rising with strength and pride. She was leading her people to a meeting that would never be forgotten. "What is our purpose this day, O People of the Place Called Olomosoug?"

And their response came back to her on the bright morning air: "We go with you to greet the Illustrious Visitors and make them welcome with friendship and gifts . . . and make them welcome with friendship and gifts!"

In Lospe's right hand, clutched among the condor plumes she was carrying as part of her gift offering to the strangers, was the silver belt buckle which had belonged to her father.

Chapter Ten

As they rode through the early morning light along the fog-shrouded dunes, Antonio on his sorrel, Pablo on his white mule, the boy's blood rose with excitement because this was the first time he'd led a reconnaissance and he remembered the old saying: "The procession marches inside you!" It seemed the entire Sacred Expedition was marching inside him, Portola's quiet admonition ringing in his ears: "Find us a route northward, and keep out of trouble!" At his side, Pablo was chuckling softly, having his laugh on the grandees, riding up front as explorer for the first time.

Underfoot grew a low sedge with here and there a gray-green loco weed with its bladder pods or a lavendar-blossomed mint whose pungent aroma increased Antonio's feeling of anticipation. Everything veiled in mist, they came to a broad lagoon. Waves reached into it with a long rippling surge. Herons stood like sentinels posted along its shores watching them. And when they arrived at a broad clear river running into the lagoon which reminded him of his native Segre running from the high Pyrenees, he felt sure something important was about to happen.

As they followed the bank of the river searching for a ford, the fog suddenly lifted and they were in the midst of a gloriously beautiful valley which led straight toward the rising sun. Brownish gray-green grass covered it solidly except where the river made a sparkling green avenue. Far away at its head rose a dark shaggy peak like the back of a huge beast and from the rugged shoulders of the beast gentle grassy hills reached down like welcoming arms on either side of the valley. Vast herds of elk—the first they'd seen—grazed peacefully around them as did antelope and deer, lifting heads curiously to observe them. Wolves and coyotes trotted unconcernedly about while overhead soared a multitude of birds including the great vultures with patches of white feathers under their wings such as Antonio had seen at the tar bog. Myriads of long- and short-eared rabbits, and squirrels and plump blue quail scurried away from underfoot, and on every side rose an invisible invitation, a restatement of that subtle compact between man and land, existing since the beginning of human creation, saying simply that here was a good place to live.

Domestic animals by the thousand might forage here, Antonio realized, and this rich alluvial soil which thrust the sweet-smelling grass up to their shoulders as they rode, could obviously produce bountiful crops. The river would provide water for irrigation as needed, and the invigorating air seemed to invite productive effort. True, the place lacked the exquisite perfection of the channel coast they'd recently traversed. But it was keenly alive, ongoing, actively connecting sea and interior, earth and sky with its many life forms, leading somewhere, promising something. It made Antonio feel like an invader no longer but a belonger, and as he looked at it with the practical eye of a Catalan yeoman who owns and works his own land, he saw that here was room for a whole society like the one in which he'd grown up, an association of independent-minded entrepreneurs who traditionally regarded their kings as co-citizens. He turned to Pablo.

"What do you say, Compadre?"

"If I was a believer, I'd say we'd found the Promised Land!" and Pablo touched that sprig of rosemary, as they called the fragrant green coastal sage, which he wore on his hat for good luck. The Indians all along the coast regarded it as magically beneficial and Pablo, partly from a reverse sympathy with "the savages," partly as if to announce his own Indian blood, had adopted it as his personal emblem.

Though their orders were to find a route northward, Antonio was so attracted by their surroundings that like a lover reluctant to leave the arms of his loved one he procrastinated, telling himself he'd dally only a moment longer, continue five minutes more. So they rode toward the rising sun from one inviting vista to another, here a charming hollow, there an upland where a man might wish to spend his life. Ahead, the high sierra beckoned like the high Pyrenees until they reached the foot of a low promontory crowned with oaks which blocked their way.

As he debated whether to continue, Antonio heard a cacaphony of human voices and wild music rising from beyond the crest and knew a band of Indians must be approaching. He remembered

This Promised Land

Portola's admonition: "Should you encounter gentiles, treat them with proper respect!" The recollection was decisive. With a "let go" to Pablo he spurred Babieca and together they scrambled up the slope to meet the unseen band on equal ground.

At the summit they were confronted by a noisy procession of humans and dogs extending for a quarter mile under the scattered oaks. On sight of them it came to a halt and set up an even greater clamor, while they drew rein and awaited developments, Antonio suddenly aware they were outnumbered by approximately two hundred to one and were far off the course he'd been told to follow.

"Look at their skins!" Pablo exclaimed as he was about to, for although some were nearly as dark as Pablo many were nearly as light as Antonio. On the whole they were taller and handsomer than any he'd seen. But what caught and held his eye was their leader. Though not distinguished by her height she wore the long cloak of bear skin which often denoted chief personages and her hair was as chestnut sorrel as his horse's, though cut short in the customary mourning, while her face was as black as Pablo's.

"By the Almighty, what have we here? Queen Calafia herself?" A surge of incredulous delight rose in him. Perchance he had discovered the supreme wonder of a wonderful land.

"Don't know about that," replied Pablo dryly, "but it's good their bowstrings are unstrung!"

He-ap, who'd been leading the procession, stopped his dance in mid-stride at the sudden apparition of two such extraordinary beings, reality proving more startling than his expectations, and glanced back at Koyo for instruction.

When she was Owotoponus and the girls bearing the gift trays continued resolutely to advance, he and the other dancers and the musicians with their flutes and clappers stepped aside and let them through, while continuing to shout with approval and blow their whistles and swing their bullroarers.

As she advanced through this bedlam, Lospe felt with a rush of joy that at last her dream was coming true. Old Quati's predictions were being borne out, for here riding toward her out of the west was the tall fair-haired man she'd seen in her sacred vision, the man her dead father also said would come some day, and who'd never been far from her mind all these years. She thought she had never seen a sight so marvelous. The rising sun was shining on Antonio's black flat-crowned hat, on his yellow hair which cascaded down his back from under the red handkerchief which held it in place, on his extraordinary clothing—leather jacket, blue shirt—and on the polished armas protecting his legs—worn shiny now by miles of weathering and contact with brush—and from saddle and leather anquera,* and metal of bit and spurs, and also the beautiful sorrel coat and yellow mane of his animal itself, so that all together he gleamed like the apparition of her dream.

Pablo was another matter, a total surprise. A black man! Was his color natural or was it paint? Was he perhaps in mourning like herself?

Her mother halted and she did likewise with Kachuku and the other girls while Owotoponus adorned with plumes and wearing his ceremonial skirt of condor feathers, bearing his magic crystal wand that captured all colors of the rainbow, advanced as prearranged. Though inwardly perturbed, Owotoponus showed no outward apprehension. He knew this moment might be decisive. His power, his preeminence in the village, even his relationship with Koyo whom he truly loved within the limits of his overweening egoism and ambition, were at stake. While fully conscious of his great capacities he assumed those of the white men must be greater or they would not be riding animals such as these, wearing clothing such as this, undoubtedly carrying deadly firesticks and those knives of the bright metal that never grows dull concealed somewhere about their persons, and perhaps with their canoes with the huge white wings waiting somewhere off shore. But at this moment he truly wanted to be friendly not only to appease and propitiate but to learn and acquire. What they had might become his. Approaching to a respectful distance he stopped and began his speech of welcome.

To Antonio and Pablo it was an unintelligible agglomeration of clickings and clackings, with many wild intonations and many gutturals and perplexing glottal stops as in the oft-repeated "A-alowow." But though his trustworthiness seemed to Antonio suspect—and decidedly so to Pablo who muttered: "I wouldn't trust him an inch! Most witchdoctors are rascals!"—there was no mistaking his friendly intent, and as if to confirm it, when he finished he made a gesture with his wand and a group of young girls bearing trays loaded with gifts advanced and set their trays on the grass in front of the two strangers and then retired, all but one.

*protective covering for a horse's rump and flanks

This Promised Land

This was the moment for which Lospe had waited. Heart pounding she continued to walk forward, while behind her she heard a great cry of astonishment rise from her people. She saw the surprised and amused look on Antonio's face just as in her dream vision, and totally forgot to be afraid. And next he was, incredibly to her eyes, separating himself from his animal—she'd thought them somehow one being—and stepping down to earth like a god descending, while another great shout of astonishment went up, and with a merry laugh he was taking off his hat and bowing in a gallant gesture of reception, and she was holding out her hand, fingers tightly clenched, and opening them, and Antonio was seeing with amazement a battered but still finely chased and brightly polished silver buckle of an antique style such as conquistadors might have worn two centuries earlier. Its tongue was missing, its framework bent but there it was—elegant evidence of work well done, a gift presented, and as he reached out, still laughing, to accept it and their fingers touched in a true first contact between their two peoples, a shout went up that made the valley ring.

From her manner and that of her people Antonio deduced that Lospe's daring action and unusual gift were entirely her own doing. Her blackened face amused him. "She looks more kin to you than to me!" he joked to Pablo. But Pablo replied gravely: "That's her mourning!" Antonio noted how she smiled resolutely, awed but not intimidated, noted her graceful figure and young breasts with the stripes of red and blue paint above them, and her bright red hair and extraordinarily large brown eyes which reminded him of Eloisa back home, with whom he danced his native sardana in front of the church in the town square. And the flicker of a flame that was more than delighted amusement arose in him.

Turning to Pablo with a raised eyebrow, he gravely deposited the buckle in his saddlebag and removed a piece of red cloth which he handed to Lospe and was rewarded by her joyful exclamation. Taking him by the hand in simple trust as if he were her father she led him to her mother "while such a din arose as to defy description," as he recorded, "and when I bowed formally before the dark-faced lady and she to me, and she gave me her hand in token of binding friendship between our two peoples, sheer pandemonium prevailed, while I thought I had surpassed all that Montalvo and all the other romancers and Torquemada and all the historians had surmised!"

Now it was his turn to make harangue. He smilingly thanked Owotoponus and Koyo for their generosity and hospitality, handed them beads, explained as best he could that he and Pablo were under command of a great chief who was leading them on a journey northward to a distant place, therefore they could not remain but hoped to return. "The people smiled," as he said later, "not understanding, perhaps secretly hoping my words were somehow an answer to a thousand questions. Unable to convince them of my intention, I began to walk slowly back to where Pablo was holding my horse and then they understood."

Tears appeared in Lospe's eyes, and after some hesitation she ran after the departing Antonio, speaking in a pleading tone as if to say: "Don't go yet!"

As he hesitated in his turn he could see the disappointment in all their faces. With firm dignity Koyo made clear she wanted him to accompany them to their village, which from the crest of the promontory he could see at no great distance up the valley snuggled against a chalky bluff.

"This placed me in a sharp dilemma, because to go by ones or twos among them, especially to their villages, was strictly forbidden lest they fall upon us and destroy us or take us prisoner, and Portola expressly warned against it when giving me permission to go exploring; yet these people were so attractive, so unusual in so many respects that the temptation to disobey was strong. Pablo, however, had his doubts. He'd not stirred from the back of old Moses where he was the focus of hundreds of eyes. He was enjoying his role of explorer but only up to a point. 'Better not go any farther!' he counseled.

" 'But the Governor told me to be friendly with any gentiles we met!' I replied. If we don't accompany them, they may take offense and turn against us, and persuade others to do likewise. What would Don Gaspar say then?"

Pablo reluctantly gave in. He riding, Antonio walking, escorted by Koyo, Lospe, and Owotoponus, they proceeded toward the village, while the throng "including a sodomite in woman's dress such as we'd noticed in several villages of the channel coast, danced and sang around us with triumphant delight. At the outskirts we came to their cemetery with the usual grave markers. Nearby was a playing field and also a large area recently burned to facilitate new growth. The streets were littered with rubbish and offal as usual and stank to high heaven, yet no more so than some of our villages at home and the people themselves were a

This Promised Land

good deal sweeter smelling than some I could remember. Their thatched houses were well made and beside each stood a small storehouse resembling a toadstool, elevated on poles to keep its contents out of reach of rats and squirrels. There were also small gardens of native plants, the first we'd seen."

When Antonio asked Lospe, who again held his hand, the name of her village she replied "Olomosoug," pronouncing it almost like a whisper, "Olomo-*show*," and by signs explained that in her language it meant "a place of new beginnings." Antonio was delighted by the name as by her brightness and wit and he noted with pleasure the charming way she wrinkled her nose when she laughed, as he tried to pronounce the name after her and failed. Lovely as the lower valley had been, this enclave at its head, cupped by hills and sierra, seemed a veritable Eden inhabited by chosen people. All his romanticism welled up and it seemed he'd found a biblical promised land and in it those ideal primitives envisioned by Rousseau—natural men and women uncorrupted by civilization.

As they reached the village, a second multitude of young and old, lame and infirm who'd been unable to accompany the others, poured out to greet them. Koyo, perspiring heavily under her bearskin cloak since it was a warm day, led the way to her house, the largest and best made of all, and graciously invited them to enter. This again placed Antonio in a dilemma since to do so would leave him almost entirely at their mercy, yet he felt inclined to risk it. "If I could win the friendship of these extraordinary people it might be of great advantage. Russians and English aside, wasn't the purpose of our expedition to win souls for Christ and subjects for the King? And these seemed exceptional candidates." But not to Pablo. "You won't get me out of this saddle!" he insisted.

"Very well!" Antonio handed him his tie rope. "Hold my horse, in any event, and keep your gun handy!"

From experience in Old California he guessed that a shot would probably send them flying in case of trouble. Yet he knew that no such terrifying shot had ever been fired in this valley and disliked the idea of firing one. As he crossed the threshold, old Seneq fell on her knees before him and tried to make him understand she'd waited for this moment and his coming signified a new day. Deeply moved, he raised her to her feet and gave her beads which pleased her enormously.

The interior struck him as surprisingly roomy and well arranged. Strong posts supported its dome shaped roof. Flexed willows served as rafters. "In the center of the floor was the circular fireplace of stone, a hole above for smoke to escape, and scattered about or hung on forked hooks which protruded from the wall frame was much gear for hunting and sport, nets, snares, hoops, sticks, balls, and there were piles of twigs and grass for basket making." Cleverly constructed wooden bedsteads stood close to the walls, each hung with reed curtains for privacy as his at home were hung with muslin or lace. "Nothing I'd seen so far gave me such a sense of our common humanity," he said later. "There were doors at east and west, windows at convenient points though composed of fresh air rather than glass, yet with shutters which evidently could be raised or lowered at will."

He noticed a young woman, little more than a skeleton, apparently extremely ill, who cowered in a dark recess and glanced at him fearfully; also a tame vulture as large as a small child. Seeing his interest in the bird, Lospe, who stayed by his side, led the condor to him by means of the cord attached to one of its legs and stroked it tenderly and let it nibble her finger to demonstrate how gentle it was. And as he watched with amused interest she gazed at him longingly, wishing she could tell him all that was in her heart. But he must know. Like the Sky People he must be omniscient.

"I realized," Antonio recorded in his memoirs, having no inkling at the moment of her deeper thoughts, "she was showing me a vulture such as I'd seen at the tar pits and also soaring above us as we rode up the valley, but now her mother was informing me I might have such a house as this and her daughter too if I would stay with them and be their companion. It sounded like something out of a fairy tale. I felt transported beyond the bounds of reality. Who in the civilized world would believe I was having such an experience? To evade answering, I laughed and asked the significance of the red hair which ran in the family, and Her Majesty answered it was a sign of divine favor, red being the color of the sun at morning and evening and of the head of their sacred vulture. Then she laughingly pointed to my blond curls and I replied they too were a mark of high favor since God made them the color of the sunlight at midday, and curled them like the clouds. This pleased them greatly, all except a youth I took to be the girl's brother since he resembled her though his hair was black. He did not join in the general approval but regarded me with suspicion.

This Promised Land

"Next I pointed inquiringly to the girl's blackened face, and the charming child replied by unmistakable signs that she was in mourning because of her father's death, for which by similar signs I expressed regret. The information and the innocent trust with which she imparted it, as if sure I would understand and sympathize, touched me profoundly.

"Unlike most we'd met, her people made no attempt to remove my buttons or take my knife but continued generous to a fault. The moment I admired an object, whether basket or bowl, her mother declared it mine. Protest was of no use. Had I a wagon I could have filled it with gifts including beautiful baskets and finely carved bowls of wood and stone, shell bead money of very high quality, beautiful blankets woven from the skins of foxes, rabbits and otters, and a cloak made from the skins of birds—its pieces delicately sewn together. Yet I saw no gold or silver. When I asked, they did not seem to know my meaning. Truly these are innocents, I thought, and I have indeed entered the Garden of Eden!"

Now Owotoponus intervened, envious of the growing affinity between Koyo and Lospe and Antonio. With an insistence which annoyed Antonio and seemed to bear out Pablo's first impression, he led the youth, Koyo, Lospe, and all their people following, to the ceremonial meeting place or plaza, as Antonio called it, nearby. "There he showed me a stick half a yard in length protruding from the earth. At first I thought it a digging tool such as they used to uproot bulbs. But then I saw that the round flat stone forming its head was not a handle in the usual sense but was set at a peculiar angle of perhaps twenty degrees from the shaft, and was stained greenish blue and had red lines radiating from a nub of hard tar at its center where the stick penetrated the stone, and the nub was decorated with shiny fragments of shell set in the tar, while in a space between two red lines was the dark crescent of a moon."

Antonio had no idea he was looking at a metaphor for the universe, that the stone represented the sun and the wooden shaft the axis mundalis connecting heaven and earth, or that Owotoponus had placed it there so ceremoniously earlier that day. Pointing to the Sunstick, Owotoponus informed him that it was an instrument of great power and sanctity, that he performed magic with it and invited him to do likewise.

"Careful, son!" Pablo muttered behind him, though lightly so as not to sound apprehensive. "Comes now the burr under the blanket! The rogue wants to test you—to see if your power is greater than his!''

Following close, Pablo and his white mule were a continuing center of attention. Pablo had long ago painted rings of charcoal around each of Moses' eyes to protect them from the glare of the summer sun and these together with the animals' long ears gave it a very striking appearance. As for Pablo himself, afraid of him yet irresistibly drawn by the color of his skin, people tried repeatedly to touch him to see if he too were in mourning and if his black would rub off. When they came too near he warned them away with a growl or offered with a smile to bite their fingers, until a little girl, boldly offering hers, received a surprising kiss at its tip—to the enormous amazement and delight of everyone.

"Put on a show that will impress 'em!" he continued now to Antonio under his breath. "Doesn't matter what but make it good!"

Wondering what might subdue Owotoponus and also impress but not frighten the others too greatly, Antonio reached a hasty conclusion. Yet it seemed a good idea. Drawing his sword, he thrust it into the earth beside the Sunstick so that its handle formed an upright cross. Then lifting the rosary cross from his breast and pointing to Pablo's gun, he informed Owotoponus that he possessed not one but three instruments of supreme power. "And when our Great God speaks," he explained by signs and gestures, "everyone on earth trembles! And now I shall let you hear what he says!" And he told Pablo to fire his musket in the air.

With relish Pablo removed the weapon ceremoniously from its foxskin sheath while all eyes watched. Checking its priming he drew back its cock, raised it carefully until its muzzle pointed heavenward, then pulled the trigger.

The report sent all but the bravest fleeing. Dogs ran howling. Children screamed. Antonio at once regretted what he'd done, wishing it undone. Something beautiful and fragile seemed broken forever as the echoes went rolling away across the peaceful hills.

Lospe shrank back against Koyo, frightened but not terrified. The hero of her dreams would be mighty and terrible. He would come with a force surpassing any her people had ever known. He would be beautiful as a tempest, or a quiet morning. What happened increased rather than diminished her feeling for Antonio and her determination to unite herself with him as best she might.

Koyo felt somewhat the same, though on a less intimate level. She'd heard the sound of the firestick described many times. Now the mighty A-alowow had come at last such things were to be expected. Owotoponus also stood his ground impassively, attempting to hide all emotion and convey the impression that he too could make the heavens thunder. Ta-apu and Lehlele likewise stood fast, fearful, uncertain. Kachuku began to whimper. Asuskwa felt confirmed in his distrust of the invading strangers. He felt sure they were bringing violence and fear to his valley, and his long struggle against them really began at this moment.

Those who'd fled soon returned, convinced that though Pablo's musket spoke with the voice of a god superior to any of their deities, it was in friendship. They danced and sang with a greater fervor to celebrate the event and propitiate the great new power "apparently believing themselves," as Antonio reported, "now joined with us in brotherhood." Still he continued uneasy at having disturbed the tranquility of the valley.

The sun was declining. Portola's admonitions suddenly recurred forcibly to his mind. He realized he'd stayed away too long, not followed instructions. But when he tried to say goodbye Koyo would have none of it. Nor would Lospe. They insisted on escorting him and Pablo back to camp. All able bodied villagers followed, and these included Owotoponus who, upset though he was, did not dare be left out. Long before they arrived, darkness fell and their way was lit by torchbearers. And as the wildly noisy and eerily lighted procession approached the camp, it roused a good deal of consternation and some disapproval, while the Indians repeated for the benefit of Portola and his officers all their dances, songs, offers of friendship and gifts. Until finally Portola was obliged to ask them to leave "lest," as he explained to Koyo by signs, "our men who have been ill be unable to sleep and our animals be disturbed and run away."

Antonio was standing beside him during the farewell. After Portola promised Koyo he would return, Antonio did likewise and told her with grave frankness he would never forget her warm and generous welcome and her lovely valley.

Lospe clung to his hand, searching his eyes anxiously for the truth. She felt her dream slipping away. Yet he in his omniscience must know best. Like sun or clouds he must come and go as he saw fit.

"I will come back!" he promised lightly, giving her hand a responsive squeeze, hoping to send her away happy, and he did intend to return, never guessing how long it would take him. His immediate concern was how to account to Don Gaspar for his overly long absence and intimate involvement with natives, and as his newfound friends slowly withdrew he began apologizing. Portola heard him out impassively, then gave him a stern reprimand.

"They might have killed you, might have held you hostage. In either case we should have been obliged to rescue and avenge you. Blood would likely have been shed. Energy and time expended, the expedition delayed, our objectives placed in jeopardy. Next time, think before you act!" Yet he was favorably impressed by Koyo and her people and intrigued by the silver buckle which Antonio made a point of showing him. "From our settlements in New Mexico no doubt," the captain observed. "Maybe it belonged to the great Coronado or one of his men—who knows?"

On joining the campfire Antonio found Pablo the center of attention for once. Questions were coming at him from every side and he was replying with magisterial calm, making their adventure seem even more fabulous than it had been. To hear him tell it, Koyo was indeed Queen Calafia and her village that "populous well-governed city surrounded by fertile fields" envisioned by Torquemada. Golden chariots drawn by gryphons lurked just over the horizon sketched by Pablo, as did the mythical Strait of Anian. "There's bound to be some treasure in that sierra," he was saying, "like those balls of silver they found lying on the surface at Arizonac not long ago, as if scattered there by the hand of God!"

"All very fine," Antonio heard Lopez observe sarcastically as he approached—perhaps aware of his coming, he was never sure—"very fine now they're safely back in camp, but suppose the gachupin and his blackbird had been taken prisoner and held hostage and we'd been obliged to rescue them?" They were almost the words Portola had used a few moments before, as if Lopez had been overhearing. Antonio realized with a shock of angry surprise just how widespread such sentiments might be. "What then, eh?" Lopez spit. "No, my comrades, a certain party thinks nothing of putting *our* necks in nooses, while *he* is safe from punishment because he's the Governor's relative!"

Antonio walked straight up to him. "I overheard what you said. Take it back!" His right hand rested on his hip within easy reach of the bone-handled knife protruding from the sash of his deerskin legging.

At that moment Rivera emerged from his tent and seeing him

exclaimed angrily: "What—at it again, Boneu? Bullying my men from your privileged position?"

Materializing as if by magic from the darkness opposite, little Fages exclaimed: "Not so!" On the prowl as usual he'd seen and overheard all.

"I was not addressing *you* sir!" Rivera snapped.

"But I am addressing *you,* sir!" They glared at each other across the firelight, bearded oldster, clean shaven youngster, old order and new, and Antonio was glad enough to let them do so. "If you doubt my word, sir, that's a question we may discuss at another time!" Fages added frigidly, leaving no doubt as to his meaning.

Rivera turned away from the deputy commander to vent his rage and humiliation on Antonio and Lopez. "Ten thousand pagans are out there!" he shouted, waving a hand at the surrounding darkness. "Save your martial ardor for them! Or it will be whiplashed out of you both, I promise!"

Fages walked slowly off without further word. Antonio went to find Costanso and tell him all that had happened.

II
The Search

Chapter Eleven

Life at the site at the foot of the chalky bluff went on much if not quite the same as always. In the fall came the annual ceremony to honor the Earth Mother. In December there was the winter solstice ritual to propitiate the declining sun and encourage its return, in spring the snake dance to placate the emergent rattlers, at summer solstice the bear dance to appease the bears prior to the annual journey by family groups into the back country. Yet if the hills could remember, as the people of the place believed, and the trees speak, they would have testified to the invisible change caused by Pablo's musket shot and the thrust of Antonio's sword into the earth. People no longer thought as before. They no longer saw the same relationships between themselves and their surroundings. It was as if the earth under their feet had turned to quicksand as they waited for the next actions of those superior beings of supernatural knowledge and power who had come among them.

Lospe prayed daily to Sacred Condor, who sees what cannot be seen by mortal eyes, to reveal to her where Antonio had gone and when he would return.

"Why don't you marry Alul?" Kachuku urged. "He is handsome and loves you. The fact he is of our lineage may be overlooked, now that everything is changing!"

Lospe shook her head. "Alul brags too much. And I have my path to follow as Quati foretold."

"What are the words of an old man long dead? These are new times with their new truth. The A-alowow have come and gone like the summer's wind. When they returned they passed us by without even stopping. You know that as well as I but you refuse to believe it. Why delude yourself with useless dreams?"

"No, for me there is only one truth," Lospe retorted, "and

one dream!'' and she resolved to hold to it tightly as she had held to the silver buckle. The other girls might take lovers as naturally as they took food, being taught early by mothers and aunts the use of contraceptive potions of mistletoe and chamise.

"The princess is putting on airs!" they derided her, as together they ground acorns and leached the bitterness from the meal by placing it in a basket lined with green grass and poured warm water over it, or rolled dice made of half walnut shells in one of their perennial gambling games. "She thinks she's going to marry an A-alowow some day! But he's forgotten her!"

Lospe pretended not to care and held her head high but at heart was deeply unhappy. Yet she resolved to remain faithful to the loved one of her dream. Wasn't he descended from sun and cloud? Were not they fated to come together? Surely he would keep his word and come back to her, unless perhaps something terrible had happened during his long journey.

When, after his altercation by the fire with Lopez, Antonio found Costanso in his tent studying his maps, the brilliant engineer-cartographer listened to his enthusiastic outpouring about the villagers but was inclined to be skeptical. "If you spent a year instead of a day with them, I daresay you'd find these noble innocents much like everyone else. Nevertheless there's food for thought in what you tell me, and I wonder what our learned men of Europe, who scoff at Rousseau as a dreamer and scribbler, would say if they knew there existed a people content with their natural bounty, dwelling as you say like Adams and Eves in a paradise?"

"While devoting themselves to the perfection of arts and crafts, ceremonies and religious practices—and a code of ethics so extraordinary they offer to share their land, houses, and women with total strangers. But how do we explain their fair skin and red hair?"

"That may be easier," Costanso suggested. "Our ships and who knows what others have sailed these waters for many years. There have been wrecks, castaways. Ortega tells me that at the tip of Old California, where our galleons occasionally stop, there are Indians with red hair and blue eyes. But I'm inclined to believe the pigmentation in this instance is so widespread as to result from nature's more normal processes."

"Could they have voyaged across the sea in their canoes from a land occupied by white men?"

This Promised Land

"It's possible."

"Some told Pablo they came first to one of the islands of the channel coast, then by a bridge formed by a rainbow to a mountaintop on the mainland, thence to this valley."

"Delightful fable! I shall record it in my diary!"

They speculated late into the evening, wishing for time for further investigation, but Portola had ordered an early departure. Ahead lay the lofty Santa Lucia Range said to be snowcapped in winter. How high was it? What would it cost in time, effort, food supply, risk of injury or attack, to cross such a barrier?

A gulf separates the explorer from the follower. Portola's problem was that he did not *know* it was possible to reach Monterey Bay by following the coast. It was not the existence of the port but its exact location when approached by land that he must discover, the uncertainties along the way which he must overcome, and he must bring his scurvy-weakened travel-weary men back the way they had come without any additional supplies, should the packet boat fail to meet them at Monterey as planned. Whatever happened, he alone would be fully accountable.

As the column splashed across the river Antonio glanced inland and saw the sun just rising over the huge dark mountain that thrust up at the head of the valley like the back of some shaggy beast. Nearer, beyond the promontory masking it from view, a column of smoke, rising vertically into the windless air, marked the site of the village. All at once something told him this place which he had discovered was his place, the one allotted him, as young Francis had been allotted his Porciuncula. Something passed from his spirit into it and from it to him, and in his saddlebag was the battered silver buckle the strange beguiling child had given him. Crespi had named it the Valley of Santa Lucia after the mountain range they were approaching but Antonio thought now it should be named the Valley of the Rising Sun, for the new illuminations it was giving him.

All day they marched along a wide sandy beach beside high dunes, occasionally detouring inland to avoid marshes and estuaries of streams, and likewise the following day. Then perceiving their way blocked once again by hills descending abruptly to the sea, they turned into a steep-sided canyon and found a large town whose inhabitants came to greet them bearing some remarkably large white clams such as they'd never seen. The place was called Pismu and its people were of the same superior type as those of Antonio's valley. Their chief proved to be a big-bellied, pompous old braggart with an enormous goiter hanging like a sack from his neck, so Ortega named him Buchon. Buchon swaggeringly claimed rulership over a wide area and as evidence of his great prestige offered Portola his two wives as companions for the night. Again Don Gaspar's diplomacy was put to the test to refuse without giving offense. At last he excused himself on grounds of religious vows taken to secure the success of his journey.

Antonio found no opportunity to talk privately with Pablo after leaving the valley, being continually scouting ahead, returning to camp late, on the march again early, and thought it inadvisable to seek him out in front of the others and publicly flaunt defiance of established codes whereby young gentlemen and lowly muleteers did not associate intimately. Though it galled his fierce Catalan instinct for social justice, he knew that such public display would only exacerbate tensions caused by his latest confrontation with Lopez and the underlying friction between Portola and Rivera. Nor would such display have suited Pablo. But going to the creek at twilight the youth found the muleteer bivouacked alone, supplementing his ration with watercress gathered from the nearby stream. In a clearing under a spreading oak Pablo had built a little fire. While watching Antonio approach he said nothing and it occurred to Antonio the black man might have thought him avoiding him during the past days, so he called out heartily:

"Compadre, let's go and discover another valley!"

"Sit down first and join me!" Pablo replied solemnly, removing his battered hat, running a hand through his curly gray hair, and laying the hat down as if in invitation.

Antonio dropped on haunches and waited. The creek ran softly beside them, subdued now in autumn. Warm sea air moved gently through the leaves overhead. Without a word Pablo ceremoniously picked up one of two tortillas which he had laid out on broad damp fans of fern and offered it to Antonio. Thinking this merely a gesture of courtesy the youth declined.

"Eat!" Pablo insisted gruffly not meeting his eyes, and Antonio deduced from his shy manner that this was his method of acknowledging how he'd stood up for him against Lopez. Keenly touched, he accepted the tortilla, wrapped it in watercress as Pablo was doing his and together they ate in silence, grace pronounced by the running stream.

Afterward the muleteer reached inside his shirt where he carried his valuables in a leather pouch strapped next his skin and removed a piece of dried root which looked to Antonio like a small shriveled carrot. "This is what the Indians of our valley call ch'pa.* It is good for every ill." Slicing it in two he gave Antonio half. "Some day you may need this. They say it has the power of life and lasts forever."

Continuing inland the expedition came to pleasant open country at the foot of dark mountains near the present site of San Luis Obispo. Troops of huge grizzlies could be seen foraging like pigs under the oaks and sycamores along the creeks. There were dozens of them in various sizes, sows, cubs, yearlings, huge old boars that weighed a thousand pounds or more. Some were gray but most were reddish brown. Deceived by their awkward appearance and shambling gait, Antonio proposed to Mariano Carrillo that they convert one to camp meat.

Choosing a huge ruddy fellow, Carrillo fired first. "Whereupon," as Antonio recorded, "the bear made straight for him at astonishing speed and nearly overturned him and his mule. My shot had no better effect but I got away without a mauling thanks to my horse's greater speed. He took nine balls, the last through his head, and even in his dying convulsion mashed under one huge paw two of the native dogs who had attached themselves to us, they screaming piteously as life left them."

When Crespi measured the fangs and found them longer than his finger, he exclaimed: "God deliver us from such as these!"

The meat was bright red, firm as pork, delicious if gamey, but thereafter they used fast horses and kept a respectful distance when hunting bears.

Proceeding westward along the Valley of the Bears as it is still called, they reached the sea at a large estuary where a great rock or "morro" rose from the water at a distance of a gunshot from shore. Though joined with the mainland at low tide, Morro Rock was in effect a dome-shaped island shining like a helmet in the morning sun.

Myriads of sea birds perched on it gleamed like jewels, while swift falcons rose and fell above it. On Portola's order they investigated the mouth of the estuary which opened beside it hoping to find the water deep enough to accommodate ships. They were constantly on the lookout for a port like San Diego or Monterey where their galleons, four to six months out from Manila on the tedious and death ridden "black current" of the northern route,

*chuchupate or balsam root

might find fresh water, food, firewood, or trees for new masts and arms, before continuing southward to Acapulco. But the estuary entrance proved too shallow. So they camped and took stock. From here the shoreline curved northwesterly around a majestic indentation fringed by grassy hills. The brush-covered ridges of the Santa Lucia Range rose steeply behind the hills. Taking the latitude, Costanso and Crespi found they were only about two degrees or 120 nautical miles from the Port of Monterey as described in Cabrera Bueno's sailor's manual.

Feeling themselves on the verge of success, they continued along the shore through the fragrant pine grove at modern Cambria, but soon the mountains closing in near the present site of Hearst Castle forced them to stop. Reconnaissance revealed no way to proceed along the water. They would have to climb the mountain wall and detour inland. Everyone must fall to and build trail for two thousand feet or more up the steep slopes of San Carpoforo Creek.

Rivera led the work party. Costanso supervised construction. And now the rivalry between the handful of Catalans, always marching with the Governor at the head of the column, and the many colonial Leather Jackets who followed—despising the Catalans as foreigners unused to frontier ways—erupted again. To tell a Leather Jacket he must labor with his hands like an Indian or a woman was tantamount to telling him he was no man at all. But for Catalans reared on their own farms where hard physical labor was the rule, trail building was simply one more task and they fell to with laughter and will, deriding their rivals as slackers.

Hacking furiously at the chaparral with his broadsword, glancing down from time to time at the glorious land that stretched below and behind—their land, his land, traversed and conquered by his feet and hands, will and sweat, Antonio again had a powerful vision of it settled by industrious thrifty Catalan yeomen like himself, and then was aware of Lopez among the others not far below, sweating, grumbling; and he wondered idly, his animosity drained away and absorbed as it were by their magnificent surroundings, what his rival might be thinking. What was his vision of this promised land? What place in it had been allotted him? And why should Lopez seem placed on earth to oppose and torment? Antonio got on well with almost everyone. Why not with Juan? And during a break in the work he brought himself at last to mention the matter to Ortega who was laboring beside him at the head of the column, sword in hand, struggling for firm footing on the unsteady slope. Ortega, crouched now, breathing heavily, wiping his brow, looked out over a realm of earth, sea, sky. The surroundings seemed to release a frankness in him too.

"Juanito's problem is himself! Make allowances!" Juan possessed no knowledge, he said, of those liberal ideas which were becoming fashionable in intellectual circles such as Antonio frequented. But Juan felt intuitively New Spain and by extension New California were rightfully his by birth. "He sees you as preempting his natural rights here."

"But nothing is further from my thought!"

"It's his thought not yours we are talking about. He thinks your recent exploration with Pablo was a preemption. That was why blind jealousy overcame him, made him speak out of turn."

"Out of turn puts it mildly. He's tried to kill me, Jose!"

"Sure it wasn't your imagination? Sometimes it runs away with you!"

"I'm sure. I hesitate to disagree because you are usually right. But this time I'm sure. There's something in Juan darker than you suspect but I can feel. It's a blind hatred, Jose, a personal thing. I feel he wants to see me dead not only for what I represent but for what I am . . . to whom does this land really belong, Jose? To us who were born in Spain? To you criollos? To mixed bloods like Juan? Or to the Indians who live here now?"

"Why, to the King, who else?"

"That's what I'm asking!"

But this was too much for Ortega. He shrugged and motioned heavenward, leaving the question there among the soaring eagles and hawks. Rivera was calling to them to get busy.

Up the route they roughed out, the Christian Indian pioneers constructed a precarious trail with mattocks and crowbars. Next day the entire expedition scrambled up it. A mule carrying the big communal soup kettle slipped and rolled crashing and bawling all the way to the bottom of a canyon, severely denting the kettle, but miraculously surviving unhurt. Nearing the crest they were treated to a panoramic view of the coastline from Morro Rock on the south to the farthest blue promontories of Big Sur on the north where the land plunged into the sea as if bent on drowning itself. Their eyes searched eagerly for the packet boat *San Antonio* which was supposed to meet them at Monterey with supplies but they saw only empty water.

* * *

Almost impenetrable wilderness greeted them beyond the summit of the range. Again cutting their way and building trail they descended into it a few miles at a time. "We were in another world," Antonio recalled, "one of breathless heat where neither fog nor sea breeze penetrated. The September sun roasted us like nuts in an oven. In these harsh circumstances we found a new type of Indian, less good-looking, and, judging from their meager huts and crude baskets and bowls, much less advanced culturally." But the Salinans were no less friendly. "They took us by the hands and led us to their humble village and there shared their pine nuts and acorns with us."

Such food was insufficient for all and since there was little time to hunt and no game apparent, the Spaniards were obliged to rely on their rations, which were running low as Rivera had predicted. He was slowly building his case against Portola, keeping his own diary which he hoped would refute that of his rival. "The leader of this expedition does not realize my pack mules need a rest!" he'd declared a few days before as if that, not the reluctance of his men to work, were the issue. "While they rest, let our Indians construct the trail! They've hardly lifted a finger so far!" When Portola declared all must fall to and do the job that much faster, Rivera took a new tack. "I call your attention to an alarming fact. Food supplies are running low as I foresaw when we left San Diego, and if my men are to labor like slaves they should be better fed or they will fall ill again!"

But Portola declared all must work for the common good, hungry or not, and there would be time to rest beyond the mountains. Rivera shrugged as if to say: "I have warned you!"

Now weakened by incessant trail building, climbing, descending, herding animals, making and breaking camp, standing guard at night, Antonio's body like many others broke out with the telltale blotches of scurvy. His joints ached and his gums bled as the dread loanda reasserted itself. "Our spirits sank as we groped our way through what seemed endless wilderness, our only certainty the compass needle pointing north."

At last they emerged into the beautiful oak-studded valley where Mission San Antonio was to stand, rested and took fresh hope. Continuing inland to avoid the skirts of the mountains they came to a much larger valley "very fertile, verdant with rosemary, sage, and wild roses," Through this valley flowed a broad shallow stream which Crespi named the San Elzeario but the soldiers called it the Chocolate River because of its muddy color. Later it would be known as the Rio de Monterey and finally the Salinas, from the salt beds at its mouth.

The River of Chocolate led them northward between tall mountains mostly devoid of trees though with good grass, until after five days to their great joy it turned westward and they smelled sea air. Next afternoon Ortega and Antonio with Yorba and Reyes were standing atop a sandy knoll later known as Mulligan's Hill gazing excitedly at what appeared to be a large open bight or roadstead.

"But, look there!" Ortega exclaimed. Southward along the shore about five miles was a promontory covered with pines exactly as described in Cabrera Bueno's manual as forming the southern reach of Monterey Bay. "And there!" Northward, farther away, was a headland which seemed to correspond to the veteran Manila captain's Año Nuevo, its northern reach. "Can this indeed be Monterey Bay?"

"Looks to me like an open roadstead!" Antonio objected. "Where's the 'well protected harbor' Cabrera describes? Or the 'very fine stopping port for China ships' Venegas records?"

When officers and fathers arrived they were similarly perplexed. Removing his octant from its carrying case, Costanso took the latitude and found it thirty-six degrees, forty-four minutes.

"But according to Cabrera it should be thirty-seven degrees, if it's Monterey!" Portola declared.

Rivera expressed the obvious. "If so we haven't gone far enough!"

"Perhaps we've gone too far!" Crespi countered. "According to Cabrera, San Diego lay at thirty-four. Actually it lay at thirty-two and a half, or a little more."

Bemused by such conflicting evidence and their great expectations, they were standing on the shore of Monterey Bay without realizing it. If you stand at the mouth of the Salinas and look out to sea, you will see how easily they were deceived.

Next morning Rivera led a party including Antonio and Ortega to investigate the point to the south. There they found the lofty pines described in both guidebooks as suitable for masts and arms, and this seemed to confirm their hopes. But where was that well protected harbor? Beyond the point was only a small cove, the present Carmel Bay, where a pleasant valley with a fine stream opened to the sea. A few miles farther the towering Santa Lucia Range began its cliff-like plunge into the water and they were forced to turn back.

Rivera made no attempt to conceal his satisfaction when he reported these negative results to Portola. He had no wish to see the man he hated succeed where he felt himself best qualified to lead. Months of strain were taxing his self-control. "There's no sign of a port!" he said triumphantly. "Once again we've been misled, and our rations are running low as I predicted while many men are falling ill!"

Unruffled, Portola replied he would call a conference next day to consider what should be done. Next day, October 4, 1769, was the feast day of Saint Francis. Following High Mass which all attended, asking God and the seraphic Francis to guide them, officers and friars met soberly in Portola's tent. He opened the discussion with a frank but unapologetic statement of their plight. Portola's reputation, not to mention his career, was at stake. But if the nightmare of failure haunted him, he gave no sign of it. "We thought to find the Port of Monterey hereabouts but such has not proved the case. Four hundred fifty miles or forty-five days' travel separate us from our base. Seventeen of our thirty-three soldiers are so crippled by scurvy as to be unfit for duty, others nearly so. Our food supply is already below a level that would sustain us comfortably during a return journey should we start tomorrow. To make matters worse, not a single Indian has appeared with food or information. This could indicate a hostile attitude. True, a ship may be on its way or waiting at the Port of Monterey. But none has appeared. Meanwhile the season is advancing. Rain and snow may soon impede our progress. In short, we may perish if we advance; we may perish if we do not. Under these circumstances, Gentlemen, and Your Reverences, the question I lay before you is simply this: Do we search farther, or do we abandon our quest and return to San Diego?"

As deputy commander, Fages spoke in favor of continuing. "If Monterey is not to the south," he argued bluntly, "it must be to the north!" His absurd daily inspections had died a natural death in the wilderness of Santa Lucia, much as Portola had foreseen, but his fiery enthusiasm remained undiminished. Costanso coolly agreed. "Since the latitude given in Cabrera's manual proved too high for San Diego, it might conversely be too low for Monterey." Crespi also recommended that they continue as far north as thirty-seven-and-a-half degrees and even to thirty-eight, a distance of about a hundred miles. Rather surprisingly considering his recent outburst, Rivera concurred. By now it would have seemed dishonorable to do otherwise. Gomez and Portola adding their approval, the decision to continue was unanimous.

Chapter Twelve

That night Lospe was wakened by Kahip's soft crying. "Why must people hurt each other?" she thought with despair, reaching out from her own sorrow to one even more unfortunate. Rebellious anger rose in her. Fully aware of the risk she was taking, she stealthily left her mat and crept to Kahip's.

As she neared the huddled shape in the darkness by the far wall, the sobbing stopped. "Come," she whispered no louder than breath. "While I quiet the dogs, you slip away!" Kahip who had sat halfway up shook her once proud and lovely head, too dispirited even to try to save herself. "Come," urged Lospe impatiently. "I'll go with you! We'll travel through the hills together and come to your home!" At the word *home,* Kahip began sobbing again. Seneq awoke.

"What's going on over there?" she demanded sharply.

"Kahip's trying to escape," Lospe replied loudly. "Fortunately for you, Old Lady, I was alert!"

After that there was no hope. At high noon when the sun could look directly down upon the Wisdom Stone, the circular judgment seat with the hole in its middle connecting upper and lower worlds, which stood at the center of the meeting place, the place where they themselves so often knelt to entreat the Sky People, as Lospe recalled with bitter foreboding, Kahip knelt terrified. "Everyone was staring with morbid curiosity. Many of them were adulterers but never had been caught. Many were too wealthy and important ever to be punished for anything. Witnesses had come to observe the spectacle from neighboring villages and even from the provincial capital at Point Conception." Owotoponus presided, plumed, painted, magic wand in hand, hateful, stern, implacable. As the sun reached zenith he raised his wand. The quartz crystal at its end sparkled with the colors of a rainbow. Twelve red arrows, one for each month of the year, discharged by his assistants, flew and pierced Kahip's crouching body. With a frightened gasp she died. Her blood seeped into the earth and left a stain that can never be removed! Lospe thought. Afterward Heap dragged the body away and burned it as those who died of snake bite or other hideous accident were burned to prevent bad luck arising from their remains, while Owotoponus delivered a discourse on mortality and the sanctity of immemorial custom.

After the departure of the Spaniards, he was uneasy at heart and had gone to Koyo and demanded: "Are you ready to give yourself to me in marriage, or are you like your daughter, in love with an A-alowow?"

"Our very existence as a people is at stake and you importune me!" she rebuked him, playing for time, hoping to escape his grasp. She'd sent word to the Tulamni to provide witnesses for the execution of Kahip but they sent word back that the execution would be regarded by them as an act of war, and they far outnumbered the People of Olomosoug.

"You are deliberately putting me off!" Owotoponus raged, seeing through her ruse but hesitating to force the issue under the circumstances.

"I am not!" she retorted. "You know as well as I we are under threat of attack! All of your great power may be needed to protect us!"

Then in accordance with protocol she sent the Tulamni word a second and third time but still they refused to appear. That left her no alternative, deeply reluctant though she was.

The battle took place on the Great Plain of the Carrizo Grass where all borders met, but at some distance from the sanctuary at the Painted Rock where no violence was permitted. All necessary arrangements were made by emissaries beforehand. After approaching within bowshot, the two opposing warrior groups stopped and tossed up sacred down signifying clouds, each side shouting defiance and invoking the aid of the Sky People.

Then Owotoponus stepped forward. Holding his basketry tray high, he challenged the Tulamni's leading magician to a contest. "What followed remains incised in my memory like the shape of a bear's paw pecked in a sacred rock," Lospe recalled. She stood watching with all her people, as did the Tulamni villagers. "Each magician was adorned with plumes and fetishes. Each held his basketry tray high to attract the sun's power. Each spoke to the Sky People in his own language of mystery and magic." Everyone watching and the vast plain too falling silent as if it also were holding its breath, the moment arrived. "The magic shot which appeared on each tray resembled seeds or fish eggs to our ordinary eyes. What it truly was, only they knew. With a simultaneous shout, they crashed their trays violently to the ground. Their invisible arrows flew through the air. Owotoponus' was the more powerful. His opponent fell senseless."

What actually happened is impossible to say. But it occurred not infrequently. Sometimes victims who had been supernaturally "killed" were "magically" restored to life, sometimes not. It was evidently some powerful form of extrasensory activity, perhaps thought projection, perhaps even out-of-body travel.

A great shout of triumph went up from the Chumash warriors as the Tulamni magician fell and they released a shower of arrows. Bitter fighting at close quarters with clubs and knives ensued. Her uncle Ta-apu, having taken momoy believing it made him invisible to his enemies and thus impervious to their arrows and blows, led valiantly. But it was on her brother that Lospe's eyes fixed. "Asuskwa's young body gleamed in the sun like a column of light. He was in the morning of his day and this his first battle. It did not seem possible that Great Sun would take him from me as He had taken my father, and my beloved!" But the spirit of the Tulamni had been broken by Owotoponus' superior magic. They fled leaving six dead. "We cut off their right hands and burned the rest. We never lowered ourselves to scalp or torture as others did. Nor did we enslave prisoners. We killed them immediately. Heaven forgive us!"

All night long the plain blazed with the fires of celebration, and there was much dancing and singing until that moment should come when all women should make themselves available to all men in traditional manner to honor Great Sun the Ruler of All Life, as at the time of the winter solstice. But first there was the solemn war dance. "Ta-apu, Asuskwa, and Owotoponus, hateful to me if now all-powerful, entered the circle of fires each carrying a feathered pole, each grunting in unison 'hu, hu,' as they slowly took steps forward, moving clockwise around the circle three times songlessly at first, and then breaking triumphantly into the song of victory: 'We shall always see the light of the Sun!' Then they drew their bows as if they were going to shoot, and boys and young men were told by elders that this signified the Sun was being born anew. The dancers proceeded clockwise—sunwise—around the circle until midnight when the solemnities were concluded." And then the highly suggestive merriment began.

In the first of these new dances He-ap played the role of a fox. He'd painted his face white and there were broad, white bands around his chest, arms, and legs signifying magic power. His neck was stained vermillion, and a headdress of twined junco fibers decorated with flowers covered the top of his head, while the ends of the fibers were brought together behind his neck and worked into a long tail-like braid, the fox's tail, which hung down behind.

At the end of the tail a small rock was inserted to serve as weight so the tail could swing from side to side.

An old man, who held a turtle shell rattle with pebbles in it in each hand, followed close behind and shook them as He-ap began to sing: "I make a big step!" jumping forward like a fox, swinging his tail. "I'm always going over to the other side!" making a jump as if over a stream, while his tail swung behind.

As he proceeded from fire to fire the verses grew more suggestive in keeping with the lusty spirit that was arising. "The fox has very black balls! He has a mottled prick! The fox does not have much hair! The fox is feeble!" People laughed with hearty approval. "The fox has a black-and-white-spotted prick! But he can't make it stand up!" pantomiming while everybody roared. "The fox has squinty eyes!" Then all at once very loudly: "EVERYBODY LIVE!" And the people echoed: "EVERYBODY LIVE!" In this way barriers were lowered and people made ready for what was to follow.

A woman must go with any man who sang to her the low wild yearning song of desire; otherwise he had the right to take her even if she lay beside her husband. Thus for one night all custom was reversed. It was now that Owotoponus had his way with Koyo. For her to put him off longer was impossible. Everyone expected it. He was the hero of the hour. But Lospe did not go with Alul though he sang to her ardently. Taken aback by her daring refusal to conform to tradition, he shrank from forcing her, and at heart she despised his timidity. And when handsome Tonto-on, the son of Shamik, boldest among many who desired her, approached but then turned aside and chose another girl, she felt a sudden unexpected pang of disappointment and an almost unbearable yearning flamed in her to be as the others, not to be different, to be joyful and fulfilled.

Lying alone in the darkness while others made love, she remembered Quati's prophecy that she must remain a virgin until fourteen—and then she would marry a Sutupaps. "And as the fires died away to sparks across the plain and the songs of delight rose around me, I thought of my sunny-haired handsome one, riding away on his beautiful beast, so gallant, so free, carrying my silver buckle. Would he ever come back? Would I ever see him again?''

Chapter Thirteen

While the conference of officers and padres in Portola's tent continued, the scurvy-ridden men not guarding the caballada, or lying groaning in pain on their ponchos, squatted on their haunches speculating as to its outcome.

"They'll vote to march on, though it leave our bones rotting in this godforsaken land!" a Catalan, Ramon Bonnel, predicted, spitting blood. Like other Catalans he'd suffered most in the beginning from the dread loanda thanks to their terrible voyage from San Blas to San Diego, and was now hard hit again, and ironically the Leather Jackets he'd scorned were now helping him stay alive by doing extra duty and out of pity aiding in small ways; and ironically some of the Leather Jackets too were disabled and some of the Catalans were helping them. From shared hardship and suffering true comradeship was being forged.

It was Camacho, a bearded colonial, who sounded the first note of insubordination. "In times like these a man must think of his own skin!"

Pablo spoke up for the poor and lowly, the Indians and mixed blood muleteers, on whom the brunt of extra duty caused by so many sick had fallen hardest. "Why should I carry them on my back?" jerking his thumb toward the tent. "What do I get for my pains, eh? Insults and poor food!" There were mutters of approval.

"If you're going to march back to San Diego alone, go ahead!" Ortega joked, intending to prick the bubble of discontent with humor.

"Think I'd be afraid to go off alone in the wilderness?" Pablo bridled. "Man, I'd get along! I'd find things to eat! The Indians would be kind to me, make much of me as they did the young gentleman and me in the Valley of Santa Lucia, eh? This way," he gestured at the scurvy-ridden camp, "I'm likely to die for God and King! What have God and King ever done for me? Not much I can't do without!"

"Watch your tongue!" Ortega cautioned.

But Pablo persisted, airily now, like a child improvising. "Rivera says he can't ride a mule in those Santa Lucia Mountains, they're so steep. Then why doesn't he walk? We Indians walk. We've always walked. I'm not afraid to live like an Indian; they'd be kind to me, honor me, maybe make me their chief!" This brought hoots of laughter. Pablo, the Ethiopian Emperor, yes, yes! "Whereas here," he continued unperturbed, "what am I? Lowest turd on the pile! You can laugh! And die!"

"So you'd desert us, would you?" Ortega inquired gravely with a wink at the others.

"Would I?" Pablo seemed to consider the possibility for the first time. "What's a man's first loyalty?"

"To himself!" the bearded Camacho reiterated and there were further mutters of approval. Ortega frowned but said nothing.

Next morning there was no one to pack Pablo's mules. "I wasn't entirely surprised," Antonio wrote, "though a little hurt he hadn't spoken to me first, even asked me to go with him. We followed his footprints along the hard-packed sand of the beach until the incoming tide erased them. 'Damn the black rascal, let him go!' Mariano Carrillo exclaimed after we'd searched the Point of Pines and found no further trace. But I could imagine Pablo walking in magnificent solitude under those great mossy trees and off into the limitless wilderness of the Santa Lucias, gun on shoulder, resourcefulness ready in both hands, perhaps finding his way back to our Valley of the Rising Sun. He knew we could afford neither time nor manpower to look for him very far!"

Summoning the entire company to hear, first Rivera, then Fages, then Portola reminded them that the penalty for desertion was death. The infection must not be allowed to spread.

Faces grim, spirits low, they resumed their march. Since the days of Cortes, the Spanish imagination had been drawn northward toward a legendary land of fabulous treasures and wonders. "A little farther north!" was the cry. Northward lay the Golden Island of California, the fabulous Strait of Anian. Now they were experiencing the suffering reality. Some were so weak they fell from their saddles unless supported by comrades.

Circling inland to avoid numerous marshes near the mouth of

the Salinas, the scouts, Ortega and Antonio leading, found a large Indian settlement among tall cottonwoods on the bank of a smaller river near the present site of Watsonville. Its people numbering perhaps 500 were totally surprised at the sight of them. "The men cried out in alarm, seized bows and arrows and prepared for war," Antonio recalled. "The women burst into tears. But Ortega showed his mettle. Dismounting and handing me lance and tie rope, he advanced unarmed, hands open in a gesture of friendship. They could easily have killed him but persuaded by his courage, thrust their arrows into the earth point down, with exclamations of approval and good will, then presented us with excellent tamales made from acorn and seed flour, our first decent food in many days."

The scouts hoped all members of the expedition might enjoy a similar treat, but when they led their sick and hungry fellows to the spot, the village was a smoking ruin, abandoned and burned to the ground. Around it stood a circle of red poles. "They have dedicated their houses to us as a placative offering," Costanso suggested somberly. "Or to their gods!" Antonio rejoined because from one of the poles hung the carcass of a huge condor such as he'd seen kept for sacrificial purpose at Koyo's house, and he explained how, as Lospe had described, the bird was strangled at a special ceremony which released its spirit to the sky while its body was buried in the earth in a sacred place and its feathers made into skirts and other ceremonial regalia. This bird was so large they measured its wingspan and found it to be nearly nine feet. They named the nearby stream the Pajaro, or bird, River.

"Groans from the sick and dying kept me awake that night," Antonio continued, "and while lying there tired and discouraged, joints swollen and aching, I imagined Pablo living like a king in some Indian village deep in the heart of the wilderness and wished I were there with him. Perhaps he would even make his way back to our valley and see my charming child. Remembering the piece of root he'd given me I got it out and nibbled at it and soon, though perhaps from imagination, felt better."

Next morning three Leather Jackets and two Catalans including his friend Yorba seemed doomed. The fathers administered last rites. "But Lopez held up, sustained by hatred, no doubt, and pride too, smiling his gap-toothed grin, playing his fiddle defiantly at mealtime, and feeling defiant myself I refused to give in, though I was pissing blood, but volunteered for the reconnais-

This Promised Land

sance Portola ordered in the direction of the coast." Rivera insisted they take extra mules as relays, their horses were so weak, and Antonio had to admit that Old Fussbudget's solicitude for animals and men was sincere, "though it was eventually to prove his undoing."

They rode toward the sea along the route followed by today's Highway 1 through Aptos and Santa Cruz, and presently saw trees of a kind never seen before. "Very tall and straight and their wood was red and soft. We called them savins* because they resembled the European cedar. From here northward they were plentiful."

After reconnoitering a barren shoreline and seeing nothing resembling the Port of Monterey, they returned to camp. During their absence the able bodied had rigged upright x-shaped leaning frames or jamugas, "like those used by women of Andalusia at the backs of their side-saddles," and additional litters so that the very ill might travel with less pain. Again all struggled forward, growing weaker, seeming destined to die by increments as scurvy, dysentery, and hunger sapped their strength and winter descended with rain and cold. Their jerked beef gave out as did their dried peas for soup. Though they killed a duck or deer occasionally, their ration was reduced to one tortilla a day and what else they could find. Rummaging through his saddlebags for trinkets to trade friendly Indians for food, Antonio came across the buckle Lospe had given him but decided at the last moment that to trade it might bring bad luck, and he wondered if she were still in mourning and what she might look like without a blackened face. "Nearly everything I owned went for food and the same held true for others. Yet wonderful to say, though drenched and chilled, the dying began to revive while the weak grew strong."

The reason was probably the horse chestnuts which hung like bronze decorations from the naked bows of the low tree. Tasting one Antonio found its moist white meat delicious. "See here!" he cried out as if he had discovered gold, which in a way he had, and all his once fastidious comrades, including officers and fathers, followed his example thus unwittingly providing themselves with the vitamins their bodies so critically lacked.

At Whitehouse Creek they found watercress and friendly Indians who gave them presents of seeds kneaded into dough balls and bits of honeycomb from the nests of bumblebees. "They were

*redwoods

123

impressive in character and intelligence," Antonio noted, "and their pyramid-shaped houses, composed of pine slabs, were as skillfully made as the thatched ones of Lospe's village. Their large central meeting lodge could accommodate all 200 of their tribe." These were members of the Costanoan family, as it is now called, a loosely linked society resembling the Chumash, who inhabited the region between Monterey and San Francisco Bay and around the bay itself. The men were bearded and wore ponchos made of carded plant fiber, which covered them from neck to waist. The women wore skirts of bark and rabbit skin capes. "They greatly excited us by informing us that four days' journey northward lay a harbor with a ship in it. 'It must be the *San Antonio*,' we all exclaimed. 'Monterey must be close at hand!' "

With relief and triumph seeming to lie just ahead, they limped forward, scrambling up and down the sides of steep canyons that opened to the sea, laboriously constructing bridges and trails across the streams and bogs, until once more their way was blocked by a high hill descending abruptly to the water. Climbing it they saw a sight which overjoyed and at the same time cruelly disappointed them. "Northwesterly exactly as described in our literature, lay six small islands or farallones, while directly ahead at a distance of some fifteen miles a long promontory resembling Point Conception, with a high white elevation at its end, jutted far into the sea."

Unquestionably this was Point Reyes, clearly described in their guidebooks. Together with the islands and an indentation ahead of them in the shoreline at the mouth of undiscovered Golden Gate, Point Reyes formed what had long been called the Harbor of San Francisco, the actual bay by that name being wholly unknown. "What we saw filled us with mixed feelings because if we had reached the Harbor of San Francisco, that of Monterey must lie behind and we had failed!"

"Still, we know exactly where we are," Costanso insisted, "and cannot be anywhere else!" His latitude for the spot was thirty-seven degrees, thirty-five minutes or virtually that of Point Reyes, and hidden somewhere in the indentation ahead or under Point Reyes itself might be a supply ship.

Torn by conflicting emotions they made camp in a deep hollow with good grass and sweet water surrounded by hills except where it opened toward the sea. They were at present Pacifica, totally ignorant of what lay so close at hand.

Next day, All Souls' Day, November first, dawned clear and

This Promised Land

warm. After Mass and a communal prayer for divine guidance, Portola said to Ortega: "Take eight men with food and animals for three days and find me a way to reach Point Reyes, or the Harbor of Monterey, or a ship!"

The scouting party proceeded along the coast until its path was blocked by still another cliff. Turning inland it began to climb a spur leading toward the top of the ridge immediately eastward. As the riders neared the crest Antonio happened to be breaking trail, forcing his way through scrub oak with prickly leaves that scratched noisily against his armas and tore at his clothes and flesh. "They had small puffy yellowish-white blossoms," he remembered years later. Thus it was he who emerged first upon the summit and saw the sight which held them breathless.

Below at the foot of the mountains, awesome in extent and beauty, lay an enormous estuary or arm of the sea. Surrounded by stately mountains, it was at least ten miles across and stretched north and south beyond their sight. Though heavy swells had been running upon the beach as they left camp, this haven lay as quiet as a lake. "Why, all the navies of the world could anchor here with room to spare!" Ortega exclaimed. They were looking down at San Francisco Bay from a point almost due west of the present International Airport.

"But this can't be the Bay of Monterey!" Antonio cried. "Nothing like it is mentioned in our guidebooks!" Gradually it dawned on them they had discovered something entirely new, a natural wonder never seen by Christian eyes till now. It was indeed a breathtaking thought and their hearts beat harder as they scanned the water for the expected ship. Though they saw none, a dozen might lie hidden in such an inland sea.

"Reasoning we could not reach Point Reyes without getting around this great estuary which must open somewhere between us and it, we descended and soon were traveling through a wondrously beautiful land," Antonio recorded, "covered with oak trees and much grass. We saw countless deer, myriads of waterfowl, and before long came to the bank of a musically flowing creek where there stood one solitary redwood towering above its neighboring oaks and sycamores. It was so big five men joining hands could barely surround it." They stopped to rest under the great tree and named it El Palo Alto, or the tall tree, likening its exceptional height to Antonio's. It still stands within the city limits of Palo Alto, shading the traveler who will stop. By this time they had met many friendly Indians who informed them that two days' travel northward was a fine harbor containing a ship. "You can imagine our delight at this news! It seemed confirmation of the earlier report and we felt confident our reconnaissance had been crowned with success!"

Returning as they had come, following generally the route of today's Highway 280 and the lake-studded valley formed by the San Andreas Fault, they reached the main camp after dark, firing muskets to herald their good tidings. Portola was so pleased he ordered a ration of precious chocolate issued them.

Next day they led the entire expedition along the route they'd discovered. On reaching the crest and seeing the immensity of the estuary below, all agreed it was a natural wonder and must have a hidden opening somewhere between them and Point Reyes. Guiding them down to the tall redwood by the stream where they made camp, Antonio and Ortega with four companions including Lopez, once more at Portola's order scouted ahead.

Circling the lower end of the bay near the present site of San Jose, the scouting party advanced up its eastern side. They found the land all burned off, almost no grass available for their animals, and the Indians for the first time openly hostile. "Assembling in warlike fashion a hundred warriors, painted and feathered, armed with bows and clubs, attempted to bar our way." When Ortega's efforts to placate them failed, he ordered Lopez to fire a shot in the air as Pablo had done in the Valley of Santa Lucia. "With great relish he did so, and they fled." Thus the first attempt by native Californians to oppose their invaders collapsed in the face of superior technology. At the moment Antonio felt only uneasiness, although later it would seem doubly evident that he and Juan had broken the peace of a blissful land and released diabolical forces.

Continuing a short distance they ascended a hill in hopes of discovering the extent of the estuary and perhaps a ship, but saw nothing except empty water and a mountainous shoreline stretching out of sight. They were near present San Leandro a few miles south of Oakland. Deciding it would take a week to circle the Great Estuary, as they were calling it, and reach Point Reyes and their time being up, they returned to the camp by the tall redwood. It was a somber moment. Discouragement gripped everyone. Still Portola was for pushing on. His response to their disappointing news had been to call another conference of officers and fathers, under the giant tree within a few yards of the later site of Stanford University.

This Promised Land

Portola had the most to lose by turning back. Viceroy Croix and Inspector General Galvez would be unhappy to say the least when he stood before them in the viceregal palace in Mexico City with explanations however reasonable. Antonio too was for pushing on. His fortunes were tied to those of Portola, and the thought of a triumphant Rivera, an exultant Lopez, was intolerable.

But officers and fathers unanimously opposed their commander-in-chief, foremost among them the jealous Rivera. "We possess neither food nor strength for further travel into unknown territory," Rivera observed scornfully, as if to a novice who could scarcely be expected to understand such obvious difficulties, "where there is little grass for animals, the existence of the rumored ship is highly questionable, the heathen hostile!"

At heart a genial man who would have preferred to avoid unpleasant scenes, Portola responded patiently. "What about the ship? What is the explanation for that widespread rumor?"

"How should I know?" Rivera retorted.

Costanso intervened: "It could be a hand-me-down from the days of the English pirate Drake. As we know, he beached his ship and spent several weeks in an inlet under Point Reyes." Costanso was for turning back and searching again in the vicinity of the Point of Pines and the coast of the Sierra de Santa Lucia. So were Crespi and Gomez. Finally Portola concurring, all votes cast in writing, the decision was taken to return and search further for Monterey Harbor in those same mountains where they had already searched, into which Pablo had disappeared.

With heavy steps the Spaniards retraced their route toward the Point of Pines, dragging their sick along, and going a little beyond it arrived safely at a campsite near the Point of Wolves*—sea wolves or lions being numerous in the waters there—on what is now Carmel Bay on November 28. The weather had turned rainy and cold. Their only solace lay in two thoughts: nobody had died or been seriously injured and they had discovered the Great Estuary which was clearly of enormous importance. "It will be a barrier to the Russians," Costanso predicted, "and a haven against the English. We must erect a presidio and mission on its shore as soon as possible, meanwhile keeping its existence secret from our enemies." He'd mapped as much as they'd seen of it

---
*Point Lobos

and its surroundings and was doing likewise with their present locality.

From the Point Lobos camp, Rivera led a scouting party south along the Big Sur Coast, swearing he would flay Pablo alive if he caught him. Most thought him dead of starvation or at the hands of Indians. But Antonio was secretly confident of his ability to survive, perhaps even to find his way back to their valley, and when he saw the track of a sandal in moist earth by a bush with some edible toyon berries he told no one. They found no harbor, nothing but precipitous wilderness where hawks screamed and waves pounded the feet of desolate peaks that plunged with dizzying steepness to a foaming sea. And when they returned, they learned that two Christian Indian laborers and two muleteers had followed Pablo's example and departed.

"If the bottom of our social pyramid is disintegrating," Costanso commented wryly, munching some of the berries Antonio brought him, "can we at the top survive?" A passage from Rousseau's *Social Contract* came forcibly to Antonio's mind. "It is freedom rather than peace, which causes a race to prosper!" he replied, and from that moment felt convinced that if this new land were to be successfully settled, it must be by free men, motivated by self-sustaining interest.

The Sacred Expedition was nearing the end of its tether. "What were we to do? Our flour was almost gone. Our supplementary diet of occasional shellfish or berries was too meager to sustain life, while the onset of winter reduced the availability of forage of all kinds. With Portola's approval, we killed a mule—an old lame stud of little use at best—but no one would eat its stinking flesh except the Catalans and remaining Indians, while to make matters worse no wild Indians who might have brought food appeared. Despite its great natural beauty, the place seemed hostile to us."

In this atmosphere Portola called a final council. Fiery little Fages, still the conquistador at heart, still ready to take up arms and push back that chaos which threatens all human endeavor, spoke first. "Give me half our able-bodied men and I'll lead them into the mountains, kill deer and bear, send meat back to camp!" Costanso calmly urged remaining where they were, asserting: "We are near the site of Monterey and a supply ship must eventually find us!" And then he courageously declared that all remaining food should be divided equally among all members of the expedition regardless of rank. This was an oblique reference to certain hams and biscuits Portola was known to be hoarding for his own table. Hearing it, Rivera thought his long awaited moment had come. "The leader of this expedition must bear full responsibility for our desperate plight. If he asks me to share blame I shall decline, for it is his alone!" He wanted those words on the record. "Indeed I warned from the beginning we should have brought more food!" This was true. But if Portola erred, it was on the side of generosity in leaving ample supplies for the sick and disabled at the San Diego camp. He could have replied that mules to carry additional supplies were not available. Instead he maintained dignified silence while Rivera completed his accusation. The two fathers then expressed their willingness to remain where they were and undergo any hardship so that the land might be Christianized. Finally when emotions had been vented and realities were considered: the sixteen bags of flour remaining, the extreme cold and wet prevailing—rain had fallen heavily on the camp and snow lay on the mountains nearby—the weakness of animals and men, and the possibility that more snow might close the passes of the Santa Lucias, in which case they all might perish, a unanimous decision was taken, once again in writing, to return to San Diego at once.

"Before we left," Antonio recorded, "a Holy Cross made of pine limbs was erected on the seashore. On it were inscribed the words: 'Dig at the foot and you will find a letter.'" The letter, buried in a medicine bottle, told of our travels, hardships, discoveries, and the reasons for our retreat. It was left so that if a ship arrived it might have news of us and might look for us as we journeyed southward."

They erected a similar cross at the Point of Pines, on the actual shore of the bay to whose identity they still were blind, and on its arms carved this message: "The land expedition is returning to San Diego for lack of provisions, today, December 9, 1769." Next day they began retracing their steps southward.

Chapter Fourteen

"But, Mother, how can you?" Lospe protested in horror as they walked toward the sweathouse by the river for their daily sauna and gossip and Koyo informed her of her decision to marry Owotoponus.

"Dear one, I have no choice. Ask yourself like the grown-up girl you are: Is it not better to make an ally of The Powerful Sorcerer than to fight him? How can any of us stand against such magic as his? Besides, since the victory on the plains, our people all but worship him. You invoke the memory of your father whom I truly loved. But when married to him I was not a chieftainess, only a wife. Now I'm responsible for the well-being of all our people and I wish to see them united and happy as in the days of your grandfather! Furthermore," she lowered her voice, glancing around to see if anyone were near, "perhaps I shall bear no more children. There are methods, as you know. In any event he has promised that your brother shall succeed me—and you your brother should anything befall my dear boy!"

"But you cannot believe a word the scoundrel says!" Lospe protested. "You will surely bear his child! That child will rule over us some day! Such is his secret purpose! He has no love for you or for our people, only for himself!"

After the marriage ceremony which was attended by chiefs from neighboring villages and the provincial capital at Point Conception, Owotoponus came to live with them in the accepted way, and it seemed for a while all might go well, until his overweening arrogance began to assert itself and he ordered Seneq: "Bring me food, Old Hag!" as if she were his slave. He was constantly, ravenously hungry, as if that too were an aspect of his insatiable egotism. Ta-apu was helpless. "Like my Aunt Lehlele," Lospe recounted, "he feared for his life, brave though he was. Who can

This Promised Land

contend against supernatural power? Likewise Alul dared do nothing. I prayed that my brother, a bearded young warrior now, would somehow deliver us, but Asuskwa held himself more and more aloof. Clearly he was brooding. Encountering him one morning among the willows after bathing, I asked despairingly: "What can we do?" By that time we hardly dared speak to one another for fear of reprisal. He said nothing. I saw by his face that his thoughts were elsewhere. Next day he disappeared. When he did not return Owotoponus demanded of Mother: 'Where is your son?'

" 'How should I know?' she replied. 'He is a grown man now. He comes and goes as he chooses!'

"Owotoponus laughed malevolently. 'Do you think you deceive me? I know what's in your mind. You hope he's fled to the wilderness and escaped my grasp. You think he's at this moment on top of Iwihinmu like your apostate husband presuming to commune with Sacred Sun! But he is not! Look!' His voice suddenly became terrible. He reached out his hand, opened his fingers wide, then slowly closed them, slowly drew them back toward him clenched tightly, smiling malevolently, so that our hearts failed for dread of what might be revealed when he opened his hand. '*Where is your son?*' he demanded of Mother in a voice no louder than a whisper.

"She cried out in fear: 'I do not know!'

"Owotoponus said softly: 'He was in the willows yesterday morning. He is here in my hand now. Were I to open it, he would never come back to you!' "

Koyo turned pale. Lospe gasped. Though she'd long since begun to doubt the integrity of all men who purported to be holy, there was no denying his fearful power. He looked at them face-to-face in turn, clearly enjoying their suffering, and in that moment she knew that he must die and wanted to kill him.

"This time I am merciful," he continued blandly, keeping his hand tightly closed. Suddenly with a motion faster than they could follow he released something. Then he turned smilingly to Lospe. "Perhaps it's just as well. Then there would be only you, My Little Flower!"

Koyo burst out indignantly: "She is too young! Besides there are the words of your own father who gave us the prophecy of the Sky People concerning her!"

Ignoring Koyo he reached and caressed Lospe's hair lightly with the tips of his fingers. "Almost ready to bloom! My father was such a wise man, I wonder he didn't pluck you himself!"

She drew back and spit. "Oh, a little wildcat!" He chuckled but his eyes flamed with desire. She decided she would run away or kill him before she would submit to him. She could not help but hear what went on behind their bed screen at night. "Sometimes he took his pleasure with Mother ritually in public on the dancing ground to entertain the populace who were grossly delighted by it all, though it was supposed to be sacred, he sliding her up and down on his huge prong like a piece of meat on a spit, they watching in supposed reverence which was in fact sniggering obscenity. How I loathed him! How I wished him dead! How I wished my brother would come home and kill him!" Owotoponus was introducing a new and grosser morality to replace the conventional ways which had existed for centuries, but the people, admiring and at the same time afraid, accepted all that he did with abject approval. "We were helpless. All of us. How can you contend against supernatural power?"

Chapter Fifteen

It was as if Portola were leading a beaten army from the field. Dispirited, spiteful, ready to blame each other, but thankful to be alive, they dragged themselves southward down the Salinas Valley toward the final humiliation of admitting defeat to their comrades and Father President Serra when they reached San Diego. The blackened grass, burned off by the Indians, yielded so little fodder that their starving animals began to nibble at each other's tails and manes. They killed a mule each day and stewed the stinking flesh in such herbs as they could find but even so it remained sickening and they had to force themselves to eat. Their sixteen bags of flour were soon reduced to ten.

Near the present site of King City they turned toward the coast, retraced their former route, and reentered the Wilderness of Santa Lucia. The cold was biting and the streams swollen from rain and snow which had fallen on the summits ahead. Skies were gray. The barren trees looked like their grave markers.

"As hunger increased, each of us became implicitly his fellow's enemy as we drew upon the same dwindling source of flour," Antonio remembered. "Our ten bags were soon reduced to five, and though these were carefully guarded, there was evidence of pilferage."

Fages raged at them. "He who steals another man's food under these circumstances is no better than a murderer!" "And should be executed as one!" Rivera echoed him. Portola would not declare what measures he would take should a thief be caught but ordered additional guards placed that night over the alforjas* containing the remaining bags. It seemed afterward to Antonio he'd forseen what followed. Lopez had dogged him on every decisive

*rawhide containers for packsaddles

occasion: at the stampede, at the tar bog, by the fire on the evening of his return from exploring the valley with Pablo, throughout the terrible rain-soaked march northward which ended in the discovery of the Great Estuary, all during the dismal return and re-search of the Santa Lucias, playing his impudent fiddle, smiling his gap-toothed grin, so why not now? "I was accepting him as my bête noire, the dark cloud over my promised land."

As they came together in the last bone-chilling watch before dawn, Ortega, acting as sergeant of the guard under Rivera's orders, went off to check the men herding the animals, warning them he'd be back in a moment. That moment dragged into an hour. While the cold crept into their marrow, owls hooted and wolves answered from the surrounding darkness, they paced up and down by the flour bags trying to keep warm, pretending to ignore each other, yet keenly alert. When Antonio stepped aside to relieve himself he turned in time to see Juan remove a hand from a bag and place it in the cartridge box at his belt.

"Put that back!" he yelled in a fury.

"Put what back?" Juan replied in a tone of injured innocence.

"The flour you stole!"

"Man, you're seeing things! There's no flour in my cartridge box. Here, look!" He flipped open the lid of the leather case and held both hands above his head invitingly.

Uncertainty made Antonio incautious. Thinking he might possibly have been mistaken, he approached and with his right hand reached into the box. Lopez seized it with his left and clamped the hand under his armpit while drawing his knife with his right, and in that instant of supreme clarity which comes before death Antonio perceived everything: flour would be found in his cartridge box, planted there by Lopez; Juan would be declared the hero who had caught red-handed the thief Fages and Rivera had branded as no better than a murderer. And in this wilderness far from home the body of Antonio Boneu would be buried with the scorn deserving a villain.

"My right arm was helpless. His was descending with my death. But we in Catalonia know the fist. Not for nothing do we live in one of the world's crowded corridors! My blow caught the side of his head knocking him down. With my foot I kicked his knife away. 'Now, wretch,' I said, 'now I shall give you your just deserts!' I'd drawn my knife. I was ready to kill.

" 'Search me! I'm innocent!' he wailed. 'For my wife and children's sake, spare me!' "

This Promised Land

Ortega came hurrying up, demanding to know what the trouble was. By then Antonio changed his mind.

"No trouble. Friend Juan slipped on the frosty ground. I'm helping him up." He'd dragged him to his feet.

"And I suppose this fell out of the frosty sky?" Ortega picked up the naked knife.

"Yes," Antonio replied impassively, looking at the blade and thinking how it would have felt between his ribs.

"I am innocent!" Juan protested. "Look in my cartridge case!"

They did. Not a grain of flour. "Had it all been a ruse to catch me off my guard and give me my quietus apparently legitimately?" Antonio wondered. "Or was it an hallucination, a chimera brought on by starvation and hate? I felt sure it was real. Yet once again, uncannily, it was nothing I could prove."

Later he unburdened himself to Ortega. His mentor replied in a thoughtful manner which at first shook Antonio's confidence. "You're positive you weren't mistaken? He claims it was self-defense on his part—that you were falsely accusing him of theft. Still," and then Antonio felt reassured, "I suggest you keep Viva," pointing to the blade whose bone handle protruded above Antonio's right legging, "handy and remember the Peruvian Stroke I taught you: under and up. It can catch by surprise and is far more effective than a direct thrust."

Next morning when Portola ordered the remaining flour distributed equally to all members of the expedition, officers, friars, muleteers, Indians—share and share alike—Antonio guessed what must have motivated his decision. "Each of us received eight small cupfuls, enough for five thin tortillas, sufficient for two days' food, perhaps three. And we were not yet halfway to San Diego!" At that same time Portola distributed his private hoard of hams and biscuit equally among officers and friars. He evidently realized the expedition was approaching a last extremity. One big storm could have trapped them fatally in the wilderness. But the weather held fair if cold and, living on berries, raw acorns, and stewed mule, they straggled over the pass at the head of San Carpoforo Creek, following the trail constructed so laboriously three months earlier, some of which had eroded from recent rains; and building a new one as needed, they descended to the sea— the blessed bountiful sea—where the generous people of the coast again welcomed them and gave them lifesaving food. It seemed a miracle had taken place. Another was about to.

While they were resting near the present site of Hearst Castle, their Indian hosts brought word that a comrade who'd preceded them was awaiting their arrival. "As our astonishment grew, they ran to fetch him. First a small black dog, waving his bushy tail like a banner, appeared from behind a nearby knoll. His color was extraordinary. Most Indian dogs were brownish gray like coyotes—indeed some kept pet coyotes—and we had never seen a black one before. The little fellow advanced toward us with an aplomb which was comical considering his size. Behind him came Pablo, great shiny Pablo, also with much aplomb, clothes somewhat tattered but looking extremely well-fed, downright sleek, gun over his shoulder, expression serenely innocent."

Preceded by the dog Pablo went straight to Portola, knelt and begged forgiveness for his absence, while the dog sat on its haunches a few feet away, never taking its thoughtful brown eyes off him.

"And why should I forgive you?" Portola demanded sternly.

"Excellency, I was searching for the Port of Monterey, eager to win the honor of being the first to find that long sought prize! Feeling hungry I rose early and took my gun—the morning I left camp so unexpectedly—and went out along the shore in hopes of finding a duck or goose in the marsh by the Point of Pines which all of us could enjoy for breakfast! Finding none, instinct told me to continue a little farther and try the marsh beyond the point, and when I found none there, instinct again suggested I'd not gone far enough. Listening to instinct as all men should, I continued and, sure enough, in the next inlet bagged a fine fat goose! 'Now, Instinct,' I said to myself, 'tell me what next, for it is time to be packing my mules and I should be getting back to camp!' 'Eat,' said Instinct. 'Eat so you will be strong and travel that much faster and work that much better all day long!' "

By now smiles were beginning to appear on several faces though not on Portola's, while Pablo continued contritely but with persuasive sincerity: "Building a fire I ate. While I was doing so three savages, attracted by my shot and the smoke of my fire, emerged timidly from the undergrowth. When by signs I made clear I would not hurt them but wished to be their friend—in accordance with Your Excellency's instructions that all pagans were to be treated with kindness—they approached and offered me some mollusks they'd just gathered.

"Remembering we'd not seen a single heathen since arriving

in that region where we thought Monterey Bay to lie, I made a special effort to be friendly in hopes of eliciting information and, sure enough, they said they knew of a well-protected harbor exactly as I described, and would lead me to it! Overjoyed at the prospect of discovering what we'd all sought so long, I was at the same time torn by my sense of duty which was urging me to return to camp. Finally I decided in favor of discovery, knowing how much it would please Your Grace, and informed my new friends I would accompany them.

"By wilderness paths they led me to their village where I was fed and honored, then to another where I was treated likewise, and then another, always assuring me the harbor I sought lay just ahead—I always torn between my desire to return and do my duty and my desire to discover the long sought prize!"

Even Portola could hardly keep a straight face by this time and the little black dog, who had sat attentively upon its haunches, opened its mouth and yawned.

"Thus tormented I proceeded," Pablo continued gravely, "through the wildest country imaginable, always honored, always an emissary of good will from Christian to heathen as our holy Fathers Crespi and Gomez have taught us to be, until I arrived at this place, where they tell me the harbor is not far away! . . . I beg Your Excellency to understand and forgive me!"

For a long moment Portola remained silent. Then he said solemnly: "God who is merciful teaches us mercy. If your instinct allows it, you may resume your duties!"

Man and dog rose to their feet simultaneously, the dog wagging its tail joyfully, Pablo exclaiming: "May the Lord reward Your Excellency's generosity! And now," he cried, beaming in triumph, "see who I brought with me!"

In answer to his shout the two muleteers and one of the two Christian Indians who deserted the camp at Carmel Bay appeared. Guided by those who guided him, they'd arrived here safely. The second Indian had sickened and died en route, though his wild counterparts did their utmost to save him.

This time Portola replied somewhat testily: "Under normal circumstances death would be the reward for your misconduct. But today, since God has brought us all safely through the terrible tribulations of the wilderness and united us once more, I shall forgive you in His name!"

"It was the blessed dog that turned the trick," Pablo explained later when Antonio asked what had befallen. "When the Indians saw that mutt attach itself to me, they decided I too was a reincarnated deity of some sort!" The dog's muzzle was prematurely gray, which gave him the appearance of a little old man, and the Indians, perhaps partly because of his remarkable color, believed him inhabited by the spirit of one of their deceased wizards and for this reason much revered him. At the first village he reached the dog had attached itself to Pablo as if by immediate recognition and never left him thereafter. As to its color, he thought an ancestor of that unique shade, perhaps a bulldog, might have been shipwrecked upon the coast. Though usually peaceful, whenever attacked El Tigre turned with fury on his tormentors and soon sent them scampering, much to Pablo's delight.

"Compadre," he concluded, "I did not inform you I was leaving, that night at Monterey, because departure without leave is a very personal matter for which a man may lose his life, and knowing your youth and rank and closeness to the Governor, I did not want to tax our friendship so heavily. But while wandering in the wilderness I often thought of you and hoped we should meet again and share a campfire!"

"But how did you keep away from their women?" Antonio inquired.

Pablo replied a little shamefacedly: "Compadre, I didn't. Part of the duties of a deity, you know! But don't tell the Governor! I'm on shaky enough ground as it is!"

"Don't worry!" Antonio reassured him with a delighted chuckle. "How was it?"

"Best thing we've discovered yet. They treat it as naturally as eating. Honestly, I had to ration myself to keep from running out of supplies!"

"Quite passionate were they?"

"You'll see for yourself!"

"Is the jewel made the same?"

"Just like we're used to, only they remove all the hair from around it."

"And the food?"

"Delicious. Did you ever hear of an Indian starving to death? No, it takes a Christian to manage that! Once I came to a village by the shore where a dead whale had washed up on the beach and the people were cutting the meat into strips, wrapping it in wild grape leaves, and roasting it over hot coals! And putting other strips in the sun to dry! I hated the greasy stuff but it filled me up, believe me!"

This Promised Land

They soon saw what Pablo's Indian friends meant by "a well-protected harbor." It was in fact the estuary at Morro Bay which they reached the following day. At the village of Pismu, Chief Buchon, he of the large goiter, welcomed the expedition with generous hospitality, and when he perceived their plight, he returned again to camp with even more food. Antonio couldn't help wondering if an expedition of invading Indians marching up and down the coast of Spain would have been received with similar hospitality.

At the Valley of the Rising Sun he of course wanted to turn aside and visit the village and make good their promise to return by paying full respects to Koyo and Lospe, but Portola and everyone else was in a hurry to get back to San Diego, so they kept on without even hesitating, "which seemed to me a very great mistake. We had given our word. We should have kept it, I thought, knowing that in such apparent trifles may rest the entire future of human relationships.

"Following generally the route taken six months earlier, well received by Indians whenever we met them, by midday of January 24, 1770 we were skirting the shore of the false bay and approaching the true Harbor of San Diego. You can imagine our feelings. Would our comrades be dead of scurvy or from Indian attack? Would a supply ship be waiting with the food and clothing we so sorely needed? How should we break the news of our ignominious failure and retreat? When at last we made out the stockade of poles and brushwood buildings on the hilltop, its standard flying, our joy was boundless. We began firing our guns. Answering fire came from the little fortress while its inmates poured forth to greet us, and six months and ten days after leaving we were back among our comrades, such as remained alive."

Chapter Sixteen

Whatever the power of Chumash sorcerers, and apparently it was considerable, it seems to have been effective principally on ground they knew well, their own physical-psychic territory.

Aware of this, Asuskwa went swiftly eastward up the river's winding gorge, after his meeting with Lospe in the willows. He carried a crushed jerusalem cricket in his packet to ward off the influence of Owotoponus. Reaching the Cave of the Condors just at dusk, he made his way through the shadows to the back wall where the ancient painting of Sacred Condor was dimly outlined in the crumbling stone. The atmosphere of silence and loneliness was both awesome and comforting, empty, yet alive with the forces of the spirit world which bring both good and evil to men.

After kneeling and breathing a prayer of permission, Asuskwa seated himself crosslegged in the gray dust at the foot of the venerable icon, fixing his eyes upon its crude outlines which bespoke its ages-old origin. Taking his magic condor stone from its down-lined pouch which he carried in his waistnet, he began to rub it reverently, while meditating on the problem confronting him in which he so keenly needed guidance. The problem—how best to destroy Owotoponus and deliver his mother, sister, relatives, and people from tyranny—seemed almost insurmountable. It would do no good to appeal to chiefs of neighboring villages, for they were all in league with their head shamans and his request would immediately be known throughout the entire A-antap organization and quickly reach Owotoponus. Similarly to complain to sorcerers in other villages would be suicidal. They would simply inform Owotoponus and measures would be taken against him, perhaps with their help. And as for rousing his fellow villagers to action as sometimes happened when a shaman exceeded his power, Owotoponus' grip was so absolute that that solution seemed out of the question. As he meditated he began to repeat slowly over and over the song Sacred Condor had given him in his original dream vision in hopes it would induce another vision which might guide him through his present difficulty:

> Out of the sun I come,
> With magic wings I sing,
> Flying where no one knows!

As the light faded from the cave Asuskwa did not feel afraid. The constant inner temperature of the earth was like a warm blanket surrounding him and the hallowed atmosphere also seemed comforting. Little by little as the hours passed and he meditated and prayed and repeated his song over and over, he felt the spirit of Sacred Condor draw closer. He could not have said how long it was when he began to rise out of his body and found himself atop a high hill watching the setting sun and out of the orb of the sun a black dot came speeding toward him. It rapidly developed into a giant condor, and in a moment more he was hearing again the whistle of mighty wings. The bald red head looked down gravely upon him as it passed, and again the sound of the wings transformed itself into the words he wished to hear:

> Flying beyond the mountains
> I reach the place where land meets water.
> There in the reeds I hear music,
> And find a new home!

At that instant he saw clearly a secluded grassy place by an eddy of clear water at the edge of a marsh where reeds grew almost as thickly roundabout as the thatched walls of a house and the atmosphere was like that of a home. Relief and gratitude flooded through Asuskwa for he knew now the first step he must take toward solving his problem. But as he lifted his head to thank the flying bird he saw only the outline of the painted one dimly lit by the dawn entering at the Eastern Window—bored ages ago to permit the sun at solstice time to reach the painting on the wall. Asuskwa sat motionless with awe and wonder, observing carefully.

When a beam from the rising sun entered the window and began to move slowly toward the ancient condor painting, he knew it would not quite reach it for this was not the time of the winter solstice, but he held himself perfectly still until the beam fell upon him, gentle and warm, seeming to penetrate him with life and hope. Rising, then, he scattered seeds and bead money before the painting and departed, feeling buoyant with strength.

He took the ancestral trail across the mountains toward the Great Valley, traveling mostly at night, the propitious time when his vision had come to him. He descended toward the Barren Lands and the Earthquake Mountains and at last entered the land of the Tulamni. Here though in danger from their scattered villages, he would be safe from the supernatural power of a greater enemy.

Proceeding with caution in twilight and dark, he made his way into that vast labyrinth of reeds and marshes that then surrounded what would later be called Buena Vista Lake, the vast watery sink into which ran the Kern and other rivers, and where there was ample food such as roots, bulbs, cattails, fish. He dared not light a fire. Kahip's people, if they found him, would gladly tear him limb from limb while he was still screaming. But he felt safe from a more certain danger.

Before long as if unerringly directed he came to the place he had seen in his dream. It was a secluded glade near an eddy of clear water surrounded so densely by reeds it seemed like a house, and through them he could hear the music of the wind reminding him of the singing wings which had spoken to him. Here he made his lonely camp.

Day by day, living and meditating, he waited for Sacred Condor to show him what to do next. Somehow he would have to acquire a power greater than Owotoponus' with which he could destroy him not only physically but spiritually, because to kill only his body would not be enough—his spirit would simply assume another form and continue its malevolent influence.

Chapter Seventeen

What Antonio and his companions found at San Diego was grimly this.

The *San Carlos* still lay at anchor in the harbor. No other ship had appeared. Eight more Catalans and as many sailors were dead of scurvy. A young Mexican servant of Serra's had been killed by Indians shortly after their departure and Father Parron wounded. Food supplies were low. Seeds of corn and wheat planted under Fages' supervision before they departed—the first inserted by Europeans in California soil—had sprung up but birds and squirrels had eaten everything and the little colony was forced to depend for sustenance on the generosity of the neighboring Indians, now docile again. Three brushwood huts including a mission church had been constructed within the stockade. But all of this became for the moment incidental to the news they were bringing. Had they found Monterey? Had they succeeded?

"All listened eagerly," Antonio recounted, "as we described a wonderful new land, fertile and mellow beyond belief, peopled by many kindly Indians including the Red-Headed Queen and her people. We told of the perilous crossings of the Santa Lucias, the open roadstead where the protected Harbor of Monterey ought to have been, the many hardships undergone, the Great Estuary attached to the Harbor of San Francisco, the almost miraculous escape from death by starvation during the return journey." Yet at the end of their narrative came the stern reminder of its result: failure.

"Why, you've come from Rome without having seen the Pope!" Father President Serra exclaimed reprovingly. "You must have passed Monterey Bay without realizing it! A harbor so well known and recorded over all these years could not simply disappear!"

Bridling, Portola and Crespi, who developed a strong respect and affection for each other during the journey, retorted: "The terrain may have been changed by earthquakes or the harbor silted up with time!"

Thus a bitter debate began. Serra and Captain Vila of the *San Carlos* felt sure the expedition had rediscovered Monterey without realizing it. "It must be the large bight immediately north of the Point of Pines—perhaps silted up somewhat, perhaps altered by earthquakes, but still there!"—and if approached jointly by sea and land, its true nature would appear. Costanso came to the support of Crespi and Portola with his records and maps. Cabrera Bueno's Chapter Four, "Coastal Sailing Directions from Cape Mendocino to Acapulco," was reopened and studied as was Venegas' *Natural and Civil History*. Emotion ran high. "Are you prepared to face Viceroy and Inspector General and tell them you've been to the Harbor of San Francisco but could not find Monterey?" Serra mercilessly demanded at one point. Honor, reputation were at stake, as were precious time and hopes, also the huge sum of upwards of 300,000 pesos already expended on the expedition, not to mention the displeasure of the King.

Loth to admit defeat but not too proud to admit a possible mistake, Portola at last agreed to march north again to the Point of Pines "though it will be like reentering Hell, and only the most powerful inducements could persuade me to undertake it! Without a supply ship it will be quite impossible!"

While the *San Carlos* or another vessel approached by sea, the land expedition would re-explore the coast and perhaps find the evanescent harbor. But for the moment any such action was out of the question. Food supplies were too low. The expedition's return brought sixty-three more mouths to feed. Unless a supply ship appeared soon, drastic steps in quite another direction must be taken.

Immediately after arrival Antonio sought out his friend Doctor Prat to tell him he was living proof of Prat's theory that fresh vegetable food would alleviate the loanda and to consult him about some troublesome red pimples which had broken out on his forehead. These secondary lesions of syphilis caused good-natured ribbing from his comrades. "Badges of manhood, eh boy? You've got the medals, I see!" But Antonio could not believe his adorable gypsy girl of Cadiz had given him the dreaded Las Bubas and wanted Prat's opinion. True, he'd noticed chancres during his voyage to Vera Cruz. But they had disappeared leading him to think himself cured.

Prat, he knew, was an expert on the fearful disease which first evidenced itself in Prat's native Barcelona at the time of Columbus' arrival there with his sailors to report to the King and Queen after his great voyage. From there it spread like wildfire across all Europe. Prat was familiar with the famous works on the subject including Ruy de Isla's *The Serpentine Disease* (Isla actually saw the sick men on the deck of the *Nina* when she anchored at Palos and observed their sexual orgies as they proceeded across Spain), Francisco Lopez de Villalobos' *On the Contagious and Deadly Pustules,* also by a brilliantly qualified eyewitness, and the famous medical treatise in poetic form by Hieronymus Fracastorius written in 1530 titled *The Sinister Shepherd* in which the hero-victim Syphilus suffers from a strange new malady sent by the gods to punish men for their presumptions.

According to Fracastorius the disease was endemic to the island of Hispaniola, or Haiti, and Columbus' men contracted it when they sailed up a river there and wantonly shot and killed a flock of beautiful azure birds, all but one who perched on a tall tree and prophesied the terrible pestilence which would fall upon mankind as consequence of their foul deed. It was Fracastorius, in his extraordinary mixture of clinical analysis and romantic poetry, who gave the disease its lasting name.

Antonio found Prat seated at the door of his hut gazing vacantly out to sea, apparently wholly disinterested in the expedition's return. Prat's usually intelligent face was lifeless, his once vigorous body wasted. As if speaking to a stranger, he asked Antonio: "Do you hear those voices?" No one yet knew that malnutrition could affect mind as well as body but Antonio got a glimmer of the truth, plus full perception of a tragedy. While ministering unsparingly to sick and dying, the good doctor had so weakened himself that the scurvy he combatted had fastened upon him irrevocably. There had been something exceptional in Prat. He'd been an explorer of a special kind. Now he was lost.

Crushed by this realization, Antonio pulled the red bandana which covered his hair lower over his forehead to hide the shameful pustules, wondering to whom he could turn for advice. Costanso suggested he try mercury ointment, the long established treatment, and finding Prat in a lucid moment obtained some from him.

* * *

Two weeks after their arrival Portola dispatched Rivera to Lower California with twenty Leather Jackets and eighty mules to bring back supplies and cattle. This decreased pressure on scanty food reserves and rid the governor of his incubus but not Antonio of his. Not only did Lopez remain but Rivera's last act before leaving was to promote him corporal. "Thus he planted his man among Portola's," Antonio noted, "as Portola, some alleged, had planted me among Rivera's, and even gave Juan authority over me should occasion arise. Ortega assured me it would not. I wasn't so sure. But for the moment there were other things to think about. Daily we scanned the sea for a ship while our food supplies continued to dwindle."

Early in March when no vessel appeared, Portola finally warned Serra: "I don't want a repetition of what happened in the Wilderness of Santa Lucia. My men were at each other's throats for lack of food. I've always believed this expedition to be in God's hands and therefore if no ship appears by March 19, feast day of Saint Joseph the patron of all our efforts here, I shall accept it as the judgment of God and march south with my people!" It would be final defeat: abandonment of New California, end of all their efforts, all high hopes.

For Serra, however, the solution was simply a matter of faith and he proposed a novena, nine consecutive days of prayer, to end on March 19. "If we have faith enough God will send us a ship!" he insisted and Portola could do no less than agree.

"For nine days we prayed as never before," Antonio recalled, "Serra exhorting us. He would stand up in front of us, bare his frail chest and beat upon its flesh with an iron scourge studded with nails until the blood ran, while his enormous voice—truly astonishing in one so small—rang out over hillside and bay: 'Christ's blood was shed for us sinners! If this wonderful land,' he gestured roundabout, 'is to become our Promised Land as God gave the land beyond Jordan to the Children of Israel, we must repent! We must become worthy! Each of us must be transformed into an ambassador of Christ!' I'd never thought of myself as an ambassador of Christ. But moved by his fervor I actually began to. I actually began to think God would send us a ship if we believed as intensely as he did! Costanso scoffed at me. 'Why should God take special notice of us? It's one more aspect of that foolish notion that we Spaniards are the divinely chosen champions of the Faith, which has got us into so many wars and other difficulties—such as this one! Claptrap!'"

March 19 dawned fair and clear. From their hilltop they could look far out to sea. All morning their eyes searched the horizon in vain. Hour by hour the deadline approached. Would God be with them? At three o'clock a sail miraculously appeared. "With one voice that was like an enormous joyful sigh, we all cried out together! Then we fired guns. Then we knelt and gave thanks!"

It was the long awaited *San Antonio* bound for Monterey with relief supplies. Riding the incoming tide, she slowly nosed into the harbor. Like the *San Carlos* she was a brig crudely but soundly built on the west coast of New Spain with a medium high poop, and a mizzenmast added behind the mainmast to increase her sailing qualities. And her captain was a Majorcan Catalan, Juan Perez.

"Thus when men tell me there is no God," Antonio concluded, "I tell them the story of the nineteenth of March at San Diego, and when they say it was Spaniards who conquered California I correct them. It was we Catalans, and a black muleteer!"

Chapter Eighteen

Each spring on the anniversary of her father's death, Lospe with Koyo would carry fresh plumes to the stone on the bank of the stream that marked the site of his funeral pyre, but this year she decided to go alone and not mention the matter lest it add to Koyo's sorrow. Owotoponus was treating her more cruelly than ever. When she became pregnant and miscarried, he flew into a rage and accused her of taking the extract of mugwort which causes abortions. In vain she pleaded her history of miscarriages. After Lospe was born she'd had three; before, two. "You don't want my child!" Owotoponus berated her savagely in front of all the family. "Deny that you don't want my child!" And then he beat her till she bled from the nose, while nobody dared intervene.

The red stone marker on the bank of the stream by the tar seep where they'd camped as a happy family so long ago was weathering, Lospe saw. Sun and time had dulled its bright paint. Winter floods had deposited sand around its base. But she smelled again the smoke of bay boughs made acrid by her lock of hair. As she knelt to pay homage, with sudden inspiration she did an unheard of thing: she prayed for her father's spirit to speak to her from the Land of the Dead and guide her, a thing most of her people would never dare to do, believing it brought the most terrible misfortune. A moment later she heard a footstep. Her mother too was carrying fresh plumes. Leaping up, Lospe took her in her arms and held her tight while they both wept.

"What are you doing here?" Koyo whispered fearfully, freeing herself after a moment and Lospe could feel her trembling. "It is not wise for you to be off alone like this!"

In this new setting she seemed to be seeing her mother in a true light, and rage and sorrow overcame Lospe at what she beheld. From a once serene and noble creature Koyo had been reduced to this poor frightened shadow of herself. Face and neck were black and blue from Owotoponus' most recent beating. Her eyes showed no hope. Fierce indignation rose in Lospe. "I am praying," she replied, "that your son will return and rid us of this monster who has fastened himself upon us and treats you so vilely. Can my brother have abandoned us completely?" And now resentment flooded her at thought of the months Asuskwa had been gone. "How can I forgive him for running away like a coward? How can I again feel the love for him I once did? There was a time when I thought him seeking strength in solitude. But it is evident he cares nothing for us who love him!"

"Hush, my child! Don't say such things! All may yet be well!" But Koyo's voice carried no conviction and her eyes did not meet her daughter's as she bent and placed feathers on the grave beside those Lospe had placed there and sprinkled soft down over all. As she rose Lospe moved to her with warm impulse and took her in her arms again and their tears fell together upon her father's grave.

"It is you we must think of now," Koyo said firmly after a moment, and Lospe heard her old serene self returning. "There is no time to lose. Go to the A-alowow. Go to the little father at the mission. Throw yourself on the mercy of the good little man in the gray cloak. Tell him everything, *everything!*" She said this last with sudden emotion that was like a dam bursting. It astonished Lospe.

"Tell him what?"

"Tell him I mistakenly betrayed my people, and you, into Owotoponus' hands, thinking I had no other course. Explain that normally our present state of affairs would cause uprising and civil war but under the circumstances I do not want that to happen and so am helpless. Tell him my present plight. Tell him my present husband confided to me: 'When their holy man is dead, the other white men will go away!' "

"Owotoponus said that?"

"Yes, he means to kill him. He sees his own power failing. He has become desperate."

"But then the soldiers would kill us!" Lospe remonstrated.

"That is what I told him. 'They will never know!' he replied. 'You will invite him here, saying you wish him to see our village, where he has never been. You will say you wish to hear about their deity who was nailed to the cross. By all report, he is without guile. He will come.' 'And then?' 'Then he will eat the camas cake you have prepared for him. After that he will sicken and die gradually as the poison slowly pervades his body, so gradually everyone will think it quite natural. And with him gone their power will die too and the other A-alowow will leave our valley, and things be again as they were. And nobody but you, my faithful spouse,' he continued, 'and I will know the reason. A secret like that will bind us more closely, will it not? Just as the birth of our son will?' 'Oh, no!' I cried out involuntarily. Then he beat me.''

Holding her close, Lospe burst out: "My poor dear Mother! But what would become of you should I leave?"

"It is you we must think of first. I have ways and means. But you must go at once. Throw yourself on the mercy of the little lame father. Tell him what I've told you. As long as you are under his protection you will be safe. Do not come back."

They embraced a final time. Lospe hid in the willows till dusk. As the bats began to fly she slipped down the valley toward the mission. Guiding her, bright in the western sky, was the Evening Star which old Quati had prophesied at the moment of her naming would lead her to good fortune, and to the fair-haired hero of her vision.

When in the previous year Father Rubio and the soldiers came and erected the cross and began building a stockade and mission on the promontory where Antonio and Pablo first met them, it caused much perturbation among the People of the Place Called Olomosoug. "We feared Sutupaps yet wanted his power," Lospe remembered. "All agreed he was omnipotent. That shot Black Pablo fired changed everything. Nothing was ever the same again. But should we welcome these newcomers as permanent settlers? My loved one was not with them, nor was Pablo. Things were changing drastically by this time and other villagers who lived near the coastal trail told us of baskets and bowls stolen and women violated. Were the white men indeed coming to steal our land as my brother often warned before he fled from the tyranny of Owotoponus? Or were they bringing the blessings foretold in legend?"

Owotoponus ordered He-ap: "Go down again to the promontory, since it was you who discovered them the day they arrived. But this time don't run away. Make yourself known. Report to me what they do. Above all observe their little lame priest. From what you say I have no doubt he is the intermediary between them and the source of their power." Absolute in his own power now, Owotoponus no longer made pretense of ruling through Koyo or the Council of Twenty. "Try to discover the secret of their firesticks," he continued, "and remember it isn't the sticks themselves but the spirit which moves them that matters most. That is where their power lies. That is why their little lame sorcerer is so important. Do you understand? Take them food. They are hungry. They will welcome you."

So He-ap went down the valley on that memorable day carrying a basket of chia meal, berries and dried cherries and at sundown returned triumphant saying he'd been welcomed and made much of by the lame holy man himself.

"How truly he spoke we did not realize," Lospe recalled, "for he was a master dissembler. Nevertheless it was from He-ap we first heard the story of Jesus upon the Cross, of the miraculous resurrection which we easily understood because it was in accordance with so many of our beliefs, also of the redemption of all people whether male or female, rich or poor—and that last was most difficult to understand because we'd heard nothing like it before, women and poor people being as a rule of little consequence among us."

"Poppycock though it may be," Owotoponus scoffed, "it may lie at the heart of their doctrine. Return. Learn more. Take others with you so that suspicion may not be roused!"

Lospe was secretly intrigued by what He-ap said. In her loneliness and near despair, feeling abandoned by her brother and loved one, heartstricken over what was happening to her mother and her people under Owotoponus' tyranny, the news that she might be loved and cared for by a compassionate deity who had taken human form was like a bright shaft of light in a dark room.

"The two old widows who often ate with us, bringing pieces of firewood in repayment, had listened as thoughtfully as I to what He-ap said. They too secretly hungered for loving understanding. They'd always been poor, their husbands sometimes were cruel, uncaring. But more importantly they were depressed by loneliness and feelings of inconsequence. They had no hunter to bring them food, no man to care. They longed to be treated as if they mattered. Encouraging them too was our long held conviction that white men would come and be our benefactors. Thus it was the lowly, the needy, the downhearted, the credulous, the oppressed who went to the mission first.

"I wanted to go in those early days but dared not leave Mother, knowing what physical and mental torture she'd suffered from our ruler after Asuskwa left us. But others went freely, taking food, finding comfort, bringing back information. Houses were being erected behind a barricade of poles, they reported. He-ap had had water poured on his head ceremonially by Father Rubio which gave him the right to go to a marvelous place called Heaven. Soldiers were using firesticks to kill antelope and elk at distances of two bowshots but nobody could tell just how they did it. And for a while all this seemed good to Owotoponus. But gradually as some people began to stay and not return, using it as a means of escaping his tyranny, he realized what was happening and turned vindictively on Mother. 'You are encouraging them to flee as you encouraged your son!' he accused her.

" 'That's not true!' she protested vehemently, driven to speak out at last. 'They are going of their own accord because they hate you! Why do you not use your great power for good rather than evil? Then people would love and respect you and not avoid you!' She was growing desperate under his persecutions. But she dared not protest to our province chief or regional council. Through the all-pervasive A-antap organization, almost before she ceased speaking, word of her protest would have been on its way to Owotoponus. And making protest even more difficult, another bad thing was happening. The old political network of authority and tradition was disintegrating under the impact of the Spaniards' arrival with their new ways and power. Every village in contact with them was in some degree like ours, every leader to some degree like Mother. Chiefs no longer cooperated as in former times.

"Mother wilted visibly under the pressures of these conditions which made a mockery of those hopes she'd held before her marriage to Owotoponus and proved me right in my warning and Asuskwa in his. And I, I remained ostracized because I'd broken age-old custom and not gone with Alul when he sang to me after the battle on the Plain of the Carrizo Grass. 'She thinks she can flout our rules!' people said of me, jealous even while suffering under Owotoponus' heavy hand. 'Now she's having her come-uppance. And her mother too! The daughter of a chief should set an example,' they said. 'Aren't her own people good enough for her?' "

Once, longing for Antonio, Lospe hung a whistling stone in a tree, hoping it would enable her to hear her voice and bring him back to her. Girls regularly used such stones to make boys fall in love with them and vice versa. Only the loved one could hear what the stone said when the wind blew through it musically. But Antonio did not hear, did not come back to her, and Lospe remained lonely as before, until that day when she encountered her mother at her father's grave, and was encouraged by Koyo to run away and commit herself to Rubio's mercy.

Chapter Nineteen

Three weeks after the miraculous arrival of the supply ship, Antonio was marching northward from San Diego, with Portola, Fages, twelve Catalans, seven Leather Jackets, three muleteers including Pablo and his extraordinary dog, Father Crespi, and five Christian Indians, thirty-one in all.

It was very much a Catalan show: no Rivera, no Ortega, no Lopez. Antonio acted as leading scout, Catalan Sergeant Puig was ranking non-commissioned officer. Leather Jackets played minor roles as herdsmen and rear guards under genial, dependable Mariano Carrillo.

Serra and Costanso had sailed for the Point of Pines a few days earlier on the *San Antonio* with Captain Perez and the additional friars he'd brought from San Blas including Rubio, Serra being too weak from scurvy and his ulcerated leg to travel overland as he wanted to and Costanso wishing to observe and map the coast from shipboard.

As the land expedition passed the Valley of Santa Lucia, as Crespi still insisted on calling it, in a misty April rain, the promontory where the mission would later stand was invisible. "We shall have a church there some day!" Crespi predicted. But no Indians appeared. "And though I made every effort to extract a promise from Don Gaspar," Antonio complained later, "that this time he would turn aside and stop, he said he was under too great pressure to waste a step, until the Harbor of Monterey should be found. So on we went and reached the roadstead at the Point of Pines on May 24 after a relatively easy trip of thirty-eight days.

Finding no ship, Portola and Antonio with Crespi walked out to the cross they'd erected on the point before leaving in December. "To our great surprise we found it surrounded by arrows thrust point foremost into the ground as a sign of peace and many small fish, and seeds and shell beads strewn around as if in propitiation. It seemed a good omen." But as they slowly retraced their steps along the rocky shore, something even better happened. "As we looked out upon the bay, while many seals and sea wolves played in the deep water below us, the truth suddenly struck us all at once that this *was* the Harbor of Monterey! Seen from this angle, it was indeed well protected from all except northwest winds, and the deep water anchorage ran right in along the rocky bluff close to shore!" Five days later the *San Antonio* anchored within two gunshots of the beach.

Brush arbor and altar were hastily constructed under a huge live oak that grew near the shore, the same under which Admiral Vizcaino conducted services during his voyage of discovery one hundred sixty-eight years earlier. Serra vested himself in alb and stole, assisted by little lame Father Rubio, then fresh from the ship, "Serra's timid shadow!" as Fages jokingly termed him, and Antonio was inclined to agree, because he seemed at first so ineffectual.

The king's bells hanging from a limb of the oak were rung, and when all were kneeling before the altar, Serra intoned the Veni Creator Spiritus, and blessed the traditional salt and water. "Whereupon we all rose and went to the large Holy Cross prepared beforehand which lay nearby and all together, each touching it with his hand, we raised this symbol of Christianity over the land," Antonio wrote. "When it was in place, Serra blessed it, chanted a benediction, and with the holy water sprinkled and blessed the earth surrounding, while we, even skeptical Costanso joining in, shouted: 'Long live the Faith!' After the standard of the King of Heaven had been raised, and Mission San Carlos de Monterey thus established, the white and gold banner of our Catholic Monarch was raised beside it accompanied by shouts of: 'Long live the King!' and more ringing of bells, firing of muskets, and a cannonade from the ship. I thought of all those who had labored and suffered for this memorable moment, and of all who would come after and be influenced by it. Tears rose to my eyes. Glory seemed in the air, destiny fulfilled."

Then Portola resplendent in his uniform of a Captain of Dragoons in the Army of America, with dark-blue trousers, coat with scarlet facings and high collar and double row of white buttons, black tricorne and drawn sword, took possession of the land in the King's name. As the royal standard was waved over him by Domingo Malaret, who followed close behind, Portola walked around upon this new addition to the realm, picking up handfuls of earth and grass, removing stones, raising his sword to the accompaniment of cheers, more clanging of bells, and gunshots. It was a moment of sweet triumph for a brave man who through patience and endurance had overcome every obstacle and won through. And the entire company shared in this feeling.

Next day Costanso chose as site for the presidio a plot of level ground at the crest of a knoll a short distance from the beach, not far from the oak where services were conducted. With Portola's approval the young engineer drew up plans for stockade and bastions, warehouses, barracks, and a church while soldiers and sailors under Fages' supervision built the first two buildings. They cut trees on the Point of Pines, transported poles laboriously by muleback, set them upright in the earth, working from dawn till dark under the eye of the little martinet until they completed both structures within twelve days.

Antonio's first enthusiasm waned with this demanding labor and he felt misgivings at thought of serving under Fages should he remain in New California "though I knew Don Pedro's bark worse than his bite. If hot tempered, he was kindhearted, quick to take offense, quick to forgive. But since he was young and relatively inexperienced, I wondered about his judgment." Portola and Costanso would soon sail away and Fages would become commander-in-chief and de facto governor. "I would be at the mercy of this youthful taskmaster of good intentions but harsh practices unless Portola took me with him as he had brought me. My future remained uncertain. I didn't inquire about it, feeling uneasy about tempting fate. I did not even ask myself the questions I knew should be asked if I were to stay or go willingly. I just let matters take their course. Next evening Portola summoned me to his tent. Parting the curtain I saw him sitting at his writing desk making an entry in his journal. Laying down his pen, he offered me a Havana but I did not smoke them as I do not now, finding it makes me cough and sneeze.

" 'I'm a great admirer of your mother's,' Don Gaspar began intimately, when at his invitation I'd made myself comfortable on one of his camp stools. 'The way Linotte held the family together after your father's death was nothing short of remarkable. With so many youngsters to look after and so little money to do it with, her hands were full, believe me, and that was one reason I took you under my wing, young man, because hers were spread so wide. You have a great deal to be thankful to your mother for!'

"'That I know well,' I replied, as the image of my tirelessly energetic, ambitious little mother joined us there beside Monterey Bay. She'd wanted the best for me, pulled every string including that of her prominent Portola relatives to advance my fortune. If she had one fault, she used to say, it was in loving my idle dreamy handsome father too well.

"'We've been through a great deal together,' Portola continued, lighting his cigar from the candle that burned on the table, regarding me with those steady eyes. 'Cadiz, Vera Cruz, Sonora, San Blas, Loreto, San Diego, and now Monterey. You have acquitted yourself well.'

"'I'm grateful to hear you say that, Don Gaspar!'

"'I purposely arranged for you to be attached to colonial troops rather than to my person because I wanted you to have the broadest possible experience, in order that you might see what it is to be a frontier soldier should you choose to remain here.'

"That startled me. 'I am indebted even further for your thoughtfulness!'

"'At the same time,' he went on, 'I retained you unofficially near me so that you might become familiar with the responsibilities of command and staff should you decide to make the Army your career. Now both of us have come to a turning point.' He looked fully at me and spoke with absolute candor. 'You may return to Mexico and serve with me there, I have no doubt, in comparative safety, comfort, honor. Here,' his eyes twinkled, 'you may remain at your own risk with only your honor!'

"Startled as I'd been from the moment he'd mentioned a choice, I found that my answer was not in doubt.

"'Excellency and benefactor,' I replied promptly, 'with deepest gratitude for all you've done, especially for your courtesy in giving me this choice, and much as I shall miss the inspiration and pleasure of your company—I believe I shall remain here.' As soon as I'd said it I knew it was right.

"He blew smoke and surveyed me good humoredly. 'I'm not surprised. If I were your age I'd do the same. May I ask your reason?'

"'I'm afraid it may sound foolish.'

"'Not at all.'

"A dozen answers crossed my mind. With intuition, perhaps derived from his candor, I chose the true one. 'This land has spoken to me.'

" 'And what does the land say?'

" 'It says it has a place for me. I'm afraid that sounds foolish.'

" 'No, not at all!' He seemed moved. 'Once the mountains and valleys of northern Italy spoke to me in that way.' His eyes shone with a faraway look. 'And when I was wounded in my left hip, here,' he touched the spot just below his belt, 'at the Battle of Madonna del Olmo near Turin and while recovering met a certain beautiful girl,' he winked benevolently, 'I thought I should remain there the rest of my life.' And then in a tone of tenderness, so that I felt the years of his youth and the great days he had seen come flooding back into him: 'This too is a beautiful land. This also is like a bride waiting.' I saw moisture in his eyes. He shrugged it away. 'But I am nearly fifty-four. My career is nearing its end. I'm thinking of returning to our Segre Valley, there to the town square at Balaguer where I first saw you as a child in your father's house. I wish my bones to lie in our native soil. But for you . . . ' He hesitated, searching for words. 'You are of the New World, I of the Old, that's the difference. You'll have your being here. We cannot change what's been or is to be. All is in God's hands.' He mused, then characteristically stroking his beard with those stubby artisan's fingers, went on in practical fashion: 'I shall miss you. I've seen you change from green youth to seasoned veteran able to fend for yourself. There is no better legacy I could leave you. Should you find root here, I believe you will prosper. Good luck, my boy. Had I a son, I should have wished him to be like you.' He rose and we embraced. 'Write your mother a letter. I shall see that she gets it.'

"Eyes moist, I walked out into the summer evening. The wind was blowing the fog in from the sea as it had on so many momentous evenings of my California life, drawing a veil over the day as over my past experience, a shroud from which, as in resurrection, tomorrow rises more beautiful than today. 'Yes,' I thought, 'this is the land of hope and promise. This is my land. Here I shall make my home!'

"Of Portolá, what can I add? How casually they treat his extraordinary achievement! He led us over fifteen hundred miles through unexplored territory without losing a man except Juan Flaco, the poor Indian who died after deserting, nor did he take the life of a single native or countenance the violation of a single woman, or the wrongful taking of so much as one basket. With final responsibility always his, Don Gaspar faced every adversity courageously, cheerfully. No eventuality, whether it be hostile

Apache, invading Russian or English, internal discord, death by disease or hunger, dismayed him. He was not brilliant but firm, enduring. In this way he triumphed greatly. Yet he sought no glory, merely to do his duty and go home."

Until the day before sailing Costanso was busy with quadrant and compass laying out the fortifications and mapping harbor and surrounding area. Antonio was already missing his company. In the formal discipline of garrison life and all the bustle of impending departure, it was not like the trail where there was time to talk.

While walking along the beach with such thoughts in the soft twilight of that last evening he found his friend, of all places, under the Vizcaino oak. Costanso was sitting on the ground, hands clasped around knees looking thoughtfully out to sea. "Yes, I too shall miss our conversations," he replied, as Antonio dropped down beside him, expressing regret at his leaving. "I'm afraid the great adventure is over for me. I'll go back to Mexico, resume the conventional life of engineer, plan hospitals, water works, remap old coasts, while you remain here among your 'noble savages!'"

"Would you prefer to stay?"

"In a way, yes. These are stirring times. Here we have been marching in the vanguard of them. Think—as I was a moment ago—of the undiscovered lands lying beyond that water." He pointed to the harbor where seals were playing in the dusky surf and the flying gulls shone white as the last light struck them. "Think what will happen when they are explored, developed. Think of the commerce. Think of the cities which must arise. Think of the ideas of Rousseau, Voltaire penetrating everywhere, even here to where we are establishing Spain's westernmost bastion. Are we not entering an Age of Reason in which men and women will throw off the chains which have bound them? England's American colonies are already demanding freedom. The downtrodden French masses are growing restive. Millions like you and me, my friend, are seeking a chance to start again, to put old mistakes, old tyrants, behind, create a better future. What better place to do so than a virgin land like this?"

Moved by his eloquence Antonio agreed, and, echoing Rousseau: "I can imagine an ideal state being created here, where people would reflect the truth that the land is the source of all personal wealth and social strength!"

"It may happen. Under our liberal-minded King Carlos we are beginning to enjoy prosperity and personal and intellectual freedom unknown before!"

"But I'm afraid freedom will be long in reaching here!" Antonio qualified his earlier vision. "The fathers will control everything for at least ten years, perhaps forever, until the Indians are Christianized and civilized and the land returned to them."

"There'll be lay communities too. Colonists will come. You will see. The friars cannot dominate forever. Our friend and countryman Don Pedro Fages will see to that, or I misjudge him. He is no fool. Nor is he afraid. He may prove a match for the crafty Serra and his Majorcan clique, insistent as they are that additional missions be established immediately though we have not the proper means to do so."

Costanso sounded radical at times but Antonio attributed it to his Catalan blood. In reality a most promising career along conventional lines awaited him thanks to his unusual brilliance. After attending the University he'd enlisted in the dragoons, then been selected for the elite Royal Military Academy of Mathematics at Barcelona where all young engineering officers were trained, then chosen for duty in New Spain. After volunteering for service on the Sonora frontier, he'd been especially selected by the Inspector General for the California Expedition. It was an extraordinary honor for one not yet twenty-nine. Costanso was typical of the talent coming to the fore under The Enlightenment: professional types quite different from the rough fortune-seekers who dominated an earlier era; and the men who finally reached Monterey with him and Antonio in this last great conquest were mostly Catalan Volunteers, yeomen stock, regular army men, not at all the ruthless adventurers from Extremadura and Castile who followed Cortes and Pizarro into Mexico and Peru.

"Now I'm about to leave, I see it all clearly," Costanso continued. "It has been for me an unforgettable interlude, for you a beginning. I'll return to civilization, marry the daughter of some prosperous colonial official, have children—to whom I'll tell stories of our talks and adventures in an undiscovered land. And you? You'll be a New Californian. Whom will you marry?"

"Whom should I? There are no white women here!"

"What about the princess with the flaming hair who gave you the silver buckle?" he bantered. "Being candid and meaning no disrespect to you and your family, you were attracted to that young lady, weren't you?"

This Promised Land

"Ah, she might be the one," Antonio retorted in kind. "Who would not wish the hand of a queen's daughter in marriage? But I'm afraid she was betrothed long ago to some dusky prince."

They talked on long after darkness had fallen, the waves lapping at their feet, the lights of the *San Antonio* rising and falling with the gentle swells, until at last Costanso stood up. "I must go and pack. Let us keep in touch. I shall be working with people concerned for the future of this land. You will be living here. We shall need all the accurate information we can get. Let me hear from you."

"And I you!"

"Let us not forget our dreams!"

"No, let us not forget our dreams!"

They embraced and never saw each other again.

Toward noon next day an offshore breeze filled the *San Antonio's* sails and as she rounded the Point of Pines, firing a last salute, Antonio was left in a new land under new leadership.

Feeling more than a little lost, at first, he worked with his fellow Catalans and Leather Jackets to construct the presidio under the harsh eyes of Fages, who seemed anxious to show no favoritism.

"Hurry, you good-for-nothings!" the young lieutenant bellowed at them unmercifully. "Russians or English may fall upon us at any time! By the Black Virgin of Montserrat,* worse malingerers I never saw!"

So they felled trees, lugged poles, erected a rectangular stockade with ravelins at each corner, mixed clay, made brick, built more buildings, dug holes for toilets, hauled earth from dawn to dusk seven days a week scarcely stopping to eat. When by Serra's intervention, work on Sundays and feast days was discontinued, Fages substituted inspection of arms, washing, and mending of clothes, bringing in a week's supply of wood for the kitchen. Thus they worked nearly as hard Sundays as other days. Yet if they stopped to roll a cigarette, he was apt to let out a flood of oaths and call them traitors.

Fages had been left in command of an area nearly half as large as Spain with twenty soldiers at Monterey and nine at San Diego. By nature touchy, he now quite naturally felt insecure as well, saw enemies at every hand, and clashed continually with the

---
*famed Catalonian sacred statue

equally strong-willed Serra, suspecting him and the friars—Crespi, Rubio, and the others, "the Majorcan clique" as he called them one day to Serra's face—of conspiring amongst themselves and with Rivera to undermine his authority and take control of the province "as the Jesuits did in Old California!" Yet minutes later he was chatting amiably with the Father President, whom he respected and even liked, about some hens who were not laying. "They are too old," Fages asserted, priding himself on his knowledge of poultry, as they surveyed the usually productive Black Minorcas scratching about their feet. "After two years they should be eaten. We've been so long delayed in our conquest of this land that even our chickens reflect it!"

Serra solemnly agreed. Rubio, his younger shadow, standing silently by as customary—as if too shy to hazard an opinion—seemed to Fages at such moments more than ever a superfluous man, a burden on the military to support and protect and the Crown to feed, representative of a young commander's many problems.

More than Portola, Rivera, or any of those early leaders except perhaps Ortega, Fages was born to explore. He was eager for new horizons, fearless, energetic, with a feeling for the land such as some men have for precious stones or women or the sea; and when his restless energy boiled over into irascibility it was not only against those under him and the fathers but all the constraints and tediums of garrison life and his heavy responsibilities.

Accordingly late that autumn when work on the presidio was well advanced and fields and garden planted at a distance of a mile inland where there was good soil, and neither Russians nor English appeared likely to fall upon them at any moment, the young commander-in-chief left Sergeant Juan Puig in charge and took six men, including Antonio and Pablo and Pablo's little black dog with the prematurely gray muzzle and solemn air who was becoming a regular mascot with everyone, on a completely unauthorized exploring expedition.

Antonio felt surprised to be included. "Don't presume on former acquaintance!" Fages' manner seemed to say and he'd been careful to watch his step.

They camped the first night near the present site of Salinas where the rich valley soil afforded good grass for their animals. The rains came early that year, the land was green, all felt relieved and exhilarated to be on the trail once more, free from garrison routine and the oppressive fogs of Monterey. "But I was careful to say little," Antonio recalled, "and dared not ask where we were going, lest Fages take it as an affront."

Next day they climbed an unexplored range lying to the east, pioneering the route up Gabilan Canyon followed later by the first coastal highway of automobile days, and descended to the charming valley where Mission San Juan Bautista and the town of Hollister would stand. Continuing a short distance eastward into a second range, they investigated the entrance to what would later be known as Pacheco's Pass as a possible route to the Great or San Joaquin Valley about which they heard from Indians, and then they turned northward through a magnificent oak and grass woodland past the present sites of Gilroy and Morgan Hill, Fages still taciturn if glad to be on the move, and near present San Jose reached again the blue sapphire of San Francisco Bay or the Great Estuary, as they called it.

"Boneu," the commander cried out, "come up here!" and Antonio spurred his sorrel alongside Fages' dappled gray, the one formerly ridden by Portola. "You were scouting here last year with Ortega. Perhaps you can show us the way now, eh?"

Antonio pointed to the green belt of reeds and inlets along the eastern shore over which myriads of waterfowl hovered. "We circled those marshes."

"And that was where you were confronted by the hostile Indians?" Soon Fages was chatting pleasantly, and Antonio realized the man was starved for companionship. With no fellow officer to talk to and unwilling to confide in friars or enlisted men, he'd been like a corked bottle. Now the cork was removed as they rode stirrup-to-stirrup through the bright autumn day. Fages wanted to investigate the Great Estuary, wanted to be first to reach Point Reyes, wanted to forestall the Russians there or if they were already there to learn of it and report to Mexico City. He wanted honor and glory, Antonio realized. He even confided his affection for the daughter of his old company commander, a certain young Eulalia de Celis, hardly more than a child, who resided with her fashionable mother in Mexico City. "She's such a beautiful thing I can hardly bear to think of her." Perhaps most extraordinary of all, this rough but intelligent man revealed he'd been born at Guizona a few miles from Antonio's native Balaguer. Like Antonio, Fages attended the university at Cervera in their peaceful countryside where it had been removed from Barcelona because of student disturbances in the cause of liberty. And he even spoke of Rousseau and the remarkable new development of Freemasonry which since the establishment of a grand lodge in Madrid was making rapid headway in military circles, condoned if not abetted by the liberalism of King Carlos.

So they advanced along the eastern shore of the bay until lack of food and time forced them to stop. Scouting ahead with Pablo for one last brief stint, Antonio saw something which seemed significant. Returning he led Fages and the others to the summit of a grassy hillock near present Oakland. From there he pointed out, westward across the intervening water, a small island later known as Alcatraz. Beyond the island lay a narrow opening between tall headlands to what seemed open sea. "We have found it!" Fages exclaimed. "That must be the entrance to the Great Estuary! And it has been waiting there for us to discover it ever since the day of creation!"

It would not be called the Golden Gate until John C. Fremont named it that a hundred years later.

Chapter Twenty

Father Rubio, the diarist, takes up the narrative now in his own words as he tells of the establishing of Mission Santa Lucia.

"As I ride south with our pack train from Monterey I feel apprehensive. Each day as my docile mule follows behind Father President Serra's, I cannot help but feel my position expressive of our continuing relationship since those university days at Palma de Majorca where he was my first professor of philosophy—on through our shared experience at the Apostolic College of San Fernando in the City of Mexico, then years of missionary work in the Sierra Gorda not so far distant, and now here in Alta California where still he is my spiritual leader. For those who will never see him I should say he is only five feet two inches tall, an inch shorter than I, frail, asthmatic, almost sixty years old, yet like many others I have grown dependent on this giant's strength and determination. Without them close at hand, shall I be able to succeed in my new endeavor?"

Father Rubio knew his limitations. Meekness and obedience not self-assertion were his strengths. "Now I must learn the grace Serra has achieved of letting God's will act through me!"

They spent that night with their hospitable Majorcan countrymen Brothers Pieras and Sitjar at Mission San Antonio de Padua de Los Robles. "Nestled in its mountain valley, it is a lovely sight, lovely as Solomon's Garden, Serra says. I never saw such oaks. Today we continued. The sun was hot, the grass short and dry for the year has not been good and the arroyos contain little water, but when our dusty column, Governor Fages and the soldiers leading, crossed the pass where the new route leaves the wooded highlands and descends steeply toward the sea, avoiding the wilderness which caused the first explorers such difficulty, the air grew cooler and there was a promise of better things. Tonight we shall stop at Mission San Luis Obispo situated in the land of the gentle Tichos* so noted for their handsomeness and friendliness to Spaniards; and our Catalan brothers there, Cavaller and Juncosa, will doubtless be overjoyed to see our impossible little Governor, their fellow countryman, whom they regard almost as a relative. At times I must confess I find Catalonian self-love a bit tiresome."

At Mission San Luis everything Rubio foresaw proved true but two days later as they proceeded along the shore, Antonio guiding them, a noble valley opened its arms as if to receive them; and inland at a distance of several miles they saw the promontory with the green oaks so often described as an ideal site for a mission. Serra's anticipation rose with Rubio's as they approached it.

"Truly we found it a marvelous spot. Situated approximately midway between mountains and sea, at a point where it is said first contact was made with the people of this remarkable valley, it offers splendid views, fertile soil, plentiful wood supply in the trees close at hand and water in the river nearby. And not far distant, its smoke clearly visible, is the large village ruled by the red-haired chieftainess jokingly called by the soldiers 'Queen Calafia' after the legendary Queen of California in Ordonez de Montalvo's absurd romance. Other villages are known to be nearby, thus assuring us a goodly number of converts, God willing. At Fages' urging, for he was in a hurry as usual, we all set to work."

Two bells, gifts of the king, were unpacked and hung from the limb of a spreading oak. While an improvised altar of brushwood was being erected beside them, an ecstasy of joy suddenly overcame Serra and he began to ring the bells while crying out in his surprisingly deep voice: "Come you pagans! Come to the Holy Church! Come to receive the Faith of Jesus Christ!"

Fages and some of the soldiers smiled behind their hands at this naive outburst, "and I myself was a little embarrassed," Rubio confessed, "though it was in the tradition of our preceptor Saint Francis who was often seized by similar ecstasies, sometimes in the midst of solemn prayer. 'Why not save your strength?' I suggested. 'There's not a single pagan to be seen!'

" 'They will come!' Serra assured me with absolute certainty. 'If we demonstrate our faith, they will come! Meanwhile allow

---

*a Chumash people

my heart to express itself!' And I felt shamed and instructed by his zeal.

"From freshly cut limbs the soldiers and muleteers including the black man, Pablo, began erecting a Holy Cross. Donning surplice and stole over his habit, Serra blessed it and hallowed the surrounding earth on which the new mission, my mission, would stand by sprinkling it with holy water to frighten away the infernal enemies. Juan Evangelista, the bright young Indian lad who was accompanying him from Monterey to Mexico City, served as acolyte.

"While the rest of us knelt before the improvised altar, Serra sang the High Mass and preached on the necessity of the solitary daily commitment each Christian soul must make to Our Lord Jesus. I surmised that in his subtle way he was referring to me and the responsibility I was about to assume. Two brothers were usually assigned each mission but none was available to keep me company. Could I measure up? Till now whatever I desired greatly, such as full responsibility for myself and others, seemed not to come to me, even to be rebuffed by my very great desire for it, while what I cared little or nothing for, such as my own life and well-being, seemed vouchsafed to me easily. Now, I wondered, was this to change? Was I at last to find my true self?"

Since the valley formed part of the famous Santa Lucia Range, Saint Lucy's Mountains, they named the mission in her honor. Appropriately for him, Rubio thought, Saint Lucy was the patroness of the eyes, "which is to say of seeing clearly, hence of inner as well as outer perception and thus of self-knowledge."

While Serra preached to them on this very subject, a half-naked woman, painted and bangled, not young, appeared at some distance, perhaps, Rubio thought, attracted by the sound of the bells or the gunfire of the soldiers (smoke from repeated volleys of musketry had taken the place of the incense they lacked) and stood watching. "After concluding the dedication Serra went toward her holding out a piece of red ribbon but she ran away, and Governor Fages, as if to say I told you so, reminded us rudely that despite all we might have heard about the friendliness of the people of this region, the natives hereabout as elsewhere were no longer to be trusted. 'Why, only last month,' he cried, 'the Sanjones attacked our mail couriers on the Rio de Monterey and two of them had to be killed. Don't be deceived by appearances! Remember they are at heart brute savages who, like animals, respect only superior force!' "

Work began immediately on a defensive stockade. It was an undertaking Rubio disapproved since it implied not love but fear. He thought it would repel the very people they hoped to attract. "A new perception was stirring in me. 'Did Jesus or Francis seek protection of stockades?' I asked myself. The answer came clearly. 'No, only of God!' And thus emboldened I questioned the proceeding.

"'What?' Fages retorted heatedly, 'isn't it enough for me to be founding a mission at such a time as this of drouth and shortage of food and lack of soldiers without you complaining about stockades? Here I am with only forty-three lazy good-for-nothings trying to defend a region half as large as Spain, charged especially with the protection of you missionary fathers, and you tell me I shouldn't build a stockade?' He grew red in the face, 'Why, your own President,' pointing to Serra, 'recognizes the necessity for stockades! Hasn't he lived behind the poles at San Diego and Monterey? Haven't you too? So why not here?'

"I wanted to reply that if a new approach were to be tried, it should be here, but timidity overcame me and I glanced at Serra who'd been deliberately withholding comment to see how I should fare on my own against our military adversary with whom I should have to deal during his absence. He generously came to my rescue. To no avail. Our tyrant remained adamant. 'You friars live in an unreal world! You pretend to abhor military force but are protected by it every day and night!' With a contemptuous glance he turned away.

"'Let him go!' Serra said quietly. 'You will find a way! Saint Lucy and the Blue Nun will guide you! . . . yes, the Blue Nun! Remember what happened at Monterey?'

"At Monterey when we were in similar predicament, hoping for converts, bedeviled by impudent soldiery, some Indians suddenly appeared, the very first we'd seen, and asked to be told the doctrine of Jesus Christ. We were astonished and asked how they knew of it. They said, 'the padre with the mamas,' the father with the breasts, had visited them and told them to come to us. 'What did she look like?' we asked amazed. 'She was dressed in blue, not unlike you,' they said, 'and wore a white cord and plain sandals as you do, and she said white men would soon come and show us the way to Heaven!'

"Serra believed it a miracle and felt sure the Blue Nun was preparing the way for us in California as she had done for our brethren in New Mexico, though I was plagued by doubts. For those who may never hear the story of Sister Maria de Jesus de Agreda, I must repeat it. One morning some strange Indians appeared at the Mission of Isleta not far from Santa Fe in New Mexico and asked to be baptized. They'd come from a region far to the east where no missionaries had been, yet astonishingly they seemed wholly familiar with our doctrine. When asked the source of their knowledge they answered: 'A Lady in Blue visited us and told us to come here and be baptized!'

"An expedition was immediately organized and accompanied them to their homeland. There our friars and soldiers were met by other Indians carrying crosses who informed them 'The Blue Lady' had appeared and foretold their arrival! They were even more amazed when they began to instruct these Indians and found them already familiar with our doctrine!

"When the expedition returned to Isleta with this news, the father custodian was so impressed that he decided to go to Mexico City and report. From there he went to Spain. In a convent near Burgos he found Sister Maria de Agreda. She was a nun of the Conceptionist Order, twenty-eight years old, handsome, rosy-cheeked, fervent. While offering herself to God for the salvation of the souls of the savages of the New World, she'd been miraculously transported, she said, to New Mexico and set down there among Indians to whom she spoke in Spanish and they understood. Having received the divine gift of bilocation as well as of tongues, she made such journeys repeatedly, being carried through the air by a band of angels.

"Witnesses testified they'd seen her come flying to them robed in blue and gray like our friars and wearing a white cord around her waist and sandals like ours, with a veil covering her head! On several occasions, frightened by her sudden appearance and not understanding her intent, the Indians shot at her with arrows, perhaps presaging her eventual martyrdom. Serra carried the small vellum-bound volumes of her famous book *The Mystical City of God* wherever he went.

"So after Fages turned away from us so rudely we prayed to Sister Maria to guide us and Saint Lucy to give us clear sight on our way. How I wished Serra could stay there beside me! How keenly I felt his strength transmitting itself to me like a tangible force! But I knew that like Fages he was eager to be gone—Fages to meet the supply ship at San Diego, Serra to board it and sail away to Mexico, there to lay before the Viceroy the full account of our grievances against our intolerable little Governor!

"I knelt and kissed my confessor's feet. He did likewise with mine. And then he said penetratingly: 'You will not be alone here! Queen Poverty and Lady Charity will grace your daily table as they did that of the Seraphic Francis in the Valley of the Nera in the fastness of the Apennines! This, my brother, is the opportunity for which long service has prepared you, for which you left your native village of San Juan not far from my own beloved Petra on our Golden Isle of Majorca, abandoned home, loved ones, familiar surroundings, and for God and King ventured nine thousand miles to this outpost at the rim of Christendom to fish for souls in the manner of our apostolic fathers! Verily you are an explorer in spirit as in flesh! Write me! Inform me so that I may have the most up-to-date information to lay before the Viceroy!'

" 'But will the mail be safe?' I questioned.

" 'Our adversary will not dare tamper with it, though he means to charge us for carrying it like the mercenary fellow he is!'

" 'How do you account for his animosity? Do you believe him infected with Freemasonry?'

" 'It is possible. That foul disease is spreading like the loanda, and may prove as virulent unless stamped out! . . . But remember I shall always be near you!' he resumed his former tone, 'I shall pray for the Blue Nun to visit you. And should you hear of my death, pray for the salvation of my soul and I shall do likewise for yours!'

"As the column departed southward across the dun-colored hills and the last imprecations of the muleteers died away, I could not help a feeling of abandonment and to allay it, remembering the joy Saint Francis found in labor of the humblest kind, I busied myself with Corporal Lopez and his men and our two Indians from Old California and our one muleteer in erecting the very stockade whose walls, I felt, would bar the people we came here to win."

Every pole Rubio cut was like a stroke of pain, every one erected like a pike set against friends. He helped tie them together with tough reeds and cut more reeds to roof and thatch the frameworks of poles that served his lonely band as houses. But hardly had the pack train disappeared than Lopez began to slack off and his men followed his example. "When I upbraided him mildly, he replied rudely that the Governor had deliberately banished him to this isolated outpost, disliking him because he was a Leather Jacket soldier of Rivera, 'who will someday return to rule all California!' and until then he did not propose to break his back for the sake of a bad-tempered gachupin lieutenant. 'My men and I already have too much to do herding animals and standing guard day and night than to labor with our hands like Indians!' he asserted. 'Furthermore we should be six istead of five which imposes extra duty on all!'

"What could I do? I'd never liked the man and would much have preferred Boneu or another Catalan as corporal for despite their numerous shortcomings they are industrious and trustworthy.

" 'How do you suppose the work is to be accomplished?' I inquired gently.

" 'That is your affair, not mine!'

"Construction of the palisade and our defense were his responsibility, as he well knew, but what was I to do? I had no authority over him, and Fages would give me no recourse. The rogue merely wanted to impose his will and drag the work along at his own lazy tempo, doing as little as possible, putting as much onto me as he could. He even spoke grandly of a day when he would live here in lordly fashion as a ranchero with his wife and daughters and own thousands of cattle and horses, as if he had a right to the very land itself! You can imagine my distress. Things were going wrong already. Was it my fault? How would Serra have handled the matter?

At night still hungry after devouring his meager ration of two tortillas and two dried figs, supplemented by fresh meat when the soldiers had luck in their hunting, Rubio stretched his body on the bare earth, having no other bed and indeed, as he insisted, desiring none, and as darkness settled down out of the wild sierra, and wolves and coyotes began to howl, with fervent devotion he thought of the Blue Nun. Perhaps she would take pity on him as Serra had suggested. He almost could see her, in the fervor of his imagination, flying toward him out of a radiant cloud accompanied by a band of angels. If he had faith enough perhaps she would come. "And by her help," he said to himself, "someday a beautiful church with long arched portico and stately bell tower will stand here, and a multitude of faithful will throng to it, perhaps to the sound of these very bells that now hang from this oak limb!"

Chapter Twenty-one

As Koyo watched Lospe's figure fading away into the gathering darkness, she felt those pangs only a mother can feel who, herself threatened by circumstances, sees her child entering an uncertain future alone.

Her thoughts turned toward her son, and momentarily she contemplated directing her steps into the wilderness and somehow finding Asuskwa there where she guessed he must be hiding, waiting, biding his time till he could acquire such power as might overcome that of Owotoponus. But on further thought Koyo realized she must face reality, and after a moment she took the path back toward the village where she must confront Owotoponus. The prospect filled her with fear. How could she face him? What should she say? But through her misgivings came the strong vital images of her son and daughter. For them she must be brave. For them and for her people, as mother and leader, she must confront this evil creature and somehow prevail at no matter what cost to herself.

Darkness had fallen when she reached the village and she hoped that Owotoponus might have joined the men in the sweathouse where they often gathered to spend the evenings and sometimes all of the night, their weapons with them, augmenting their maleness by this close association, exchanging their homosexual love, guarded by sentinels, ready to rush out if necessary and repel sneak attacks by neighboring villagers. Her hopes rose when she entered the house and found only Lehlele and old Seneq, who had returned on a visit from the mission, seated in conversation after the evening meal.

"Where have you been, my sister?" Lehlele advanced to her lovingly, taking her by both hands, gazing into her eyes, guessing, it seemed to Koyo, at the truth.

This Promised Land

"With the Sky People watching I went to lay feathers and pay homage at the grave of my loved one."

"But what kept you so late?" Lehlele's gently searching eyes seemed to find an answer. But Koyo hesitated to say it.

"Sorrow. The darkness seemed to speak to the sadness in me, to comfort me. For there are times, as you know . . ."

"There are times when you know people are speaking a falsehood!" Owotoponus exclaimed sarcastically as he entered the doorway, animosity evident in tone and movement. These were the days when, to humiliate her as his jealousy increased, he was going off alone into the willows with He-ap, then vaunting their sexual prowess afterward, so that gossip rose behind Koyo's back as she walked along the lanes of the village. "You too thought to escape me!" His voice accused her. "You thought you would join your son whom you imagine safe beyond my power. But I merely hold him in a trap like a rabbit, helpless until I want to take him!" He smiled his sardonic smile and waited. Though her heart pounded, Koyo's purpose remained firm and she did not reply but gazed steadily at him. "Where is your daughter?" he prompted cruelly, his voice no louder than a whisper.

For a moment Koyo was tempted to lie to him, to do anything that might contribute to Lospe's safety. But then she thought: No, I must face him; I must confront his evil. Even if it costs me my life, I must dispute his terrible power and do my utmost to dispel it. "She has gone to the mission as others have gone to escape your grasp!"

At that old Seneq, who'd remained unusually quiet, let out a cackle of satisfaction.

Although Owotoponus suspected the truth, he was a little dumbfounded by Koyo's outspoken fearlessness, and for a moment hesitated, and in that moment Koyo saw a hope that was like salvation.

"You may kill me if you like, as you did my father, as you did my husband, you murderer. But it will not end there. My son, my daughter, my people will in the end rise up against you and throw off your yoke. You cannot with all the power in the world suppress them cruelly forever . . . !" And then with inspiration born of desperation she added: "For there is a higher law than your magic!"

Owotoponus laughed scornfully. "Do you think you can frighten me? Thus the cornered always squeal and the frightened cry out when they have no other recourse! Have you forgotten so soon what I did to the Tulamni sorcerer on the Plain of the Carrizo Grass?" And after letting that sink in for a moment, he added in his menacing whisper: "Have you forgotten this?"

Stretching out his right hand, he opened its fingers toward her while watching her malevolently, slowly drew them back toward him, in the way which had so terrified her before. But this time she did not blanch. Transcendent courage filled her.

"You may take my son! You may take me! But you will not prevail . . . not ever!"

Old Seneq rose from where she'd been crouching by the embers of the fire. She had returned from the mission to gather her last belongings in preparation for a permanent move there. With a fierce gaze she leveled a crooked finger at Owotoponus. "I lay my curse upon you, Evil Being! My daughter may do as she likes! But I shall accept no more abuse from you! . . . There's another holy man in this valley who does not speak with a wicked tongue, and to him I shall listen henceforward—not to you!"

Resolutely, self-centered as ever, the old woman turned her back upon them and began gathering her possessions, while Owotoponus was left with clenched fist, and Koyo turned silently away from him.

Chapter Twenty-two

To make matters worse for Father Rubio in the beginning, not a single Indian came to his new mission, though smokes of their villages could be seen at a distance, and mindful of the strict rule against proselytizing or in any way invading their privacy, he did not approach them but waited for them to come to him.

With makeshift plow fashioned from a tree limb drawn by two mules he plowed the rich loam by the river, his lame leg giving him much pain. Aided by his two faithful Christian Indians and Tobias, the muleteer, he planted wheat and barley and brushed soil over the seed with branches, there being no harrow, while the lazy soldiers watched, "yet even though we blessed wild laurel leaves," he wrote, "and placed them in the sown earth and prayed to Saint Joseph, patron of New California, for the success of this first crop, months must pass before it matured. Fages had spared me only the meagerest supplies. Sugar and chocolate were all but gone. Our flour was running dangerously low. Now in winter there were no berries to gather. Soon we should, it seemed, be starving as game retreated warily to the fringes of the valley and became harder to kill. And all this time though I prayed continually that it might happen, not a single heathen came near." It was as if an invisible wall surrounded him as real as the stockade he'd helped to build, and it was with utmost difficulty he prevailed upon Lopez and his men to abide by the injunction that they were never to invade the Indians' villages but let them come voluntarily to the mission.

"One day nearly overcome by despair I had gone a little distance out among the oaks of the promontory and flung myself down upon the earth, arms outstretched in the form of a cross, and in agony of spirit prayed: 'Show me what I must do, O Lord, to deserve Thy Grace!'

"Rising I saw a solitary heathen woman watching me. Instinctively I opened my arms in a gesture of welcome. With delight I saw her begin to move toward me. Then with horror I saw she was in reality a man dressed as a woman and realized I was encountering a sodomite such as with unspeakable vileness they maintained in all their villages. Aversion was my instant reaction. Then Saint Lucy gave me clearer vision and I recalled Saint Francis first abhorring then administering to the leper he encountered on the road near Assisi, as God brought him painfully to an understanding of the meaning of charity, and my heart went out to this unfortunate creature who stood before me, his face and manner expressing torment and need. The Lord has sent me my leper! I thought, rejoicing.

"Embracing him I knelt and kissed his feet, much to his consternation, and then accepted the basket of seeds he was bringing as a gift. He impressed me as remarkably alert, clean despite his outlandish appearance, and with no offensive odor.

"Escorting him inside the stockade, while the soldiers stared and smirked, making obscene remarks as they recognized the nature of his profession, I showed him our church and the Holy Cross. He seemed to grasp quickly what we were about, and by signs explained that he had watched from afar and now wished to accept our faith.

"I was overcome with joy that the Lord had sent me such a willing first convert. Suddenly it dawned on me that perhaps the Blue Nun had heard my prayers and in the fastness of the wilderness been at work upon the souls of the heathen, preparing them to receive Christian doctrine. I felt overwhelmed with grace and fell on my knees and gave thanks aloud, praising God and rejoicing that at last His work at our lonely outpost had begun. This brought more frowns and smirks to the faces of the soldiers who thought we should treat all Indians with reserve lest they become too familiar.

" 'He may be a spy!' Lopez objected. 'Is it not strange only one has come? Where are the others?'

"But after questioning him and finding he'd indeed often observed us and our activities, I was convinced of his innocence.

"Improvising an abalone shell as a font, I baptized him with water from the river, which pleased him greatly since, he informed me by signs and gestures, it was sacred to his people and came from the sun which they worshiped. Explaining he was now reborn, I gave him the Christian name of Junipero in honor of my preceptor now on his way to Mexico City, Corporal Lopez standing godfather grudgingly enough, still disgusted by the poor creature's former occupation and freakish appearance. 'You are moving too fast in your zeal!' he complained. 'This fellow may not be at all what he seems.' But I reproved him for lack of faith and gave Junipero a red ribbon and some blue beads and invited him to stay with us. He replied he must return to his people but would soon come back and I urged him to bring others who might wish to receive the faith.

"That night I wrote my father confessor in Mexico telling him of my first conversion and all that had happened since he left me.

"Hail Jesus, Mary, and Joseph!
"Reverend Father Professor and President Fray Junipero
Serra.
"My Very Dear Friend:
"Today, thanks be to God, we baptized our first convert. With deepest respect for the tradition you have established in this province I named him Junipero in honor of Your Reverence. As I kissed his bare feet I felt ashamed I wore sandals, remembering how the divine Francis went barefoot as these Indians when he started his missionary journey. May God help me to greater humility! He is the one you tried to welcome the day of our arrival here but who ran away. Indeed he was initially sent to spy on us but, seeing us day after day at our devotions, became inspired, I have no doubt by the intercession of the Blessed Virgin and of Sister Maria de Agreda her handmaiden, to come forward and commit himself.

"He tells me the Indians think we Spaniards were born from she mules because we have no women with us. Since you asked me to keep you informed, I respectfully urge your Reverence to request the Viceroy to remedy this deficiency, which militates against the best interests of God and King, by sending us settlers with wives. The presence of women among us will go far to reassure these simple souls that we are not to be feared. Yet a beginning has been made and for that I rejoice. I suspect additional reason for their aloofness, and this I hope to determine and report to you.

"The state of our food supplies is deplorable. The vegetables are thriving under our close care but our grain which is beyond reach of constant oversight is being destroyed by birds and squirrels. We shall soon like John the Baptist be reduced to living on locusts and wild honey, except that neither exists here, there being no honeybees as at home and the locusts, if present, all hibernating.

"At times cold winds blow down upon us from the north and snow lies deep on the sierra. Other days are like the best on Majorca when sun, earth, and sea air mingle with most pleasant consequence.

"Then I agree with you that this lovely spot, midway between San Diego and Monterey, may be central to our California Dream. Here Christian and pagan may come together in harmony and beauty and God's will be done in a virgin land!

"Lopez, as you foresaw, is a problem. Yes, he is indeed here under a sort of banishment, being in great disfavor with Fages particularly, he tells me, because of trouble between him and a favorite of the Governor's, young Boneu, the Catalan, that tall blond fellow related to former Governor Portola who was among the soldiers who helped us dedicate the mission and continued with you and Fages to San Diego. Boneu uses his connections to advance his own fortunes unscrupulously, Lopez claims, though I do not quite believe him. He claims that both Fages and Boneu are Freemasons, which I also doubt, though I do suspect our Governor of dangerous thoughts. Why our Gracious King, God Save Him, should favor antireligious Catalans over others of his subjects is a mystery though I suppose it's because of his French blood which is so close to theirs.

"Such gossip aside, I like Boneu. I noticed during our journey here that he was particularly considerate of the lowly, the Indians and muleteers, and I should much have preferred him to Lopez as corporal. Lopez had the gall to say the other day that unless Indian women come to the mission soon for the pleasure of him and his men, as is so common at the presidios, they will go to the nearest village and lasso some! When I threatened him with a heavy penance, he laughed: 'Father—we are but men, we are not saints like you!' The impudent rascal! Thus he undermines my authority and corrupts others. Even his Catalans have become lazy-good-for-nothings. Yet there is a kind of scurrilous integrity about him. He is unashamedly what he is and insists he intends to settle here some day 'when Don Fernando Rivera becomes Governor!' as he confidently predicts.

"The French alarm clock you loaned me serves me well. I rise at midnight, recite Lauds and Matins, remain at devotions until nearly dawn, then rest briefly to have strength for work. Most difficult are my terrible moments of self-doubt. Then feelings of utter worthlessness overcome me and I hear that insidious whisper in my ear: 'Nicolas, it is all of no avail! You will never succeed! You belong to me!' I seize my crucifix and pray, focusing all my thoughts on God until the voice of the Evil One is stilled!

"It will give me great pleasure to hear that Your Reverence is in good health, likewise your California Indian servant, young Juan Evangelista. Good-bye! May the day come when I send a young girl to the City of Mexico to be our first little Indian nun from California! Is it not a privilege to play a winning game against the Evil One for the souls of thousands of pagans? What a glorious contest! I feel fortunate to be a participant, however humble and unworthy!

"May God protect you from all danger and bring you safely to these shores again!

"From this valley and new mission of Santa Lucia in New California, February 19, 1773.

"Your most affectionate brother and servant,
"Fray Nicolas Rubio"

Chapter Twenty-three

When Rivera obstinately refused to come north to Monterey with the supplies and cattle he'd brought to San Diego from Lower California, Antonio and Fages sailed south on the *San Antonio* to fetch them. After delivering welcome provisions from San Blas, the pint-sized frigate was carrying back a cargo of salt mined from the beds at the mouth of the Salinas. With them went Ramon Bonnel and three others to help bring the cattle and additional supplies north. As the sturdy little vessel was running close hauled before a westerly breeze, she passed the mouth of the Valley of Santa Lucia, and at sight of those grassy hills reaching down like open arms from the shoulders of the dark sierra, Antonio felt an unspoken invitation to return and see Koyo and Lospe again.

"Whatever happened to the silver buckle that red-haired black-faced princess gave you?" Fages chaffed, as if guessing his thoughts.

"I've still got it!" he replied resolutely, wondering if indeed he had.

As they entered the narrow mouth of the harbor at San Diego, the high bluff of Point Loma towering on their left, at their right the flat sandy island which would one day be the U.S. Naval Air Station, nothing seemed at first to have changed. Directly inland the stockade stood up its hill, royal standard flying, huts of Indian converts clustered nearby. But there was one great difference.

"Look!" cried Bonnel. "Black cattle!" Grazing in the lush lowlands toward the false bay were a number of the predominantly black Andalusian strain, though with many reds, duns, and piebalds among them. Those grazing shapes were firm proof the land was being domesticated. But Fages flew into a fury at sight of them.

"That execrable Rivera has kept them here to spite me, while our northern missions and presidio have gone without!"

His companions got ready to witness a real blowup when he should face his old enemy. What followed far exceeded their expectations when Lopez and not Rivera met them at the beach.

"Where's your Captain?" Fages demanded, repressing his rage with difficulty. For the governor of a province to be greeted at a post of such importance by a mere corporal seemed a final affront.

"In Old California, Your Excellency?"

"And what's he doing there?"

"Securing more cattle and men, Your Excellency!" Juan was standing rigidly at attention, trying to be the soul of deference.

"Where is Sergeant Ortega?"

"Likewise in Old California, Your Excellency."

"And who is in command here?"

"I am, may it please Your Excellency!"

"You!" Fages exploded, and when he had subsided enough to speak coherently he demanded: "And who does Captain Rivera think rules this province?"

"I don't know, sir!" replied Lopez, bumbling at last despite his best efforts to be discreet.

"So much the worse for you, for you shall find out!"

When word of this spread among the Leather Jackets of the garrison, they felt convinced they could expect nothing but harsh treatment from their Catalan overlord. Underpaid, underfed, longing to see their homes again and now fearful of further abuse, that night nine of them deserted and headed eastward into mountainous wilderness intending to reach Mexico via the Colorado Desert and Sonora. When Antonio broke the news to him next morning, Fages was beside himself. "It is the plot, it is the plot!" he yelled, accusing the friars of conspiring with the soldiers to embarrass him. He saw his authority crumbling away. How could he exercise command if he could not control his men? Yet if he pursued the runaways, bloodshed might ensue and the incident be enlarged to his further discredit. Sensing his predicament Antonio suggested in reasonable fashion: "Why not ask Father Paterna to act as mediary?"

"And become beholden to the Franciscan hierarchy which opposes me?" Fages was still fuming.

"Isn't it better than bloodshed?"

Antonio's logic was inescapable. Swallowing his pride, Fages approached the affable Paterna a favorite with the soldiers, and asked deferentially: "To avoid bloodshed would Your Reverence be willing to act as intermediary, in the King's name, with the scoundrels who have fled, and persuade them to return?"

Paterna obligingly agreed. Accompanied by two Leather Jackets to give him credence, he followed the runaways, parleyed with them, and persuaded them to return, while Fages vented his rage on Lopez, accusing him of instigating the desertion, despite Antonio's remonstrance that it was hardly likely Juan should devise such a method of bringing trouble upon himself.

"Ah, but there's no bottom to that rascal's deviousness as you've often said yourself!" Fages retorted. "And I shall take him and his henchman Nunez, that burley galoot with the wandering eye who led the flight, back to Monterey with us where we'll keep them on short tether!"

Helpfully at that moment Ortega arrived from the south with additional soldiers and cattle as well as confidential dispatches which he handed Fages. After a brief reunion with their old companion during which they learned that Rivera was indeed at Loreto intriguing for Fages' removal, they started for Monterey with their cattle and new recruits leaving Ortega in charge.

Fages with the dependable Malaret and Bonnel led the march while other soldiers were dispersed as guards along the pack train. Lopez and Nunez, the ringleader among the deserters, were assigned demeaning positions as herders helping the cowboys who'd arrived with the cattle, and Antonio and his friend Yorba brought up the rear following the caballada and cattle herd where they could keep an eye on everything ahead. Antonio who'd never participated in a big cattle drive before was fascinated by what he saw. The newly arrived vaqueros were a colorful carefree lot bubbling over with jests and laughter, their weather-beaten trail hats cocked at rakish angles, their long hair dangling below shoulder blades. They wore the ubiquitous short pants with long underdrawers, once white, exposed at knees and tucked into the usual leggings. Around their waists like corsets were broad leather belts which helped their bodies serve as snubbing posts when they lassoed on foot.

Antonio noted the graceful way these free-spirited fellows handled their charges, treating the cattle almost as if they were human, urging them politely yet firmly forward with softspoken words, keeping a respectful distance, allowing a recognized leader, a huge red ox with horns like the spreading branches of a tree, to set his own pace, prodding the slow movers when necessary with a shout or crack of their rein ends against their armas.

Their gear resembled his: high-cantled, high-horned saddle; reata coiled at right side; rusty spurs with huge rowels attached to heels of leather shoes. And their horses were mostly chestnut sorrels like his Babieca and he recalled Ortega saying that of the sixteen originally brought to Mexico by Cortes ten were of that shade, while five were dappled grays like Portola's stallion now ridden by Fages.

As for the cattle, they were predominantly of the black De Lidia strain which furnishes bulls for today's bull rings and their long white horns curved menacingly forward and up. But most were not large by modern standards, weighing no more than seven or eight hundred pounds when mature; yet they were rangy and very tough.

By eerie coincidence, just as the herd reached the old campsite in the grassy hollow where the stampede had occurred two years before, a fierce black bull broke away and started back to join those left at San Diego. Lopez who was nearest darted in pursuit. In sudden alarm lest he was using this ruse as a means of escaping, Antonio instinctively drew his carbine and shouted: "Halt!" But the other, reata out and whirling, intent upon his quarry, did not seem to hear.

With marvelous dexterity Lopez's loop encircled the running bull from the rear, passed forward along the entire length of its body as if the animal were running through a hoop, dropped over its head and deftly caught both forefeet, which were abruptly pulled from under it as Lopez drew hard on his reins and set his horse back on haunches amid approving shouts from the cowboys. The bull after turning a somersault measured its length in the grass. It was the famous abrazo todo, or total embrace, the most difficult of all throws.

"Which were you going to shoot, the bull or me?" he called out tauntingly as Antonio sheathed his gun. And again it seemed as if Juan was a pest who would not go away, always marching with him into his promised land, forever plaguing him, impudent, indestructible.

That night by the fire Juan taunted him in further ways: "This is not a land for the foreign born but for us who have the native skills it has taught us! The day will come when we will take what is rightfully ours! We shall populate these fertile valleys. You gachupins have held everything in your hands too long!" Antonio for once did not respond. He realized he'd reserved no place for Lopez in the community based on social justice he was imagining for his new land and the omission troubled him because he found himself feeling something like fondness for his old adversary.

Beyond present Los Angeles they followed the route of today's Highway 101 along the west side of the San Fernando Valley through Calabasas and Thousand Oaks. Mingling with the cowboys and Lopez, Antonio experienced the sensation which marked his later life—that of being among a herd of moving horns advancing into virgin grass, his only boundary the horizon. At times the gentle red ox who led the way at a steady pace would be so close he could rest his hand on the great horn nearest him. As he felt the horn rising and falling in his grasp, he sensed without actually knowing it that he was in touch with a force which extended back through ages of time, through farm lot, manor field, kraal, and steppe to those original wild cattle of Asia, Africa, and Europe now come like him to a new continent.

On reaching the Valley of the Rising Sun, they made camp near the spot behind the dunes where they'd camped two years earlier. Antonio was hoping the People of Olomosoug would come and greet them and when no one appeared, he wondered with foreboding what was keeping them away. Beyond the promontory where the mission was to stand he saw no sign of life in the direction of the village, and though it was perhaps due to his angle of vision, the dark head peak no longer seemed to extend welcoming arms. He resolved that in the morning he would investigate, but after supper Fages drew him aside and confided the secret news carried in the dispatches Ortega had handed him. Among them was a letter from the Viceroy ordering him to explore the Great Estuary immediately and find a route to Point Reyes without delay. The estuary was considered of such strategic importance that no public mention had been made of its discovery "lest our Russian or English enemies learn of it before we can take steps to occupy and fortify it. So we must move along smartly, my friend, and you will have to defer your sentimental reunion with your red-haired girl friend to another time!"

"But we promised these people we would return and repay their kindness," Antonio protested as if from reasons of policy. "Yet each time we pass we fail to keep our word, though we all agree a mission will stand here some day. What good will it do us to prepare against foreign enemies if we create hard feeling here where we live?" But Fages was adamant.

* * *

Leaving Lopez and Nunez and the cattle at Monterey under supervision of Sergeant Puig, Fages and Antonio hurried northward with a small party including Pablo and Father Crespi. This time they went all the way up the east side of the bay past the present site of the University of California where they camped overnight and got a fine view of the sunset through Golden Gate. Next day they reached the narrows at Carquinez Strait where the bay draws to a head. Unable to cross for lack of a boat they turned inland along the bank of what appeared to be a giant river entering the estuary from the east. In reality of course it was two rivers coming together, the Sacramento and San Joaquin. Tasting its water they found it fresh and Crespi christened it the River of San Francisco because it flowed into the estuary connected to the harbor by that name.

Continuing eastward along the foot of Mount Diablo past the present sites of Martinez and Antioch, they entered a marshy valley of enormous dimensions stretching north and south farther than they could see. It was Fages, the explorer, who cried out: "Look there, ahead!"

What they had thought a line of white clouds across the eastern horizon was in fact the summit of a gigantic snowcapped mountain range which resembled the Pyrenees though far larger in scale. They were looking at the Sierra Nevada and their eyes were the first Europeans' to see it.

Defeated again in their attempt to reach Point Reyes, they returned to Monterey, where Fages prepared to deal with their two troublemakers. "I'll put Lopez in command of the guard at the new mission which Serra in his blind zeal is forcing me to establish in your Valley of Santa Lucia, and keep that burly rogue Nunez and his wandering eye here under mine!"

"I don't see the logic in making Lopez corporal of the guard at the new mission," Antonio argued, secretly miffed at not being assigned to the post himself. Here was his chance to achieve his long-held desire.

"Very simple," Fages replied firmly, outwardly oblivious to Antonio's desire. "Serra is forcing me to establish an outpost which should never be established under our straitened circumstances. A disastrous failure will be no fault of mine, as I shall make clear, and it may expose these Franciscans for what they are—for what I've presented them to the Viceroy to be—Jesuits at heart who wish all power for themselves and their pets like Lopez and Rubio. Haven't they consistently defended their precious Juan against me, as witness Paterna at San Diego? Now let them live with him! No friend of mine will be involved! While we keep a sharp eye on Nunez here! Once a deserter, always a deserter, is my rule of thumb!''

Establishing the mission, as we have seen, and leaving Lopez and Rubio there, they escorted Serra to San Diego and watched him sail away to Mexico where he would do all in his power to discredit Fages, and then circling back by inland routes, searching for deserters, they became the first white men to enter the southern end of the great San Joaquin Valley.

Standing in Tejon Pass where the Sierras join the Coast Range, they looked down upon an unexplored wonderland of marshes, lakes, rivers, grassy plains gleaming in the still November sunlight, teeming with elk, antelope, wildfowl. And more than ever it seemed to Antonio that a race of giants was needed to befit such a mighty land, free people, new, unfettered, and more than ever he longed to identify with it, if he could but find the right mate.

Descending the pass they came to the shore of a lake surrounded by a labyrinth of reeds and marshes not far from the present site of Bakersfield. There they discovered a large settlement populated by a handsome race of exceptional stature and grace who welcomed them warmly. These Southern Valley Yokuts lived in houses made of tules arranged in squares like city blocks and beside each, built upon poles, was a spherical storehouse containing kernels of wild rice, bulbs, the eggs of turtles and wildfowl, and dried cattails.

After the usual exchange of gifts, the Yokuts informed them they were not the first white men to appear there. Others had come from time to time. This convinced Fages he was on the trail of deserters and he pressed for more information. A white man, the Indians said, had married one of their women and was living not far away. But when they undertook to lead them to him he could not, whether by accident or design, be found in the maze of reeds and treacherous marshes.

''At least we know where they hide!'' exclaimed Fages grimly, ''and in these tulares a whole army of them could disappear and not be found!''

But the Tulamni, as the Yokuts called themselves, were familiar with the people of the coast and in particular, Antonio learned with surprise, those of his valley whom they called Tokya and with whom they'd had warfare. They exhibited two withered hands as trophies of victory, causing him renewed concern for Lospe and her people. "The longer I was prevented from returning, the more I thought of her place as mine." And his hopes rose as the Tulamni spoke of a trail which would lead them toward the coast.

Turning westward as the Tulamni directed, they crossed a low range and came to a desert-like plain out of which rose a solitary rock the size of a castle and in the side of the rock was a large oval opening into which they rode. A strangely mysterious atmosphere hung about this lonely place. It was as if some ineffable essence of Owotoponus' magic air shots, of the great victory led by Ta-apu, of Tinaquaic's ill-fated adventure in search of self-realization, of Kahip's tragic hopes lingered there, as perhaps they did.

Inside the rock the explorers found themselves in an amphitheater of stone, its walls decorated with paintings of extraordinary color and design such as they had never seen. They were looking at an aspect of the lavish, even passionate use of color and line by native Americans and preeminently the Inland Chumash of whom Lospe's people were part, and Owotoponus' talent a prime example. Though unintelligible to Fages and Antonio, the paintings nevertheless conveyed a powerful sense of artistry and imaginative reach. They were in fact visualizations of those supernatural forces which in the Indian mind governed the universe. They also constituted a kind of planetarium or star map on which were recorded not only sun, moon, prominent planets, and constellations like the Pleiades and Scorpio but historical phenomena such as Halley's Comet, eclipses, and explosive supernovas of past ages.

"It must be a place of great importance," Antonio commented, "a natural church, perhaps, and these are its stained glass windows. Do you feel the power in that stone?"

The usually matter-of-fact Fages agreed. "My skin prickles with superstition! These," pointing to the fantasic paintings of whirling red and yellow sun discs, dark crescent moons, fiery comets, and strangely misshapen figures of polychrome animals, birds, reptiles, and still other creatures of inhuman and yet human appearance, "are no doubt their sacred idols." They dubbed it The Painted Rock and scratched their names and the date beside one of the paintings.

This great journey of discovery was exciting Antonio by enlarging the outlines of his new land and his experience upon it, and he hoped it was bringing him nearer his heart's desire. Pushing westward, they soon began to sense the presence of the sea in the increased moisture of air and density of vegetation and two evenings later were sitting to table inside the stockade at Mission San Luis Obispo with the Catalan fathers Cavaller and Juncosa.

"What news do you bring us, Don Pedro?" the friars eagerly asked Fages, their countryman, of whom they were very fond.

"Brothers, I've been forty days in a wilderness," he responded jocosely, blossoming under their warmth. "It is you who must tell me things! The mail couriers have been passing. What news do they bring? Is your Father President returned from Mexico City bringing my promotion—and his blessing?"

"If it be God's will miracles may happen!" They smiled, understanding his true meaning. While too loyal to Serra to speak openly against him, Cavaller and Juncosa sided with their countryman in his controversy with the Franciscan hierarchy. Thus within the religious establishment there was a division between the Majorcan clique—Serra, Crespi, Palou, Rubio, and others who controlled—and the non-Majorcans who must do their bidding. Yes, there had been difficulties at Mission Santa Lucia. Brother Rubio, alas, zealous but not overly strong, was having trouble with his soldiers. There was a serious food shortage. An evil witchdoctor was causing dissension at a neighboring village and some of its inhabitants had sought refuge at the mission.

But when Antonio suggested it might be wise to investigate, Fages flared up: "No, let him stew in his own juice! It's no brew of mine! And let Lopez stew with him! When they've mired themselves inextricably, as Juan did in the tar bog, so all may see whose fault it is, then will be time enough to extricate them!" Antonio still did not agree but there was nothing more he could say.

"I'd almost swear," observed Fages looking at him with a twinkle, "that there was some hidden reason for your wanting us to retrace our steps all that way!" And Antonio was obliged to blush.

Back at Monterey they found more bad news. The burly malcontent of San Diego, Nunez, and two other disgruntled Leather Jackets had stolen mules the night before, one of them Antonio's speedy Diablo whom he'd left behind to recuperate from a strained foreleg, and disappeared. Sergeant Puig, feeling undermanned, had not organized a pursuit.

Promoting him corporal, Fages dispatched Antonio with five Catalans, including the crack marksman Malaret, on the trail of the runaways. They followed the tracks eastward from the grazing lands at the present site of Salinas over the hills along the new route toward the Great Estuary. Antonio was thoroughly familiar with it after two explorations but soon saw that the fugitives were not, for they wasted time in useless detours until at last they hit upon the East Pass, later Pacheco's Pass, leading to the interior valley and tulares.

Close behind now, as he could tell by the fresh earth thrown up by their hoofprints and not yet dried, Antonio and his men caught sight of them at a distance in that long grassy apron which descends to the floor of the San Joaquin Valley near the present site of San Luis Reservoir.

Spurring their horses they raced down the slope but the deserters took alarm and spurred their mules too. They had chosen to steal mules which in the long run would prove hardier and better keepers than horses but in a short run were at disadvantage.

The race continued across the plain toward the River of San Francisco as Crespi named it, later the San Joaquin, where a dense growth of willows and cottonwoods promised refuge. The pursuers gained steadily. But dusk was falling and the haven along the river loomed near. Urging their mounts to a final effort, the Catalans came within gunshot and Antonio called upon the fugitives to stop and surrender in the name of the king or be fired upon. The two rearmost halted but the burly figure of Nunez on Diablo held on.

Antonio reached a bitter decision. "Wing the mule!" he ordered Malaret.

The long-barreled Ripoll musket made in their Pyrenees foothills spoke and Diablo's hindquarters crumpled. Nunez, pitching headlong, recovered quickly, and as the mule lay struggling, snatched his musket and fired from behind its back, the ball whistling close to Antonio's head. Deploying his men with an oath Antonio moved to outflank his adversary, but taking advantage of the momentary delay, Nunez darted into the undergrowth and disappeared.

They searched in vain that evening and next morning. No trace of him could be found in the reeds and marshes. Finally deciding he might have drowned or been sucked into a mire, they abandoned the hunt and returned to Monterey with their prisoners, leaving Diablo behind with a ball through his head.

For that reason and others, the homeward journey was far from a happy one for Antonio. True he'd discharged his first mission as corporal creditably. He had even sacrificed his mule in hopes of taking Nunez alive as ordered. But a sense of impending doom which centered about Fages and by association himself rested upon him heavily. How could they go on like this with men deserting right and left and the powerful Franciscan hierarchy working against them? And his rising desire to be united with Lospe remained as frustrated as ever.

Chapter Twenty-four

Serra disliked writing but I always enjoyed it,'' Father Rubio continued his narrative of his mission experiences, ''and I began to enlarge my diary into a full record of events which I hoped might form the basis for an archive. I also began my dictionary in the native tongue, thinking one day to translate the catechism into it. Under my Junipero's tutelage, I learned rapidly. He would point to something, pronounce its name, and I would say it after him and write down the word just as it sounded. Thus 'head' became *chilipi,* 'knee' *mogomel,* and so on. I must confess I never heard so many scrambled consonants or glottal stops! Similarly I taught him Castilian which he learned quickly and could soon speak nearly as fluently as I.

"On the day following his baptism my convert returned with two old widows, infirm but ambulatory, who brought me acorn meal and a few pine nuts which were a welcome addition to my diet.

"As we stood before the Holy Cross and I explained how Christ had died for their salvation, they were both deeply moved and asked to be baptized. I gave them some brown sugar and named them Maria and Marta.

"With the assistance of my two Christian Indian laborers and Junipero, they began to build themselves a conical-shaped thatched hut just outside the gate of the stockade and thus our little colony of converts began. How we should have survived without their help, I don't know. Our remaining food was almost totally consumed but they brought us theirs and showed us how to forage for bulbs and roots, and I received these gifts joyously, remembering how Jesus and his disciples and Francis and his, lived by the charity of others, exchanging things of the spirit for those of the flesh.

Robert Easton

"I was from the first, of course, eager to visit their rancheria but to do so was forbidden all of us except in cases of extreme emergency such as soldiers in pursuit of criminals or runaways, and in any event I did not wish to appear with a military escort or seem too forward in any way lest I discourage their coming to me freely, as we should always come to God. From them I learned the chief reason their people hesitated to visit us was fear. From informants up and down the coast, they heard how our soldiers, feeling themselves secure, had become arrogant and no longer respected women and property but raped and stole at will; and none of the native leaders came to see me now because of bitter discord in their village where a powerful witchdoctor who hated and feared us was attempting to assert authority over their chieftainess of legendary fame.

"Daily I instructed my little flock in the blessed doctrine, my heart lifting as their voices sang with mine each morning at first light

> Here comes the dawn,
> Making way for the day!
> Let us all say
> Hail, Mary!

"Then one day a very elderly woman, white haired, barely able to walk, appeared. The others welcomed her with great veneration, explaining she was the wife of a highly respected former chief, mother of their present one, the fabled red-haired queen. With Junipero interpreting, the old lady informed me there had long been a tradition among her people that white men would come and be their benefactors, and before she died she wished to see me and embrace our faith in which she believed lay much power. Her name was Seneq. I baptized her with the water of their sacred river and gave her the Christian name of Engracia, signifying she had, through faith, received grace at last. With sprightly independence she said that conditions at her rancheria were such that she no longer wished to live there and accordingly took up her abode with the old widows and Junipero.

"As the spring wore on, she was followed by others. One was a woodworker named Wima much interested in our methods of construction, a skilled cabinet- and bowl-maker, quick to learn, as indeed they all were, easily repeating after us all we said and not forgetting it either. More houses were erected and our village grew. And as I went about my work, sometimes I astonished my flock by bursting out singing with joy. I felt my cup running over. Sometimes I seized two sticks and scraped them together in imitation of a violin, and did a little dance, while the Indians said among themselves: 'He has the Sacred Madness! He must be respected!'

"And then one evening while I was at prayer Junipero brought to my room our most unusual visitor so far. She was a girl of thirteen or fourteen, slim, beautifully formed, eyes large and intelligent, hair bright red, bearing regal, but with no more covering over her upper body than they usually wore so that I was obliged from modesty to look at the ceiling while addressing her lest the Devil intervene between us. Junipero explained she was the daughter of the chieftainess of his village, the legendary Queen Calafia, and had come to us in distress to seek refuge. My heart leaped. If we'd caught the daughter, the mother might follow, then the entire community!

" 'Come forward my child and do not be afraid,' I said kindly.

"When she advanced into the light of the candle burning on my priedieu, she showed no fear whatsoever but looked at me boldly as if appraising an equal. Sensing her fearlessness and strength, my immediate thought was that the Blue Lady had sent us our first little Indian nun, for just as Saint Clare, Francis' first female disciple, a beautiful young creature like this, had come from a fine aristocratic house, leaving behind the privileges and pleasures of this world for eternal life in the next, so perhaps this princess had emerged from her brushwood palace to embrace the life of the spirit!

"Now she was looking at me beseechingly like a child in need. Her voice was harsh and guttural as they all were.

" 'She says she's in great danger,' Junipero translated, 'and that you are too! They are plotting to kill you!' "

"Why should her people want to kill me?" Father Rubio asked. "What has happened?" Junipero in turn put his question to the girl who was standing before them in the candlelight.

"The wicked sorcerer who rules my people regards you as the heart of the power that keeps the soldiers here," Lospe replied. "When you are dead, the others will go away, he believes, and the mission fall into ruins and things be again as they were." And Junipero faithfully translated word for word.

Rubio fought down a feeling of dread. "Was I to blame?

Where had I fallen short? How would Serra have handled the matter?" he asked himself. "In my innocence I thought I was establishing good relations with her village, from where so many before her had come to us, though I had never visited it, preferring that its inhabitants come voluntarily to me as customary.

" 'You say *he*,' I asked the girl. 'Is not your ruler your mother?' She shook her head fiercely and explained in bitter tone the usurpation which had taken place. 'Many, my mother among them, want you to remain,' she concluded, 'but they are afraid He Who Oppresses Us will destroy them if they speak out. They want to come to you. They want you to come to them. But they are helpless!'

"As Junipero finished interpreting her words, all uncertainty left me, for I saw how, like the blessed Saint Francis so often vilified, I might become a means of establishing love where there was hatred, harmony where there was discord. I remembered how our first brethren were reviled, robbed, stripped naked, whipped, and martyred for the very reason I was now standing in this very room in this very valley, namely the Love of Our Lord Jesus Christ; and I remembered how, gradually, as they persisted, never resisting, suffering all things gladly, the feeling against them reversed itself, and where they had been reviled, they were revered—and by the same people, too! Might I not do likewise? Or were all such examples to be mere words for books or lips to repeat?

" 'I shall go to your village,' I said, 'and let your people see I mean them no harm. By God's grace I shall heal the breach that has opened among them and thus bring them all to our fold!'

"When the girl understood what I said, I saw by her eyes God had inspired me with correct thought. Yet I also sensed carnal danger. Her look was so openly grateful and loving that a shameful flush tried to creep into my face. Junipero protested: 'They may kill you!'

" 'They will not kill me!' I assured him. 'Now you must take this child back the way you brought her'—he had easily parted the loose poles in the stockade wall away from the mounted sentry patrolling outside—'and make her comfortable with old Engracia who you say is her grandmother in the hut near the gate. Tell her not to fear. God is her protector now!'

"She looked at me with sweet gratitude. Then her expression changed abruptly and she spoke grimly. 'She is afraid the wicked sorcerer whose power is very great will pursue her even here and harm her,' Junipero explained.

"Instinctively putting my hand out in a gesture of protection and turning my eyes full upon her, thinking I'd never seen a creature so fresh or so lovely, asking the Lord to forgive me, I touched her bright red hair. 'Do not fear! You will be safe with me!'

"A feeling of tender joy such as I had never known ran from my fingertips into my heart, and as if to mock me I heard the soldiers' ribald laughter from their hut above the sound of Lopez's impudent fiddle.

"'Warn her to avoid the soldiers!' I instructed Junipero.

Rubio had never known passionate love of woman in the flesh, or felt the tender adoration of a daughter. What stirred in him after Lospe left him seemed both. Was the feeling sacred or profane? He was tempted to rush to the river and immerse himself naked in its cold water "following the example of blessed Saint Francis in the snow at his lofty hermitage near Chiusi, thus rigorously disciplining 'Brother Ass,' as he termed his body." But somehow it seemed sacrilegious to do so, degrading by implication an innocent child who'd come to him for protection, sullying by gross implication what ought to be pure and holy.

"As for going in person to her village, I had no doubt. I must do so. I must do it at once and alone. If not, those conspiring against me would, sure that the girl had warned me, think me afraid. She'd said as much. 'They think you are hiding behind your wooden walls because you fear them!' But if I went to them boldly and alone with only God's help, they might think me come in wrath to punish them and so great was my power I did not need even one soldier to protect me; and when they discovered I came in peace and forgiveness, their relief would be so great their hearts would be opened and they would be changed, while at the same time those who favored me would be encouraged; and thus finally all might be united and brought to our fold. I slept fitfully that night, waking often to pray for strength.

"'You must have a military escort as regulations require!' Lopez informed me next morning when I disclosed my purpose, 'Otherwise you may be harmed.'"

It was that critical moment which often intervenes between resolution and action. Rubio was tempted to give way. Who was he to break regulations? Who was he to go alone to a hostile village and meet there with Brother Hatred, possibly Brother Violence, perhaps even Brother Death? But then he remembered his resolution taken months before when Fages cautioned him in similar terms and he asked himself if Francis or Jesus ever sought the protection of soldiers or stockades, and now once again the answer came clearly: "No, only of God!" Yes, the walls must go down! He must break through to his goal, the sheep he had come to gather!

Summoning all his resolution he replied: "Corporal, I shall not be harmed and I shall not need an escort!" And the moment he said it he felt unlimited strength.

Lopez was greatly amazed. "But the Governor has given orders! So has the Viceroy! Not even the Father President may leave a mission without escort!"

"So have I been given orders!" Rubio raised his crucifix and held it toward him, and for a moment they gazed into each other's eyes. Then Lopez subsided, grumbling that he wanted his men to witness how Rubio had overridden his objections, that he was not responsible for what might happen to him. And then he grew argumentative. "Isn't this the very thing which causes the worst disagreements between soldiers and missionaries? that makes the Governor complain to the Viceroy how you religious undermine his authority? as you yourself have told me? Isn't it the chief reason your revered President Serra is in Mexico City at this very moment seeking redresses?" Lopez had an incorrigible way of penetrating to the heart of matters, as Rubio noted.

"What you say may be true," he replied mildly, not wishing to continue the debate, "but now let me tell you what is going to happen today as God and Our Blue Lady have vouchsafed to reveal it to me."

When he disclosed his plan fully, Lopez exclaimed: "At least ride a mule! Next to a gun, they fear the mule most!"

"A gun!" Rubio snorted. "Again, the gun! Are all our actions to be measured by the gun or some other instrument of intimidation, such as a long-eared mule? Is love never to have its way?" Lopez was silenced. "I shall go afoot," Rubio repeated, "and Junipero shall guide me!"

Chapter Twenty-five

When Fages received one of Rubio's letters of complaint he would chuckle derisively: "Serves the little Majorcan right if the mestizo corporal gives him fits! These religious must learn it's the military, not they, who run things!"

Then late one afternoon the couriers from Loreto, travel stained and weary after the 1400 miles to Monterey, brought him a letter of another kind. After reading he grew thoughtful. Next morning he summoned Antonio to his quarters in the west or seaward wing of the presidio.

By one of those strange coincidences, a few days earlier while rummaging through his belongings to find something trade to Indians for food—hunger was once again acute—Antonio came across the tongueless silver buckle Lospe had given him. Each time he saw it, it brought back with a little pang the thought of her tender sweetness and the trusting touch of her hand, and his dream of the beautiful valley. But this time a sudden new impulse seized him.

Carrying the buckle across the parade ground to the shop of Tony Murillo the blacksmith, he asked: "Tony, can you make me a tongue for this?"

"Here we are suffering the greatest hunger ever," the broad-shouldered smith exploded, "reduced to subsisting on milk and herbs salted with tears of longing for something better to eat—no bread, no chocolate, no sugar—and you importune me with an old broken buckle! Now, if you'd handed me a fat goose . . ." But he was intrigued. "This looks like fine Zacatecas silver," he commented approvingly, "where did you get it?"

Antonio explained. "Maybe it belonged to one of our early conquistadors in New Mexico, to Coronado himself."

Impressed, the blacksmith shrugged. "I have nothing to match it! I'm a blacksmith, not a silversmith!"

"Oh, the ship is coming, Tony, you know that, and then you will be busy as a beaver. Now, in your spare time," handing him a little tobacco, "why not have some fun with something precious? Do the best you can, eh? An iron nail maybe?"

Forty-eight hours later Murillo had contrived a tongue for the buckle from the steel of a broken awl. When Antonio expressed wonder and admiration, the smith replied simply: "Steel is better than silver. Without good steel, our silver is worthless. Isn't that what our feisty little Governor is always telling us? even though his days are numbered?"

Next morning when Fages called him in Antonio saw at a glance he was seriously troubled yet heard him say almost lightheartedly as if he did not really care: "I am to be replaced. Serra and his friends have done for me, Skinny. I shall be returning to Mexico with all my men. Rivera will succeed me. And it may be better for you, my countryman, to return to Mexico with me!" His eyes leveled with Antonio's as he faced the hard truth and he grimaced a little at thought of the man he detested supplanting him. "Our Country Cousin has no love for you, either!"

Four oppressive years of conflict with Rivera and Lopez came flooding over Antonio and threatened to submerge him too. But after the first shock of dismay he took heart from Fages' cheerful grimace. His friend, for such he was now, hard beset, was still game. Perhaps it was that gameness that decided Antonio. If Fages was not giving up, why should he? And then the idea came. "I'm nominally still one of Rivera's men. Haven't I a right to stay here then?"

Fages looked at him quizzically. "You still want to be a Californian, after all you've suffered in this godforsaken land of hunger and desertion?" He placed a forefinger alongside his prominent nose, tapped twice and smiled, shaking his head disbelievingly. "Yet to be truthful I feel the same. Haven't I too pounded the saddle thousands of miles over her lovely landscape? Haven't my sweat and hopes gone into her? I'll be back! You can count on it!" He stuck out his chin and said jauntily: "Fortune's wheel may take another turn, my countryman, for you as well as me! But meanwhile, where would you hang your hat?"

"Why not Mission Santa Lucia?"

"What do you mean?" exclaimed Fages in astonishment.

"Why not?"

"Replacing Lopez?" Fages stared as the idea sank in. Then a

delighted smile broke over his face. "Yes, why not? Rivera is coming overland from Old California to assume command here. Thus he is bound to stop at Santa Lucia. There he will hear from Juan that I have mistreated him, which is false, that I have exiled him, which is true. What will our Country Cousin's reaction be?" He frowned a moment, then found an answer. "He will be angry that his pet has been abused. He will wish to retaliate. But he will not dare be too severe for the same reason I've not been overly hard upon his men. I have demoted none of them, you notice? Even with deserters I've been more lenient than I should. For who knows when, as now, situations may be reversed and my men come under his command, or his again under mine ... Yes, and there is further reason to expect mildness. Serra who's made him what he is will be watching his conduct closely. He will wish to appear benevolent, deserving. He will, however, wish to retaliate in some way. And against a favorite of mine ..." He looked sharply at Antonio. "Is your mind made up?"

"Yes."

"Good boy! Then let us wait, while I think ... Meanwhile," he added mischievously, "there's another alternative. The Viceroy's letter informs me that married men and those about to be married may remain here ... So if you would care to find yourself a bride? Such as that little princess of your adored valley? Your countrymen have shown you the way, haven't they?" Indeed they had. Nearly a year before, Yorba of Barcelona, Arus of Gerona, and Butron of Valencia had become the first whites to marry California Indian girls, the rites solemnized in the mission church at Carmel where Serra and Crespi had long since moved Mission San Carlos to get their converts away from the attentions of presidio soldiers and to find better water and farming land; and on what he proclaimed grandiloquently as "a historic occasion truly uniting California and Catalonia!" Fages stood godfather to all three. Then carried away by his own rhetoric, the fiery Catalan asserted: "You are giving substance to the fancies of the romancers who told us centuries ago about beautiful women of dusky hue who inhabited this wondrous land of California, and in their tales married them to princes of white blood!"

The three bridegrooms were now living contentedly in a little colony of their own houses outside the mission stockade, the very first settlement of its kind in the province. But Antonio stoutly denied any such intention though in fact he found it exemplary.

"I just like that valley, Don Pedro. It feels like home. You know what I mean?"

"Yes," said Fages laughing outright. "I know what you mean! She's worth a little trouble. Such glorious hair, oh my! Not to mention other attributes! I wonder how she looks without charcoal on her face? But let me think. Maybe we shall put one over yet on those two scoundrels, Lopez and Rivera!"

Chapter Twenty-six

Paralyzing fear crept up in Rubio as he and Junipero approached the village at the base of its chalky hillside. A band of armed men had suddenly appeared upon their right about a bowshot distant. Keeping them always upon their left or bow side, this menacing group matched paces with them watchfully, and Rubio wondered if he possessed the courage to welcome an arrow into his flesh—Brother Arrow, as Saint Francis might have called it. And the thought of the saint gave him such joy he felt exalted beyond fear.

"Who are they?" he asked.

"They are those who hate you and adhere to the sorcerer who is your enemy!" Junipero's voice trembled.

As soon as he learned of Lospe's flight, Owotoponus dispatched these bowmen to keep an eye on the mission and give warning of any approach by the A-alowow, and he raged at Koyo: "Are you so foolish as to think your daughter can escape me?" But she held firm in her new resolve and replied calmly: "My daughter is protected by a power stronger than yours!"

As Rubio and Junipero drew nearer the village, a much larger group, wholly unarmed, came joyfully to greet them, crowding around in welcome, touching Rubio's robe with wonder, exclaiming with delight over Junipero's tunic and loin cloth.

"Where is the sorcerer?" Rubio whispered.

"Who knows!" Junipero looked around fearfully as if Owotoponus might spring from the earth by magic. "All is confusion as you see!"

"And their chieftainess?"

Junipero shrugged. All was confusion indeed. Owotoponus at that moment was saying sardonically to Koyo: "Our little friend is coming as I predicted. This is the moment for you to prepare the poisoned cake!"

"I shall not prepare it!" she retorted defiantly.

"Do you wish to continue to live?" But she detected that trace of uncertainty in his voice.

"It is your own safety you should be thinking about," she rejoined, "for the little man is coming to take vengeance upon you for your wickedness!"

"Then I shall prepare it myself!" He touched the sorcerer's bag he wore strapped to his upper leg containing the powder of the death camas and the ground bones of rattlesnakes.

"If you do I shall tell him!"

While they were clashing in this fashion the people surrounding Rubio and Junipero were moving forward with them as if by common consent until they reached the plaza near the house where the two were talking. Glancing out the window and seeing them approaching like a massive retributive force, panic for the moment overcame Owotoponus and he rushed away, leaving Koyo disbelieving, yet filled with hope. With a prayer of thanksgiving she hurried to join those who were welcoming Rubio.

"What happens now?" he whispered to Junipero as the crowd stood back and looked at him expectantly.

"They expect a demonstration of your magic power, as was performed here years ago by the soldier of the First Expedition!"

Rubio had often heard the story of how Antonio thrust his sword into the ground to form a cross and terrified everyone by having Pablo fire a shot into the air, telling them it was the voice of God. "And the recollection," as he said, "of this transgression inspired me now with quite a different idea, thanks to Saint Lucy!"

Raising both arms high he waited until everyone fell silent. Then clasping his crucifix in both hands, he sank to his knees and began to say the Lord's Prayer in Chumash, Junipero participating at his request, it being among the first things he'd learned from his convert and in turn taught him. *"Dios cascoco upalequen Alaipai quia-enicho opte; paquinini juch quique etchuet cataug itimi tiup caneche Alaipai . . ."*

When the Indians heard Rubio speaking reverently in their own tongue, gasps of astonishment broke from them. He seemed magically inspired, and as he continued, first a few, then many, began to repeat after him and Junipero: *"Ulamugo ila ulalisagua piquiyup quinsceaniyup uqui amog canequi que quisagiu sucuta-*

najun utiagmayiup oyup quie uti leg uleypo stequiyup il auteyup. Amen."

Then the little priest rose, joy rising in him too for it seemed his faith had been justified, and made the sign of the cross over them while murmurs of wonder and admiration arose on every side.

Witnessing all this, Owotoponus, who'd hidden in the sacred ravine in his moment of panic, gathered himself with the courage of desperation. But before he could act, Koyo stepped forward. "Auburn haired, rather more handsome than beautiful, not of impressive stature, I knew her instantly by her commanding presence," Rubio wrote. "Stripped of all the absurd trappings of romance, I saw this legendary queen as she truly was, a bereaved wife and mother, a leader struggling against difficulties which threatened to overwhelm her."

Koyo spoke in subdued yet forthright tones, her old serenity returning: "As we all see, the white men have kept their promise. They have come back in peace bringing good tidings. Let us rejoice!" She didn't even glance at Rubio but the unspoken understanding passed between them that Lospe had delivered her warning to him and was safe at the mission.

Before she could say more, Rubio became aware of the impressive figure of Owotoponus approaching from the declivity beyond the plaza. "Even without Junipero's whisper I should have recognized him instantly. He stood nearly six feet tall, was remarkably well endowed with the organs of manhood, and came forward authoritatively as if just arriving from some important business elsewhere.

"Adroitly he tried to turn the tables on me. Addressing me through Junipero he complained that my visit was long overdue, that I seemed to them to be hiding fearfully behind the walls of my stockade, but now that I had at last emerged they welcomed me wholeheartedly, were honored greatly, a feast of friendship had been hastily prepared of choice food and drink of which I must partake. He hoped, I surmised afterward, his consort might have relented and placed poison in a cake as he'd ordered, or that I might, believing it poisoned, show fear and discredit myself in the eyes of everyone by refusing to eat it.

"Through clever speaking he assumed charge and now led me, she following, to a commodious dwelling adjacent to the meeting place where he ordered her to serve me food. Without a word she offered me a single freshly prepared cake resting in the center of a basketry tray of great beauty. And without a word I accepted it, knowing it might be poisoned yet having faith it wasn't. Even now I had no certainty, only faith... Nagging at me was the fearful doubt that everything I was doing might be an enormous presumption, each step leading me toward disaster. I summoned all my will for purity of thought, so that my vision of the right course might be maintained. And as I unwaveringly took the bread and broke it I thought of it as the Body of Our Lord which was given to me so that I might have everlasting life."

But what followed was even more extraordinary.

"Raising my crucifix I blessed her household. Tears came to the good woman's eyes. As she started to kneel to thank me, I did so more quickly and kissed her feet, inviting her to visit my house, she much taken aback. Then turning to the naked Judas at my elbow, I, even as our Lord, embraced and with forgiveness in my heart kissed him on both cheeks, saying: 'You too visit my house!' And he also was utterly taken aback and rendered speechless."

Even so Rubio's walls did not quite come down, for though many accompanied him to the mission, many, including Owotoponus and Koyo, did not. Her spirit renewed, Koyo decided to remain in the village. She felt unwilling to abandon the field to Owotoponus and determined to contend against him for the sake of her people and the rights of her children to succeed her.

"Nevertheless," as Rubio wrote, "there followed a golden time and we began to build our New Jerusalem."

Chapter Twenty-seven

Day after day Asuskwa lived alone in his hiding place in the dense reeds by the edge of the marsh waiting for Sacred Condor to show him what he must do next. From time to time he took his magic stone from its pouch and rubbed it reverently, while focusing all his thoughts on what he hoped to achieve. Somehow he must find a way to destroy Owotoponus not only in body but in spirit. At such times he often thought of the white men who invaded his valley, particularly the tall one with the blue eyes and yellow hair who had stood so close he could smell his nauseating odor, and after laughing and dissembling in such friendly fashion, terrified everyone with the thunder and lightning from the firestick of his black companion.

Thinking also of the silver buckle his sister had given the invader, Asuskwa felt he'd known Antonio all his life and always hated him. Almost alone from that first day of the A-alowow's coming he'd recognized their overwhelmingly destructive power, a power which might prove greater even than Owotoponus'. And as he thought about this now, a completely new idea entered his mind. If he could somehow acquire the power of the white men, might he not use it to destroy that of Owotoponus and dissipate it permanently, so it could not simply assume another form and continue its evil influence?

The idea seemed a revelation. It seemed the sign from Sacred Condor for which he had been waiting.

But how could he, a fugitive in a foreign land, a hunted outcast, acquire the white men's terrible magic? It seemed utterly impossible.

He seldom ventured far from the hiding place in the reeds which had been shown him in his dream. He dared not light a fire which might reveal his presence but subsisted on raw bulbs, roots, and cattails, minnows, turtles, and birds' eggs, and as the lonely days went by he became intimately acquainted with the life of the marsh around him—the green-winged mother teal who each morning came paddling close to the bank looking for shoots of grass to eat with six tiny yellow ducklings following her, the brown weasel who slunk by him hungrily eyeing the ducks, the red-winged blackbirds who balanced precariously on the reeds above his head burbling their spring song of oblivious delight, and particularly the young doe who came down as warily as a shy girl each evening from the neighboring grassland to drink. She awoke his tenderness as he watched her advance a step at a time, looking this way and that, testing the air with her little black nose. She was a hunted creature like himself, afraid for her life. When he watched her drink, lowering her head momentarily for a sip just as he did, raising it quickly for a look about, as he did, he realized how much alike they were. His heart went out to her and when she stole silently away he felt lonelier than before.

He began to anticipate the doe's coming, to wait for her as for a person, and to observe with pleasure her lithe graceful movements, delicate testings of the air with that moist black nose, quick, nervous switchings of her tail across her delicate white rump. If he spoke to her, it seemed she would answer, and he began to wish that some actual connection might be established between them.

The one day he sensed a strange new presence. The mother teal paddled hurriedly away into hiding with a warning note to her children to do likewise. The red-winged blackbirds above his head fell suddenly silent, then exploded into noisy flight.

After Nunez escaped Antonio's posse by hiding in the dense growth along the river, he made his way warily southward down the Great Valley toward the marshlands which were becoming known as a refuge for deserters. Like Asuskwa he dared not light a fire and dared not use his gun to kill game for fear of attracting attention. Some Indians of the valley were friendly, he'd heard, others hostile, but he could afford no chances. Traveling by twilight, subsisting like Asuskwa on bulbs, roots, lizards, turtles, birds' eggs, bulrushes which he gnawed hungrily, berries, rose hips, he went slowly along, growing daily weaker from ravenous hunger, more desperate for solid food, until he decided that if he did not eat meat soon he would become too weak to travel and must risk a shot. He'd seen antelope, deer, and elk at a distance but never within range. Crawling into a dense thicket of tall reeds where a trail led to water from the neighboring grassland, he waited in ambush.

Asuskwa could almost have reached out and touched him. Trembling inwardly from excitement for he knew immediately this was the opportunity Sacred Condor had sent him, Asuskwa nevertheless held himself motionless, every sense, every muscle alert, watching, waiting, observing everything, while the white man with the blue eyes and offensive odor began to do something to his firestick.

Nunez was reloading his bell-mouthed trabuco or carbine blunderbuss. First removing a paper cartridge from the leather case at his belt, he bit off the paper at the bottom, poured a little powder into the firing pan and—as Asuskwa's eyes remained fastened on him but narrowed, so as to diminish their impact lest they alert the other by their intensity—as Asuskwa watched he placed the butt of the weapon on the ground, where a ray of sunlight struck the initial "N" composed of brass nails embedded in the stock and made it gleam suddenly. Then Nunez poured the remaining powder into the muzzle and rammed paper and ball down upon it with the iron rammer attached to the barrel. Then he examined the piece of flint held by the jaws of the cock, as Asuskwa had seen Pablo examine his before firing that shot which so terrified everyone, and finally he pulled back the cock with his thumb as Pablo had done, and waited. They waited together a long time a few feet apart.

Asuskwa saw it all in his mind before it happened. He knew this vision was the waking dream Sacred Condor had sent. Great joy and confidence rose in him, along with great sorrow and bitter revulsion at what he so clearly foresaw. When the young doe came warily down to the water for her evening drink, she came a step at a time as if sensing danger. Once she stopped and seemed on the point of turning back, and he found himself hoping she would turn back, but on she came, a thing of such beauty she made his heart ache, and as she lowered her head warily to drink, Nunez raised his gun and fired. The sound deafened Asuskwa but did not frighten or deter him.

As the Spaniard bent over the body of the dead doe, a red arrow buried itself between his shoulder blades. With a gasping intake of breath that was like a sob, he flung up both arms and fell face downward over the body of his victim.

Moving rapidly, Asuskwa removed his arrow, breathed a silent prayer to the deer spirit, then undid the belt with its attached cartridge box, noting with dissatisfaction it had a buckle such as his father had brought from Muwu long ago and his sister had cherished and given to the young white man with the yellow hair, and then at last he picked up the heavy gun.

He knew instantly with a surge of fierce delight that he now held in his hand the power that was greater than Owotoponus'. He felt himself rising to meet his destiny, however difficult it might be. With the help of Sacred Condor he might now return and destroy the hated tyrant who caused his father's death, and would cause his if he could, while shaming his mother and enslaving his people.

Carrying his gun and wearing his cartridge belt, he quickly made his way to a new hiding place lest the Tulamni be attracted by the shot. That night he started his homeward journey. Next day, on reaching the vast empty Plain of the Carrizo Grass near the site of the solitary Painted Rock, he loaded the carbine exactly as he had seen Nunez do. Raising it to his shoulder he aimed it at a chalky stone as Nunez had aimed at the doe. When he pulled the trigger the stone disintegrated. Elated, Asuskwa hurried on his way.

Chapter Twenty-eight

Rubio's goal, like that of every other Franciscan in California at the time, was to make Indians into Christian citizens so that in ten years he could turn over his mission lands and improvements to them and move on "while the mission itself, its walls quite down, became their parish church.

"Thus each day at dawn Junipero, acting as my majordomo and alcalde of our Indian community, rang the large, or Angelus, bell which, with its smaller companion, was now removed from the tree limb and hung on a crossbeam in front of the new and larger church we were building."

Roused by its notes his neophytes gathered around him in the morning twilight and, facing the dark sierra over which the sun was just peeping, offered their morning prayer.

> Here comes the dawn,
> Making way for the day . . .

And as this greeting rose upon the air of his lonely valley at the edge of the wilderness, it seemed to Rubio a sweet echo, far carrying, of that divine ave with which the archangel saluted the Virgin, announcing the dawn of a new spiritual day.

Afterwards each household sent to the communal kitchen under the ramada for its share of breakfast gruel containing seed or acorn meal, roots, bulbs, bits of everything nutritious that could be found, for all worked for the common good in this time of continued want; and after breakfast Junipero, enormously proud of his office, rang the smaller bell announcing work time. Women and girls went to gather firewood, forage or tend garden. Men and boys helped Rubio build the new church, while Junipero lightened their labor with his panpipe.

"First we set forked sycamore poles in stone-lined holes nine feet apart, then filled the spaces between with smaller poles stuck upright close together but not reinforced by stones. When these interior walls were erected we plastered them inside and out with mud and added a central row of larger posts to carry a ridgepole. Then we were ready to lay the stone foundation around the outside and upon it an outer wall of adobe brick."

Fortunately he'd found proper soil close by for brickmaking. A trough of suitable dimensions had been excavated at the spot. Dry grass was readily available as binder. "When earth and fragments of grass were thrown together into the trough and water added, men and boys vied to tread this mixture into a proper consistency, knowing they made the material of which Our Lord's house would be constructed."

At mid-morning Rubio met under a tree with all his charges over five years of age to instruct them in Christian doctrine, teaching it as the rule required in their language as well as Castilian, and they learned to repeat after him the Sign of the Cross, the Lord's Prayer, the Hail Mary, the Creed, the Confiteor, the Act of Contrition, the Acts of Faith, Hope, and Charity, the Ten Commandments, the Precepts of the Church, the Seven Sacraments, the Six Necessary Points of Faith, and the Four Last Things.

"From the beginning I made it clear that until baptized they were free to come and go, to travel as they wished, but afterward they might leave only with my permission. Yet in those first happy days, all aglow with hope and faith, we had no difficulty."

Daily repetition, he found, impressed even the dullest minds while the brightest were incited to learn more, and thus he discovered the exceptional characteristics of his newest pupil, "our potential first nun from New California, the chieftainess' daughter. Her name is Lospe which she says means flower and I must say she blooms like one."

" 'What is God?' she suddenly inquires.

" 'Why,' I reply somewhat startled for I cannot remember any of them asking such a question before. 'God is love, my child!'

" 'What does he look like?'

" 'What does love look like?' When she cannot tell me, I say: 'Thus we recognize God but cannot describe him!'

" 'Where does he live?' she persists.

" 'He's evidenced by all created things! His abode is in Heaven where we pray to him!'

" 'Then he is like Kakunupmawa!' she exclaims triumphantly, 'our Ruler the Sun!'

" 'But isn't there one great difference?' I correct her gently. 'Did Kakunupmawa ever descend to earth, be born of a woman, suffer and die for your sake?'

" 'No, but he shines upon us every day. He is not remote and mysterious.' Her acuteness is astonishing. Suddenly she asks: 'Do you know a tall soldier with blond hair?'

" 'Why, yes, I know one.'

" 'Where is he?'

" 'I do not know.'

" 'Is he coming back here?'

" 'How can I tell, child?' I chide her, suspecting the truth for the first time. 'What has a tall blond soldier to do with Christian Doctrine?'

"Each day she grows in beauty, and though Valenzuela and Cota or any of our unmarried soldiers would gladly take her as his Christian wife, the Governor approving, she will have none, saying she is betrothed in her heart to another. When I ask who, she blushes and replies shyly: 'He is not here! But he will come! He is searching for Monterey!'

"And so, concealing my smile, I learn the truth. One of the members of the First Expedition, probably brash young Boneu himself, captured the child's fancy, and there is more to her love of things Christian than I first supposed, and a twinge of jealousy and disappointment goes through me.

"Yesterday she led me into a new world. With her grandmother we had gone to seek out the bulbs of the blue brodiaea or Indian Onion, and soon we came to an enchanting hollow such as the one, she says, where she was born, right on the ground, right out of this earth. She ceased speaking and as we three stood there quietly together in the sunlight among the blossoms I heard the song of a lark which seemed to celebrate her words. The truth came to me with overwhelming vividness, and I knew for the first time what the divine Francis meant when he spoke of his sisters the birds, his brothers the grass blades.

"At last my eyes were opened and I saw how earth, sun, bird, grass, myself, girl, old woman, distant sierra—all were one. I understood the love of God for all things natural and human in perfect wholeness as never before. And moved by a sudden impulse I lay down and kissed the warm earth, much to the delight of the other two who said they did so regularly.

"As Saint Augustine writes of his soul, I write of these things in all humility. I've decided to make my diary a journal of daily events in the fullest sense, a record of spirit as well as of substance. How else may the whole truth be told?

"I sleep on a deerskin stretched tightly over a simple wooden frame my Indian carpenter has made me and I cover myself with a rabbit blanket of beautiful patchy brown and white just as they do. I write with the sharpened quill of a raven they found for me. Without their help not one of us Spaniards could have survived. The gentle bands of elk and antelope are no longer to be seen. The soldiers' guns have scattered them. Nor are deer readily apparent. This makes it difficult to secure meat for our table. Yet I am glad for the sake of the animals, I love them so. There is a little flock of quail—our sisters the quail!—which survives in the shrubbery along the river where we go daily to draw water. I've given orders that no one is to harm them.

"Soon I shall have no flour to make altar breads and the mice devour what remains. I wrote Serra: 'Please send us a cat! And some chickens! I would give anything for a fresh egg!' And I complained about my ragged habit. 'It is so full of holes my skin shows in several places. Savages are hardly less naked!' But then I admitted to a very pleasant visit from Brother Cavaller of Mission San Luis Obispo de los Tichos.

"I didn't realize how lonely I was until I saw him riding up. He came with one soldier, Brother Juncosa remaining in charge during his absence. Since Cavaller is the first of the brethren I have talked to in the months since Serra left me, we never stopped. He has considerable difficulty learning the Tichos' many tongues since no less than five dialects are spoken by those who come to him, and much the same is true here. He brought me a copy of *Agricultura General* which will be helpful in our farming and gardening. He says that without food and trinkets to offer, of which he still has a supply, he would be pounding cold iron so far as converts are concerned. I told him of a kind of miracle which happened here March 19. On that feast day of Blessed Saint Joseph, patron of our new land, a flock of twittering swallows came and built their nests under the eaves of our unfinished church. I thought it a good omen.

"Next to the Great Nay Sayer I fear our soldiers most. While returning from foraging with her grandmother, Lospe was accosted by Tipo Valenzuela who seized her roughly and would have had his way with her, but the old woman struck him over

This Promised Land

the head with her digging stick, which sent him reeling, allowing the child to free herself and run, Tipo in hot pursuit, to the hut of her old friend Wima, my carpenter. Wima has known her since she was a baby and is contemplating baptism without urging from me. Admitting her, then bravely interposing himself at the door, he was savagely beaten by Tipo. Hearing an uproar, I rushed to the scene. There I encountered Lopez who accused me of interfering on behalf of the Indians. 'It is the girl who should be disciplined for being so provocative! What do you think my men are made of?'

"For their protection I have taken Lospe and Engracia, her grandmother, into my house. They occupy the room adjacent to mine intended for my brother companion, whenever he may arrive and I hope it is soon. Junipero sleeps as guardian at their doorway. Nevertheless the soldiers jeer at me saying: 'Padre, you have taken a concubine!' "

Chapter Twenty-nine

As Asuskwa reentered the coastal ranges he proceeded more carefully. Now that he was again within Owotoponus' territory he might be struck by one of the magician's invisible air shots, or attacked by him in the guise of a grizzly bear with poisoned claws or a rattlesnake with similarly deadly fangs. Taking a rarely used trail where he might pass undetected, he climbed through silvery piñon pines and passed the summit near a mighty outcropping of rocks known as the House of the Sun. They arose mysteriously out of a high meadowland like powerful spirits emerging from the earth, warmed by the sun all day long and far into the night, and feeling strengthened by their presence, Asuskwa descended into the depths of the river's gorge which would lead him toward home.

From time to time he stopped and with satisfaction admired his newly acquired gun, running his fingers with pleasure over its shiny steel barrel and brass butt plate and the brass nails of the initial "N" embedded in its stock.

He knew he must kill Owotoponus but under what circumstances or when he did not know. For that he would need further guidance. Utmost care and correct procedure would be required. In a world where everything, even rocks, was alive with intelligence and power and intimate relationships, this most talented and powerful being could be dealt with successfully, he felt sure, only in the most extraordinary fashion, and at moments his heart misgave him as he faced a future where no one had preceded him.

Accordingly he stopped again at the Cave of the Condors and, avoiding looking at the presumptuous masterpiece of Owotoponus on the upper lip as he entered lest it bring bad luck, once more seated himself crosslegged in front of the ancient painting on the inner wall, this time with his gun resting across his knees.

All night he sat there meditating and praying, hoping to see a vision, hear a song, but none came, absolutely nothing, and in the gray light of morning he was still sitting there feeling discouraged, his body aching with weariness, when once more the rising sun entered the Eastern Window and put forward a single ray like a probing finger into the cave. Suddenly alert and fascinated, Asuskwa watched the finger of the sun come searching slowly across the powdery gray dirt of the cave floor, as if trying to find the painting on the wall. But it still was not the season of the winter solstice when that would happen. Then of course the first rays, on that shortest day of the year when the great orb of the god had reached its southernmost point, would shine directly in through the window upon the ancient painting, and prayers and sacrifices would be made in order to encourage it to return northward with its lifegiving force. As he watched with fascination the probing ray came gradually to where he was sitting, and when at last it rested fully upon his gun, making the metal gleam, it stopped as if unable to go any farther

All at once the manner in which he must kill Owotoponus became perfectly clear to Asuskwa, and at that same instant, as his spirit rose with elation, he seemed to hear a high musical whistling sound as of air passing through giant wings. For just an instant more the power and talent of Owotoponus appeared to him like a mighty mountain in the distance, lofty and insurmountable. "But my destiny is remorseless," he thought, "so I must be strong!"

Before departing he made the vow which was to have far reaching effect, and as he passed the painting by Owotoponus at the cave mouth he found it no longer filled him with apprehension.

Chapter Thirty

And now the Devil began to lash his tail in earnest," Rubio continued, "but subtly so that we could not tell at first what he was about. The girl's mother brought the news. She came at midday when they seldom traveled and we ourselves were at rest. Though it was hot, she wore the bearskin cloak donned for important occasions and her best bone and shell hairpins denoting wealth and status. 'I wanted you to hear it from no one else!' she announced gravely when her daughter led her joyfully to my door. Her husband-against-her-will, the wicked sorcerer, was dead, she informed me solemnly. Her son had returned from the wilderness and killed him."

As Koyo spoke tears welled from her eyes, for she knew that something great if also malevolent had been removed forever and the world changed by that amount.

"The news though sad was good," Rubio continued. "I'd long hoped to attract her to my flock thinking that, once she came, all remaining at the village might follow, and the wicked fellow be left, like His Satanic Majesty when cast from Heaven, writhing and gnashing in impotent despair. Despite my kiss of peace he never ceased conspiring against me. Now all difficulties seemed removed. Yes, she was free to remain with us. She hoped her sister and brother-in-law and their daughter would soon follow. Her son, greatly revered for his act of courage, would succeed her as chief. At last her people were freed from bondage and she and her daughter reunited.

"I blessed her and joined my tears of gratitude with hers and Lospe's. All difficulties seemed removed but one. The young man had used a gun to kill the wizard.

" 'Are you sure?' I asked, alarmed. I foresaw what this might portend. For an Indian to possess a gun was as forbidden as for him to ride a horse or mule, those three chief instruments of conquest and domination being reserved strictly for people of reason.

"She was sure. Owotoponus, as she termed him, had emerged from his dawn bath in the river just as the rising sun was touching his body and her son had shot him as if a ray of the sun had killed him. 'Thus his evil spirit was utterly dissipated forever.' Where the youth acquired the gun, she did not know.

"A few minutes later when I attempted to explain all this to Lopez it was the gun which preoccupied his attention, as I foresaw.

" 'This means but one thing,' he announced harshly. 'We must recover it before he turns it against us, and see the villian promptly punished!'

" 'Villain? Punished? What are you talking about?'

" 'If he can kill a witchdoctor, he can kill a Spaniard, can't he?'

" 'Why should he kill a Spaniard?'

" 'He's hated us from the first, from what they say. And, Father, how do you suppose he acquired a gun?'

" 'I've no idea,' I replied. 'Perhaps some deserter... But would a deserter have shown him how to load and fire it?'

"Lopez shook his head at what he seemed to regard as my abysmal innocence. 'A deserter might not have lived to conduct such instructions, though I suppose,' he added caustically, 'you will take the Indians' part as usual and say it was all the soldier's fault, murdered though my poor comrade may have been!'

" 'Where are you going?' I demanded as he strode away.

" 'I am going to teach your friends a lesson!' he flung back.

"In vain I pleaded. In Lopez's view, heathen were no better than vermin and must be exterminated when need be. I know that sometimes we hate what we are, and it may have been Lopez's Aztec blood speaking against itself. Still I was appalled at the intensity of his hatred. The man was beside himself. He saw our occupation of this land threatened, even of his plan to bring his family here. Mounting three of his rowdiest fellows on mules—armored in leather jackets, bearing shields, lances, swords, muskets, pistols, full regalia—and leaving instructions not to allow me custody of my Constanza or I should have ridden after them I was so perturbed, he galloped hotfoot for the village.

"Asuskwa received them with cool dignity. Lopez rudely demanded the gun. The youth explained he'd used it to kill the wizard because it was necessary to overcome his great power with one even greater, and that then he had divested himself of it, entrusting it to his guardian spirit, believing it an instrument of incalculable evil for which he had no further use. This seemed to my good corporal an unlikely story. He again demanded the weapon and when Asuskwa could not produce it, he and one of his men, Barca, a Catalan, entered the house—the same I entered in the name of Our Lord—to search for it, while the others held the youth outside at pistol point.

"Inside they found the chieftainess' beautiful sister known as Lehlele. Inflamed at the sight of her, Lopez attempted to have his way with her. Hearing her screams, Asuskwa attempted to come to her aid. In the ensuing scuffle, Valenzuela's pistol was discharged, wounding the young chief slightly in the hand; while Lehlele fought off Lopez, and his companions urged him jeeringly on. 'Stick her with the white man's truth!' they shouted obscenely. 'That will quiet her!' Those were their very words! I put them down with trepidation. But they were said. They are part of the history of this valley. Ruthlessly Lopez raped the poor creature. And her husband entering at the other door attempting to prevent it, Barca grappled with him and stabbed him to death. In the uproar the young chief escaped.

"Furious, in retaliation they ransacked the house and many others, taking whatever valuables attracted their fancy: bowls, baskets, headdresses, carved wood and stone miniatures; and also brought back the head of the dead man still dripping blood, its features contorted in lasting hatred, which they placed on a paling at the gate of the stockade, boasting they had 'taught the savages a lesson!' as Lopez proclaimed.

" 'Indeed you have!' I retorted scathingly, beside myself with anger and outrage, while the lament of the women rose around us wildly. 'You have shown them exactly how to behave, and we shall reap the consequences! Look at those pitiful creatures!' pointing to Lospe and her mother who were prostrate before the bloody head, lacerating their faces with fingernails, mingling their blood with that which dripped from it.

" 'The gun—!' he began but I cut him off: 'Why didn't you believe the young chief? Why should he lie? Did he offer resistance? For shame! And as for this innocent man you killed, whose bloody head cries to God from these holy precincts, whose only crime was trying to defend his wife, your action will bring down not only heavenly wrath upon us but that of all his people! Nor will I absolve you from your sin!'

"He was thoroughly frightened, I could see, but it gave me small recompense. Going to the grief-stricken women and the others from our native community who had gathered to view and mourn the macabre display, wailing and tearing hair and flesh, I attempted to console them. 'I shall go to the village myself and try to make amends!'

" 'No, no!' Lospe and her mother cried together. And then the mother, reasserting her role as chieftainess, urged that the guilty be punished and justice be done for her people's sake. But finally she insisted again: "Do not yourself go to the village! You might be killed! They will be too upset to listen to what you say! Let us go instead! We speak as one of them! You would only aggravate matters!' At last they convinced me.

"They went to the village. In an action to my knowledge unparalleled in the annals of this province, they pleaded with their enraged son and brother and his distraught and angry people for our sake. The killing was a terrible mistake. It was entirely the soldiers' fault, which even they now repented. I had threatened to punish them with my sacred magic. They had been carried away. The gun was to blame—the evil gun used in overcoming the evil spirit of Owotoponus. I had nothing to do with the matter. I had tried my best to prevent it. 'Hasn't he always been our friend?' they argued. 'Didn't he come fearlessly to you bringing the cross, thus breaking the hold of Owotoponus over you, providing a refuge when we had no other? Is he not generous with beads and ribbons?'

"At last they convinced them we should be forgiven. Yes, that for the sake of peace and to avoid further bloodshed the Indians should show compassion toward us Spaniards!

"Tears came to my eyes when I heard of it. 'Long ago they saved our bodies with their generous gifts of food,' I thought. 'Now they are saving our souls!'

"Are we entitled to so much? I fear we are not. I fear the price for Lehlele, for her husband, for all the other innocent victims has not been paid.

"Asuskwa continually urges Lospe and her mother to return to him, while they urge him to join them, and Lopez wonders gloomily as to the whereabouts of the gun. The slightest incident, I feel, will again cause violent discord."

* * *

Asuskwa began to plan a general uprising against the white murderers and rapists but the superior weight of his mother's authority and his love for Koyo and his sister overbalanced these thoughts in his mind. Newly come to power, he was uncertain exactly which way he should go. As the days passed and he waited for a sign from Sacred Condor as to what he should do next, he endeavored to unite his people as they had been in the days before the white men came and Owotoponus destroyed their unity.

Chapter Thirty-one

Our occupation of California was more precarious in that spring of 1774 than at any time since the days of the First Expedition," Antonio wrote. "Because of the scarcity of food, Fages had been obliged to implement the scheme he proposed to Portola at the crucial conference before the retirement southward from the Point of Pines in December of '69. Remembering the Valley of the Bears, he and I and a party went down there with pack mules and for several weeks hunted grizzlies successfully, obtaining enough meat to keep the northern missions and presidio going until supplies might arrive by ship."

Word of this expedition reached Lospe and she was tempted to run away and try to find Antonio. But the state of affairs at mission and village was so delicate she dared not leave and go off alone. And Antonio too was similarly tempted toward her but Fages kept him busy conducting pack trains.

There were further threats to the occupation. Without ample food or trinkets to attract the Indians—or unfavorable conditions in villages such as Lospe's to impel them to come—the missionaries made little headway with conversions. "Nowhere in New Spain were baptisms slower than in California," Antonio noted. "A whole year passed at San Diego without one. At Monterey six months went by before Serra and Crespi could claim their first. After years of such meager results the Father Superior at the College of San Fernando in Mexico City, headquarters for all missionary effort in California, freely predicted the missions would fail and the friars be blamed, much as Fages was hoping."

Fages' predicament was dire. Plagued by deserters, with only a few loyal men to count on, he was faced by scores of thousands of potentially hostile natives who could, as he liked to say, "sweep us away," were it not for their fear of guns, horses, mules as Lopez likewise insisted to Rubio.

Transportation was another problem. Of the original five hundred horses and mules brought north by the Sacred Expedition, many had died. Replacement had been insufficient. "There was also a lack of animals for breeding purposes," Antonio recalled. "Meanwhile supply ships failed to arrive or were delayed by bad weather. But overriding all others from the viewpoint of higher authority was the matter of costs." Upwards of 400,000 pesos, or nearly twenty million in today's U.S. dollars, had been expended in exploring and missionizing the new province, not to mention the goods and animals taken from the former Jesuit missions of Old California or substantial monetary contributions from religious sources. "And all this for fewer than five hundred converts in five years, for no economic return whatsoever except a few shiploads of salt, for dubious protection against dubious encroachment from Russia or England, for two hundred seamen and soldiers dead or missing and four vessels lost, as Viceroy Bucareli pointed out!" The able viceroy, descendant of noble families of Florence and Seville, representative of Italy's and Spain's best brains, was saying that an early abandonment of the province might be expected.

"For the Land of the Great Dream, as for Fages who presided over it and who therefore must accept major responsibility for its present state, the future looked bleak indeed. As it did for me, his countryman and comrade!"

To a lesser degree the same was true of Serra who presided over California's spiritual destinies but who, by going to Mexico, had been able to convince the authorities that it was Fages rather than himself who was to blame for present difficulties and that a change to Rivera would correct matters.

It was against this rather desperate background that the Father President arrived back at San Diego in April, disembarked and began an overland journey northward to visit missions, while his vessel continued to Monterey. At Monterey Antonio was going about his duties as corporal in a kind of limbo as result of Fages' enigmatic assurances regarding his future, waiting to see what would happen when Rivera or Serra arrived.

"Sometimes I traveled inland the fourteen miles to check conditions at the grazing lands, becoming known as the Royal Rancho [near the present site of Salinas] where the presidial herds were kept. The cowboys who'd come north with Fages and me looked after them, living in brushwood huts, fearful of Indian raids, guarded by a detachment of soldiers."

On other occasions he led a working party including Pablo and other muleteers and their pack animals to the mouth of the Salinas to gather salt, and sometimes he took a foraging party out along the shore of the Point of Pines, along what is now the scenic Seventeen Mile Drive toward Pebble Beach, to gather shellfish. And more than once he followed the well-beaten trail under the great mossy pines of the point itself over the hill to Mission Carmel. There, suddenly emerging as if from a cave into light, he saw the stockade and neighboring huts of married soldiers and Indian converts standing on their promontory above river and bay, and beyond them Point Lobos, the Point of the Sea Wolves, where he'd camped in what now seemed glorious old days with Portola and Costanso.

Remembering his idealistic talk with Costanso beside this same shore, the current petty intrigues between Fages, Rivera, Serra, himself and Juan Lopez seemed a terrible comedown. Was all heroic exploration, all high hope to be reduced to this? Where were his dreams? Unwittingly in a dark moment he shared with Lospe's people a deep-rooted pessimism. Things were getting worse, as old Seneq had often said. Old days were better. The world was running down. Virtue was ebbing away. Another flood was coming. And in this feeling Antonio and the Indians were not greatly different from Rubio who saw in Saint Francis and Jesus a wonderfully better time. Nor indeed did they differ from many people today who think of a golden age gone by.

"But as I looked again at the curve of the bay in the bright morning, the beautiful land around me green with renewal, the calm sea so limitless in its immensity and power, I shook off such thoughts. The trouble was not in my circumstances but in myself. Here was another chance! Here, all around me, was an everlasting promise!"

His companion on many of these assignments was a young Majorcan of about his own age named Benito Ferrer. Ferrer was one of those new recruits who'd come north with the cattle drive. He was slightly but firmly built with bushy dark hair, sharp black eyes, and a pleasant yet wary manner which neither intruded nor held back. One day while they were standing side by side relieving themselves, Antonio happened to glance down and notice that Benito was circumcised. Seeing his look of astonishment, Benito flushed—and instead of offering his usual excuse that the mark of circumcision was merely an accidental scar confided that he was a marrano, or secret Jew. "My ancestors came to Majorca, the golden island, when the Jews were expelled from Palestine by the Romans. They settled at a seaport which we now call Palma, where they became merchants and traders."

At the time of the expulsion of all Jews from Spain by Ferdinand and Isabella in 1492, a tragedy triggered largely by the groundless suspicion that a Jewish physician had poisoned the royal son and heir, Benito's family was faced with the grim choice of leaving a land they'd regarded as their home for nearly fourteen centuries, or converting to Christianity. They chose to convert, outwardly at least. Following a usual practice they sent their eldest sons into the church without informing them of the family's continued secret adherence to Judaism, thus lulling suspicion while swelling the ranks of the clergy.

Despite a strict ban on Jewish emigration, as the persecutions of the Inquisition persisted into the 1500s, some members of the family forged or obtained false papers, took names of dead Catholics from tombstones, paid bribes, used any means necessary much like some Russian Jews today, to escape and so came to the New World. There, in spite of the activities of the Inquisition which followed the Spanish conquests, they became merchants, doctors, lawyers, and even government officials and military leaders in the Viceroyalty of Peru or the Audiencia of Mexico. Benito had not needed to go to these lengths. Outwardly conforming in every respect, he simply enlisted as a good Catholic Majorcan Catalan in the elite Free Company of Catalonian Volunteers and thereby went to his promised land at the King's expense.

"What is it like to have been born a Jew?" Antonio asked him frankly.

"I digest my food as you do. If a tree falls on me I'm likely to die. But sleeping or waking I'm listening for the knock at the door or the step of the approaching boot which leads to the rack and the stake, the auto-da-fé of the Inquisition."

Antonio shuddered inwardly at thought of the heavy burden this sensitive youth must wear every day, just as he wore his clothes.

"But you're a loyal subject!"

"That makes no difference. I may be denounced at any time for allegedly refusing to eat pork or because my foreskin is not like yours."

Unlike most Majorcan Jews, Benito's branch of the family became farmers and lived in the interior of the fertile island not far from Serra's later home at Petra. By that time, after many centuries of intermingling, most of the people of the island as well as many upon the mainland, including most of the middle class and many members of the aristocracy, had Jewish blood. And this was true even of the great King Ferdinand. Even Columbus might have been included in this category, and almost certainly six of his sailors were Jews.

"Serra's people were conversos or converted Jews," Ferrer confided, hungry like Antonio for someone to talk to of home. "It's well known among those of us who live in the neighborhood, though of course the church hushes it up. It may account for his great zeal. There is nothing so great as the zeal of a convert. The most terrible enemy we Spanish Jews ever had was the converso Torquemada, the Grand Inquisitor!"

"And do you think Serra an Inquisitor?" asked Antonio, amazed, remembering with a shock something Fages had told him.

"Not as a rule. But the potential is always there. The House of the Inquisition in Mexico City has many arms. It is like the octopus we caught among the rocks of the shore yesterday."

"Why did you come to New Spain?" Antonio asked.

"Why, to be freer. To enjoy better opportunity. Why did you?"

Antonio decided to ask Fages if Ferrer might accompany him to Mission Santa Lucia if the enigmatic scheme for arranging that happy event ever materialized. He still could not fathom what Fages' plan was, as they waited for Serra or Rivera to arrive.

Chapter Thirty-two

As Serra rode up on muleback, Rubio and his converts were singing a Te Deum in welcome from the steps of their newly built church. Rubio had given the structure its orientation facing eastward toward the sunrise and the head of the valley he'd learned to love and to which he'd committed his life. Far back in that Valley of the Rising Sun, as he liked to think of it, there was a cave, Lospe told him, where the sun entered just as it did the doorway of his church and touched a sacred painting just as it did the cross on the altar of native stone where the flame he and Serra lighted that first day under the oak still burned with a power Rubio hoped would be everlasting.

"What marvelous changes you've wrought!" his Father Confessor exclaimed looking around as they embraced. "And you yourself, my brother, seem to have grown a little, am I not correct?"

Rubio glowed at this praise yet wondered if he truly had measured up. The walls of his stockade had not come down. He seemed far from the ideal vision they'd shared on that founding day nearly two years before, and he was prompted to confess some of the things he'd managed badly or failed to do.

But Serra replied encouragingly: "It may be that when we feel unworthiest we are most blessed!"

"How can that possibly be?"

"It may be God's way of opening our hearts so that He may enter in. Do not be overly concerned about what you call your failure to establish perfect harmony with your pagan neighbors. God will use you in His way in His own time. Yes, your walls, visible and invisible, will come down, believe me!"

Serra sang the High Mass of thanksgiving while Junipero, his namesake, served him as acolyte. Afterward in the privacy of the padres' quarters the Father President revealed what he'd accomplished in Mexico.

"The Viceroy granted most of our requests. Baptized Indians are to be entirely under our control. Immoral soldiers are to be removed from missions. Rivera is to succeed Fages as Governor. Ortega was my first recommendation but His Excellency objected that Jose, being merely a sergeant, was too low in rank despite his many qualifications. Still I think we shall be satisfied with Rivera, despite his somewhat rustic character."

At this point Rubio took the opportunity of suggesting that Lopez be replaced by Antonio, explaining his many difficulties with Lopez and the incorrigible nature of the man. "Boneu is a corporal now and from the first attracted me by his considerate treatment of the lowly, whether pagan or Christian." Serra readily agreed to the proposal, expressing indignation that Fages should have disregarded Rubio's many protests. "He doubtless wanted you to get into all the trouble you could. But, very well! I shall speak to Rivera regarding Boneu!" Then he broached the subject of Junipero's sodomy and Rubio replied frankly: "Apparently he has been reborn in Christ. He plays his role as my mayordomo and alcalde among the converts ably, though he is oversensitive about trifles. Just the other day, for example, I found my spectacles missing. When I queried him, since he alone has the run of my quarters, he denied any knowledge of them. Later I found him parading in them among his people in the village outside the gate, posing as 'The Alcalde with Four Eyes!' When I reprimanded him he became quite sullen and resentful!"

"Are you alert against the spread of his vice?"

"I regularly ask the prescribed questions in confessional: 'Have you touched the lower parts of a man wishing to commit a sin?' And so on."

Serra sighed. "It is the curse of the New World. They say it's even worse in Peru than in New Spain. But we shall extirpate it, for it is an abomination unto the Lord as the Scriptures say!"

They shared a frugal meal of fresh lettuce from Rubio's garden and cakes of wild seeds, supplemented by tortillas, chocolate, and figs from Serra's packs, topped off by their mutual weakness, snuff, "a treat I'd not enjoyed for many months," as Rubio recorded.

Serra's Indian servant from Carmel, Juan Evangelista, was still with him. Juan was returning quite the civilized young man. He'd been introduced to the Viceroy. The Archbishop had confirmed him. He wore clothes like a Spaniard. He smoked cigarettes. Serra was very proud of him, Rubio could tell, though Rubio found him insufferable as he strutted about boasting of all he'd seen and done. "Not to be outdone myself I exhibited my protégé. At her request I'd baptized Lospe, giving her the Christian name of Clara, after the sainted Clara of Assisi, Francis' first female disciple, hoping she would follow the footsteps of her namesake into the sisterhood of our order and always be the light of the world. She learned everything so readily that I taught her Latin as well as Castilian. She could recite her catechism in three languages, knew the location of the Holy Land, Madrid, Mexico City, the principal nations and seven seas, and I explained to her the nature of eclipses and other celestial phenomena so she would no longer be bound by her people's superstition concerning such matters by which their sorcerers held power over them. Thus gradually I opened her eyes to my world as she opened mine to hers. Through this lovely child I perceived the interrelationship of all created things as never before. She also helped me greatly with my dictionary of her language and I was amazed at the subtleties of a tongue in which pronouns were parts of verbs and in which, by varying emphasis, I could imply a variety of meanings at several levels of comprehension. Their elite had even, I discovered, devised their own language, a kind of court language, which no one else could understand. 'Isn't all this indicative of a high degree of civilization?' I asked Serra.

"He was impressed by her beauty and intelligence, I could see, but when she recited her catechism first in Spanish then in Latin he was quite overwhelmed. Blessing her he asked if she wished like Juan to visit Mexico City and see its great buildings and be confirmed by the Archbishop. She surprised us by saying she preferred to remain where she was.

"Afterward I explained with embarrassment about the soldier to whom she was betrothed in her heart, perhaps Boneu himself. 'No need to apologize,' Serra answered with gentle humor. 'We've always faced such competition from natural impulses and always will! It can be one more bond between us and this new land!!' "

Before leaving he gave Rubio a beautiful oil painting on canvas done by a skilled artist of Cuernavaca depicting Saint Lucy full face, her great eyes accentuated like those in Byzantine portraits, for placing above the altar of his new church, "and though it represented a debt of eighteen pesos charged—in his shrewd way," Rubio noted, "without any authorization from me!—against my account, I said I was delighted to possess it. Saint Lucy indeed had clarified my vision. I told him how she and the Blue Nun had guided me."

" 'Always press forward, Nicolas! Never turn back!' Serra counseled me as we said farewell. His indomitable spirit seemed fresh as ever, though I feared for his frail body."

As soon as his vessel the *Santiago* unloaded her cargo at Monterey, supplies would reach Mission Santa Lucia, Serra promised, as well as the brother companion Rubio had so long awaited. Their dreams seemed within reach.

Two days later, to Rubio's surprise, Rivera and a party of soldiers arrived, also en route to Monterey, where the aging captain would assume the governorship. Rivera's fussiness and indecision astonished Rubio, "and I wondered if we were to be better off with him than with Fages. Fernando de Rivera y de Moncada he styles himself fully, now that he is Governor. Yet he could not even make up his mind where to pitch his tent or whether to dine with me or not, finally writing me a letter, as is his custom apparently, though he was sitting only a few yards away, stating that he did not wish to be guilty of the impropriety of reducing my meager rations—lest, of course, it be a blot on his record that might someday be used against him! He is too old, well into his mid-sixties now. He should have remained in retirement at the little ranch near Guadalajara he described to me with affection—when taking protocol by the horns I went to him and we enjoyed a pleasant chat. But the Viceroy recalled him to service, and now to the governorship which he secretly coveted so long. Yet now that he's obtained it he seems to feel uncomfortable with it! I wish he were thirty years younger! They say that in youth he was a fine leader and performed many notable exploits. Lopez filled his ear, of course, with what lies and half-truths I could only imagine. That irrepressible fellow has the audacity to tell me to my face that the time will come when 'We shall have our own mestizo padres here and you can go home across the water!' as if I were an interloper.

"I can scarcely bring myself to relate what happened next. While joyfully dwelling among us, joining our daily worship, expressing a desire to learn our doctrine—and persuading many others to do likewise by reason of her example and great prestige—Clara's mother fell ill of what seemed no more than a common cold. Suddenly she grew worse. When all native remedies Clara applied had no effect, I consulted my copy of the *Florilegio* and decided to administer horehound as Esteyneffer recommends. But as I looked down at the poor creature gasping for breath, her breast heaving like a bellows, I saw that Sacred Death, our ultimate visitor, had been before me."

Thus Koyo became the first of many to succumb to the white man's diseases against which Indian bodies offered no natural defense. Next day she died of what Rubio called congestion of the lungs but was undoubtedly pneumonia. "Five days have passed," he went on sorrowfully. "Some of our converts blame me for her death. Her son, according to Junipero who visited him—the youth himself has never set foot here—says we Spaniards have caused his mother's death, that our evil presence has killed her. His patience has come to an end, Junipero says, and quotes him: 'I have accepted much. I cannot accept this!' I shudder to think what may happen."

Clara, heartbroken but dry eyed, wanted her mother's body burned on a funeral pyre as her father's had been. Asuskwa demanded that it be returned to their village for burial. But she insisted her mother had died "while on a journey"—meaning in search of the Christian faith—and thus by tribal custom was entitled to cremation where she died. "The girl's own faith was absolute!" Rubio recorded with quiet wonder. It was based on deepest needs for survival. Rubio and Christianity represented to Clara the new, more powerful, more enlightened way, the way which had led her from oppression and danger to freedom and safety. And when with the others she and Rubio began to collect wood for a funeral pyre, she did not shed a single tear.

"My mother has gone to join my father in the Land of the Dead," she told him, describing her pagan heaven for him in hauntingly beautiful terms, "and that is good because they loved each other very much and to be separated so long was very hard for them!" He controlled his emotion with difficulty and confided to his journal that night: "The dear child believes that when she goes to our Christian Heaven she will meet her parents there 'because the Land of the Dead is really Heaven by another name!' I have not the heart to correct her theology. 'My brother is wrong,' she staunchly affirms, when informed what he is saying against me. 'Hatred is blinding his eyes!'

"And when again this morning he sent for her to leave me and join him, she would not go.

"Meanwhile there is renewed talk of the accursed gun and sentries are on the alert."

Chapter Thirty-three

The presidio at Monterey did not stand then where it does now but half a mile nearer the beach on the crest of that knoll where Costanso located it and where its original mission church may still be seen.

As Antonio was crossing the parade ground in front of the church at mid-morning on his way from the warehouse to the guardhouse by the gate, he encountered Serra. So small, so frail looking, coughing from asthma, limping, a running sore on his leg, the little figure seemed to the youth more an act of will than a man. Purpose so great it was palpable emanated from his fragile body, as did enormous kindness and simplicity. How then could Serra be a merciless Inquisitor?

Antonio remembered him pounding the flesh of that frail chest till it bled, and felt awed in the presence of such a complex personality. "Good morning, young man!" the Father President greeted him warmly. "I found they've not forgotten you in the Valley of Santa Lucia!"

Startled, Antonio replied: "Why, Father, that is indeed gratifying!"

"And have you been behaving yourself here?" Serra gave him a humorous and at the same time penetrating look.

"I have tried to!"

"That may prove to your advantage!"

Afterward he wondered what Serra meant and for a moment was tempted to run after him and ask but thought better of it. There was a formidable sternness underlying that mildness and he remembered Fages telling him that while a missionary in the Sierra Gorda of Mexico Serra had become an informer to the Inquisition. "It's well known, but few will admit it." Were any of them now, Christian, Jew, or Indian, to be deemed guilty in

This Promised Land

his eyes of any deviation from doctrinal belief or practice, he had the power to bring down the full weight of that terrible body upon them. "He named names," Fages said. "Suppose one had been yours?" Antonio shuddered inwardly at the recollection. Then he remembered what Benito Ferrer recently confided to him and decided not to run after Serra, for if the Father President were to know all that was in his mind he would undoubtedly feel obliged to inform against him. Antonio had no intention of rotting in a dungeon. His problem was becoming more than ever how to reconcile his intellectual convictions with his religious faith. Already he sensed that the church which gave such great initial impetus to the Conquest was not the wave of the future in the New World any more than in the Old. He even suspected it might prove ineffective with the Indians whose way of life he'd begun to admire. The new wave was coming from a different source, the one he felt stirring in himself as in Costanso and Fages, a reasoned enlightened approach to social justice and political and spiritual freedom. Inquisitions had no place in it. So he continued toward the guardhouse wondering what Serra meant.

Serra was even less forthright with Fages. He revealed nothing to the young governor about Rivera's imminent arrival to supplant him, nor did Fages, playing tit for tat, mention a word about the Viceroy's letter containing that very news. They were like two diplomats knowing what's in the other's mind but pretending not to.

"Ah, Don Pedro, my son!"

"Ah, my dear Father President, delighted to have you back! A successful visit, I trust?"

"Beyond expectation, thanks be to God!"

"You cunning little devil," Fages said to himself and inquired politely when the vessel Serra left at San Diego could be expected.

While they were talking the *Santiago* rounded the Point of Pines, guns firing, bringing not only lifegiving supplies but the province's first colonists. Antonio rushed with the others to the beach to stare as the longboat touched the sand and the first white women to reach California stepped ashore. They were the graceful Josefa, young wife of Doctor Jose Davila; Anna Maria Chamorro, matronly consort of the sturdy smith and farrier Fernando Chamorro; and, most notably in the eyes of all young men watching and cheering, the two unmarried Chamorro daughters Maria and Cipriana, a lovely sixteen and eighteen. They seemed to Antonio like two Aphrodites appearing from the sea. Yet though he soon gained favor in the eyes of these young goddesses, as he could tell when they danced the fandango in the celebration which followed, Antonio found his heart elsewhere and his thoughts kept turning to that elaborate stratagem by which, Fages assured him, he would be posted to Mission Santa Lucia if only he remained silent and let matters take their course. "Look, look!" someone cried. Rivera and his party were riding in at the gate of the fort.

When the new governor summoned him a few days later, Antonio noted that Rivera's beard was grayer, his manner more pompous, his uncertainty more pronounced, and sensed that beneath his grave exterior was a man who is beyond his depth and knows it. His voice sounded more like someone playing a commanding role than actually commanding. "Since Captain Fages tells me you wish to remain in this province . . . when the ship is unloaded, Corporal Boneu, I shall send you," with a look which Antonio thought stood for reprisal, having no idea Serra had suggested the assignment, "with a pack train to Mission Santa Lucia." Disbelief nearly overwhelmed him. "There you will replace Corporal Lopez." It was too good to be true. By what magic had Fages managed? "And we shall see how you do there! I want to caution you: arrogance on the part of the heathen is not to be tolerated. There's been some unrest. Lopez took measures he found appropriate. Things must be firmly controlled," Rivera searched for properly stern words, "if you are to remain happily under my command!"

"Excellency," Antonio replied solemnly, as if dismayed at the prospect of exile at lonely Santa Lucia far from the fandangos of Monterey, while his heart leaped for joy, "I shall do my utmost to deserve your confidence!"

His parting with Fages was something they discussed with relish in later years. It was one of those occasions which can be fully appreciated only from the perspective of time.

"Why are you so surprised?" Don Pedro exclaimed triumphantly now. "Did not my stratagem succeed, simply by keeping our mouths shut? A damned difficult thing for me, as you know!" He spoke as if it were Antonio's future rather than his own which mattered, and Antonio was moved by his generosity.

"This is not good-bye, Don Pedro. My heart tells me you will return."

"You can bet on it! And I'll bring my bride, my sweet, my beautiful, my dove-like Eulalia! Oh, wait till you see her! And

This Promised Land

we'll all join hands and dance a sardana in the middle of the parade ground!... Meanwhile," he continued scornfully, "as I foresaw you'll have nothing to fear from our Country Cousin. I've taken his measure. He will not wish to make trouble. Besides, he knows your connections in high places and," he grimaced in his comical but determined way, "mine!"

Thus it happened that early in June Antonio was leading a mule train loaded with supplies southward along the Salinas Valley.

With him went three Leather Jackets intended by Rivera to keep an eye on him and by pure happenstance Benito Ferrer went too, also dour young Father Espinosa, arrived on the *Santiago* and destined to keep Father Rubio company, and heavy company it seemed to Antonio, for Espinosa was one of those haughty Castilians who always appear to be looking down their noses at the rest of the world and disapproving what they see there. Antonio was apprehensive, too, as to what he might find at his new post. Rumors had disturbed him. But he was wearing his newly renovated silver buckle and it felt like a good-luck piece. It too would be returning home. And with the caballada were his five cattle, also a prized possession. Since there was almost no money in circulation, soldiers were paid in goods and credits, and with an eye to the future, he'd begun taking part of his corporal's wages of 400 pesos annually in the form of calves from the presidio's rapidly increasing herd. He now owned four heifers and a young black bull, all descended from those Fages and he with Lopez and the cowboys brought north, all branded with his initials in the form of a crude *AB* traced with a hot poker on their left hips.

The trail no longer ran through the Wilderness of Santa Lucia but straight down the valley to the side canyon leading to Mission San Antonio, and thence down its smaller valley back to the Salinas near the present site of Paso Robles, and on south as the highway goes today over the easy summit to the lowlands at Mission San Luis Obispo and the Valley of the Bears.

"What I learned from Fathers Cavaller and Juncosa at San Luis didn't allay my apprehensions," Antonio recalled. "Their information, though in arrears, was a tale of discord, violence, uneasy peace. 'And the red-haired chieftainess,' I asked, 'what of her?'

" 'We are not sure. But it is certainly her daughter who has taken refuge with Rubio.'

" 'Her daughter?' I must have started visibly, judging from the way they looked at me.

" 'Yes, her only one. Grown to womanhood, now, and very

beautiful, by all report. You remember her?' "

" 'Yes, I remember her!' "

The buckle has been right, he thought. It's been that piece of her I've been carrying all along and it told me when to return.

Antonio had never seen the valley in that magical season between spring and summer when the larks are rising, the nesting quail are calling their single sweet note, full ripeness of land and year lie just ahead, and as the column swung out onto the mesas above the long curve of the sea and that white ribbon of beaches he'd marched over with Portola and Costanso and he could see once again the tall dark head-peak and lovely hills descending from it like embracing arms, he sensed he was coming home at last.

Pablo seemed to feel the same and even El Tigre wagged his tail. Pablo had taught the little black dog to ride behind him on his white mule and even to stand up there on its hind legs, balanced by putting a forepaw on each of his shoulders, resting a small gray muzzle on one, so that the dog too was eagerly peering forward as they approached their goal.

"Remember that day we first rode into this valley, Compadre?" Antonio asked.

"Compadre, how could I forget?" And Pablo touched the sprig of rosemary he always wore in his hat for good luck.

Rising above the oaks on the promontory, a column of smoke showed them the site of the mission.

"Strange," Antonio said, knitting his brows, "that there should be so much smoke at mid-afternoon. It's more than a kitchen makes and they shouldn't be burning grass at this season. There's blackness in it, too, as when brush is burned. I wonder what it means?"

III
Clara and Antonio

Chapter Thirty-four

He came riding out of the west, out of the afternoon as in my dream vision, and as he turned to speak to Pablo, the sunlight struck the buckle at his belt, making it sparkle like a star, and I knew it was my buckle and he was wearing it!'' Clara would tell it that way to her grandson.

For Rubio, eagerly watching beside her, the pack train seemed the culmination of his lonely trial, for he perceived clearly the gray robe of Espinosa behind the leading figure of Antonio and he knew that in the packs of the mules were the supplies that would insure the life of his mission. Were it not for his deep-seated apprehension of what might happen as result of Koyo's death he would have been completely happy. They were just leaving the dying ashes of her funeral pyre as the train arrived.

For Lopez the arrival seemed the happy outcome of plans made with Rivera, and as soon as he was back in Monterey at the side of his mentor, he would begin his long-awaited return to Loreto and reunion after five years with his wife and daughters. At last he and Rivera had the hated gachupins, Antonio and Fages, where they wanted them.

To Benito Ferrer the isolated valley appeared an ultimate haven in his long flight from bigotry and fear of persecution.

To Pablo the Zambo it was a place where in future a man might be judged for what he was, not by the color of his skin, while enjoying a bit of song, a bit of a smoke, and a bit of a woman.

But to Antonio as he led his column up the slope toward the crest of the oak-studded promontory welcomed by cheers, gunshots, and the shrill neighs of animals greeting his from the corral next the mission compound, it was a homecoming, and he was looking for a special face. Instead he met Lopez smiling with obvious satisfaction.

Old grudges had no place in Antonio's present mood, however, and he greeted his perennial adversary heartily: "Well, Juan, the last time we embraced, that cold night in the Wilderness of Santa Lucia, it was as enemies. This time shall it be as friends?"

"Man, all I ever meant was to have a little fun!" Lopez was ready as ever with a plausible explanation. "You just took it too seriously!"

Juan knew he held the upper hand now. Antonio seemed to be truckling, and his satisfaction grew to exultation as they gripped each other, for a proud gachupin had at last sought his favor and was even bringing him a letter. Opening it he read what Rivera had written while his men began helping Antonio's unload the packs.

Pablo and his dog quickly became a center of attention. Among those gathering around them, Kachuku was giggling with particular amusement. She'd come to mourn at her aunt's funeral pyre, and like Clara had been lifted from depths of sorrow to heights of joyful excitement by the arrival of the train. But Clara shrank back now, brimming full though her heart was. Her first impulse had been to rush to Antonio and take his hand as she'd done in the beginning and had thought all the time since she would do at this moment, but shyness overcame her.

Antonio, glimpsing, recognized, saw her drop her eyes, understood, felt his entire being rise toward hers, as he listened to what suddenly became the insignificant chatter of Lopez. Smacking the open letter across his palm obnoxiously Juan resumed: "Colonists are coming. To make this place secure for their settlement I am to remind you that firm measures against the gentiles must be continued."

This irked Antonio further. "But why did you start with such violent ones?"

"I? You began it all, my friend, with that shot you fired here years ago!"

Controversy flared anew. Glancing toward them, Rubio saw with his new clarity of perception that they stood for two irreconcilables: Antonio the tall and fair European invader, Lopez the stocky Aztec-eyed proto-Mexican, challenging the established order which for nearly three hundred years had kept his kind under its heel. After welcoming Antonio warmly Rubio was doing likewise to Espinosa and had almost brought a smile to the young man's dour face. "He is depressed after his long journey. I must cheer him up!" Rubio decided, as usual thinking of others first

This Promised Land

in terms of what he might do to help them. "Is this where I am to live?" Espinosa complained, looking at the barren lodging of upright poles toward which Rubio was conducting him. "I'm afraid we are short on comforts," Rubio apologized. "This is not Mexico City."

At the Mass of Thanksgiving which followed, Antonio and Clara stole glances at each other while Rubio spoke of gratitude, of joy, of hope, of faith, the two of them kneeling among the congregation on the earthen floor, she in red skirt and blue chemise which Antonio thought most fetching. He like the other soldiers was wearing his leather jacket over his uniform, hat hanging from a button at the back of his left shoulder. In her eyes he rose head and shoulders gloriously above all the others while Espinosa warned of the dangers of sin and the importance of confession. As they were leaving, Antonio found opportunity to speak to her.

"Are you not the girl who gave me this silver buckle long ago?" touching it with his forefinger.

"Yes, I am she!"

"I have carried it from one end of this land to the other, and see, it has only gotten brighter!" He laughed as if at were all a joke but she sensed he meant much more and a song began to rise in her heart as she forgot her shyness and even the presence of everyone but the two of them.

"I was saddened to hear of your mother's death," he continued, gravely now, but what he wanted to say was: You are more beautiful than I ever imagined, and you have a delightful way of wrinkling up your nose when you smile! Instead he went on: "I shall always remember your mother's kindness and hospitality. And I regret what is reported to be the hostility of your brother. I hope it is not true?"

"Unfortunately it is true," she replied forthrightly.

"If I knew the reason perhaps I could alter it."

As if they had known each other for years, she found herself telling him about Asuskwa, his long-held antipathy toward whites, the death of Owotoponus, the murder of Ta-apu, the mystery of the gun.

"And what did happen to the gun?"

"He hid it in a sacred cave, dedicating it for safekeeping to his guardian spirit."

"Why?"

"He follows his dream!"

Then she heard the words fall miraculously from his lips as if preordained.

"And you—what dream do you follow?"

She flushed and dropped her eyes. "Some day I may tell you!"

"They tell me your name is Clara now," he persisted.

"Yes, I've been baptized."

"How did it make you feel?"

She glanced at him boldly and laughed. "Wet!"

After the service as they were putting away their vestments in the sacristy, Espinosa expressed his surprise to Rubio. "I noticed the Indians did not come forward and kiss your hand."

"And why should they kiss my hand?" asked Rubio in astonishment.

"Why, so you can tell who has attended and who has not!"

"But none would dream of not attending. It is the greatest moment of their week! Besides, I know them all by sight. One glance, one feeling, tells me who is there, or who from illness or other grave reason is not!"

Espinosa shook his head as if with patient understanding for an older man's failing comprehension. He was a generation younger than Rubio, not yet forty. "The new procedure is becoming widely accepted, as new conditions dictate. Aren't you too trusting?"

"Why, I don't think so!" Rubio replied, easily disconcerted where his own conduct was concerned, wondering if indeed he was becoming blind again. He was anxious to please his new companion yet irritated by what seemed presumptuous criticism. The young man seemed to have been born from another race of beings somehow oblivious to spiritual truth.

Thus inexorably a new pattern of human relationships was being imposed upon the land, displacing those which had been before it, sometimes to be different from them only in degree, sometimes in kind, and as yet the land itself remained apparently unchanged, accepting patiently as it had for countless ages what was being done upon it, giving no sign that it knew or cared. The arrival of the *Santiago*, fully loaded with supplies and settlers, had been a turning point in its history too. The Spanish occupation was an established fact. New things would be happening. Impalpably this feeling spread among both whites and Indians, perhaps to the earth itself.

This Promised Land

* * *

One evening Kachuku brought Lospe word that her brother wanted urgently to see her. Since she had previously refused to come to him, he would meet her in the oak grove some distance from the village in the direction of the mission. It was a spot they both knew well. They'd played in those oaks as children and their family owned one enormous tree in the middle of the grove to which they possessed full rights of harvest, collecting its acorns every fall and regarding it as one of their special connections with their Earth Mother. This great tree emerged from the ground like an enormous hand with five huge branching trunks for fingers which, spreading outward with the centuries, had grown so large and gnarled and heavy that several had come down like weary arms to rest themselves on the earth. As a child Clara had climbed into them and pretended she was a bird or a squirrel. Sitting there hidden among the leaves on summer afternoons as the sunny breeze blew up from the sea, she first heard the voices of the Sky People "who," as she said, "speak to each of us in their own way, telling us we are members of a single family but have our separate ways to go in the circle which has no end."

Afterwards she asked old Seneq: "How did we get here in the first place?" and her grandmother told her the story of Lizard and the Rock of Creation.

It was this tree in which she'd hung the whistling stone in hopes its music would bring Antonio back to her, and it had brought him back. Thinking of these things in the early morning light she waited under it for her brother, smelling the nostalgic odor of the smokes from the village fires not far distant, anguish tugging hard at her heart as she felt the deep division within her between old ways and new. She loved both, she wanted both. She felt there was room in the valley for them both. Mingled here they could constitute a new way. Wasn't she herself evidence it could be done?

Asuskwa came so softly to her over the carpet of dry leaves she hardly knew he'd arrived. His face showed a new gravity and determination which, she realized, reflected his new responsibility and increased manhood. Tears rose to her eyes as they met. She saw similar moisture in his. Taking her in his arms without a word he held her close against the firm young body she'd always adored.

"Come home with me," he said gently. "Our house is waiting."

She was strongly tempted, tempted to turn her back on everything new and different she had begun to be, even on the man she loved, and return with her brother to what seemed for one shining moment the perfect magic of their childhood. Then with an agonized sob she burst out:

"I cannot! Though I love you I cannot!"

"Why not?" he urged gently, holding her tenderly.

"Because water which flows down a river can never return!"

"And do you love the A-alowow so much that you can abandon me and all the life you were born to?"

"No, no, no!" she cried out. "Brother, it is not that, not that at all! I want to mingle our way with theirs, their way with ours. I want them to be like us, we like them!"

A coolness crept into his voice as he released her. "Even after what happened to our mother, our uncle, our aunt you can say that?"

His tone aroused her and she retorted: "Remember we are not without our own misdeeds. Have you forgotten the Evil Sorcerer who tyrannized us? But let us not think of him! Let us think instead of our own father, who explored new ways, thought new thoughts!"

"Speaking of him," Asuskwa retorted coolly, "I hear that the new leader of the soldiers is the young man with the yellow hair to whom you gave the buckle which belonged to our father?"

"It is true."

"I suppose you are in love with him?" They were adversaries now, she realized.

"As my dream vision revealed. You follow your dream, why should I not follow mine?"

"You would marry an A-alowow?" He looked down thoughtfully into the leaves and when he looked up she saw the face of a stranger.

"Yes!" She said it defiantly and as she spoke she felt cut off irrevocably from him and their past life together. For another moment he was silent while the leaves rustled above them. The talking wind seemed to be trying to tell them something.

"My heart tells me the white men will bring untold ruin upon our people. For the last time," he said ominously, "I ask you to come home with me!"

Meeting his eyes squarely, she slowly shook her head while a sharp dread rose in her that they might indeed be speaking together for the last time. "I shall pray for you," she said softly, "I shall always love you."

"If you loved me you would come home with me!" he answered harshly. To Asuskwa her refusal was a final blow. He had lost mother, uncle, aunt—though Lehlele was still alive she was kept in seclusion until her child should be born—and now his sister. He felt sorely beset. Having overcome one mighty enemy, Owotoponus, he was now confronted by another even mightier, the Spaniards, while trying to hold a fragmented community together in a society he sensed was fast disintegrating under the impact of enemy invasion.

It seemed to Lospe as she went homeward down the valley with aching heart that night had fallen though it was not yet midmorning. Her thoughts were in turmoil. She felt as if she had been cut in two.

After the departure of Lopez and his men with the empty pack train northward for Monterey, Antonio sat with Rubio on the sunny bench in front of the church. Newly arrived chickens, the Black Minorcas, clucked and scratched around them. One of two cats Antonio had brought, the big brindled gray one, was curled contentedly in Rubio's lap, softly purring under the stroke of his hand. "I know we shall get along," he was saying, "I told Father Serra so when he agreed to arrange your assignment here!"

"You and he arranged it?"

What had seemed to Antonio his and Fages' victory over Rivera and Lopez suddenly became the secret triumph of Rubio and Serra over them all, and he felt humbled by the beneficence of this little man he'd misjudged as ineffective.

"My Indians are at heart gentle, peace loving," Rubio went on, "as I think you understand. Oh, they can be exasperating! They can lie. They can steal. They hold grudges like children over slights real or imaginary. Junipero still hasn't forgiven my reprimanding him after he took my spectacles and paraded in them among the converts. And I never shall get used to the way they answer nature's calls innocently as animals wherever they happen to be. But this is their way. Many of ours must seem strange to them! Time and love can change all. And now, my boy, I shall give you my blessing. I must go and plant the seeds and cuttings you brought me. Even in New Jerusalem we must eat and drink, you know. One last thing before we part. Regarding a possible attack by Clara's brother upon us, let us put it from our minds lest thinking bring it to pass. None of them would dream of taking up arms against us were it not for our outrageous provocations against them, for which I fear atonement has not been made. Let us, rather, resolve to make amends, to create good will and thus avoid further strife!''

Rubio gently set the gray cat down on the ground, and Antonio went off to inspect the premises of his new command. He wasn't sure Rubio's beatific sentiments would make effective field strategy and was determined that his responsibility for the security of the little settlement be fully discharged.

Exchanging an informal word with Ferrer, standing guard at the gate, he turned to his left as he emerged from the stockade, thus putting the Christian Indian village at his back, and went toward the new soldiers' quarters with its separate stockade where Pablo and Junipero were directing a group of Indian men and boys in the final stages of construction. The project had been started several weeks before at Rubio's insistence in order to remove the soldiers from the confines of the mission compound and close proximity to his neophytes, and thus allow both groups greater privacy. Serra and Rivera had approved the project, and Lopez in an uncharacteristic burst of energy promptly implemented it in order to impress his superiors. Only a bit of sloping thatched roof and a few upright poles of the palisade remained to be set in place "before the Apaches come!" Pablo was joking.

"Better if the roof were tile, eh?" Antonio commented. "Then it would be proof against blazing arrows should things come to that. But let's not borrow trouble!" He lent a hand with the pole Pablo and Junipero were erecting. Junipero did not join in the conversation and Antonio thought he detected a sullenness in his manner as Rubio had mentioned. Engaging him in talk he handed him a little tobacco afterward with a wink and encouraging word to Pablo.

Continuing his tour of inspection he skirted the long rectangle of the main stockade on its west or seaward side and, with an eye to the strategic defense of his post, continued inland past the corral which joined the compound on the south and began to climb the grassy slope which rose gently toward the neighboring hills. After climbing some distance he reached a point he thought would give him the overview he desired and turned. Directly below him, the elongated rectangle of the main stockade with the new smaller one to the left of its entrance and the Indian village and sweathouse to the right by the river, formed a kind of headless cross with truncated arms. Where the head should have been, at the tip of the promontory, the river curving around beneath it, was the cluster of live oaks. Upstream was the green patch of vegetable garden within its enclosure of poles and adjoining it the grain field with its yellowing mass of wheat.

He saw three figures moving out along the slope above the grain. These were Rubio and two Indian boys going out to plant the grape cuttings he had brought. Far away across the river at the base of the hills opposite were the horseback figures of Cota and Morin hunting the antelope and elk which had grown scarce, and he thought how the valley had changed since he first saw it.

To his left the caballada and cattle herd including his own animals grazed in the lush bottom land, guarded by Labra and Ruiz, and beyond them on the river was the ford he'd crossed with the pack train and which Lopez had recrossed that morning returning northward. Far away toward the distant sea above the line of white dunes he could see the pack train crawling like a worm along the mesas of the coast, and remembered Lopez's final taunt: "Let me tell you where the colonists are coming from who'll settle this valley! Not from Madrid, my friend, but from Loreto, Sinaloa, Sonora! And Governor Rivera the criollo and I the mestizo shall lead them!" These colonists would form part of his future, Antonio thought. As would Juan. Incorrigible Juan, with his two missing front teeth and impudent fiddle. Disappearing from his life now, yet never to leave it, he felt sure.

The cackle of chickens, the talk and banter of the men at work upon the new quarters, the voices of women and children calling to one another from among the dome-shaped huts of the Indian village, rose to him pleasantly. All at once he had a sense of life being lived, and something of that feeling which had come to the first people to see this place thousands of years before him, who had stood not far from where he was standing, came to Antonio. This was his place. Here he hoped to spend his life.

Turning he saw, eastward toward the dark mountains, the enclave of the upper valley which had first enchanted him, and faintly visible against the hillside where the river emerged from its gorge, the smoke of Clara's village. Somber thoughts came to him. Imagining how he would attack the mission if he were Clara's brother, he decided he would use a two-pronged thrust, one descending along the slope where he stood to strike the compound from the rear, the other advancing along the dense cover of the river bottom to strike from the front. How could this best be countered? He decided to give the matter further thought. He wondered when he should see the girl again.

Strategic considerations firmly in mind, he descended the slope to where Rubio and his helpers were planting the grape cuttings. One Indian lad preceded the little padre with a hoe to scoop shallow holes as he directed, Rubio following with a basket of cuttings slung in the crook of his left arm. Bending, he placed them one by one in the sandy soil which was still moist from the late rains, and kicked the loam over them. The second lad completed the fill-in.

"How long will it be till the first wine, Father?" Antonio asked.

"The drainage is good, the east and west alignment of the rows will be right for the sun, the climate is neither too wet nor too dry," Rubio explained. "They should prosper. Three years to the first drop, God willing!"

"I make you a proposal. Let us drink it together!"

"Here or in Heaven!" Rubio replied joyfully, raising his right hand as if offering the cutting it held to the Almighty for approval.

Antonio continued down the slope to inspect the grain crop and vegetable garden and note possible avenues an enemy might use if approaching under cover of the growth along the river. Asuskwa had been described as both courageous and bold and Antonio guessed he would have a worthy adversary.

Making his way under the trees and through the undergrowth which lined its banks he came to the river and, being thirsty, knelt to drink. The water was cool and sweet as life itself. Refreshed, he stood a moment bemused by the music of the stream, the secluded beauty of his surroundings, looking, meditating, and while he was doing this he saw upstream the figure of a young girl emerge from the willows, slip off her blue chemise and red skirt, stand for a moment naked and then slip easily into the water.

Clara had no idea of his presence. The long walk homeward down the valley after the painful meeting with her brother depressed her. She'd not yet had her purifying daily swim. Turning aside from the trail on sudden impulse, she determined to have it. And when she saw Antonio swimming smilingly toward her, she strangely felt no fear at all, only joyful recognition that their moment had come at last. As they swam toward each other it seemed prearranged that they should meet in this way in the water which flowed from the Heart of the World and merge themselves in it body and spirit.

Afterward as they lay together on the sunny bank she asked him shyly: "When did you first love me?"

"When I first saw you! When did you first love me?"

"In my dream!" And at last she told him of her dream vision.

"And I laughed at you?"

"Yes, and I was quite vexed!"

"Now I shall laugh again. But don't be vexed!"

When he had kissed her once more, she said: "What a nice feeling!" because the Chumash like many Indians did not kiss. "Do all white people do this?"

"Yes," he replied smiling delightedly. "But only I do it to you!" And again he demonstrated this fascinating new procedure. Then again he took her to him passionately and the life force surged up from him to her, with love and delight, again and again; and Father Rubio watching—he'd come to the river for a drink—departed silently, feeling as if he had tasted a special kind of wine. "A miracle!" he said aloud to the listening grass, "a beautiful miracle!" And realized that what he was saying was sacrilege.

"I can't, I can't!" Kachuku burst into tears. Under stress she usually tended to lose her presence of mind, and every time she began to recite for Father Espinosa who'd assumed instruction of the newest neophytes: "Honor thy father and mother that thou mayest be long lived upon the land which the Lord thy God will give thee!" she broke down at recollection that her father had been murdered and her mother was held in disgraceful isolation until the unwanted child should be born; but Espinosa misinterpreted her disturbed state as foolishness and scolded: "The others learn readily enough. Why can't you?"

"Not severity, Brother, but love," Rubio interposed. "Love is what she needs!"

"But why not as at other missions place her in a separate class for the stupid instead of where she disrupts?"

"Because they are accustomed to doing things together. That way they encourage one another. To separate her would upset her the more." He explained to Espinosa what had happened to her father and mother.

"But if we are lenient with some," Espinosa insisted, "how can we be firm with the many, especially now when an attack is impending? Besides, if our neophytes see we are not resolute, they too may be tempted to turn against us! And therein lies also the matter of the close proximity of our village of converts to the stockade," he continued imperiously as if he not Rubio or Antonio were in charge. "At other missions converts are removed to a greater distance for reasons of security, lest their dwellings become a shelter for those who wish us harm!"

Rubio rebuked him gently. "I must agree with Corporal Boneu!" Clara, bringing tortillas and chocolate to their noonday meal, thrilled at the sound of her lover's name, as Rubio continued. "To remove our converts would be interpreted as a sign of mistrust. This is a time for us to be open and outgoing!"

But still Espinosa was not mollified. "How trustworthy is Boneu's judgment? Isn't this his first command? Is it quite wise to rely upon his youthful views?" And then Clara felt the eyes of the new father upon her and with a woman's intuition knew instantly of his secret lust, and as she was withdrawing heard him say: "Isn't it time we built a dormitory for the unmarried girls and young women as is customary elsewhere?"

She wondered why Rubio did not sense Espinosa's hypocrisy. But now that she was possessed of the revealed mystery of Antonio in the flesh, there was such joy in her heart that she could not care greatly about anything else but their next meeting.

Word came that Lehlele's child had been born with a white skin. She had strangled it and committed suicide by taking momoy. Sentries were doubled at night, two mounted men patrolling the perimeter of the mission compound in opposite directions. Work on the women's dormitory or monjerio began, partly to placate Espinosa, partly because of the expected arrival of the settlers who might provide a maestra to supervise and teach the girls.

Antonio after conferring with Rubio rejected the idea of going to the village to see if preparations for war were in progress. Such a visit would be an offensive action, they decided, which might cause the very thing they wished to avoid, and at the end of the conference Rubio said gently: "You haven't attended confession lately, my son. Is there some little thing you would like to tell me?"

And such was his penetrating sweetness that Antonio blushed and said: "Father, I love the girl. I want to marry her."

"Governor Rivera is your commanding officer," Rubio went on with a composure which surprised even himself. "With his permission, perhaps you can."

"I know. But I can't bring myself to ask him. At least not yet."

This Promised Land

"Then give yourself some time!"

"But I want her right now!"

"The impatience of youth, my son! The impatience of youth! All things come to him who waits! But," and Rubio next said something he never thought he would be saying, "when you go swimming, perhaps it would be better to go alone!"

And Antonio, flushing furiously, paid penance for a misdemeanor Rubio took it upon himself to forgive in this way.

The settlers Rivera recruited in Old California, Sinaloa, and Sonora arrived in September, winding in over the tawny hills in a column including women in bright red and blue skirts and colorful rebozos.

"Look, white women!" Clara cried, eager to take Kachuku's mind off her many sorrows, and together they rushed with the others to observe the wondrous spectacle, crying out in greeting: "Love Jesus! Hail Mary!"

Ortega was leading the party and they watched him embrace Antonio with strong affection. Then for three days there was merrymaking. Bullocks were killed and roasted on spits and there was dancing and horse racing. These colonists, thirty-four in number, were on their way to Monterey but after persuasive talk by Rubio and Antonio some elected to remain and settle in the beautiful valley. Among these were the blacksmith Jose Diaz and his kindly wife Eugenia. Eugenia, having no children of her own, volunteered to take charge of the monjerio. The one-room structure of pole and thatch had been erected not far from the church to the left of the main gate and Clara, Kachuku, who was as yet unbaptized and so had no Christian name, and the other girls and young unmarried women now slept there, locked in each night by padlock and chain. Patiently Rubio explained that everywhere in New Spain as in Old it was customary for fathers to lock daughters in their rooms at night, and since they were his daughters and the daughters of Christ, he was merely doing something that was customary elsewhere. But all the girls were eager to marry Spaniards, thinking it would unite them with the great new power and allow them to enter an apparently more wonderful world. Clara in particular resented the locking in and managed to slip out between two loose poles of the wall and meet Antonio as other girls did their lovers until Espinosa discovered the loose poles and insisted to Rubio they be replaced and strongly bound.

Under the gentle guidance of Eugenia Diaz the girls were

taught to dress and behave in Spanish fashion, to cook, sew, sing, make candles and soap, and later to spin and make cloth which they much desired. And in light of all these activities the dark threat of attack by Asuskwa and his allies, for it had been rumored that he was gathering the disaffected from other villages, faded away. Asuskwa was already showing those qualities of generalship which were to make him famous. He would not attack when expected but would wait until the moment was right.

"I knew in my blood he was coming," Clara said afterward. "I knew the price for Ta-apu, for Lehlele, for Lehlele's strangled child, for my mother—the price for life taken and not given—must be paid. It was what my brother meant but did not mention during our meeting under the oak. It was what Rubio meant when he said more than once: 'I fear atonement has not been made!' And on my own part, whenever I thought of my Asuskwa and my Antonio, a terrible dread gripped me lest they come to blows and perhaps kill each other. I tried to warn Rubio. 'Poor child!' he said when I finished. 'How you must suffer from such heavy thoughts!' He was thinking of others first as usual, rather than his own danger, as his sympathy went out to me. 'But we must put such fears behind us. Unless God guard us, who can? Remember the story of Saint Francis and the Robbers? How when they had waylaid and were about to kill him, they were overcome by his sweetness and humility and instead gave him the alms he had not asked? My dear child, the Lord knows our needs better than we do! He may give us alms such as we have never asked!'

" 'But my brother is not like those robbers!' I replied. 'He will not be deflected from his purpose. His hatred for white men is as deep as the life in him. Sooner or later he is coming. But I do not know when.' "

She had forgotten the Torch of the Sun. The sun carried a torch on his daily journey, and by lowering his thumb allowed more of it to burn and thus made greater heat on earth, and this heat could be controlled by evil shamans who knew how to influence the wind . . . or by the Great Ruler Himself.

For three stifling October days the heat increased and no air stirred. This was the result of an atmospheric condition which would later be called an inversion layer. The air seemed to be locked still in the valley, as the girls were locked in their monjerio at night, gasping for breath in the darkness.

This Promised Land

Tossing restlessly that last night, Clara finally dozed off. She dreamed that the terrible hot wind, the Breath of the Torch of the Sun, the killer wind which came from the desert to the east, had begun to blow. Its first breath was cool as death, its second a withering blast. When she was a child it had come and killed all the little birds and withered the leaves on the trees. Now in her dream she saw with horror a giant condor come and perch on the Holy Cross in front of the new church and begin tearing at the cross with its beak. And suddenly the cross became the dead body of someone very dear to her whom she could almost but not quite recognize. In horror and dread she tried to cry out but could not. She lay watching helplessly while the bird tore with its huge crooked beak at the flesh she held so dear.

And when she awoke gasping, the terrible Wind of the Torch of the Sun was blowing. It came searing like fire through the poorly chinked walls of the monjerio and through the thatch of its roof and suddenly Clara knew this was the time, this was the moment of blood and death when the price for Ta-apu, for Leh-lele, for the strangled child, for her mother would be paid ''and by those not to blame but by others, for such is the way of this world!

''I jumped up and rushed to the locked door. I screamed and beat upon it with both my hands. The girls woke around me and asked what was the matter. But no one outside heard me because of the wind. As I stood there beating and screaming I smelled the first smoke and heard the warriors' first wild yells!''

Waking, Antonio saw the thatch of the new barracks roof above his head was alight with fire and the hot wind was fanning it into a sheet of flame. ''Up, fellows!'' he shouted, springing from his bunk as sparks fell around him, hearing as he rose the savage yells above the fierce roar of the wind and crackle of flames.

Morin who slept nearest the door had already seized his musket and was dashing outside. An arrow met him. He staggered back across the threshold crying in a voice Antonio would never forget: ''Compañeros, they have killed me!''

As he was speaking a naked Indian appeared in the doorway. Antonio fired and he fell which caused those behind to draw back. Taking advantage of the respite, he and Ferrer and Labra hurriedly donned their leather jackets. Seeing that Morin was quite dead, Antonio seized his gun and cartridge belt and followed the others out of the burning building.

The hot darkness was filled with arrows, stones, and fierce yells. Shadowy figures danced at the edge of the light cast by the flaming barracks and stockade. Everywhere there was fire. The main stockade too was ablaze, Antonio saw, as his heart sank. "There must be hundreds of them!" he thought. And his next thought was for the girl locked in the monjerio. She might already be beyond saving, as might Rubio, Espinosa, Eugenia, Jose Diaz and the other settlers. There was no sign of his two mounted sentries and he guessed, with rising foreboding, they might be dead. "The livestock in the corral will have been driven off or killed too!" he thought. And at this moment of near despair he heard behind him a reassuring growl that he knew well. He'd quite forgotten Pablo.

Turning he saw what looked like a bear in a leather jacket, lumbering along, little black dog trotting unconcernedly before him, musket in one hand, circular shield in the other, an arrow protruding from the center of the shield. Pablo's hut next to the barracks had gone up in flames, and he was furious at those who'd disturbed his slumbers so rudely. Together the four men surged through the remnant of burning stockade into the mission compound. The long central warehouse and sleeping quarters occupied by the fathers was ablaze but the church at the near end of it remained untouched. The monjerio was also intact, Antonio saw with relief. "This way!" he cried and led a dash for it.

At the door they met brave Doña Eugenia and her husband Jose, arriving from their cabin beyond, and with a united effort Jose and Antonio broke down the door. Out poured a flood of terrified girls, Clara leading. Her face blanched as she saw Antonio. An arrow had cut a furrow across his forehead and blood poured down his face. "To the church!" he shouted above the terrible wind and pointed. "The church is of adobe! It will protect you! Run quickly!" She and Doña Eugenia led the way, and the rest followed, other settlers joining, and as they ran they saw before them, silhouetted against the flames near the foot of the Holy Cross, two figures locked in struggle. One was Rubio, the other Espinosa. As Antonio ran up to them Rubio broke free. "Paying no more attention to Espinosa and me than if we were not there, he began walking with determination toward the flaming gateway of the stockade.

" 'Don't go that way, Father!' I cried out and tried to stop him. 'They will kill you!'

" 'Let go, my son!' he answered in a voice of such exaltation

This Promised Land

as I had never heard, brushing my hand aside, his face radiant. 'At last, you see, the walls are coming down! Quite down!'

"Holding his crucifix high in his right hand, he advanced toward the flames and the savage horde beyond them, crying out in a voice that rose above all the turmoil and even the hurricane: 'Peace, my children! I bring you peace!' And then he began to sing! What could I do? I ran on! The last I saw, arrows and stones rained around him but none struck him as he advanced singing into the fire!''

At one side of the church a new sacristy was under construction, its adobe walls waist high; at the other was the smouldering remnant of the old one, used also as office by the fathers. Each could be entered from the church by a side door. Ordering Pablo, Labra, and Ferrer into the uncompleted one, Antonio dashed with Jose Diaz into the ruins of the old, and protected by its remnant of wall, as were Pablo and his party by the rising bricks of theirs, all began to fire at their enemies; while inside the church Espinosa led the women and girls in prayer.

"A hail of arrows and stone came back to us," Antonio recalled, "and Jose and I were struck repeatedly on our bodies, but thanks to our heavy jackets, none wounded us fatally, while the light from the burning buildings illuminated the scene so clearly that our enemies dared not approach closely. I could see dead lying on the ground and howls told of others hit by our fire. Thus for a time we held them off. Then a burning brand struck the thatched roof of the church. While clambering up to put it out, Jose received an arrow in the leg just above the knee. Even so the courageous fellow would not leave me. Far from it! Though unable to stand or sit upright he continued, half lying, to load his carbine and that of poor Morin which I'd brought from the barracks, and hand them to me, then reload mine, and so I kept up a fusillade as if from several rather than one alone; and when he began to weaken from loss of blood and I exhorted him to crawl inside the church for help and he found himself too feeble to do so, a certain girl, watching from the doorway, seeing and overhearing, darted out, disregarding the arrows and sparks from the flaming roof and helped him inside."

A moment later Clara took her place beside Antonio despite his objections. "Wearing Jose's protective jacket, she held out his carbine for me to reload after I fired mine. When I commanded her to return inside, she shook her head. This was no time to argue. Soon she was snipping open the cartridges with her teeth as she saw me do and loading the weapons herself, saying never a word, delight of battle shining in her eyes."

During a lull in the attack Antonio shouted above the wind: "Pablo, how goes it?" And from the other side of the church came back a resounding roar: "Merrily, Compadre, merrily! Soon we shall begin to sing, eh?" Next, Antonio heard the booming voice lifting in the words of the ribald old ballad Pablo learned as a waif on the docks at Vera Cruz where he sang for coins tossed by sailors and soldiers, throwing the stanzas out now into the darkness as if they too were musket balls.

> Ye mariners of Spain
> Bend lustily your oars,
> And bring us once again
> Among our favorite whores!

Inside the church Espinosa was invoking heavenly aid, his words shaking with fear: "Let us ask Our Heavenly Queen to look with favor upon us, slacken the fury of our enemies, give us victory over them! With this intention, I propose to fast nine Saturdays and offer Mass in her honor nine times!"

From the dark perimeter beyond the flames Antonio and Clara could hear voices raised, encouraging one another for a final assault. Among them they recognized with a mutual glance of amazement and horror Junipero's. But there was one which dominated all others, invoking the attack in tones of utmost ferocity.

"Who is that?" he asked.

"That is my brother!" she replied grimly, biting her lips.

"What is he saying?"

"He is saying you are afraid to step forward and meet him face to face!"

"Tell him the time will surely come when that will happen. Ask what he has done with Father Rubio!"

And when the attackers heard her voice, there was a yell of vindictive rage. Asuskwa's rose above all the others calling upon her to be true to her blood and leave Antonio and come to him. She shouted back that she would never do so. In reply came a shower of missiles. But encouraged by the steady fire from both sides of the church, the final attack never materialized, and as day broke and the wind dropped, Antonio and Clara looked into each other's eyes and knew they were bound henceforward by something more than love. Blood streaked his hands, face, clothing. Hers were stained with Jose's blood and the soot and ashes from the burning roof.

Daylight also revealed the ruin around them. Except for the church not a building was standing in what had been the mission compound. But the dome-shaped huts of the Indian village were untouched. Guided by Junipero the attackers had stealthily infiltrated and intimidated the converts into non-resistance and some into joining them, much as Espinosa had feared, before launching their attack upon barracks and mission. The rest was a smouldering desolation. Stockades, corral, chicken pen, everything.

Throughout the morning arrows and stones discharged from a distance fell upon them in desultory fashion and Antonio wondered what would happen were they to be besieged much longer, for their ammunition would soon be exhausted and they were already feeling thirst and hunger. He speculated aloud that Asuskwa might use his gun to snipe at them from a distance but Clara said her brother would never do that because it would dispell the magic power which had enabled him to kill Owotoponus. Toward mid-afternoon, when Antonio heard a distant shot, he thought she must be mistaken. Looking out upon the valley, he saw a band of horsemen galloping toward them and realized with a surge of joy it was the couriers carrying the mail from Monterey to San Diego. Because of increasing danger from attack along the way there were four of them instead of two, and at sight of this cavalcade, which might be prelude to more, the besiegers melted away into the trees and river bottom.

Leading the couriers was Corporal Yorba, Antonio's old friend and companion of the Conquest. "In the name of God, man," Yorba called out in dismay as Antonio emerged from the ruins to greet him, "what terrible calamity has happened?"

Terrible calamity it was, and yet similar ones occurred at San Diego and San Gabriel Missions and there would be threats and forays against San Luis Obispo, San Antonio de Los Robles, and even Carmel as the tide of resistance rose. Antonio estimated afterward that the attackers might have numbered as many as three hundred, assembled by Asuskwa from all neighboring villages and even joined by Tulamni from the interior valley.

While he and Yorba were talking, Espinosa and his flock were emerging like terrified sheep from the fire-blackened church, bearing with them not only the wounded Diaz but Estudillo the carpenter and Sanchez the stonemason, both injured earlier in defending their houses. At that moment a number of Christianized

Indians approached from the direction of the still standing village, calling out to Antonio not to shoot, explaining they had been intimidated and rendered helpless to resist by the ruthless attackers. They offered to join in pursuit of them.

Singling out one of the lads he recognized as having helped Rubio plant the grape cuttings, Antonio asked: "Where is the Little Father?"

The youth shook his head with what appeared honest conviction. "I do not know!"

When others came up, Clara asked the same question and received a similar answer.

She led some to look for Rubio while Antonio led others in what he feared must be a tragic search for his two sentries. He found the body of Cota near the corral, that of Ruiz near the ruins of the soldiers' barracks. Both had been stripped of clothing and horribly mutilated. But their guns and cartridges lay strangely untouched.

Clara came running back crying in agonized tones: "We've found the Father!"

Rubio lay naked partly in the water of the river with which he had baptized his converts and which was known to them as The Tears of the Sun. Heavy blows had crushed his skull. Face and body were disfigured almost beyond recognition. Women were sobbing wildly around him. Clara began to shake with grief as she looked down at him. Taking the girl in his arms Antonio tried to comfort her. "He is in Heaven. We must not cry about that!" And Espinosa added sanctimoniously: "He has found what he sought—he is among the blessed martyrs!"

But Clara flared out at that: "Do not speak so! It is sinful! He did *not* seek death! He sought life—a life more beautiful and wonderful and unselfish and innocent than you will ever dream of!" Espinosa was taken aback and fell silent.

That afternoon they recited the rosary over Rubio's shroud-wrapped body. Next day they buried him in the earthen floor before the altar of the church of his dreams "and with him," as Antonio said, "my three good fellows who laid down their lives with his that the rest of us and his mission, and this province, might live, and so what is alive is paid for by what is dead!"

Among the charred ruins they found a letter to Serra at which Rubio had apparently been at work when the attack came.

"I love this place, yet I must fear even my love for it, for I remember how Francis admonished the Brethren to love no place too much but always be ready to move onward!"

Chapter Thirty-five

In the months that followed, the face of the land lay calm, and aside from the converts at the mission, few Indians were seen. The changes slowly taking place in the valley would mark another turning point for all its inhabitants but especially for two among them.

Antonio received permission to marry Clara the following spring. Father Serra, who'd come down to supervise the rebuilding of the mission, readily agreed to perform the ceremony.

"Naturally, my son! Was not a chief reason we entered this land to cherish its people in the love of God of which holy matrimony is a most sacred aspect?"

After that Rivera could hardly have withheld his approval even had he wanted to. Still painfully ill at ease—he was seriously considering leaving the governorship and taking holy orders—Rivera nevertheless hurried down from Monterey in bitter mood with fourteen men soon after the battle, to wreak vengeance on the perpetrators of Rubio's heinous murder, and with Antonio he visited all neighboring villages in search of hostiles. At the Place Called Olomosoug they found only blackened ruins. Foreseeing their coming Asuskwa burned the village to the ground and with a remnant of his people fled into the back country. All that remained was the Wisdom Stone, the circular Judgment Seat, standing alone in the middle of the plaza with the hollow through its center which had once united the three worlds. "What is it?" Rivera asked. But Antonio did not know.

Searching further they found Junipero who'd been partially disabled by a musket ball through his left side and taken refuge at the neighboring village of Geep, up the ill-fated North Fork, and when they came to him he was an abject sight, begging for mercy. Apparently his treachery resulted entirely from wounded pride.

He'd brooded over the injury to his vanity suffered when Rubio rebuked him before the converts for taking and wearing his glasses, as "the Alcalde with Four Eyes," and in revenge had gone secretly to the conspirators and guided them to the mission the night of the attack.

Serra and Rivera disagreed sharply over how to deal with him and the three others who confessed to murdering Rubio. Rivera insisted all be shot or sent to Mexico in irons. Serra insisted all be forgiven. "Else how can we preach the religion of Jesus Christ? Harshness will drive them away! Mercy may bring them to us!" Much to Antonio's surprise Espinosa agreed. He'd felt sure the dour Castilian would join Rivera on the side of severity but instead Espinosa pontificated: "Brother Rubio would have wished it so!" Long afterward Antonio realized that Rubio alive was of little use to Espinosa, but Rubio dead could be of inestimable value as a symbol of martyrdom. All unconverted Indians remaining in the valley and all of the converts who'd defected were now anxious to make peace, and tactfully handled, as Espinosa surmised, they might flock to his fold in greater numbers than ever before. Rivera gave in.

Incredibly, therefore, within a few months not only the murderers but many others who participated in the attack were attending Mass, and soon Junipero was alcalde once more, limping slightly from his wound as if in sympathy for the little lame man he had betrayed. He professed to a new piety and led an exemplary existence as far as outward appearances went.

Antonio and Clara were married on April 10, 1775, Serra uniting them according to the Roman ritual, they kneeling on the earth which not long before had received the blood of both their peoples. He wore the silver buckle she had given him. It had become an emblem of their fate. Outside the air was sweet with the odor of fields of wildflowers. Burning on the altar was the flame Rubio had lighted and hoped would never go out, and afterward the bells rang which he and Serra had hung from the tree limb on that first day.

To satisfy Clara who insisted upon it they married themselves afterward when they were alone in the manner of her people "so that both ways may be united in us!" Taking his hand she placed it over her heart. Then they pledged themselves to one another by saying simply: "I love you and wish to live with you in marriage!"

After this intimate ceremony Clara insisted there be the traditional public one at the site of the old village, and to it came all the Indians remaining in the valley. While Serra discreetly turned his back on the whole affair they celebrated with feasting and singing, games and gambling and trading, and the wonderfully lewd dances such as the Fox Dance which Junipero as He-ap had performed that night long ago after the great victory on the Plain of the Carrizo Grass; and afterward when Antonio sang to her in the low sweet song of desire she had taught him Lospe, Clara now, did not hesitate to go to him.

Their union, the first intermarriage to occur in the valley, became a symbol for the uniting of two worlds and the peaceful coexistence which might henceforward mark its life, and consequently many Indians decided to come to the mission to live or remain in their outlying villages rather than flee to the wilderness.

Following the precedent established at Carmel in Fages' time when he encouraged the three Catalans to marry Indian girls and Manuel Butron was allotted use of a plot of land in the valley by the river below the mission, Antonio was allotted a plot by the river becoming known as the Santa Lucia, just east of the mission where it may still be seen, and thus he became one of the first to till the soil of California in his own right. Using first a pair of mules, hitched to the plow with Pablo's help, later two black oxen which he broke to the yoke, he tilled the loamy soil and felt himself embodying the dream Costanso and he had conceived and Fages had fostered of a Catalonian California composed of small landowners tilling their own earth with joy and pride, creating the social unity and strength discerned by Rousseau, for as Antonio confided to his memoirs "a nation of yeomen will be strong, loving their land as themselves, whereas a nation of grandees not in touch with the earth and its proceedings but separated from it by arrogance and love of ease will eventually decline."

He sowed corn and wheat, Pablo and friendly converts helping, and he and Clara lived in a hut of poles and thatch which Wima, her old friend and defender, the village carpenter, and Estudillo, the new carpenter from Sinaloa, helped them build in the row with others facing the church inside the reconstructed stockade. Its walls had risen again and so this aspect of the peaceful coexistence envisioned by Rubio remained only a beautiful dream.

Clara and Antonio lived so simply their descendants could hardly imagine it, having never experienced anything like it. Wima made them two stools and a bedframe over which they laced the red hide of a steer. The furnishing of the room spoke of the two worlds united there: rabbit skin blanket, rolled reed mat for pillow and a similar mat for sleeping, steatite bowl for cooking beans and the comal or flat stone with handle for toasting tortillas, baskets to hold and serve food; but metal spoons and ladles, pottery bowls, jars, and cups, two glasses and an iron grate made by the blacksmith Jose Diaz.

On the wall hung their most prized possession: the crucifix Serra gave them as wedding gift. Like his, its two arms were of unequal width, the higher shorter, and the hands of Jesus were nailed to the higher one. This patriarchal cross, its form dating from earliest Christian times, was a replica of the foot-long one Serra had carried with him since youth and placed upon his breast at night when going to sleep, and they prayed together under it at morning and evening.

With clever fingers Clara soon made them a cradle of willow for the baby she felt was coming. To commemorate the event she also created a beautiful basket of willow and sedge root and juncus grass in the manner Koyo and old Seneq had taught her, design and decoration arising from her innermost being, yet following the dictates of her people's traditions, embodying horizons broken by hills and treetops, dark interlinked diamond-shaped design of a rattlesnake's back, the zigzag path of the lightning, the dark shape with outspread wings of the condor or as white people would later say, the thunderbird. And she planted a garden as old Seneq had done in the now vanished village, and grew herbs and roots, especially the ch'pa with its lifegiving powers, Antonio describing to her how the piece Pablo gave him sustained him in the terrible winter march north from Monterey. Clara from her native knowledge also began to synthesize what would later be known as the Spanish- or Mexican-Indian herbal lore and folk medicine, using plants such as the yerba buena and lemonade berry of long established beneficence, consulting with old men and women at the mission's Indian village as to the best way to concoct and use those potions once the sole province of the curing shamans and still known to a few old people.

By Indian standards the couple were considered very wealthy and were looked up to admiringly by Clara's people, obsessed as most of them were with money, status and power. And because of Antonio's high social standing and Clara's chieftan's blood they were similarly looked up to by most of their Spanish neighbors.

Pablo soon followed Antonio's example. From the first he'd

felt an affinity for Clara's people, finding them much like his mother's velvety-eyed Siboneys; and though Kachuku was young enough to be his daughter he confided to Antonio his readiness to assume responsibility for her future.

"And what does the young lady say about it?" inquired Antonio in considerable amusement.

Pablo looked sheepish for once. Having faced hardest obstacles, he was daunted by this tender one. Removing his hat the suitor nervously fingered the sprig of sage worn there to ward off the Evil Chance, while his little black dog sat patiently on its haunches as if waiting for its master to make up his mind. Pablo continued meekly: "I haven't asked her. I was hoping your wife would do me that favor?"

Kachuku readily accepted him. Pablo's ebony skin and the esteem in which he was held helped make him a desirable husband. And after all, wasn't he a member of the gente de razon?* Neither of them converted to Christianity but they continued happily living in sin in the Indian village outside the gate of the stockade, professing their intention to be baptized eventually, fume and fulminate though Espinosa might in the meantime.

Truly those were years of hope and glory. A dark corner had been turned. Supply ships came regularly. Settlements were established at San Jose and Los Angeles. "And as our own little community grew and spread outside the walls," Antonio wrote, "my vision seemed possible of attainment. I was named acting alcalde, Jose Diaz and Emilio Estudillo councilmen. We had no official standing. It was all impromptu, informal. 'Yet by the First Law of the Indies,' as I reminded the others, 'a town shall have a plaza as well as a yard and garden plot behind each house, councilmen, mayor, plus an agent of the King. Our time will come!'"

It might not be the New Jerusalem of which Rubio dreamed. But it would be a beginning. "And then as if to encourage us word came of the revolt of the English colonies at the other side of our continent, and our good King joined with them against their English masters, and we, even we in our new province at the rim of the world were subjected to a tax of two dollars each to defray the King's expenses in that faraway war at the side of the beleaguered colonists and our French allies; and so I was em-

---

*people of reason: all non-Indians, including blacks and mixed bloods boldened to think privately that, while kings fought amongst themselves, the cause of liberty had spread to a portion of the earth on which I stood!''

Then tragedy struck them. After much difficulty including incessant bleeding Clara was delivered of a boy. He was baptized and named Gaspar after Antonio's mentor and surrogate father Portola. But he died on the fourth day. That his invisible syphilis might have caused the death of his son, Antonio never guessed. All outward manifestation of the dread disease had disappeared. And afterwards it seemed as if Clara would never conceive again. At night in tears as she clung to him in the darkness she would whisper: "I want a son! I want him to be tall and gallant like you!" The words tore at Antonio's heart and he answered: "God may yet be merciful to us!" At first her faith was absolute. She prayed to the Virgin Mary to give her that son she craved so desperately. But as the years went by her faith in the Virgin's efficacy in matters of fertility began to diminish and she turned to the remedies her mother had used, powdered sage leaves and tea made from the wild cucumber. When they also proved ineffective, two ideas began to shape themselves in her mind: one that God no longer looked with favor upon her, the other that there was truly something inimical to life about the atmosphere of the mission, as her brother had so strongly affirmed. And ever so little she began to think of him and her old way.

Periodically over those years there were attacks but never in such force or organization as that first terrible one. These were probings, forays, horses were stolen, cattle butchered, defenses tested, nerves kept on edge, and this was true up and down the coast and it was said that hidden in the fastness of the wilderness and moving freely up and down the vast interior valley where he found many allies among the unchristianized tribes, Asuskwa was becoming a mighty leader single-mindedly dedicated to driving the Spaniards out of the land or killing them all.

Whenever they visited the site at the foot of the chalky hillside where the village once stood and saw there only the solitary Wisdom Stone where her ancestors had sat in judgment during time immemorial, Antonio and Clara found lying across its top and pointed down the valley in their direction a red arrow. The sight of the arrow roused her to anger. "He hopes to intimidate us. He thinks this place is his. But it's mine as much as it is his! And it was he not I who destroyed our village!" And the tiny glimmer of an entirely new idea began to shine in her mind, which she did not confide even to her husband.

From time to time Antonio heard from Costanso. His friend was in Mexico City busy with many important engineering projects and also advising the Viceroy on various matters of policy. Costanso was urging that the existing presidios at San Diego, Monterey, San Francisco, and the one to be established soon at Santa Barbara be strengthened with additional armament, troops, skilled artisans. "Equally important, as I'm sure you'll agree" he wrote Antonio, "I've suggested bolstering civilian communities such as yours with additional colonists." Costanso also recommended a program for encouraging integration of Indians with gente de razon. Though his advice was largely ignored, there was a trickle of new settlers.

One day a group came riding in and among them were two young men and a young woman who'd journeyed all the way from the city of Monterrey in the province of Nuevo Leon near the border of Texas. Monterrey was known as the Jewish capital of New Spain and these were cousins of Benito Ferrer who'd heard from him of the opportunities offered by New California and decided to emigrate. The two brothers made application for plots of land such as Antonio and Pablo had received while their capable sister Ester set up housekeeping for them in the cabin Benito, with the help of Antonio, Pablo and other friends erected in the tract set aside for settlement.

Antonio also heard from Fages. Fortune's wheel was turning, as his fiery friend predicted when they said good-bye. Fages had married his beloved, ravishing, youthful Eulalia and, with powerful backing from his father-in-law and others close to the Viceroy, was now a lieutenant colonel serving as commandant at the frontier presidio of Pitic in Sonora.

During these transition years Antonio's major adversary became Espinosa, now Father Superior. Sensing their personality differences as well as Antonio's resentment of church domination, Espinosa did his best to thwart the young settler at every turn.

"Corporal Boneu," he said one day, "your animals are eating grass which belongs to the mission for the benefit of the Indians."

"Precious little benefit the Indians are getting from it under your jurisdiction," Antonio was tempted to reply, "and there is enough grass out there for all the cattle in Spain anyway," but instead he politely inquired what the Father Superior had in mind.

"You should move them elsewhere!"

"But where, Your Reverence?"

"That is no concern of mine!"

"Well, it is of mine," retorted Antonio, nettled. "By the Laws of the Indies we settlers have rights too! Everything is not for the church! I depend in considerable degree upon my animals, who were purchased by my labor and have increased upon the common pasture, and as my family increases, as I pray to God it will, I shall need them even more!"

During those first years his stock with their ⱯB brands—the letters neatly affixed, now, with a stamp iron and officially registered at Monterey—had grazed indiscriminately with the mission herd, but now the inevitable processes of growth and differentiation were at work.

"You settlers are insatiable!" Espinosa rejoined. "Always wanting more! I have brought the matter to your attention. I leave it to you to settle. I should rather not consult the Governor!"

The matter rankled. Other settlers including Benito Ferrer and his cousins owned livestock in considerable numbers and needed additional pasture. But the area set aside for common use was not enough, and as the mission herds totaled well over two thousand and the settlers' animals more than five hundred, friction between the two groups increased.

Then events played into the settlers' hands in a remarkable way, and the next time Espinosa raised the issue Antonio was able to reply with confidence, knowing he would prick the friar where it would hurt: "I shall speak to our new Governor about it!" For now in the autumn of 1782 Fages had returned in triumph. "You might say he returned over the body of our old adversary," Antonio recalled, "for he was the first to see Rivera's remains, and someone else's I shall mention."

It happened in this way. Rivera was bringing a party of colonists to the province along the desert route from Sonora through what is now southern Arizona and had reached the villages of the Yuma Indians on the Colorado River where there were also two recently established Spanish settlements. Among the colonists in Rivera's party were Paloma, wife of Juan Lopez, and their three daughters, one hardly more than an infant, and among the soldiers escorting them was Juan himself. When they reached the Yuma villages and the recently established settlements of San Pedro and La Concepcion, they stopped to rest and pasture their animals. Then the colonists proceeded under special escort while Rivera and Juan with eighteen men lingered to graze their stock even

This Promised Land

longer upon the Indians' lands, thus fanning feelings already smouldering, for the Yumas' corn fields and mesquite groves had already suffered severely under the mouths of the settlers' livestock.

"Rivera might have been more considerate of the rights of others, less concerned for his own animals and men," Antonio recalled. "In any event the Yumas laid their plans well." First they fell upon the Spanish settlements on the west or California bank and destroyed both, killing all the soldiers of their garrisons and all male settlers and four missionary priests including the famous explorer Garces. Then they fell upon Rivera's camp on the east or Arizona bank and after a bitter fight killed everyone there.

When word of this terrible disaster reached Pitic in Sonora where Fages commanded the presidio, he assembled a hundred Catalans and Leather Jackets and hurried across the 500 barren, nearly waterless miles to the scene of the massacre, and as he went he enlisted eighty Indian allies, Papagos and Pimas, and took care to give their chiefs handsome gifts of beads, baize, boxes of cigarettes and treated them with the respect due fellow commanders. "From the day he set foot in California Fages had shown himself adept at dealing with Indians," Antonio recorded. "They admired his hearty fearlessness and offered him their women in token of esteem. He got on better with them in many ways than with his own men." But he was changed now and managed well with both.

Reaching the Colorado he found five hundred Yuma warriors assembled on the opposite bank. "Some were armed with guns. Many rode horses. Flushed with their recent success they taunted and jeered. One chief, he could see, wore Rivera's uniform." It was a formidable array. But skillfully mixing negotiation and gifts with firmness, the once fiery hothead coolly secured the release of forty-eight captive women and children, and at the site of the final battle he found the remains of Rivera and Lopez. He identified Rivera by an old break in his right shinbone, Lopez by those two missing front teeth.

"As I looked down at them all enmity left me and moisture came to my eyes," he confided later to Antonio, "for these were my comrades in arms who died bravely doing their duty far from home!"

"Then you acted on my behalf, too," Antonio replied, similarly moved, "for I would have done likewise, though I must confess there were times when I wished Juan dead sooner!" All the vicissitudes of their long rivalry poured back over him as he heard Fages' words, and he felt true pity and regret for his old bête noire. Fages buried the bones where he found them. Then the incredible saga of derring-do which brought the little Catalan back to the governorship really began. Returning with his freed captives to the outpost of Sonoitac, he sent the bereaved women and children on toward the Royal Presidio of Altar under escort, while with the rest of his men he turned back for the Colorado to secure release of additional captives and to investigate the ruined Spanish settlements on the west bank which he had not yet visited.

Approaching cautiously he was able to cross the swollen river without opposition though smoke signals could be seen rallying the Yumas from their villages up and down stream. He'd caught them by surprise, they supposing him gone for good. When all of them had assembled and confronted him, they numbered about fifteen hundred, not counting their allies, and thus though the odds arrayed against him were not so great as those arrayed at critical moments against his models, Cortes and Pizarro, they were great indeed; and in this way Pedro Fages realized his boyhood dream, because there in the hostile desert amid lizards and rattlesnakes, without inducement of gold or silver such as motivated those earlier conquistadors, inspired only by ambition, honor, duty, and a desire to emulate, he became in many respects the man he hoped to be.

"If the Yumas acted under great provocation and fought valiantly, it was beside the point of his exploit," Antonio always insisted in later years.

As Fages stood facing his adversaries he was deep in their territory five hundred miles from his base. If he hadn't burned his ships behind him, like Cortes, he was nearly as completely isolated. At his back raged a river where two pack mules had just drowned, at his front loomed overwhelming odds.

With his men he spent that night expecting an onslaught, horses saddled, bridles hanging from saddlehorns, muskets primed. But the Yumas were too wise to attack an enemy prepared to receive them, and a series of negotiations punctuated by skirmishes followed in which ten more female captives were recovered including a mother named Maria with a baby. Though like other white female captives she'd been made to work, Maria hadn't been molested sexually, nor had the others.

This Promised Land

Negotiating, fighting, foraging by day, pasturing horses and mules under guard, watchful day and night for ambushes, constantly menaced by an able enemy who outnumbered them twenty to one, Fages and his veterans held firm in their position on the California bank until that crucial moment when they must make a sortie to investigate the ruined settlements six miles downstream and if possible recover the bones of the dead.

Leaving the camp in charge of Catalan Sergeant Noriega, he took forty-four Catalans and Leather Jackets with him. Searching the ruins they recovered the bones of Fathers Diaz and Moreno and the bodies of Fathers Garces and Barraneche. They placed the remains of the priests in a large wooden cigarette box wrapped tightly with jute cloth. The bones of the soldiers and settlers were collected and burned and their ashes placed in two leather sacks.

"Fages also recovered the great bell of the town of San Pedro," Antonio recalled, "and put it in a hamper on a mule and was thus returning successfully when a messenger met him with news that his camp was under heavy attack." Upwards of fifteen hundred Yumas and their allies including two hundred horsemen had fallen upon Noriega's Catalans and simultaneously upon the Leather Jackets guarding the caballada. "But our lads received them warmly, killing several some almost within the camp itself, and holding off the others with accurate fire."

Spurring forward Fages' party completed the repulse. Having thus vanquished his adversaries and secured the release of the last of their captives, Don Pedro retired two hundred and fifty miles to Mission Caborca, from where he sent the unfortunate women and children and the box containing the remains of the fathers and the two leather bags containing the ashes of the settlers on into Sonora under escort, while with thirty-nine picked men he turned back once more for the Colorado.

By now six months had passed and it was March, freezing cold at night, blazing hot by day. He found the river in flood but, discovering a ford, led his men, their animals swimming at times, across to the California bank in the face of the hostile Yumas, who now apparently were too astonished by his daring to resist him, and he proceeded boldly through their villages. After traveling without respite for two days and nights with no water for his nearly exhausted animals, Fages passed out of Yuman territory and in due course despite the godforsaken nature of the desert terrain reached Mission San Gabriel and relief. But this was merely an interlude. As Antonio said: "My son will not believe it. He claims it's impossible—a tale made up out of that fusty yarn of good old days; but I reply that in those days all things were possible because they were necessary!"

After resting briefly at San Gabriel, Fages retraced his route across, as he said, "land so desolate birds declined to fly over it" in order to effect a rendezvous at the Colorado with a force coming from Sonora to the east bank for concerted attack upon the Yumas. But the river being in flood and the Indians nowhere to be seen, the attack was deferred till autumn when the water would be low and the Yumas once again among their fields of squashes, watermelons, musk melons, and corn.

En route back to San Gabriel, Fages heard that tribes in the mountains toward San Diego were restive. Thinking he might quiet them and also wishing to explore new territory, he turned westward toward the coast "passing through some of the terrain we explored in '72 while on our journey to Monterey which took us by the Painted Rock," Antonio noted, "crossing high summits with pines and meadows which were like blessings to his weary animals and men and finally reaching the mission and presidio at San Diego safely, all Indians proving friendly." From San Diego he continued north to San Gabriel.

In August he set out with a strong force to keep the rendezvous at the Colorado with the troops from Sonora. As they approached the river—Fages now having been in the field nearly a year and traveled nearly 3000 miles over the roughest terrain imaginable—a messenger met him with word of his appointment as governor of New California. So there at the desert camp of Saucito under a cottonwood tree not far from the present site of Palm Springs he took office. "That was the happiest moment of my life," he told Antonio, "with the exception of my wedding day, for in both instances I came to bliss after long deprivation and suffering!"

All of this Fages confided when they met again after eight years in the compound of Mission Santa Lucia. As new governor, Fages was making his way northward to Monterey inspecting missions and presidios, and his journey had become a kind of triumphal progress as word of his exploits preceded him, also word that he himself was greatly changed for the better, and certainly Antonio found him much more tolerant and good humored, his impetuosity replaced by tactful restraint. As result of the Yuma Massacre, Fages expressed concern about the security of the coastal settlements, and particularly Antonio's exposed outpost. "If they ever unite here as they did on the Colorado they might push us into

This Promised Land

the sea!'' he declared. The massacre had cost more than thirty soldiers, not to mention colonists and priests, and he recalled a time when he and Antonio were holding the entire province with about that number. "All our adversaries have ever lacked is leadership and determination!" And Antonio replied that now perhaps their adversaries had overcome that lack in the person of his wife's brother, and he related details of the attack on the mission about which Fages had heard even in Mexico. Don Pedro agreed to strengthen the mission garrison and announced he would promote Antonio to the rank of sergeant, while trying to influence the Viceroy into granting pueblo status for the mission's civil community, thus encouraging settlement and strengthening defense.

Against such background it seemed too self-seeking to broach the subject of a place to graze his cattle apart from the mission herds and Antonio decided to defer the matter to another time.

"What happened to Lopez's widow and children?" he inquired.

"They came on to Santa Barbara when the presidio was established. I saw them there as I passed."

And Antonio was startled at the thought that perhaps his dealings with matters concerning Juan were not yet at an end.

"She's a good looker," Fages added. "No doubt she'll find another husband."

Espinosa's attitude toward their new Governor amused Antonio mightily. Espinosa was all smiles and courtesies to the man he once joined his fellow friars in condemning. As for Clara, Fages professed himself totally charmed. "What a princess you are!" he said to her face. "Antonio, you must bring her to Monterey when you come! And we shall dance in the plaza, eh, as I predicted?" His Eulalia and little son were to join him there. He expatiated on Eulalia's youthful beauty, the child's delightful ways. When Don Pedro first returned from California and was being lionized as a frontier hero in drawing rooms in Mexico City, especially that of her father, his former commanding officer, he'd fallen in love with her all over again. She on her part was enthralled by this romantic figure, hero of many adventures in a legendary land. When they married she was sixteen, he older than her mother. Except for the greater discrepancy in age, it was a story not unlike Clara's and Antonio's, with the further exception that Eulalia's aristocratic Barcelona family was influential in Madrid and Mexico City and had helped secure Fages' advancement.

"Yes, bring Clara when you come to Monterey!" he concluded with his old impetuosity. "She'll hit it off with Eulalia!"

Clara proposed a startling solution to the grazing problem. The tiny new idea which had begun to shine in her mind had grown to full light, and while she and Antonio were on one of those visits to the site of her village which she insisted more frequently in taking, she pointed out that if their animals were to graze there, they would be separated from the mission herds and have a marvelous pasture all their own. "But who would look after them?" he objected.

"Perhaps we could build a house here?" And she pointed to the old plaza with its Wisdom Stone around which the grass was growing higher and upon which the red arrow rested.

At first he shook his head at such a preposterous idea. "I would have to retire from service. Besides it would not be safe!" And he indicated the arrow.

But she persisted, pointing out further that once their animals were removed here, there would be ample pasture for those remaining behind including both mission and settlers' stock, and thus all would be well served and Father Espinosa quieted. Her simple logic made him listen. And when she saw he was listening, she moved on to her main point. "I'm afraid I shall never conceive while we live where we are. There is something unhealthful in the atmosphere at the mission. My mother died there. So did our son. So did our beloved little father with the lame foot. It is a place of death, my loved one, and for us to create new life in such a place is hard. But here," she gestured at the beautiful amphitheater of hills and sierra surrounding the upper valley, "here my being quickens!" And she pointed out to him the hollow directly across the valley where she had been born, and while trying to make him understand her feeling, her voice rose into the narrative almost like the song of joy which Koyo had sung that morning of her birth, and he listened with wonder. "I was born," she said, "at the season of the flowers or as we would say now April. Mother felt the pangs come upon her when she was over there in that grassy hollow searching for succulent brodiaea bulbs. Realizing I was on my way, she scooped a shallow hole in the soft earth, lined it with grass blades, warmed it with fire kindled with the two sticks she always carried for that purpose, and composed herself tranquilly, breathing a prayer to Sun and Sky Coyote, and Sacred Moon who referees their eternal guessing game

This Promised Land

in their crystal palace in the sky, about which I shall tell you later.

"I slid easily into the world. Removing the membrane she saw I was a girl and was glad because she wanted a daughter. Since my brother had begun to walk she'd miscarried twice. She shaped my nose in customary fashion, molding it between thumb and forefinger—yet white people think we naturally have handsome noses—and next she took me down to the river and washed me in the water that flowed from the side of Iwihinmu, the sacred mountain which stands at the Heart of the World where I shall take you some day. And then she continued homeward singing a song composed as she went along:

> Ha-ha-ha, ho-ho-ho!
> Who is happy? Who is happy?
> I am happy! I am happy!
> I bring new life! I bring new life!

"Mother smiled at people who came hurrying out of their houses to congratulate her. Some of them admired her song so much they offered to buy or lease it but she shook her head good-humoredly and went on singing, holding me out for all to see.

"My grandmother greeted her angrily as she crossed the threshold of our house. 'I warned you not to go off by yourself! It's a wonder you're both alive! Here, let me see!' And she examined me meticulously from head to toe. But instead of approval she grumbled: 'Well, it's about time! I don't know what's been going on inside you! Heaven knows you've been taking your husband aboard your canoe often enough!' We were very frank and open in those days and nothing remained unsaid as among Christians."

Seneq was especially cross because the special hut built for childbirth had gone unused and the midwives and older women been denied their customary participatory functions. "You didn't even cut the umbilical cord with the proper cane knife!"

"No," Koyo replied resolutely, "I did it with my teeth. Do not be upset, my mother. This child will thrive. She is truly a child of the earth!"

"With the help of my Aunt Lehlele," Clara continued her tale, "whose time was also nearly due, they wrapped me in a wildcat skin and strapped me to a cradle carrier made from the forked stem of a willow, while my grandfather, old Masapaqsi, rose from the bed where he'd been resting his rheumatic legs and tottered forward to see me. He had been up early as usual to pray to

Morning Star and said afterwards I was his answer.

"Squinting down through bleary eyes, he suddenly straightened up as if he'd seen a remarkable sight and exclaimed: 'She must be named immediately! Where's her good-for-nothing father? That gadabout is never on hand when we need him!' He and my father never got on, being totally unlike. They soothed him with word Father had been sent for, also my uncles Tinaquaic and Taapu and all our other relatives including Cousin He-ap, and of course old Quati, the astrologer priest, who would name me.

"Quati took his time arriving as usual. A substantial part of his income came from donations received on these occasions and he wanted everyone to be present before he appeared. He'd been our holy man for nearly as long as my grandfather had been chief, and during all those years no event of significance—not a naming, not a marriage, no war or trading expedition—had occurred without his consulting the Celestial Beings first and naming the auspicious day. But his power was, as I have told you, benign and not like Owotoponus', evil." And Antonio nodded to show he understood. "As Quati entered the eastern door, he moved ponderously because of his great weight and age. His hair was white and over it he wore a headdress of owl and magpie feathers symbolic of those who know and speak. Around his huge waist was the skirt of condor plumes representative of the power which sees what cannot be seen by mortal eyes. And elevated before him in his right hand he carried his sacred cord of condor's down signifying clouds and celestial power. Everybody fell silent as he advanced toward my cradle. Bending over with great solemnity he placed his sacred cord in a circle on the earth around it. That circle represented the eternal round, the unbroken continuity of all things which now included me.

"They said that for a long time I did not move or make a sound. Actually I was asleep. Then suddenly I opened my eyes and squirmed. Immediately Quati proclaimed in a loud voice: 'I name you Lospe—meaning flower—because you were born at the time of the flowers!'

"Straightening up he made a ceremonious gesture with both hands toward these hills which were as you see them now gorgeous blue with masses of lupine, orange with poppies, yellow with violets, white with snowdrops* and evening snow. 'Like the flowers she will have a happy life!' he announced gravely. And

---

*popcorn flowers

This Promised Land

that has proved true in some ways. 'Morning and Evening Star will lead her to good fortune!' And that also has proved true. 'The Star That Never Moves shining all night when she was born will bring her power!' That too has proved to be the case you will say, thinking me determined to have my own way. Then Quati cleared his throat and added thoughtfully: 'But since Great Sun, Our Ruler, takes as well as gives, her days may be like those of the flowers her sisters, beautiful but brief!' And that has proved quite false. As you see, here I am!''

And when he heard this charming recital Antonio understood his wife as never before and was so favorably impressed that he began to think seriously about ways in which he might bring his livestock to the upper valley and establish some kind of residence there where Clara could feel at home in familiar surroundings and perhaps conceive the son they both craved so desperately.

Pointing to the arrow lying on the Wisdom Stone, he asked: "What about that?"

"I am not afraid," she replied simply.

Chapter Thirty-six

The presidio at Monterey had changed considerably since Antonio helped to build it. Its original stockade of poles was now a wall of stone and adobe brick twelve feet high, and though its buildings continued to surround a rectangular plaza or parade ground, all were of adobe and some were roofed with tile rather than thatch. On the west side of the rectangle toward the sea in company with the dwellings of his officers was Fages' spacious new hacienda. It was whitewashed inside and out, boasting carved wooden grills over its windows, enclosing a patio and garden, all created especially for his Eulalia, the first white woman of fashion and high social standing ever to visit the province.

There was a board floor, the first Clara had seen. Heavy wrought iron sconces holding tall thick candles enhanced the walls and there was handsome furniture including armless chairs with leather cushions Don Pedro's craftsmen had made in an attempt to duplicate the luxurious furnishings of the palace in Mexico City where Eulalia had been brought up. In his absence she greeted Clara and Antonio warmly.

"You are just in time!" she exclaimed with girlish excitement. "There's to be a ball tonight in honor of the visiting French officers!" Antonio had noticed the two tall-masted ships in the harbor flying French colors and wondered at their presence. A Manila galleon had stopped the year before but no foreign vessel had ever touched a California port. "Monsieur le Comte de la Perouse, their commander, is very à la mode as are his companions!" Eulalia bubbled on. "They have stopped here to study our land and its people as they circumnavigate the globe in the interests of knowledge. Isn't that exciting? They will be charmed to meet a genuine native princess like you, my dear!" And she pressed Clara's hands between hers with extravagant enthusiasm.

This Promised Land

The two had become friends earlier when Eulalia and Don Pedro stopped at Santa Lucia on their way northward from Loreto where he'd traveled to meet her, and she had made Clara promise to come to Monterey. "Today they are visiting the mission at Carmel, under Pedro's guidance, to see the Indians and meet the fathers. And yesterday we enjoyed the most wonderful picnic by the shore on the Point of Pines!"

Returning at that moment, Fages embraced Antonio and after kissing Clara's hand inquired: "Eulalia, have they seen the children?"

"They're grownups! They're not interested in children! I'm sure they're much more eager to hear about your excursion with the officers, as I am!" And she made a face, so that Antonio was surprised and Clara shocked for like all Indian women she adored children, and indulged and spoiled them but in a wise firm way. Far from the dovelike creature Fages once described to Antonio, Eulalia was an outrageously spoiled child of luxury and indulgence, as willful as she was beautiful, and truly she was already bored by life in the rustic presidio as by her much older husband. Thus it was he who led Antonio and Clara to the nursery to see their newborn daughter and young son, she refusing with an impetuous toss of her head to accompany them when he did not first oblige her with an account of his day's activities.

"You must forgive Eulalia," he whispered. "She's so used to having her own way she flies into a temper when she doesn't get it, yet I can't let her rule me!"

Their quarrels were becoming a scandal. When she first saw the presidio and found it anything but the romantic capital she'd imagined, Eulalia flew into a tantrum and demanded to be returned to Mexico City; and when her outbursts proved of no avail, she accused Don Pedro of infidelity with her Indian servant girl and barred their bedroom door against him. Finally having to be away on business and not daring to leave her alone, he broke down the door and dragged her off to Mission Carmel where he left her in charge of the fathers, she behaving so wildly they thought her possessed by the Devil. She even demanded a divorce, a thing absolutely unheard of in New California, but in due course all quieted and she admitted the accusation against Indezuela, the servant girl, was a fabrication and contritely bore Don Pedro their daughter, while secretly never abandoning her determination to be gone from Monterey and from him. Aware of some of this, Clara and Antonio found her charming but not quite comprehensible, yet her impulsive warmth and generosity were unmistakable. During her overland journey to Monterey she'd been so moved by what she took to be the unfortunate nakedness of the Indians that she began to give them her clothes, until Don Pedro cautioned her that no such garments could be obtained where they were going and that if she did not stop she would be left half naked herself.

As they were in their room dressing for the evening's party, Clara was seized by an uncharacteristic attack of misgiving. "I'm afraid I shall embarrass you before all these fashionable people!"

"Nonsense," Antonio retorted reassuringly. "Look at yourself in the mirror!"

Her dress had been smuggled up from San Blas on one of the supply ships and he'd asked Jose Ortega to buy it when the vessel stopped at Santa Barbara, Ortega now being commandant there. It was of finest taffeta, cut in the latest style, dark blue with a brocaded pattern of delicate white and red flowers, tight bodiced, full skirted, short sleeved. It cost him fifteen sea otter skins of the finest quality.

"But I don't know how to dance as they do!" she persisted.

"More nonsense," he repeated with assumed roughness. "I've shown you. We have practiced. Let the music lead us!" Yet he himself was unsure how the wives of Spanish officers would react to the presence of an Indian woman as a social equal. For both of them it would be a trial. All would depend, he realized, on the mood of that unpredictable spoiled child Eulalia, and when they entered the drawing room he felt Clara trembling on his arm. Eulalia came right up to them in genuine admiration and extending both hands exclaimed: "My dear, how stunning you look! That chaplet of seashells is just perfect on your red hair!" and taking her from him added: "Let me introduce her, Antonio!"

Delighted by an unconventional situation where she could play a leading role, she led Clara to the wives of the officers of the garrison and introduced her with impish delight as "the daughter of the famous Queen Calafia for whom California was named!" and though they might otherwise have snubbed her because of her Indian blood, under the warm eye of the governor's lady they dared not; and as for the French officers and scientists they were entranced. Here was the very thing they were circumnavigating the world to find, truly such a creature as their philosophers Rousseau, Voltaire and Diderot had postulated. And from that moment Clara became the sensation of the evening. They were fascinated by her dignity and beauty and her delightful way of wrinkling her nose when she laughed. When not dancing with her, they queried Antonio as to the progress of Spanish settlements, methods employed in military operations against the natives, the nature of the land and its fauna and flora. Among them were an astronomer, a mineralogist, a botanist, and a doctor of medicine, also the vice consul for Russia, Monsieur de Lesseps, who was later set ashore at Kamtchatka in Siberia and carried to Paris the records of the expedition to that point. Their dashing commander, the Count of La Perouse, not a large man but resplendent in white peruke, inquired particularly as to the manners and customs of the Indians of Antonio's part of California which unfortunately he would be unable to visit because he was departing tomorrow to cross the Pacific.

"Do you find them as a whole adaptable to civilization or is your wife a charming exception? I notice she even speaks some French!"

His home was at Abri, not far across the French border from Catalonia, and he spoke with an accent not unlike Antonio's.

"It depends on what you mean by civilization," Antonio replied candidly, seizing this opportunity to express some of his new ideas. "If you mean nobleness of spirit including reverence for the beauty and harmony and mystery of the universe, I find them already more civilized than we!" This impressed La Perouse strongly. He was a man of the new Enlightenment, inspired quite literally by Voltaire, searching for values beyond those of known civilizations. Rounding Cape Horn he'd sought them at the Island of Juan Fernandez, or Robinson Crusoe's Island, and later at the Sandwich Islands as the Hawaiian group was called, and then far north at Bering's Sea and Nootka and now here, believing as Costanso and Antonio had once speculated that somewhere in a new world a new type of man might exist. But he had been keenly disappointed by the Christian Indians seen that day at Mission Carmel, finding them, as he said, "more like slaves on a West Indies plantation than free souls" and the fathers "overzealous in their paternalism however well intentioned" and thus he was encouraged to hear from Antonio that in their natural state the Indians might be quite different.

Meanwhile the gaiety of the party increased. As heedless of consequences as she'd been in championing Clara before the other women, so was Eulalia in her delight in the company of the dashing intelligent Frenchmen whose language she spoke fluently. She found them dazzling in their blue uniforms, golden epaulets and powdered wigs, their talk of Paris and the bon ton; and they, after many months at sea, were starved for the companionship of such a woman as she. This was particularly true of a certain young Lieutenant de Clonard, as was plain to see, for she danced with him repeatedly and their eyes said much which words could not, and Antonio gathered from comments he happened to overhear that this was the culmination of an infatuation which had grown rapidly during the ten days of the foreigners' visit.

"How does La Perouse strike you?" The voice of Fages broke in upon him gruffly as he was watching Eulalia and De Clonard, and he wondered if Fages too had noticed what was so obvious. He would have had to be blind not to. Yet the governor was under instructions to receive the expedition with exceptional hospitality since France and Spain had been allied in the recent war against England and La Perouse represented an answer to England's Captain Cook and his voyages of exploration and discovery which had captured the attention of thoughtful people throughout the civilized world. La Perouse had adopted Cook's dietary measures which resulted in the complete elimination of scurvy during long voyages, and had discussed with Fages Cook's remarkable observation of the transit of Venus from Tahiti which had resulted in more accurate determination of the diameter of the sun and its distance from the earth. An international community of scientists and intellectuals was emerging which freely exchanged information and ideas, and La Perouse was bringing this new development for the first time to California shores.

"He strikes me as a good man to have on our side in a fight," Antonio replied. "He was telling of his campaign against the British during the late war at a place in the far north called Hudson's Bay."

"A gallant exploit, wasn't it!" Fages seemed deliberately to ignore what was going on before his eyes in the figures of the minuet and take refuge in a man's world of military achievement. "Rammed his flotilla in there through the ice! Put the Redcoats to flight! Landed his troops, captured both forts! He's on our side in other ways too!"

"What ways?"

Fages leaned closer and lowered his voice. "Like us he is held by the Mystic Tie. Yes, he too is a Freemason. I've grown well acquainted with him during the past few days. He belongs to the Nine Sisters of Paris, the most eminent lodge in all France! And like us," Don Pedro continued, dropping his voice still further, "they oppose despotism! There is talk of a revolution in France which may duplicate that of England's American colonies! It even has the backing of some aristocrats! A certain Marquis de La Fayette, who also fought on the side of the colonists, took back with him firsthand knowledge of what liberated men can do! And would you believe this, at the death of Voltaire they conducted a fantastic ceremonial at which Greuze the court painter was present, also an emissary from the rebellious English colonies named Franklin. They went so far as to lay a crown at the foot of Voltaire's portrait! And during the banquet afterward the first toast was to America!"

"And the authorities permitted it?"

"The authorities refuse to take it seriously. They believe it is nothing but a pastime of the intelligensia and constitutes no threat!"

Violins and guitars played on. The party continued until nearly dawn. Every one of the visiting Frenchmen insisted on dancing with Clara in order to say afterward they had danced with a genuine Indian princess; and Antonio thought, as he glimpsed her radiant happiness, that he was witnessing a miracle of acceptance in which the elite of the world were meeting, and suddenly he saw that if this could truly happen all the people of the world could be as one. Eulalia's delight in the success of her protégé was so obvious as to be almost embarrassing, and Antonio found something else disturbing in it, as if it were an aspect of the giddy girl's infatuation with her Lieutenant Clonard.

After the final toasts Antonio and Clara retired to their room aglow with excitement and pride. "You never looked more beautiful!" he exclaimed. "Nor you more handsome!" she replied with similar ardor and their mutual desire rose until it was fulfilled. It seemed to Antonio only a moment later that the sound of a man's and woman's voices raised in bitter altercation waked them. "Why, it's Eulalia and Don Pedro!" Clara whispered.

So it was indeed. Antonio thought he never had heard such vituperation and screaming, such slamming of doors, and recalled that when the padres were keeping Eulalia at the mission in Fages' absence she'd thrown a tantrum right in the middle of the Mass. "Well," he said, "there's nothing we can do about it!" And feeling themselves delightfully snug and fortunate by contrast, they kissed in that wonderful way he'd revealed to her.

* * *

When he and Fages talked business next morning, Don Pedro explained to Antonio what happened the night before. Infatuated by her young lieutenant who was indeed charming, Eulalia giddily made up her mind on the spur of the moment to run off aboard his ship. "Perhaps down to Mexico, perhaps on around the world, I can't quite make out!" Forewarned by the selfsame Indian girl she'd falsely accused but who did in fact love him, Fages intercepted her at the beach. Disguised as an Indian herself she was stealing through the dawn to a rendezvous with her lover, whose launch was waiting. Back up the hill, struggling and screaming, Fages dragged her and locked her in her room. "You can't imagine what hell that woman has put me through!" he confided. "Why, she even wrote the Viceroy saying I was ill and should be relieved of my duties. Yet I continue to adore her!"

All at once he seemed broken and tragic, and Antonio felt deep pity for him. Sensing that the festivities were over in more ways than one, he decided to lay before him the matter of grazing his stock at a place removed from the mission herds at Santa Lucia.

"By all means your proposal is worthy of consideration," Fages replied when he'd heard him out. "Who has a better right to use the King's grass than we who secured it for him! It's the same way here, if anything more so since Serra's death. And I find this Lasuen no easy nut to crack, either. But since this proposal of yours sets a precedent, I shall need the approval of the Viceroy. Let me have it in writing!" And then Antonio handed him what he had written, foreseeing just such an eventuality. It said simply:

Sir:
    I, Antonio Boneu, a soldier attached to the Royal Presidio at Santa Barbara, now serving as Sergeant in command of the outpost guard at Mission Santa Lucia in the Country of the Olomosoug, appear before Your Worship with the greatest of due honor and say: I have my horses, mules, and bovine stock at said Mission, and because they are increasing and I have no place to graze them, likewise no hut for myself to care for them, I request Your Worship's charity to assign me a place six leagues distant from the Mission at the head of the Valley of Santa Lucia, at the site formerly occupied by the Indian village called Olomosoug, which was destroyed at the time of the troubles in 1774 and has not been reoccupied. Thus I can do no harm to the

rights of its inhabitants nor to those of the Mission, nor to any other person. Thus I humbly beg that Your Worship see fit to grant my request for this privilege, and if so I shall receive a precious gift.

I swear I make this request without malice or for private gain other than for the need of myself and my family and my animals aforesaid, and I promise to cherish the land and its fruits.

"This is fine and I shall approve it," Don Pedro said when he had read. "But how will you manage to attend your animals and also see to your duties as soldier?"

"I shall soon have twenty years of service behind me and shall request retirement on half pension. Pablo, too, is ready to call it quits. At least he may be entitled to alms? He will help care for the animals."

"Very well!" Turning to his desk Don Pedro wrote with customary directness:

Presidio of Monterey,
September 23, 1786:

I grant the petitioner permission of having his horses, mules, and bovine stock at the place called Olomosoug and its environs, provided no harm is done to Mission Santa Lucia nor to the pagan Indians of the vicinity, and there must be someone to watch over his stock and dwell at this place.

Pedro Fages

"There," he said, handing it to Antonio. "Now you are a ranchero. Keep that paper. But do not act upon it until I have the confirmation I mentioned."

Thus he handed Antonio his future. And at that moment Eulalia began to scream again.

Chapter Thirty-seven

Asuskwa was becoming a political as well as military leader as he ranged the hinterland encouraging the wild tribes to resist the Spanish invaders. His perception had been enlarged by his sufferings and wanderings, and he was the first native chieftain to realize that the people dwelling between the Sierra Nevada and the sea could be one society. Really he was California's first Indian governor, at least in spirit. His message was simple: unite and resist. The examples he cited in support of his argument were persuasive: his attack on Mission Santa Lucia which had cost the Spaniards dearly and the Yuma Massacre which had destroyed them totally. "We must learn to plan carefully," he counseled, "and to strike at the right moment with overwhelming force. Since we far outnumber our enemies, only apathy and lack of common purpose keep us from annihilating them or driving them out of our land!" But here he ran into difficulties for the concept of "our land" was very limited in the minds of most of his hearers. No region in North America contained more diverse ethnic groups and territories and no region was more densely populated than what is now California. Nearly one-third of all the Indians in what later constituted the forty-eight United States lived there, and this large population, numbering perhaps 400,000, was like that of a later California descended from a variety of ancestors. In the north were people of Athabascan, Algonkin, Yukian and Lutuamian stock, most quite different from their neighbors in speech and customs, and also in the north as in central regions were various groups of the large and widely scattered Penutian family including Costanoans of the San Francisco Bay area; and in the south there were similarly diverse branches of Shoshonean stock; while scattered up and down the entire region were members of the Hokan family. Like nations today each of these jumbled groups had historically followed its own way, alternately fighting and living peaceably with its neighboring tribelets, never quite able to unite for any purpose other than trade or religious observance, or occasional intermarriage. Each spoke a language—more than 100 different tongues could be counted in all—unintelligible to most of its neighbors and within the various groups there were such differences in dialect from region to region and even village to village that communication was very difficult. Asuskwa was obliged to use signs and interpreters everywhere he went. Further complicating his problem, each group was highly ethnocentric in the manner of humans since time immemorial and thought of itself as "The People" or "The Human Beings," as his own villagers had once thought, holding itself superior to its neighbors and reluctant to unite with them in any common effort.

By council fires, at trade meetings and religious festivals he nevertheless argued that they must rise above such differences or succumb to the tide of Spanish invasion. But many who listened were busy with other matters, or they coveted the beads and other gifts received when they traveled to the missions of the coastal strip. One chief of the Northern Valley Yokuts objected: "You expect us to fight your battles for you, but you are just working off an old grudge while asking us to pull your chestnuts out of the fire! The white men will never find their way over here. It is too far!" But Asuskwa answered calmly: "They will find their way everywhere and they will take everything, for they are as ravenous as a raging wildfire!" And then he would speak convincingly of his own experiences and bloody betrayals at the hands of white men. And when another chief argued: "You expect us to contend against guns with bows and arrows?" he replied by citing what he had done with bows and arrows and stones during the attack at Mission Santa Lucia. "There is a great evil in guns," he added, "which is why my men and I never use them. Why should we weaken our strength with what we know is bad?"

Thus he kept the vow he made before the sacred condor painting on the wall of the cave never to use a gun except to kill Owotoponus, and he never allowed his men to employ guns or lances or horses against the Spaniards, even after others obtained these through theft or capture and used them effectively; and this strange obstinacy and purity of intent added a mystique to his cause, making it seem special to many who learned of it and began to feel as he did.

Thus with a hard core of faithful warriors from his native village, landless, homeless, dispossessed but fiercely committed to revenge, he began to forge a resistance which would continue and be the longest and bloodiest of its kind in the annals of what is now the United States.

In 1788 there was a night attack on Mission San Luis Obispo with fiery arrows in which two neophyte Indians were killed, one soldier wounded and a dozen horses driven off. In 1795 a party of soldiers and neophytes sent across the bay from San Francisco to investigate disturbances in the interior were set upon and roughly handled. The bravery with which the Indians fought astonished the Spanish commander. In 1798 a large body of Indians surrounded Mission San Juan Bautista not far south of San Jose but were driven off with substantial losses on both sides. In 1804 there were frightening rumors of an approach against Mission San Gabriel and the little walled pueblo of Los Angeles by a horde of Indians from the Colorado region, and in the following year a punitive expedition against the hostiles of the Tulares in the great central valley resulted in bitter fighting when the Indians were found to be entrenched in pits cleverly concealed from which they discharged arrows and into which the soldiers' horses fell and were disabled. Bloody hand-to-hand fighting with swords and lances, clubs and knives ensued.

Other native leaders were often mentioned as being involved in these operations, but it was Asuskwa who was the moving force behind them all, and though he refrained from attacking the mission in his native place—knowing it to be reenforced and expecting him—and merely sent his sister those mysterious but unmistakable warnings in the form of the red arrow left upon the Sacred Stone, it was naturally to his native land that his thoughts turned often. He saw that there the Spaniards were indeed weakest and that a concerted blow at the relatively narrow corridor they held between mountains and sea might cut their chain of settlements in two, leaving those in the north isolated from those in the south, and enable a well organized and vigorous attack to defeat them utterly, as the Yumas had utterly defeated the Spaniards and destroyed their two villages and Rivera and Lopez and all their men.

And all during this time his personal conduct enhanced his efforts. He behaved modestly, never asking advantages for himself but only for the common cause, never married or had anything to do with any woman or man sexually but remained single-mindedly devoted to his goal, and it was noted with approval that he worshipped his native deities regularly including the Great Condor whose lesser embodiments could be seen soaring every day over the region he wished to unify, as if adding supernatural mystery and power to his cause.

Eary in the summer of 1791, the year they received word of the revolution in France, Antonio and Clara began to build the house she had dreamed of at the site of her old village. It was made of fireproof, arrow-proof adobe brick with a tile roof and resembled on a small scale a mission compound or presidio rectangle. Its exterior windows were narrow slits through which guns could be fired and it stood naked and alone on the site once occupied by the plaza of her village, and at the center of its enclosed courtyard was the Wisdom Stone.

The work was done with the help of Pablo and his four sons and of friendly Indians who were repaid in beads, cloth, wheat or beef from Antonio's rapidly increasing crops and herds. And some Indians, unhappy with life under Espinosa, stayed away from the mission and lived in huts by the river where Pablo had built his first shelter while he and his boys cared for the livestock; and other Indians drifted down from the hills to join those already there so that before long there was a native community or Indianada at what was becoming known as Rancho Olomosoug.

In the following year when Antonio received permission to retire at half pay, the house was completed and they moved to it. Despite some misgivings on his part as to their safety, Clara was anxious to be gone from the vicinity of the mission and to dwell in what she felt was the fresh, free and fertile atmosphere of the ranch, believing that there she would conceive and bear the son they both wanted so badly. Antonio felt some additional hesitation about leaving the settlement and the causes which engaged him there but he was willing to make any sacrifice for his wife's welfare and the chance of their having a son. Besides, as he told himself, the separation from the pueblo community would be only a matter of a few miles and thus more apparent than real. Furthermore by occupying his grant, or concession to pasture his livestock on the King's land, he would be pioneering the way toward greater independence and increased opportunities for all. And so he went gladly and encouraged her in her belief, and as her time drew near she resolved the child should be born in the way and place that she had been. She prepared herself with determination for the event, and when she sensed it near she went off alone without telling anyone to the hollow across the river. There in the grass of the earth, as she had been, her son was born, and when she came back with him in her arms and Antonio met her joyfully, she was singing the song Koyo had sung at her birth. "Thus he will truly be of two peoples," she said, "and of this place! Let us give him two names, since he is of two worlds." So they named him Helek or the hawk in her language, for a hawk knows its own way; and Francisco after the saint and the great bay which Antonio helped discover, for they hoped that the child too would be a discoverer at heart.

For the first naming ceremony old Quati's younger son Tilhini—the antithesis of Owotoponus, kindly, thoughtful, patiently wise in the ancient lore—who'd come to live at their Indianada, officiated as Quati had once done; and for the second they reluctantly carried the child to the mission where Espinosa duly sprinkled water and named him, shrewdly asking if they were dedicating him wholeheartedly to the Christian way. But they kept his Indian name secret from Espinosa and from everyone except Pablo and Kachuku who witnessed that earlier ceremony, because as Clara pointed out to mention it would bring bad luck.

And to justify her hopes the boy throve wonderfully and showed no signs of ill health. Clara kept him first in the cradle carrier made of willow such as she'd been kept in for the first three months following birth, then in the larger Y-shaped cradle board which had a tule mattress and similar sun shade. The child was wrapped with a diaper of soft absorbent dry moss, which was changed often, while to prevent chafing and rash his little bottom was powdered with powdered steatite, which is to say talc; and he was laced into his cradle with a very special deerskin band about an inch and a half wide with shells sewn on it such as Indian women wore to wrap the long braid that hung down the backs of their heads. As soon as he was able to toddle he was freed from the cradle and allowed to go naked in the warm healthy air.

Clara never disciplined her little Francisco except by deprivation of privilege when necessary, never struck or punished him physically in any way, but lovingly and firmly reared him as she had been reared, building that confidence which is so essential to a child's stability. At first Antonio was amazed. Having suffered many sound beatings as a youth he believed them essential to progress toward maturity. But in keeping with his admiration for his wife and her people he let her have her way, and the boy was brought up Indian fashion but as a Spaniard too.

"I see in him the new man," Antonio wrote Costanso, "of whom Rousseau wrote and you and I talked, not to mention Fages and La Perouse! He is the man for whom this glorious land is destined!" The irony of this statement in light of what lay in store was to be remembered later.

It was at this time that Clara began to participate fully with her husband in the daily life of the ranch, breakfasting early, riding out side by side with him on her white-footed bay mare which he'd named Princess, joining in the roundups held each fall and spring, learning the ways of animals upon the land, and how to use a reata and to shoot pistol and musket, and even to kill a running steer from horseback with one blow behind its head while riding astride at full gallop knife in hand, and to take counsel with her husband in all practical matters, and in this athletic and businesslike companionship she set a pattern which other California women would follow.

She observed closely the methods of slaughtering cattle for their hides and tallow, accompanying the men and animals to the matanza or killing ground by the river a short distance downstream from the hacienda. After each animal was lassoed by head and feet, stretched flat upon the ground and its four legs tied in a bunch together, its throat was cut and hide quickly removed and staked out to dry. Then the fat was rendered into tallow in huge iron try pots and poured into big leather bags for storage until shipment.

And at the threshing season in midsummer, Clara also attended while the wheat and barley were threshed out upon hard ground by the feet of scores of mares with cropped manes and tails who raced around and around a circular corral. When they became dizzy from circling in one direction, they were turned and driven in the other.

"Poor victims, I protest for them!" she interceded laughingly. "They work for you men until they are dizzy. Why not make your stallions do a little?" But Antonio replied, laughing with her, that such practice could not be tolerated because it demeaned males at the expense of females, and when she asked him why the manes and tails of the mares were always cropped and made into ropes, reins and halters, but never those of stallions, he replied: "Because then the mares would take a dislike to the stallions and no longer look up to and respect them!"

"But I should love and respect you no matter what the length of your hair!" she retorted gaily. "I think your policies toward mares are cruel and unjust!"

In turn she showed him her favorite places and he learned to know the land intimately through her eyes. "This was where I first saw you in my dream," she said, taking him across the river to the hilltop where old Quati had sat shining like a polished stone while the sun of that new day rose upon her life, and Antonio marveled at the magic of the place and the mystery which seemed still to pervade it as he gazed at the surrounding panorama and heard her explain the significance of the three worlds into which she'd been born.

Then she led him to her father's grave marker and recreated for him the terrible drama which had transpired there, so that he could almost scent the bittersweet fragrance of the funeral pyre with its bay bough and lock of her hair; and then she led him up the river into the strangely haunting back country, condors soaring above them, until they came to the waterfall cliff over which the river plunged, and she showed him the great birds perched at the edge of the precipice wheeling this way and that with outstretched wings as the sunrise fell upon them, and it took his breath away. He felt gripped by something of their supernatural power which seemed to come from prehistoric ages, and as she had done as a young girl, he began to feel he was observed by mysterious eyes, as a member of a community of all living things.

Then she took him deeper into the wilderness, on toward the Heart of the World, and they walked hand in hand by the rushing stream under the dark trees where she had walked with her father, till they emerged upon the summit of the sacred mountain. Then he could see the full scope and splendor of the land which was now his land, of which she and he were part, from the offshore islands to the snowcapped mountains. Overcome with awe and feelings of thanksgiving he took her hand again and they knelt together and gave thanks for all created things to the Christian god and the god of the mountain.

Clara was filled with immense happiness by this. She felt at last she was sharing her innermost being with her loved one, and when that night they made love on the grass it was with renewed ecstasy.

"Can it be that we shall create a new world from our own separate ones?" she asked him.

"Yes, it can be!" he replied tenderly.

On the way home she took Antonio to the Cave of the Condors and showed him first Owotoponus' innovative masterpiece on its outer lip, at which he expressed amazement, and on the inner wall the crude condor figure of such great antiquity, at which he expressed still further wonder, but when he saw lying in the gray dust before it the bell-mouthed trabuco or carbine blunderbuss with the initial "N" embedded in its stock in brass studs, he uttered an exclamation of recognition and astonishment. Full recollection of the escape of Nunez came back to him. He also understood as never before the character of the mortal adversary who was his wife's brother, and beyond antagonism he felt a new and enlarged respect for Asuskwa.

As he stooped to pick up the gun, Clara intervened. "It would be sacrilegious!" she warned, and he obeyed her admonition, realizing its wisdom.

She explained what had traditionally taken place at this spot at the time of the winter solstice when the sun entered the Eastern Window and placed its finger upon the painting of the ancient condor upon the back wall, and was persuaded by ceremonies and prayers not to continue its southward journey but to stop and begin to travel northward again, bringing light and warmth and life. "Sad memories of things now lost," she concluded in a moment of somberness.

"But our son shall know of them," Antonio responded determinedly, "and remember and understand!"

"Yes," she said, "he will be a great man like you, but in a new way!"

Frequently in earlier years when Antonio came riding from the settlement of Santa Lucia to visit his ranch, he would ask Pablo if he feared living there as caretaker comparatively alone and defenseless, and Pablo would shrug and touch the sprig of rosemary in his hat. "I hear from the Indians that Asuskwa is alive, armed, and planning to come back into this valley, but I am not what he wants. He is waiting for bigger game, Compadre!" and then Pablo would look away into the distance as if the bigger game were off there somewhere. After visiting the sacred cave, Antonio thought he fully understood the meaning of Pablo's remark. The disciplined restraint of Asuskwa continued to impress him deeply. Here was indeed a man who could keep to his vows and wait.

One morning a few days after their return home he and Clara were sitting at early breakfast when little Francisco came rushing into the room brandishing a bright red war arrow in one small hand, crying out in delight: "Look what I just found!"

"Where did you find it?" Clara demanded, her voice rising with alarm.

"On the Wisdom Stone!"

"Impossible!"

But he insisted and taking them there, showed them where it had been lying. In the dust beside the stone in the center of the courtyard they saw the print of a naked foot.

"It's he!" Clara cried out involuntarily. "See how the big toe of the left foot splays away markedly from the others? He broke it as a boy clambering down to raid those condor nests I showed you on the waterfall cliff!" And her face clouded. "That is his footprint. I would recognize it anywhere. He thinks to intimidate us. But he will never do so!" she affirmed grimly, lifting her face to the sky.

But the child did not understand all this. He was fascinated by the arrow.

"Can I have it?" he begged.

For answer she snatched it from him rudely and snapped it in two pieces across her knee and flung it in the dust with an execration. "He shall not frighten us from this place where we live, which we have worked so hard to attain, which he abandoned after staining us all with blood!" And impulsively she seized her child and clutched him to her with unreasoning possessiveness so that he fussed and disengaged himself.

Antonio meanwhile, filled with alarm and dismay at what seemed an incredible intrusion into the locked and guarded compound, picked up the pieces of arrow and examined them. Their design was the one common among his wife's people: point of chert, foreshaft of chamise painted bright vermillion, mainshaft of reed banded red, black, and green; while the fletching was of three split tail feathers, an eagle's, a hawk's, and an owl's. "He might have killed me with this but he did not," he thought, marveling. How had the intruder entered? No one could tell. The dogs had not barked. Pablo and his sons had been up and about at intervals during the night as always but saw or heard nothing. And Antonio felt again that strange feeling he'd had in the backcountry that he was being observed by mysterious eyes.

"Can I have an arrow like this one?" his son begged. Playing with the boys of the Indianada, Francisco had already learned to shoot with his toy bow the arrows with wooden points hardened in a fire that killed rabbits and squirrels at short range.

"The time will come, the time will come!" Antonio temporized uneasily, as his eyes met those of his wife above their son's head, in unspoken concern.

It was not long after this that kindly old Tilhini, advising and guiding the boy in the Indian way as his parents wished, made him an adult's bow of beautiful polished juniper reenforced with deer sinew, and taught him how to shoot by holding it almost crosswise in front of him much like the crossbow of Europeans, as Antonio noted.

Chapter Thirty-eight

But no attack came and as they reached the year 1811 it seemed to Clara and Antonio and the members of their little community that none ever would. Their enclave at the head of the valley had prospered enormously and the mission a few miles away was now the richest in the province. Its herds like theirs had increased astonishingly and Antonio's enterprise evidenced itself in other successful ways, so that as he rode down the valley on a fine May morning it was with a pleasant feeling of anticipation regarding the business which lay ahead for discussion with Father Espinosa, business which involved them both in a new and interesting manner.

As he rode along, his spurs jingling pleasantly to his sorrel's jogtrot rhythm, the fields at either side burgeoning with wheat, barley, and corn reminded him of Mission Santa Lucia's new wealth and the almost incredible extent of its herds of cattle, horses, and sheep which now totaled nearly 60,000. Ahead of him the vast structure of the mission complex rose like a castle in the morning sun. It was something far beyond Rubio's wildest dreams, a monument to Espinosa's stern ambition and shrewd management, and yet it was a monument to Rubio too, for in the thatched huts of the Indian village at its gates were two thousand baptized converts many of whom had flocked to the fold as consequence of what they believed to be his blessed death and martyrdom. It was in no small degree also for Rubio's sake that they labored in the vineyard and orchard he had planted, now also grown beyond all expectation, and at the magnificent new church, the largest and finest in all the province, being erected in his memory.

Antonio had timed his arrival for eleven o'clock when he felt sure that Espinosa and his young assistant Father Rafael would be at their middday meal, and as he approached the front of the unfinished church he was greeted by friendly Indians who called out the traditional "Amar a Dios!" to which he replied in kind with a smile for he felt these people to be related to him by deep experience as well as marriage. He'd come to regard their subservient condition as an unfortunate change from their natural state, and at his Indianada tried to provide a viable alternative for both converted and unconverted. He knew that many converts were well satisfied with their life at the mission and even joined in its defense and in counterforays against their hostile relatives. But still he felt the general state of their affairs to be unjust and their future highly uncertain, and in this feeling his wife fully concurred.

Dismounting he tied his horse to the hitching rail under the drooping green branches of a pepper tree. Nearby the great stone fountain played musically. As he turned to enter the inviting shade of the long arched portico, he noticed a young Indian woman sitting in the stocks in the blazing sun outside the jail. Her bare head and feet were within the boards, indicating punishment for a severe misconduct, perhaps adultery, perhaps attempted murder. But since this was no uncommon sight in the domain of Espinosa as at other missions and there was nothing he could immediately do about it, Antonio merely compressed his lips and entered the cool shadows of the portico.

Its graceful arches ran across the front of a large quadrangle formed by the mission compound, of which the uncompleted church served as a kind of cornerstone. This quadrangle measured 500 feet on each side and included storerooms for supplies, tools, and farm implements, a blacksmith shop, workshops for spinning and weaving, candle making, soap making, pottery, and leather work. There was also an infirmary and a building for young unmarried men to match the monjerio at opposite back corners of the square, as well as the padres' quarters and guest rooms which fronted on the portico. All were of adobe bricks roofed with tile except the church which was of brownish gray field stone from a quarry Father Rafael, the master builder, had discovered in the nearby hills.

Passing into the interior cloister Antonio was in a secluded courtyard where multicolored hollyhocks bloomed in a garden plot and the fragrance of honeysuckle climbing the walls pervaded the quiet air. Espinosa and Rafael were at a table under one of the arches which surrounded this sheltered retreat. Since the close presence of girls was now strictly forbidden by regulation, young boys were in the act of bringing them tortillas and hot chocolate from the kitchen and Antonio accepted their invitation to sit down and join them.

"And what did you think of the proposition the young American sea captain made you, thanks to my suggestion?" he began pointblank, prepared for what was to follow since Espinosa could be as roundabout in business affairs as he was direct in matters of doctrine and discipline. The aging Father Superior's hair was turning gray and he was nearly bald but his expression had lost none of its severity.

"I've been so busy with my spiritual duties," he sighed resignedly, "that I've scarcely had time to think about business, and now it is pine trees I have on my mind. Aren't there some growing on your place?"

"And why pine trees?"

"Large beams are required for the ceiling of our new church."

"Seven years you've been building your monstrosity and now you want to crush it by heaping trees on top?" With a wink at young Rafael, Antonio turned upon Espinosa in the half facetious, half bitterly serious manner established between them by long usage. "Why are you determined to build the largest church in all the province in our secluded valley? Is God bigger here, better here? No, you are here! That is the true reason! And you've gotten so rich in your illicit trade with foreign ships, at which everyone winks an eye, you think you can afford such foolish grandeur! I predict it will come to no good!"

Espinosa shrugged and flipped a rolled tortilla toward one of the waiting Indian youths who opened his mouth and caught it between his teeth with an impish grin. "Regardless of your impertinence, Brother Rafael must have beams—must you not, Brother Rafael?" he said with patient resignation. Diego Rafael who was pretending to be neutral during this exchange was in fact a gifted architect and engineer as well as master worker in stone. He was a Gallego or Galician from that stony northwest corner of Spain where even the corncribs are graceful expressions of the mason's art and his skilled thoughts and hands, guided by Espinosa's stern ambition, had created not only the new mission quadrangle but the extraordinary new irrigation system.

With Indian labor Rafael constructed a stone dam in a canyon in the nearby hills from which a stone aqueduct brought a steady clear flow to a large stone reservoir upon the hillside overlooking the mission. From the reservoir part of the water went to turn a grist mill while the rest continued to the large octagonal stone fountain that played under the pepper tree in front of the church, from where it ran into a long open lavatory or trough with sloping stone sides. There, as if on the banks of a stream, women might scrub their clothes while they gossiped within the shadow of a Holy Cross made from massive limbs. Finally the water flowed on to nourish orchards and vegetable gardens.

Rafael was a quiet man, expressing himself best in work of this sort, and the loquacious interchange between the other two made him feel uncomfortable. With the help of the famous compendium by Vitruvius, the noted author-compiler of the age of Caesar Augustus, Rafael was creating in the new church something even a Roman emperor might have found appropriate. Above a classical Greek façade embedded in an otherwise Moorish front, four domed towers were rising slowly skyward, framed by scaffoldings of poles, grouped around a central or fifth tower. This latter would be far grander still, groined and vaulted like a cathedral's apse, and it was to be painted blue inside like heaven and be surmounted outside by a golden cupola like the throne of the Almighty.

"If it be deemed desirable," he replied gently and tactfully to his superior's question, "we will support the roof of the nave with beams."

"And so you see, we must have trees!" Espinosa turned back to Antonio with weary patience.

"Very well. You will find some directly up the river floor. Six miles above my house."

"But aren't those the crooked ones? These must be mountain pines, tall and straight."

"Indeed you are insatiable! To get those you must travel six miles more and climb. Send you majordomo. Pablo will show him."

"But Brother Rafael wishes to select the trees himself!"

"I don't think Rubio ever envisioned anything so elaborate as this sepulchre you are creating for him!" Antonio burst out.

"We will improve on Rubio's vision," Espinosa replied imperturbably. "The dear man was if anything to modest."

"Not a failing you will succumb to! How do you expect to transport such loads? There's no road or trail, nothing an oxcart might follow."

"Since it is all for God, God will provide a way."

"And will God also reimburse me for my trees?"

"We can consider them part of your annual tithe. Each could be worth five head of cattle!" Espinosa riposted with sudden shrewdness.

"Ah, so? And is this the manner in which you dealt with young Captain Sedley?"

"The American told me you yourself were harder to deal with than a clam!" Espinosa retorted in a further penetrating thrust, and Antonio acknowledged this with an incredulous smile and a shake of his head at Rafael, as if to say that some people are incorrigible.

Two days earlier he'd happened to go with Pablo and Pablo's four sons—the four acorns, Antonio called them, because they were the brown-black color of acorns which have lain upon damp earth—and four pack mules to the estuary at the mouth of the river to gather salt, and while they were loading the mules, they saw a ship approaching swiftly on the northwest breeze. As she cleared the point Antonio had named for Portola and dropped anchor in the shallow bay, he saw she was a brigantine with a new and trimmer line than any he'd observed before, flush decked, gracefully raked, sharp in all respects, and she flew the Stars and Stripes which he'd heard about but never seen.

With Pablo and the four boys and their animals, he stood still upon the beach and watched while she lowered a boat from under her starboard guns, and a big comber soon delivered it almost at their feet. Its crew who evidently knew their work were half-naked Kanakas, he noted, as Hawaiian Islanders were called, and their stalwart young captain wore the new-style revolutionary long trousers as well as black cocked hat and dark-blue cutaway coat. In company with his taller, older, more traditionally dressed companion—a Russian, Antonio judged by the black shapka which covered head and ears even on a spring day—the young captain advanced and greeted him heartily with a: *"Ha, Señor, Los Anglo-Americanos con los Hispano-Americanos, bella union!"*

"Bella union, hombre, bella union!" echoed Antonio thus firmly establishing a phrase that was to become a political rallying cry in future decades, and for good measure adding a heartfelt: *"Viva el liberalismo!"*

But since Americans were reputed to be liars and cheaters and were strongly suspected of desiring to take over the province, Antonio was on his guard. Yet there was something powerfully disarming and ingratiating about the gutsy fearlessness of this youngster with the strange long trousers. He acted as though he owned the world, cheerfully, and was entitled to do so.

Horatio Sedley was just nineteen, the age Antonio had been during those great days of the Conquest, and had commanded his own ship for three years and been to China. He was distinguished by that ruddy complexion known to Spanish Californians as "English," and his eyes were as blue and his hair as yellow as Antonio's. He'd exhausted most of his Spanish vocabulary, in that first exuberant outburst and his supercargo, the courtly Kalenin, in fact a Russian factotum from Sitka in Alaska, continued the dialogue in more formal tone.

Their vessel, he explained, was the *Enterprise* from Boston by way of Cape Horn and the South American ports, thence to the Sandwich or Hawaiian Islands, and then up to Sitka where at New Archangel Sedley had sold the Russians New England furniture, shoes, stockings, ladies' fine handkerchiefs, hammers, nails, saws, picks, shovels, knives, guns, and ammunition and such food as he could spare to the total value of some ten thousand rubles, as Antonio learned later. The *Enterprise* was now come down to California under contract with the Russians to hunt and trade for sea otter skins and take on grain. Since these latter activities were known to be strictly forbidden by Spanish law but nevertheless regularly engaged in by fathers, soldiers, and settlers, Kalenin and Sedley avoided the ports of San Francisco and Monterey, where there were presidios and officials, and came to the secluded anchorage at the mouth of the Valley of Santa Lucia. Besides a crew of many races they carried fifty Aleut Indian otter hunters and in addition to those trade goods already mentioned tobacco, cottons, and deal boards. "We believe mutual need creates mutual benefits," Kalenin explained judiciously. "Ourselves, we lack provisions such as meat, eggs, vegetables, salt, and above all fresh water."

Antonio was favorably impressed by what he sensed to be the significance of this occasion. "Well, you have come to the right place and the right man," he replied with candor. "I have the best otter skins you will find on this entire coast, and the same goes for my vegetables and beef. As for salt, you may see for yourself that I hold it in my hand," indicating the mule packs, "and here is a sweet river. I am a rancher and sometime trader and have long advocated freedom of commerce. The life of our province is stifling for lack of it and we must act for ourselves since our reactionary Government cannot or will not act for us! There was a time when we had great kings, but now . . . !" and he threw up his hands, "we have none!"

"By heaven, you sound like a Boston patriot!" exclaimed young Captain Sedley.

"Well, I come from Catalonia," replied Antonio warming to his subject, "where people are enterprising like you Americans. And, by the way, I contributed money to your fight for freedom, as I now contribute to the Spanish struggle for liberation against Bonaparte!"

"The devil you say! My father fought under General Washington!"

"Yes, I believe liberty should be fostered everywhere, even in Russia, begging your friend's pardon, and the capture of Madrid by that upstart Napoleon and his placing his brother on the throne is something I cannot condone. But as result of such turmoil, our ships do not come from Mexico or Manila as they formerly did and our commerce is in decline. Thus we must rely on your help as you once did on ours!"

By the time Espinosa and his escort of Indian converts and curious townspeople arrived to welcome the strangers, they had reached an understanding with Antonio.

"And if I refuse to let you have my pine trees, will you sentence me to the stocks like that poor woman I saw outside the jail just now?" Antonio resumed his conversation with the friar.

"It's a possibility," Espinosa responded blandly, sipping his chocolate, "but let us always remember that we sentence ourselves."

"I shall remember that!"

"And meanwhile," resumed Espinosa, "I'm tempted to report you to Governor Arrillaga for illegal trading with foreigners!"

"Ah, but you won't," retorted Antonio, "for you have profited greatly, thanks to my young captain! You sold him every one of your otter skins for six dollars and will profit more when he returns from his southern hunt and buys your grain to take to the hungry Russians of Sitka. Lucky for you I had no grain to sell him myself! As for meat and vegetables, you can't blame me if he preferred mine to yours!"

"I wonder if he will stop at Santa Barbara during his southern hunt?" Espinosa mused, as if Antonio did not exist.

"No, he won't stop at Santa Barbara for there is a presidio at

Santa Barbara and although Captain Arguello is favorably inclined toward trade with foreign ships, he would not dare flout the law openly. But Sedley will stop at Capistrano where like you the fathers know how their bread can be buttered!"

"I shall impose a severe penance for your impertinence when you come to confession," Espinosa replied, rounding on him sternly, "if you ever come! And I hear that your wife teaches your baptized son idolatries from the old Indian religion! Let Brother Rafael be my witness!" And then relaxing and placing both hands upon his well-filled belly he gazed not at Antonio but at the pigeons cooing about the dovecote on the roof.

"And I shall report to the Governor your dealings with the American smuggler and his Russian friend who is without doubt a spy sent to observe our scandalous lack of defenses!" Antonio retorted. And thus they reached their usual standoff, neither able to gain lasting advantage.

After taking leave of the friars Antonio continued to his former house in the town which was now occupied by his friend Benito Ferrer and Ferrer's wife Maria Ester and their three children. Though it was siesta time he guessed Benito would be engaged in some profitable activity. In fact he found him listening to his young daughter Maria Ana recite her reading lesson. Despite the smoke he'd noticed emerging from the chimney as he approached, there were no signs or odors of cooking in the house, and suddenly realizing it was Saturday, Antonio came to the conclusion Benito and his family were practicing their Judaism in secret by observing a Sabbath fast, and he remembered Benito telling him long ago how marranos or secret Jews in Mexico as well as in Spain outwitted the spies of the Inquisition by worshipping in secret, lighting their candles in closets, koshering their meat, sweeping their houses well on Fridays, observing the Sabbath by not working, putting fresh linen on their beds and wearing clean shirts like Christians.

"When fasting during the Day of Pardon and at other times," Ferrer said, "men who appeared in public would keep toothpicks in their mouths in order not to arouse suspicion, making it seem they'd just eaten, while women kept fires going in kitchens so that smoke would emerge from chimneys as if meals were being prepared. Or they complained of stomach troubles as excuse for not eating." Even so the police apprehended many who were dragged off to dungeons, often to wait years before trial, and then be tried in secret without opportunity to face their accusers before being burned alive, or strangled, or condemned to service as oarsmen on ships where few survived "and this was true even of the Manila galleons on this coast," Benito noted.

In lesser cases victims were often sentenced to wear humiliating garments of coarse cloth with pictures on them of demons pushing heretics into hell's flames, and a high peaked cap like a dunce cap. "Women too were subjected to these tortures and indignities as well as being raped or forced to grant sexual favors to their jailers," Ferrer confided further to Antonio's horror, "and the final test for men was the examination of the penis by a team of three doctors to see if it had been circumcised. We tried to fool them by making the incision longitudinally instead of around the organ or by saying it was a scar, and one imaginative fellow claimed he'd had it done at the request of his loved one who was a Jewess." But such ruses seldom had any ameliorating effect and sentence was pronounced regardless.

Antonio kept these confidences and they cemented a friendship. He'd long suspected his house was now secretly used as synagogue by Benito and his family and his cousins and their wives who with him operated the community's only store, but he had no proof and cared for none, but only the pleasant conviction that things were so and his old friend worshipping as he saw fit right under the nose of Espinosa. Though the Inquisition still functioned from its dread headquarters on the Plaza de Santo Domingo in Mexico City and though the Father Superiors of California continued to be its designated representatives, the liberalizing forces of the Enlightenment spreading worldwide from the explosive impulses of the French and American revolutions were reaching the remotest frontiers, and in New Spain no one had been condemned since the Franciscan Rafael Cristo Rodriquez, a dozen years earlier, was sentenced to the stake after confessing to practicing Jewish rites in secret.

In another two years from the moment in which Antonio and Benito stood the Inquisition would be abolished and its fearful hand lifeless forever. But no one knew this now, and as if to allay suspicion Benito's two sons were at work as usual on the plot of riverbottom land he leased from Antonio, and Ester was quietly spinning coarse wool into yarn in a corner of the room. Excusing himself for interrupting the lesson in progress, Antonio said: "Some day we shall have a school in this community!"

"I should like to teach it," Ferrer replied warmly. "Too many of our young people are growing up in ignorance despite individual efforts by parents. It's one more sign of the backwardness of our present condition and the need for change. But you did not come here to talk philosophically," and he asked the others to leave them alone. Then Antonio said:

"Amigo, I bring news which may be useful to us both. Before the American captain departed he offered to buy as many otter skins as I might accumulate before he returns. And if, working among the townsfolk as you know how to do from your store, you will accumulate all you can, we shall share and share alike at ten dollars each for a prime pelt—lesser amounts for lesser grades."

"Isn't ten dollars rather a low price?" Ferrer objected. "They tell me skins are bringing up to a hundred and twenty dollars when they reach China."

"That is something we can negotiate. It may depend in part on what luck Sedley has on the channel islands and farther south. His new method of taking otter with his own crews has yet to be tried."

"I predict it will work very well," replied Ferrer. "Our handicap has always been that we lacked means of taking them in quantity because of the haphazard approach of our Indian hunters with bows and arrows or nets and lines. But these fellows with guns are trained especially for the business. What about the authorities, though?"

"You know as well as I they'll wink at it. Governor Arrillaga has said himself: 'Necessity makes licit what is illicit.' And of course they'll profit too."

"But Russians are involved this time. Isn't that significant?"

"Yes, they're eyeing us for a takeover. I'm sure of it. So are the Americans. They've recently moved their capital from a place called Philadelphia to one called Washington, which is farther west, Sedley told me, and their purchase of Louisiana brings them to the coast north of us, where the expedition under their generals Lewis and Clark recently appeared, as you know. But what interests me is their alliance, at least in this business, with the Russians."

"What's the reason for it?"

"Very simple. The Americans need a greater volume of skins than we can furnish with our old-fashioned methods, and the Russians can provide it with their skilled Aleut hunters. On the other hand the Russians can't trade at Canton, but American vessels are allowed to. So, on a share-and-share-alike basis, as Sedley explained it to me, it works beautifully for both parties."

"And where does that leave us?"

"He'll take all we can sell. We simply need to increase our kill."

"Well," said Ferrer, "it reminds me of back in Fages' time when private enterprise made such favorable beginnings here in the fur trade. It's one more thing gallant Don Pedro should be remembered for, rest his soul. For several years, if you remember, the Manila galleon took back a rich cargo of pelts to the Philippines in hopes of trading them to China for the quicksilver so badly needed by our gold miners in Mexico to reduce their ore. But the chuckle-headed Philippine Company, government chartered, mind you, refused to wake up to the fact that a market existed for otter fur in China, and nothing came of it."

"Monopoly is a curse. It is to commerce what despotism is to politics."

"Which reminds me," continued Ferrer, "there are other reasons for getting ourselves on the good side of these Boston men. Word has reached me of that continuing unrest in Mexico I told you about. The winds of liberty may reach even here, and we should be looking for friends who may prove helpful should our commerce with San Blas and Manila continue to decline. Heaven knows I could use more goods for my shop. People are hungry for everyday necessities, a pair of shoes, let alone such luxuries as a silk shawl!"

"Well, Captain Sedley is the man to bring them to us. He will be on his way to China after he leaves here."

And when they had planned further dealings with the enterprising young American, Antonio rode back as he had come that morning, reflecting on how the amplitude of his valley was creating new freedoms and new opportunities of various kinds for all who dwelt there except the Indians of the mission who continued to seem to him skillfully and brutally exploited by Espinosa.

Chapter Thirty-nine

When Captain Horatio Sedley returned from his southern hunt three months later, he immediately invited Antonio and Clara aboard to inspect the goods displayed in his trade room. But the news he brought was even more exciting than silk stockings.

Off Lower California where otter were extremeley plentiful he'd fallen in with a Lima ship which informed him of an uprising in Venezuela against Spanish rule. "A group of patriots led by a young fellow named Bolivar has seized control of the capital, Caracas, and declared the entire province independent. They're talking about a revolution that will free all South American countries and unite them in close relationship to the United States!" Sedley declared proudly. Yet this paled beside what he next revealed. "Mexico herself is aflame! A priest of mixed blood named Hidalgo y Costilla has placed himself at the head of an army of mestizos and Indians. Revolt is sweeping the land!"

"I cannot believe it! It's too good to be true!" Antonio exclaimed, seeing his dream of freedom for his promised land nearing reality.

"Now let me ask you," Sedley urged, "why doesn't California follow suit?"

"Maybe it will. But you mustn't ask me to commit treason just yet!"

"But in due time?" the young captain urged, eyes sparkling.

Antonio shrugged but Sedley read his answer in his face.

For their entertainment Sedley had prepared an otter hunt to illustrate his new methods, and now pointed to the water. Skimming over it in tiny skin boats or bidarkees made from the intestines of whales, his Aleut Indian hunters soon surrounded one of a number of otter remaining in the bay. When it rose for air, they gave a tremendous shout frightening it so that it dove again before breathing fully. Soon it lay exhausted on the surface. Then they shot it through the head with remarkable accuracy, killing it instantly so it did not sink, while leaving the fur virtually undamaged.

"Speeds things up wonderfully," Sedley explained with pride. "Instead of taking a skin every hour or two as they used to do with spears, each crew takes two or three." As well as smoothbore muskets the stocky Aleuts with their Oriental eyes were using a new firearm called a rifle. Antonio had heard of rifles but never seen one. Sedley explained how their grooved barrels imparted a spinning motion to a ball, giving it much greater range and accuracy. "They will improve our efficiency even more remarkably!"

"But won't you soon kill all the otter?" Clara interposed with some concern.

"Impossible!" Sedley laughed. "It would be like exterminating the water itself. Look!" Between them and Point Portola several dozen could be seen basking on their backs, diving for shellfish or cavorting about on the surface as they played with one another like dogs or children unconcerned as if no danger threatened.

But Clara was not so easily put off. "Before the Spaniards came, elk and antelope were plentiful in our valley. Now they're all gone. And now you Americans have come, will the otter also go? I was taught," she said gravely, "that the animals with whom we share this earth are our brothers and sisters, and we should take only those we need in order to survive."

Smiling at such innocence, Sedley presented her with the freshly taken skin, calling her attention to its marvelously rich dark brown color, showing her how when he breathed on it to test its perfection its hair lay down evenly in every direction. Such skins, he explained, were highly valued in China. "Emperors and mandarins and their wives wear them in the form of beautiful robes, or as capes, or as trimmings on fine silk gowns. So do all the rich people. Isn't that right, Boris?" he asked the murderous looking Siberian Russian halfbreed who supervised the Aleut hunters and had handed Sedley the skin. Boris nodded as if incapable of speech but his eyes gleamed with ferocious understanding.

"I wonder if it is because we are related to the Chinese that we too cherish the skin of the otter?" Clara wondered aloud as she touched the beautiful fur. "There is a tradition among my

This Promised Land

people that our ancestors came from across the water in that direction."

"As these did?" Sedley pointed. "It's certainly possible." Busily stoning the deck were three small men even more strikingly Oriental looking than the Aleuts. "They're from Japan. We found their junk adrift off Point Conception having lost its rudder in a blow. They were trying to anchor her in sixty fathoms against a lee shore with a rope run through a hole in one of their stone anchors. The rest of the crew were lost but we managed to save these three."

Hole. Stone anchor. A strange idea flashed like a meteor across Antonio's mind. It seemed answer to a question which had long nagged at him. "What do those stone anchors look like?"

"Like a wheel with the center cut out. Weigh about 350 pounds. The Chinese use them too. I've seen plenty of them at Canton." And Clara and Antonio listened while Sedley described almost exactly the Wisdom Stone which since time immemorial had stood in the center of the meeting place at the site of her old village and now rested in their courtyard. Vessels from both Japan and China, Sedley assured them, following the current that circled the northern Pacific just as Manila galleons did, could reach their coast with relative ease. "No doubt in my mind they've done so for centuries!"

Later findings would support Sedley's conjecture. As early as the fifth century A.D. the Chinese knew of a strange land lying far to the eastward across the ocean. In 452 a Tibetan Buddhist priest named Hwui Shan sailed off with several companions to spread Buddhist doctrine. In 499 he returned with an astonishing account of his travels as far as 20,000 li or about 7,000 miles east of the Chinese mainland. Hwui Shan accurately described the Aleutian Islands and Alaskan coast and their people but most remarkably he told of life in a place that seems to have been Mexico.

And as for the ancient stone anchors, those found recently off the California coast were identified as being of a fine-grained gray limestone known to exist in large quantities near the Shantung and Liaotung peninsulas of China but nowhere in California. One had rested on the ocean floor perhaps as long as three thousand years judging from the type and thickness of its encrustations. Another was found in shallow water where perhaps Clara's people found theirs, or perhaps it was given to them as a ceremonial gift by a captain who came ashore at the mouth of their valley.

Sedley's statements about the doughnut-shaped stone anchors confirmed Clara in her belief as to the mystical and perhaps magical origin of her Wisdom Stone, come to them from the west across the sea; but what he heard excited Antonio's imagination in another way. His wife's ancestors had evidently been sitting in judgment for ages not upon a symbol of their three worlds as they supposed, but upon a practical device from another continent which had reached them by who knew what means, and yet seemed to say that one people could reach out to another, as he Antonio had done, in undreamed of ways. And he felt encouraged about the future and his part in it.

"At the fiesta day after tomorrow when we celebrate our son's coming of age, you will see the stone for yourself!" he told Sedley, after relating what he knew about it.

Antonio and Clara weren't even sure the guest of honor at their party, their son, was going to be present.

"Where do you suppose he is?" she asked anxiously the day after their visit to the ship when less than twenty-four hours remained until the festivities were scheduled to begin.

"Off on one of his mad fool jaunts," Antonio replied disgustedly, "just to make us feel upset and to call attention to himself! I swear we've spoiled that boy nearly rotten despite all our good intentions and best efforts!"

Francisco had been absent ten days, no one knew where, and what was to become of their only child was a question they were continually asking themselves. Though they saw clearly he had inherited their venturesomeness and stubbornness, he did not seem interested in following that middle way they thought they were establishing for themselves and for him, a mingling of white and Indian worlds to produce something new and hopefully better. In fact the boy felt oppressed by his father's many achievements and high prominence and by his mother's ancient lineage among a people now in disorder and decline and determinedly sought his own path. He had no desire to be the symbol of a union between two worlds, two ways of life, two races—some fabulous new synthesis as his parents seemed to regard him. All he wanted to be was himself, whatever that was. He'd hunted with the lads of the Indianada until he could put an arrow through a deer's heart, learned to use musket and pistol almost as well as his father, listened patiently to Antonio's declamations about the importance of Rousseau, Voltaire and Montesquieu and dutifully read *Don*

Quixote and *Robinson Crusoe,* had ridden with Pablo and his sons and his father's vaqueros until he could lasso wild cattle and horses and even grizzly bears, and with old Tilhini he'd visited the sacred caves of the backcountry so dear to his mother and seen their extraordinary paintings and even scaled the summit of Iwihinmu and beheld all the world, but still this had not satisfied him because it was not his world.

Seeking his roots further he journeyed south to the great promontory at Point Conception about which his mother and father had spoken so feelingly and there at the end of the land, the point of departure for the Other World, he stubbornly felt compelled to go even farther, because visible out there lay a lonely island which appeared like the hump of a whale emerging from the waste of the gray sea. The island fascinated Francisco for it was the place where the first white man to come upon that coast long before his father's time, Juan Rodriguez Cabrillo, the intrepid captain, lay buried. He'd heard from his father how Cabrillo came sailing up that legendary coast only fifty years after Columbus landed in the New World. Rounding the promontory which would later be called Conception, the mariner sailed on into uncharted seas until a great storm overwhelmed him, smashing him against a rib of his tiny undecked ship, breaking his shoulder blade and forcing him back to take shelter behind the lonely island at which Francisco gazed. And there the brave man had died of his hurt. And at thought of this a compulsion seized the youth such as had seized his mother and father at other places in other ways, and with Indian companions he went by canoe to the beckoning island which would later be called San Miguel, and in its lonely dunes and grass, among gulls, seals, and barking sea lions he became the first to search unsuccessfully for Cabrillo's grave.

Afterward he danced in the fashionable parties at Santa Barbara and Monterey but they did not provide the answers he sought. So now he was traveling with stubborn insistence in search of the almost legendary wild Indian capital of Tehame known to lie somewhere in the distant interior. Tehame was said to be a center of resistance against the white man, a hideaway for deserters and outlaws, also a great trade center to which people of many nations came and the commerce of the mountains and deserts met that of the coast. It was also rumored to be the headquarters of his famous uncle Asuskwa.

Increasingly the romantic, eccentric, rebellious figure of Asuskwa about whom he heard from so many sources, whose red arrow he had found on the Sacred Stone, captivated the youth's imagination. His parents would say little about his uncle and he sensed their disapproval, but from old Tilhini and others he learned the truth: Asuskwa was alive, powerful, threatening. Like himself Asuskwa seemed a seeker, like himself aloof from other men and shy with women, like himself dedicated to attaining some great purpose. So he set out with eagerness on his newest quest, hoping to penetrate to the heart of the wild Indian world as it was now constituted, discover the whereabouts of his uncle, and perhaps find himself there.

He did not tell his parents where he was going, knowing it would disturb them, but leaving after dark crossed the ranges by the light of the moon, traveling as an Indian, naked except for his waistnet in which were his personal belongings, some gifts, and the nutritive oldtime seed meal Tilhini provided him. At dawn he was approaching the Great Plain of the Carrizo Grass where he saw the Painted Rock rising like a monument and remembered stories his father and mother had told him about it, but holding unswervingly to his course, following those trails he'd heard described so often he could almost have taken them in his sleep, he passed over the Earthquake Mountains and entered the Great Valley and the labyrinthine wastes of the tulares.

There was little danger of his being mistaken for an interloper as he penetrated the wild and hostile interior. His hair was not red like his mother's or blond like his father's but black like an ordinary Indian's, and he was not tall and thin like Antonio or lithe and graceful like Clara but stocky and somewhat fleshy like Koyo. Making inquiries, his credibility certified by his appearance and impeccable credentials as the son of his mother and grandson of Koyo, his skin like theirs a color betwixt light and dark, Francisco came at last to the place he sought, the secret inland capital.

It was on a peninsula like an island extending into a vast expanse of marsh. It could be approached only by a narrow isthmus easily defendable against attack. It was a spot almost completely hidden and virtually invulnerable, and there he found assembled amid an exciting stir and babel of voices many kinds of people he had never seen before: Wintun and Maidu and Shasta from the north, Mojave and Cahuilla from the south, even Paiutes from beyond the Sierra Nevada; and when a band of Shoshones rode in from far to the east from what is now Wyoming, they created a sensation for they were not only mounted upon beautiful spotted horses but carried new guns acquired in trade from British and

This Promised Land

French and were anxious to exchange their beads, furs, and precious stones for the highly valued iridescent abalone shell and other products of the coast such as finely carved redwood miniatures and beautiful baskets and rich red cinnabar, and of course the horses stolen from ranch and mission herds.

Mingling with the throng Francisco passed as one more newcomer, keeping on the lookout for his uncle who would have no idea who he was. He made further inquiries and at last a stocky man not unlike himself in appearance was pointed out to him eloquently addressing a group of chieftains with signs and words, and as Francisco edged into the circle of listeners he understood that Asuskwa was exhorting them to unite and resist the Spaniards. And a strange twinge went though him because he realized that the Spaniards were in part himself. But he kept quiet and listened. "Who does their work? We do! Who dies of their diseases? We do. Who takes our land as well as our lives? They do! And yet, my brothers, apathy and disunion are more to be feared than the white men. How many of them are there? Not more than two thousand. How many of us are there? Twenty times that number. United we can overpower and destroy them and regain the land which is rightfully ours!" But one by one the listening chiefs drifted away, Francisco noticed, from the middle-aged rebel with the wild eyes who was his uncle to the places where trade was in progress, and when none was left, he advanced and identified himself to Asuskwa.

"I am your nephew. White men call me Francisco. But in our language I am the Far Flyer." He did not use his actual Indian name of Helek or The Hawk, fearing it would bring bad luck.

"Welcome, Far Flyer, many times welcome!" Asuskwa exclaimed, amazed and delighted, his heart overflowing, thinking of course the boy had come to join him. His disappointment at the indifference of his recent listeners was dissipated in a flash. Here seemed to be his dream coming true, here at last was reunion with his sister, his people, his ideal. Embracing Francisco he exclaimed joyfully:

"You remembered the red arrow?"

"Yes."

"It delivers its message in many ways. And by the custom of our people I am the one who instructs you in such matters!" Asuskwa continued with satisfaction. "Welcome!"

But Francisco had seen the glazed eyes of those who had left the circle and begun to suspect he was listening to the advocate of a lost cause, much as he admired his uncle's independence and fortitude, and there was something else which troubled him even more. Seeing his doubtful look, Asuskwa said carefully:

"Will you join us?"

All at once Francisco replied: "No, I cannot."

"Why not?" Asuskwa's face fell.

"I am half a white man. I cannot turn against myself. Yours is a cause for those pure in blood as well as in spirit, and I am murky in both."

The depth of this comment struck Asuskwa forcibly and he was silent. Then: "Why did you come?"

"I came seeking the truth. I also came bringing a message. My uncle, I have come to propose peace between you and my family and my people. Isn't it better that we should live together side by side in this ample land rather than fight each other?"

Remaining noncommittal and wishing to test the youth, Asuskwa, now turning skeptical, said: "What power have you that shows you and your proposal worthy of serious consideration?"

Francisco thought quickly. In his waistnet among the gifts and personal belongings was the pocket compass Antonio had given him telling him that with it he could never lose his way.

Taking it out he said to his uncle: "My power resides in this magic needle. It points always to Polaris—Sky Coyote—and because of this, Sky Coyote, the benefactor of mankind, is my special helper." Thinking swiftly Francisco continued: "And it was Sky Coyote who sent me here to give you this and to say that if your power is greater than mine, then make the needle point to your helper, Sun! Here, take it!"

After a moment of hesitation for he sensed a good deal more in this young man than he had thought, Asuskwa gingerly took the strange looking compass and rotated it, turning it first sidewise, then upside down. Still its needle pointed north. Yet he felt sure he could not lose this contest for power which had suddenly arisen between himself and his nephew, because an object placed in water, he knew, would have its power neutralized. Accordingly, he proceeded to the spring at the heart of the island-like isthmus, accompanied by Francisco and many others who by now had gathered around them, and placed the compass in a clear eddy of the spring, while everyone watched excitedly to see what would happen. The needle still pointed north.

Asuskwa was shaken to the core. Picking up the compass with

a grim face he held it up to the Sun, then put it back into the water. Still the needle pointed north. Then he knew he had lost, and a bottomless sense of despair crept into him. Francisco picked up his compass and repeated his plea for peace.

When he finished, Asuskwa replied gloomily: "No matter what your Sky Coyote wants, it will not bring back the land as it was, our people as they were, the happiness which we cherished. No, Sky Coyote already sides with the whites, and with your mother. It is too late. But I shall continue to put my faith in Sacred Condor, and perhaps we shall someday see who is more powerful, he or your white men's gods! Now go!"

As Francisco journeyed homeward he felt despondent. He also felt compassion for his uncle. He'd been strongly drawn to the man, yet sensed the doom Asuskwa seemed to carry within him. This quest too had failed. And Francisco decided bitterly there was nothing else to do for the time being but return and face the conventional life his parents were preparing for him, which he loathed and which oppressed his spirit.

Imperceptibly to themselves, Antonio and Clara were becoming reactionary in their attitude toward their son who in what they considered blindly selfish ways seemed determined to escape their grasp and his filial responsibilities. They had taken great imaginative and risky steps forward in their youth such as Francisco was now taking but they had forgotten this, and being as they thought realistically concerned about the continuity of their ranch and their dreams they hoped Francisco would marry Constanza, the daughter of the rancher Estenaga who had established himself in the neighboring valley to the south.

Estenaga was also an important official at Santa Barbara and to be connected with his family could be of advantage in the colonial society which was rapidly developing and stratifying, whereas to marry an Indian or even a mestizo girl would be counterproductive for Francisco in a white man's world, a step backward as even Clara believed. Because now the Indian way was becoming lost and discredited, something far different than it had been in her youthful days at those gloriously promising moments of first contact.

Constanza Estenaga was warm, sweet, sensible, and seemed to Antonio and Clara an ideal counterweight to what they regarded as their son's irrational impulses and wild ideas.

They were at breakfast when Francisco entered the room, naked except for his waistnet, bronzed, and travel stained, his flesh reddened by the ochre with which he had smeared his skin to protect it from sunburn.

"Where on earth have you been and why are you undressed in this wild fashion?" his father exclaimed angrily, while Clara stared in silent wonder.

"Father, I have been exploring the Indian way," Francisco replied, noting his mother's eyes shining with pride and amazement, "and I have learned much."

He kissed their hands as customary but found it impossible to say that he was returning disappointed from a quest in which he'd hoped to find his true identity, and that his parents loomed as almost insurmountable obstacles in this path because they had followed so fully ways he might have taken himself.

"I have been to Tehame."

At this Clara and Antonio started. Francisco might almost as well have said he had been to the moon. No one they knew of had ever been to Tehame. Even the existence of the pagan stronghold was in doubt, as its implications were sinister. But there was something in Francisco's manner which convinced them he was telling the truth.

"And what did you do at Tehame?" his father asked in a more subdued tone.

"I talked with my uncle."

"Asuskwa? What did he say? How did he look?" Clara broke in excitedly.

"He looked well. He asked me if I remembered the red arrow."

"And what did you answer?"

"I answered that I remembered. I told him how you broke it across your knee and threw the pieces in the dust."

"What did he say then?"

"He said nothing. But his face darkened with thought." And Clara's face showed her misgivings as she heard this. "I said that you loved him and urged that there be peace between him and us, and his people and ours."

She gasped, for it was what she hoped he had done.

"What is your uncle planning to do?" Antonio asked gravely.

"He is urging a united attack by many nations which will annihilate all Spaniards." And Francisco told everything that had happened to him at Tehame, so that Antonio's eyes were opened to the magnitude of his son's achievement in successfully visiting this enemy citadel, while Clara for the first time saw that her son embodied not a new way but the same painful dilemma which had once torn her apart and still tormented her at times: whether to be Indian or Spaniard. Yet she could not resist venting her vexation at the anxiety he'd just caused them: "You might have told us where you were going. You might have considered us just a little! We've been on pins and needles! Everyone is coming to your birthday fiesta today. And these are nice people for you to meet! Someone besides rattlesnakes and wild Indians! So that you may take your rightful place in society among the gente de razon!"

"Don't worry, Mamacita!" Francisco replied dutifully. He had decided to placate his parents until he should discover a new path that would lead to his true self. "I won't disgrace you!"

Encouraged by this Clara went further. "Constanza Estenaga is coming. She's a lovely girl. The kind your father and I wish you would marry!"

"Yes," Antonio chimed in irritably. "Clean yourself up and get rid of that dirt and paint!"

But this was too much for Francisco and he exploded in disgust. "Constanza! How well I know her kind! So genteel! So refined! So dead!" And without asking permission, he stalked from the room in a fury.

"What do you think?" Clara turned apprehensively to her husband.

Antonio shook his head. "I do not know what to think. But his journey to Tehame was a brave achievement."

"At this rate I fear he will never settle down!"

"We must be patient and see what develops. But now let us get ourselves ready. Our guests will be arriving soon."

Chapter Forty

Outside, two Indian lads under the direction of Pablo were tying up a corner of the huge canopy of sail cloth which shaded the courtyard to protect guests and especially dancers from the hot sun, one corner having been loosened in a gust of breeze, and in the outdoor kitchen under its brushwood arbor where cooking was done in fair weather, Kachuku assisted by girls from the Indianada, was preparing tortillas and barbecued chicken and trays of sweetmeats and of eggshells filled with perfumed water for breaking gaily over unsuspecting heads during later stages of the frolic. And in the huge stone-lined pit reserved for such purpose the chunks of beef wrapped Indian style in wild grape leaves were quietly roasting covered with ashes and earth, where they had lain all night on the warm coals.

Observing these things while waiting for their guests to arrive, Antonio continued to feel disturbed about Francisco's future but there was no further time for such concern because a motley procession was approaching the hacienda. First came Espinosa and his flock of mission Indians, the Father Superior, wearing his black hat with its broad flat brim, riding on his white mule surrounded by Indian vaqueros mounted on horses despite the continuing yet generally ignored ban against any but gente de razon doing so. Others were on foot, men in cotton or woolen tunics and loin cloths, women in similar tunics with skirts and many of the girls in colorful petticoats and white bodices and red or blue rebozos like women of the town, and their black hair cut off at a length equal to half their height and floating over their shoulders charmingly.

As he looked at this approaching medley Antonio reflected that here as in those first days of the Sacred Expedition were the elements which had constituted the heart of his experience ever since: himself the soldier layman, Espinosa the missionary cleric, the Indians, the land. And a central conflict now as then was still the struggle for dominance between laity and clergy with Indians and land as all but silent bystanders. That continuing conflict between church and state was embodied in his perennial quarrels with Espinosa. Yet he must give the devil his due. The man was a master executive. Not only that, he had become by necessity a farmer, orchardist, viniculturist, livestock grower, master of loom and tannery, and grist mill, doctor, architect, judge, diplomat, trader, business manager as well as missionary priest. Yes, Espinosa had taken those idealistic visions of Rubio and enacted them into a massive reality. Like life itself that reality was imperfect. But there it was. Why did it disturb him so? Antonio wondered. And with what seemed sudden insight he decided it must be because the church, guardian of the individual's unique importance in the eyes of God, surely one of the most revolutionary and liberating ideas to come upon the face of the earth, the church was at the same time the jailer of the individual's mind and spirit and, in the case of these Indians, his body too. And the distastefulness of the latter seemed to Antonio so abhorrent it overshadowed the glory of the former.

"Well, I see you continue to mount your cowboys on horses despite regulations!" he could not help needling Espinosa.

"As you do yours, because how else can we manage our vast herds since the gente de razon will do no work!" the friar retaliated.

"Be welcome!" Antonio laughed. "For today we shall put aside all differences!" And he ushered the father toward the refreshment tables under the shady portico of the inner courtyard and after warm welcomes indicated to the others the area where games and dances were already in progress among the Indians of the Indianada and food and drink were being served under direction of Pablo and his sons.

Hard upon the heels of father and Indians came the townspeople, curious to see the house of a famous man, hungry for experience and food, eternal recipients they suddenly seemed to Antonio. Once he had embarked with them on a communal adventure with such high hopes but now they seemed to be resting on their oars, succumbing to ease of existence, benign climate, letting Indians do all their work even to farming their land for them on shares, while they danced and made love. "Except for a few I could name," he'd written Costanso in exasperation, "they have gone to sleep in our Promised Land! Here on soil so fertile it can yield two and three hundred fold when properly worked, the chief crop they produce is children. Their fecundity in that respect is unbelievable! Families of fifteen or twenty are becoming the rule. Yet I love them still. How can I do otherwise? Some are my old companions. All came here with high hopes as you and I did. So I forgive them their dolce far niente though such sweet idleness irks my thrifty Catalan spirit and, I fear, bodes no good for the future!" Yet riding among them as he was thinking this he saw the refutation of his fear. Benito and Ester Ferrer were moving like a nucleus of self-containment and individual enterprise, as if holding themselves tightly inviolate in their secret Judaism, an island in the midst of this lax gentile flood. "And who could be more industrious?" Antonio thought.

With Clara at his side he welcomed one and all uncritically as friends and neighbors and invited them to share refreshments and join in the games and impromptu dances and horse races.

And then came the fashionables, the gentry, appearing in casual disarray and gaiety, some riding in brightly caparisoned shrilly squeaking carts drawn by pairs of oxen, some on prancing steeds, their saddles embossed with silver, laughing, singing as they came, for this was a time of music and delight. Among the first were Don Lazaro Estenaga and his wife Victoria and their lovely gentle Constanza, also Sedley and Kalenin riding the horses Antonio provided for them. They were followed by some sailors and men from their ship including the ferocious looking Boris. Antonio directed the sailors and attendants to the greased pig chases and the baiting of young bulls in progress in the nearby arena and welcomed the principals with heartfelt warmth. Clara too greeted them with natural ease and cordiality. Now in middle age she was still slim and graceful. She wore a beautiful gown of white lawn with full sleeves. Around her straight red hair at the forehead a chaplet of sea shells announced her race without further comment—in contrast to the elaborate lace mantillas and rebozos of the other women over hair curled into ringlets. Nevertheless, like Antonio, she was firmly convinced these were the people with whom her son must unite. They represented the new way, and she felt instinctively her son must follow it in order to insure the future life of their land, this place where she had been born, which had belonged to her people since time immemorial. Through him it could pass to her descendants and thus in effect to her people's and a continuity be preserved.

This Promised Land

Lazaro Estenaga was a suave but likable Andalusian, a small smiling man, not entirely scrupulous but wealthy and influential. Antonio had decided to overlook his faults in favor of his virtues. Lazaro was master of supplies and business manager at the Santa Barbara Presidio, a position of much responsibility and power, but it was through his wife who was related to the family of the late Viceroy Bucareli that he acquired the concession known in new pious style as The Hills of the Purification, in the valley to the south, and became the first of those to dwell in town and have ranches in the country. His wife was a large woman with brown hair and snobbish cold eyes who like her husband felt impressed by Antonio's influence and prestige.

Francisco was bowing dutifully over the genteel white hand of Constanza, taking it by contrast into his rough dusky one, again concealing his true feelings, wishing he were on some adventurous quest rather than in this situation he loathed. But to Constanza, who'd heard of his wild roamings, he was an exciting romantic figure, and her heart raced at the touch of this son of a conquistador of noble class and a mother who was said to be a princess in her native right.

After Clara and Antonio led the way in dancing the first set, accompanied by Victoria and Lazaro and other older couples, the young people took over while their parents retired to the sidelines to talk and watch. The hardpacked earth of the courtyard made a firm flooring under their feet. Music was provided by an Indian orchestra playing in the shade of the portico in the manner Antonio and Clara had taught them, but some used native four-holed flutes and the musical longbow played like a jew's harp with one end in the mouth, as well as violins and guitars. Mission Indians and some of the guests with their own mandolins and guitars joined them as the merriment grew.

Watching Francisco and Constanza in the graceful figures of the contradance, Antonio could not resist a feeling of pride rising above earlier disappointment concerning his son. He had wished him to be graceful and red-headed like his mother or tall and blond like himself, as intrepid as Fages, as wise as Portola, but there he was looking like just what he was, a mixed blood, a mestizo of predominantly Indian appearance; and as Antonio thought this he also saw that Francisco was a true child of the land and a brave fellow who sought his own way, and it suddenly came to Antonio that Francisco *did* represent a new way, *was* the new man he and Costanso and Fages had so often envisioned.

And thus by irony a miracle had come to pass in a manner unsuspected. And Antonio felt humbled and illumined.

At the refreshment table Sedley and Kalenin were talking with Espinosa and Estenaga about the uprising in Mexico, Estenaga having broken the latest news. Couriers passing from San Diego en route to Monterey confirmed the report brought by Sedley. Mexico was aflame. Revolutionaries were slaughtering landowners and priests. "What does this mean for us in New California?" Antonio asked. Estenaga shrugged. "If the insurrectionists prevail, it may mean trouble!" All eyes met with understanding except those of Espinosa, and Antonio chaffed him: "You better watch out, padre. Down in Guadalajara they are cutting off the cojones of fellows like you!" But Espinosa riposted: "Don't blaspheme, Freemason! God and King will yet prevail despite you and your kind! I on my part have just heard that Governor Arrillaga has declared that greedy ranchers must reduce their herds again, for they are consuming the grass needed by the missions for the good of the Indians. So you can start making your plans!"

"Let me show you the Wisdom Stone," Antonio said as diversion and taking the others to it waited eagerly while Sedley examined it. "It's no doubt a stone anchor," the young captain declared. "They look just like this. Rounded. Tooled. Chinese or Japanese. But how did it get here?" Antonio repeated the known history of the judgment seat upon which his wife's ancestors had sat for centuries. Estenaga and Kalenin expressed amazement. Espinosa interjected his opinion that like the paintings and idols in the caves of the back country it was just one more example of heathen superstition and idolatry.

"Oh, here come the Arguellos!" Clara interrupted and Antonio went with her to greet the new arrivals. No family in California was more beloved and respected. Stout broad-shouldered Jose Arguello began his service as an enlisted man like Antonio, a tie which bound them, and he too had risen through the ranks, his gracious wife Ignacia and their growing brood beside him. While he was commandant at the San Francisco Presidio the events occurred which gave birth to the province's most famous love story. Dashing Count Rezanof, Imperial Chamberlain at the Russian Court, had taken charge of the Tsar's North American affairs and come down by ship from Sitka, the very first Russian to set foot in New California. Ostensibly Rezanof came to pay a courtesy call and buy grain, but secretly to observe the state of Spanish defenses and the possibilities for a Russian takeover. But that day

This Promised Land

he met Conchita Arguello in her father's presidial house, he became a lover. She was fifteen, he forty-two and recently widowed. His tales of court life dazzled her. Concepcion, to give her her true name, was of course of the Roman church. He adhered to that of Constantinople. Nevertheless they became betrothed. The count sailed back to Alaska intending to return via Siberia to Saint Petersburg and thence to Rome to obtain the Pope's permission for their marriage. Next he planned to go to Madrid to smooth relations with the Spanish court regarding California. And finally to Mexico City and then to San Francisco to claim his bride. Five years had passed. Conchita had given him a golden locket containing a strand of her hair. Rumors reached her of his death which she refused to believe. Her beauty had been arrested in the bud like a flower half opened, and nothing could conceal the tragedy of her melancholy.

Approaching with her now came another young woman, slim, dark haired, dusky skinned, plainly dressed. Rebellious vitality smouldered in her fiery dark eyes, a contrast to the gentle melancholy of Conchita Arguello. They brimmed with life as did the voluptuous figure of this strange girl.

"Who is she?" Clara asked, and Ignacia Arguello replied:

"She is our daughter Juanita Lopez."

"Lopez?"

"Yes!" And Ignacia related a story which was to reverberate in the minds of Clara and Antonio as long as they lived.

After the Yuma Massacre, the colonists who'd proceeded unaware of it toward Mission San Gabriel, reached there in safety and among them were Juan Lopez' wife Paloma and three daughters of whom Juanita, hardly more than a baby, was youngest. With others of their party they continued to Santa Barbara where they became its first settlers. And there Juanita's mother and sisters had died of a fever and the kindly Arguellos had taken the orphan child into their household and treated her as one of their own daughters. But as Clara and Antonio looked at this fiery girl with straight dark Indian hair whose eyes seemed to mock theirs as her father's had done, they felt an almost superstitious foreboding. It was as if their old adversary had risen from his grave. And as the party wore on and night came and the gaiety increased, this feeling seemed justified.

There was suddenly a loud burst of applause and approving outcries and they saw that, daringly alone, Juanita was dancing the fiery jarabe or hat dance, in which with clicking heels and flashing eyes and sinuous body movements a girl invites her admirers to pair themselves with her in a representation of a more intimate union. But the decision is hers. She can refuse or accept whom she chooses.

One by one young gallants approached and placed their hats hopefully upon Juanita's dark tresses, and one by one she ridded herself of these encumbrances with a saucy toss of her head, to shouts of laughter and outbursts of applause. But now Francisco, their own Francisco, was approaching swiftly from behind and placing his low-crowned sombrero upon her dark locks which matched his own, and she did not reject it as music and cheers rose to crescendo. Next they were dancing together, their eyes and hearts speaking to one another through the pounding rhythm. While gentle Constanza Estenaga's eyes grew dark with the pain of rejection and tongues wagged, and Clara and Antonio looked at each other.

When towards dawn the party ended for that night and they retired to their room she said to Antonio:

"That Lopez girl is out to get Francisco. Could she really be the daughter of our old enemy?"

"Don't worry. Francisco's a level-headed young fellow or he wouldn't have got himself to Tehame and back," replied Antonio, ignoring the thrust of her question. "He knows his own mind. Any youngster likes to kick up his heels a little at a party with a pretty girl!" But secretly he was thinking: "Is Juan striking a final blow at me? Or is it simply the inevitable process of circumstance and coincidence?" He could not be sure. But his heart beat with uneasiness and he did not tell Clara what he truly feared.

Next morning Antonio rode out to look at the ranch with Sedley who like many others stayed overnight in guest rooms and outbuildings or tents of their own. Kalenin remained behind, being slightly indisposed after the night's revelries in which he'd participated fully. It was only the second time Sedley had ridden Spanish style. Although he readily understood the reasonableness of the cowboy saddle with its broad working seat, high pommel for roping and cantle for support, and long stirrups in which a man could balance himself for action, he had difficulty comprehending the heavy cruel-looking spade bit and the neck reining, until Antonio explained that the bit was not designed to punish but was carried lightly upon the tongue as a signal weight to the touch of the reins, and the reins also touching the neck lightly, signalled the animal with minimal effort and maximum speed which direction to go.

Antonio then took the opportunity to ask some frank questions. "The revolution in Mexico aside, many of my countrymen fear an American takeover of California but I am more concerned about the Russians. Tell me your honest opinion."

"Every Russian in Sitka would prefer to be here if he could!" Sedley gestured at the surrounding scene. "They think that all you Spaniards do is enjoy the climate and make love!"

"And what prevents them from taking us over?"

"Fear of an international quarrel. But now they've organized their Russian American Company with the Tsar himself as stockholder, they are on the move, and I think you will hear more of them!"

"Are there many troops at Sitka?"

"Hardly any. But they would not be likely to use regulars, should they decide to move down upon you, but promyshleniks."

"Promyshleniks?"

"Yes, irregulars. Like Boris, that Siberian halfbreed you saw on the deck of my ship. He's typical. Wolves are mild by comparison. It was his kind who subjugated Alaska. Crossing in skin boats they subdued the Aleuts and other tribes with such ferocity as you cannot imagine."

"Indeed! And would you Americans help us forestall such an attack?"

"Well, I cannot speak for Washington but I think Boston might—such of us as happened to be upon your coast. We have a strong liking for it, indeed feel at home here, and we foresee a fine market for our products, as for yours, in mutually advantageous trade. Our manufactories will need your hides, tallow, hemp, and other raw materials. You will need our finished goods. All this in addition to the present fur trade which should continue for many years. So indeed I see a bright future ahead—such as that!" And he pointed up the river valley where the fog which had come in from the sea during the night was beginning to withdraw, allowing the sunlight to enter as if an awning were being pulled away. "What a magnificent prospect! Are those peaks your boundaries? How many acres do you own?"

"I have no boundaries and I own no acres." Antonio explained the nature of his tenure.

"By the Almighty!" Sedley exclaimed. "Maybe we had better

not take you over, for if that were to happen I should be the first to squat on you!" He laughed.

"Squat on me?"

"Yes. Settle without title. Preempt your property. Seize your land simply by occupying it."

"Is that how you do things in America?"

"We do nearly everything in America," Sedley chuckled. "Right or wrong. It is a consequence of liberty. Some day those consequences may overtake us, but as yet we are young and free with plenty of room for expansion, so we do not worry. But you, my kind friend, are in a different situation. The predators are eyeing you and you have weak defenses. I urge you again to give serious thought to working for a liberated California which may become part of our United States. Indeed I wish all Mexico would join us, should the revolution there succeed, so that we might become one great commonwealth expressive of the rights of man!"

"You speak to my heart!" exclaimed Antonio, clasping him by the shoulder, "and if I had a daughter I should want you to be my son-in-law. Are you married?"

"No, but I hope to be after this voyage!"

"Tell me about your plans while I ponder your recent suggestion!"

"Well, I shall sail from here to Sitka, unload my grain for the starving Russians there, proceed to Canton with my furs, sell them to the Chinese at a handsome profit of which the Russians will share half, return to Sitka with a rich cargo of silks and teas, cottons and spices, rugs, jewelry and other valuables, and then stop here on my homeward journey before proceeding to Boston—where I shall arrive a year and a half from now and turn a profit, God willing, of 400 percent on my backers' investment."

"Remarkable. For you people, difficulties seem but opportunities. How I wish we had more like you! But now one last confidential question. Is it true General Washington is a Freemason?"

"Yes, though he has long been dead. Our present President Madison is favorably inclined and so are many of our leaders, as were others of our founding fathers. And so am I!" said Sedley forthrightly.

"And so am I!" Antonio gripped his hand in the fraternal clasp. "Most extraordinary! Saint George's, Barcelona!"

"Saint Andrew's Lodge, Boston!"

"In freedom's name, may god witness!"

"I'm sure he will!" said Sedley matter of factly but with perfect confidence.

They had toured the upper valley at a comfortable gait and were returning toward the oak grove against the hillside not far from the ranch buildings where Clara had played as a child, where she had held that last decisive conference with her brother, and where the picnic would take place. Joining them as they moved toward it were many of the principal guests on horseback or in oxcart, young gallants racing and prancing their mounts, girls in bright dimities coquetting afresh and Antonio noticed with renewed misgiving that Francisco was riding beside Juanita Lopez, deeply engrossed in conversation with her. Something about the way she sat her horse reminded him unpleasantly of Juan, but her seductiveness was quite her own, and as he mentally undressed her his blood stirred with old fire, and he could well understand what seemed the infatuation of his son.

As he and Sedley approached the grove where Pablo and Kachuku and numerous helpers had been at work since dawn, the fragrance of roasting meat and oak wood coals greeted them and they saw the carcasses of three beeves turning slowly on spits over the huge pits and the red and white table cloths spread upon the grass. "It is Homeric," Sedley exclaimed "and I shall describe it in the drawing rooms of Beacon Hill!"

Dismounting they handed their tie ropes to waiting vaqueros and joined the festive throng, Sedley seeking out Kalenin and Antonio greeting Lazaro Estenaga and Victoria who were just arriving. Girls were now joining hands and dancing around the roasting bullocks, singing and laughing, tossing flowers and bits of fragrant sage into the pits of coals, while the young men prepared a rooster race. A cock was soon buried alive with just its head showing, and the eager contestants galloping by at full speed leaned down from their saddles and tried to grasp its bobbing head. When young Aidan Estenaga, Constanza's brother, finally snatched the bird bodily out of the ground, he was immediately surrounded by other gallants who tried to grab it away from him so that blood and feathers flew, much to the amusement of the onlookers. Next Francisco performed an even more difficult feat. A peso was placed flat on the earth. Racing by at dead run, he reached down from his horse and picked it up with his fingers. Everyone expressed admiration for this daring exploit but Constanza's was tentative for she was uncertain how it would be

325

received, while Juanita's was unrestrained as if certain of welcome; and another twinge went through Antonio as if indeed Juan were goading him from the grave. Yet to those who congratulated him on his son's performance he said proudly: "The lad's just returned from Tehame, you know!" and he told what Francisco had found there. Their faces showed their grave interest, for the threat of another Yuma Massacre was in everyone's mind. Because it hadn't happened didn't mean it would not happen, and what occurred at Yuma Crossing continued to haunt the Spanish California frontier as the Custer Massacre was to haunt the American frontier west. Both tragedies caused innumerable bloody reprisals or preemptive attacks on blameless and peaceful Indians as well as hostiles, and Arguello told how an expedition setting out from Santa Barbara had searched the tulares in vain for the location of Tehame, killing eight hostiles while wounding many more and capturing twenty-two runaway mission Indians. "We must take your boy with us as guide next time!"

"If he would go. He's a strange one in many ways. He has his own code of honor," Antonio continued still proudly, "and he might feel it a betrayal of trust to accompany such an expedition."

Arguello, frankly broaching a subject usually discussed behind Antonio's back, asked: "Is it true that your wife's brother is a leader among the hostiles of Tehame?"

And when Antonio said that it was, he could see on the faces of several of his hearers that they thought this the reason his hacienda had never been attacked while others suffered. But he felt it fruitless to try to explain about the red arrow and the whole tragic history of Asuskwa and his relationship with Clara, and with himself, and so did not try.

Concepcion Arguello, her lovely violet eyes cast down, was sitting quietly as a widow among the mothers and duennas. "Did she learn anything from Kalenin about Rezanof? I saw them deep in conversation yesterday and again just now," Antonio asked Arguello in intimate tone when they were alone for a moment. Her father shook his head and his broad shoulders seemed to Antonio to sag visibly under the weight of his daughter's woe. "The count is said to have died in Siberia en route to Saint Petersburg. That's the story we always hear. But she'll never be convinced till the locket she gave him is returned by his hand or another's. Then she will believe him false or dead."

Clara was talking to the girl as they sat on the grass in the shade of the oaks, trying to cheer her and make her feel part of the festivities, and seemed to be succeeding. But when Juanita Lopez sat down beside them Clara's own cheer left her for she now saw in Juanita a deadly threat to her plans for Francisco and Constanza and the future life of the place she loved so strongly. And though she knew it was wrong to feel vengeful, she hated the daughter of the man who raped Lehlele and murdered Ta-apu and brought that untold misery upon her village which had at last separated her from her brother and divided and dispersed her people irrevocably. When Ignacia Arguello openly chided Juanita for being so forward with Francisco, Clara could not help a secret feeling of satisfaction. But the girl tossed her head in response and her eyes flamed with rebellion, and a fear went through Clara lest Francisco find this spirit more to his liking than the gentleness and amiability of Constanza. And she could not find a kind word to say to Juanita.

As they returned toward the hacienda after the picnic, a messenger rode up with word that Governor Arrillaga was feeling better and would soon arrive. Everyone of importance between Santa Barbara and Monterey, the two seats of provincial society, had been invited but the aging governor had sent word he was unwell. As the news of his imminent arrival spread among the guests it added new and greater significance to the festivities.

Sensing his mother's disapproval and hurt by her snub of Juanita, Francisco decided on a course of defiance and an exciting idea came into his head. In the confusion attendant upon the governor's arrival he slipped away.

The ruler of California arrived with cavalry escort. Papa Arrillaga, as he was affectionately called, made a splendid figure in full uniform of dark blue frieze with tails and turnbacks, benevolent smiles for everyone, plus sweets in his pockets for children which he handed out generously. He was an old bachelor, fat, amiable, very popular. Ignacio Vallejo, Antonio's old friend from Monterey, commanded the detachment accompanying him, and since the visit was a social one Ignacio had brought along his young son Mariano who was a great favorite with the governor, and also Mariano's cousin Juan Alvarado, the two boys dressed in miniature uniforms serving as mascots for the troop. Antonio paid dutiful respects as did Clara and they led Arrillaga and Ignacio to places of honor beside them in the viewing stand which had been erected overlooking the arena where the events of the afternoon were to take place.

Again townspeople and mission flock had gathered, Antonio and Clara insisting that Indians from mission and Indianada be invited to attend each day and encouraged to perform their native dances, and these were in progress in the open ground surrounding the hacienda, likewise impromptu horse races, rolling of dice, chasing of greased pigs with kinky tails, attempts to climb greased poles in hopes of securing coins at their tops.

"Where's Father Rafael?" Antonio asked Espinosa, after the padre had in his turn greeted the visiting dignitaries and taken his seat. "Neither today nor yesterday have I seen him!"

"He's up the river cutting pine trees," Espinosa replied with a heavy sigh. "The work of the Lord must go on even while we revel. But he fully expected to return by now. I wonder what's detained him?"

"Perhaps he's cutting more trees than you agreed to!" Antonio needled him.

"Which reminds me I saw that book our Russian visitor presented you with yesterday," Espinosa retaliated. "It looked strangely like Rousseau!" And it was true the courtly and sophisticated Kalenin, himself fluent in French, had presented Antonio a volume of Rousseau in that language containing *The Social Contract* and other writings. "Such as are proscribed by the Index and subject to confiscation by order of the Inquisition and Holy Office!" Espinosa added pointedly while Antonio, turning away to speak to Vallejo, pretended not to hear.

When the honored guests were seated and the rest crowded and perched upon walls and roofs of outbuildings, a wild black bull with menacing horns was released into the arena by Pablo and his sons amid cries of approval and expectation. The magnificent creature epitomized brute strength and courage. But with almost impossible dexterity, avoiding its charges with marvelous skill, the four sons lassoed it and tied its legs together so that it lay helplessly bellowing with fury in the dust of the corral. Amid even louder and more expectant cries, a mighty grizzly, reddish brown like that first one Antonio had seen in the Valley of the Bears so long ago, was dragged in prone upon a cowhide, where he lay hogtied like the bull. He was so large and heavy that two horses straining to their utmost at the ends of reatas could hardly move him along. Going to a place in the hills they knew to be frequented by bears, Antonio and Pablo and the boys had, during the preceding week while Francisco was away, captured the beast in preparation for today's celebration. When surrounded by them it rose on hind legs in its fury, and Antonio made that crucial first cast which must capture one dangerous forepaw with its five-inch claws. That done, Pablo captured the other. This effectively neutralized the mighty creature, and his head and hind feet were soon encircled by the ropes of the boys and he was stretched flat and hauled off to the ranch on the hide where he now reclined.

When bull and bear were joined by a foreleg to a foreleg with a stout leather rope twenty feet long which was greased with tallow so that the bear could not haul it in hand over hand, all other restraints were removed and the two ferocious creatures were free to go at each other. Sensing freedom rather than combat, however, they scrambled to their feet and looked around bewildered. Mad cheers of excitement rose from the spectators but Antonio sickened at thought of what was to follow. It was a proceeding dear to his countrymen in which he unwillingly concurred. "I never condoned it, but you can carry out your objections only so far if you are to function effectively as a member of the society in which you live," he noted afterward, "and this is particularly true on a frontier, where a person is dependent upon his fellows for survival." He knew that a fiesta without such a contest would have been no party at all in the eyes of most of his guests.

As bull and bear got to their feet it was his fellow white-skinned Christians who howled loudest for blood. As if to spite them the bewildered animals continued to ignore each other. Riding up to the bull Pablo whacked it smartly across the nose with the end of his reata, and maneuvered swiftly out of the way. With a snort all passivity left the huge creature as result of this insult. Supposing it to have been inflicted by the bear, who'd sat down and begun licking one paw, the bull gave a bellow and charged. With marvelous adroitness the huge grizzly leaped upon the bull's back and fastened its foreclaws in its nose. Bellowing with pain the great black bull tossed and turned in fury but there was no dislodging its rider, who soon tore off its nose, ripped out its tongue, blinded it, and then severed its throat with mighty claw strokes so that blood spurted in all directions. This gruesome spectacle delighted almost everyone but it disgusted Antonio and he loathed himself for conforming to the popular taste in this fashion.

As if sensing his feeling a figure leaped lightly into the arena.

It was Francisco. In his hand he held of all things Antonio's sword of the Conquest which had once been thrust into the ground here and over which Pablo had fired that first disturbing shot. Antonio had taught him how to use it long before but for several years it had lain untouched among faded uniforms and other memorabilia, while Francisco's eccentric yearnings led him elsewhere. Now sword in hand, amid unbelieving cries and fearful protestations, the boy advanced upon the murderous bear. Beneath his seemingly madcap action lay a desire to prove himself in the eyes of Juanita, whom he was determined to possess, and to defy in company with her the conventional society which turned up its nose at them both. And beneath, too, lay something of Antonio's feeling of disgust at the cruelty and unfairness of what had just occurred. Sensing this latter intuitively, pride surged up in the father as he watched his son.

Astonished at sight of a creature so strange, the bloody bear rose towering upon hind legs for better perspective. Awesome intakes of breath were heard as it reached full stature, six, seven, nearly eight feet. Francisco surveyed his adversary coolly. Then darting in swift as thought, he delivered a thrust such as Antonio taught him. With a dreadful roar the bear made a rush. But Francisco sprang back just in time and as the bear was brought up short by the rope which tied it to the dead bull, he delivered another thrust.

Thus they fenced. At times the bear nearly had the youth in his grip as he had had the bull, and at those moments Antonio's heart nearly stopped, while the onlookers fell silent with apprehension. Frustrated at last by its fruitless efforts, the bear rose again upon hind legs, tottering now, blood pouring from its wounds, and defied its enemy to approach. Francisco swiftly circled it, confusing it further, then with a daring thrust ran it through the heart and it dropped with a groan.

Bravos were deafening. Women tore off their rebozos and waved them like flags, all except Clara who shared her husband's views. The rest flung fans and flowers into the arena while men tossed in their hats and cheered.

Standing beside his dead adversary, Francisco received this acclaim with a modest bow, and then a Quixotic notion seized him and as if he were a matador in a bullring he bent and amputated the bear's short thick ears and brought them not to Constanza, not to Governor Arrillaga, but to Juanita and laid them at her feet.

This Promised Land

* * *

Now it seemed to Antonio as to Clara that Juan truly had risen from the grave and struck back at them, publicly humiliating them through this madcap if gallant action of their only son which made Juanita the queen of this joust, belle of the ball. But the end was not yet. The insatiable crowd was shouting for more. "Colear! Colear! Tail the bull! Tail the bull!" they cried.

Never satisfied they wanted to see Francisco tail down a living bull in the customary way as final evidence of his coming of age. A fierce companion to the one just killed was being held captive in the adjoining corral for this purpose. So Antonio repressed what his overflowing heart was urging him to do then and there. Carried away he'd leapt into the ring to be beside his brave son.

"Colear shall it be?" he asked, wondering if Francisco had strength for such a further test. Sweat was pouring off the boy. The blood of the bear was on his hands and on his sword. He was breathing heavily. But there is no energizer like admiration.

"Colear!" he nodded laughing, his eyes searching beyond his father for Juanita's, and in them Antonio saw his son taking his fated way.

The youth looked fresh as morning as he mounted his horse. Like Antonio's of oldtime it was a chestnut sorrel with cream colored mane and tail, and the animal seemed to catch the spirit of the occasion and snorted and pranced while its rider remained elegantly poised. At a sign from Antonio the bull was released from the neighboring corral and made for the hills at top speed. But the sorrel brought Francisco alongside with what seemed effortless ease. Leaning from his saddle the boy grasped the bull's flying tail and with a dexterous motion clamped it under and over his right thigh, hard against his saddle, at the same time spurring the sorrel so it darted ahead, and the bull was turned head over heels and, as Francisco released the tail, hit the ground with a resounding thud which raised dust.

Huzzahs were deafening. Acknowledging this wild applause, Francisco gravely lifted his hat as he came trotting back, while the chastened bull rose unsteadily and was guided by Pablo's sons to its corral.

And now, at last, with fond paternal pride from which he excluded every other thought, Antonio drew from his pocket the silver buckle whose history almost everyone knew, for it had become part of the lore of the valley, and stepping forward to greet Francisco as he dismounted, the governor and all principal persons of the province watching, he said: "My boy, now that you have proven yourself worthy to succeed me, here is the most precious gift I can give you. This is the link between your mother and me. It represents a union of which you are the beloved result. I give it to you as token you are a man who can carry forward with honor the life we have bequeathed you!"

Clara tried to explain the significance of all this to Governor Arrillaga who was becoming a little senile.

Francisco held the buckle aloft for all to see and it shone brightly in the sun as did all hopes at that moment except those of Constanza Estenaga. Then kneeling, Francisco received Antonio's blessing, then that of Father Espinosa. At that moment a strange cry of astonishment began to ripple through the crowd. Glancing in the direction in which all heads were turning, Antonio saw, emerging from the mouth of the river gorge and advancing down the valley toward them, a remarkable procession.

At its head walked Father Rafael with workmanlike strides looking neither right nor left as if intent upon some important purpose. Behind him came an enormous pine log carried in horizontal position on the shoulders of a file of Indians, and behind it another, and behind that a third, and at the end of the procession limped a tall gaunt ragged figure, hair straggling down from under his tattered fur cap and mingling with his nearly equally long beard which was as fair as Antonio's.

Abe Jenkins' deerskin shirt was in shreds. With one arm he cradled a long barreled gun. With the other he waved to the watching crowd with extraordinary aplomb, calling out jauntily in English: "Howdy, folks!"

"An American, by Jove!" Sedley exclaimed.

Purposeful Father Rafael and his logs kept steadily on their course toward the mission, for he and Espinosa had instructed their Indians that, once cut, these were holy logs destined for the Lord's House and must never touch ground until they reached its sacred precincts, thus assuring continuous and rapid transport of heavy loads over difficult terrain. But the wild looking stranger turned boldly aside and came toward the crowd of spectators. Tongues wagged, questions flew. Who was this? Yet another Yankee? Coming from the interior? What did it mean? Was he the advance scout of a force approaching from that direction? Was this the long feared American takeover?

This Promised Land

Abe Jenkins' story was simple if wonderful, as Sedley translated. He'd come overland from Missouri with Lewis and Clark to the mouth of the Columbia or Ouragan, as it was originally called. Encamped there for the winter, Jenkins became restless during long months of rain and inaction, and having quarreled with his sergeant decided to desert and make his way southward to the Spanish settlements in the fabled land of California, which even to him had an almost mystical attraction as a place of eternal sunlight and wealth. Jenkins recalled Captain Lewis saying that the Spaniards fought bravely against the English in the recent war for American independence and in his simple yet shrewd way he thought they might receive him as friend and ally.

Making his way southward along the valleys tributary to the Ouragan, he was well received by Indians he met. A scrawny crooked man, well versed in wilderness ways, he knew their universal sign language and also a few words of their lingua franca acquired from Sacagawea, the Shoshone woman who guided Lewis and Clark. "But as I was about to enter the Great Valley of California," he continued, "near the base of that lofty snowcapped mountain where it begins, my luck deserted me and I fell in with a warlike tribe who compelled me to join in a campaign against their neighbors to the east." The Modocs took him into a desert region of low gray bushes which they called the Antelope Plains, actually northern Nevada. "They thought old Rigor Mortis here," patting his long-barreled Kentucky rifle, "would bring them victory." The campaign against the Paiutes consisted of a series of inconsequential skirmishes and was followed by almost interminable ceremonies and negotiations after which Jenkins insisted on release from his obligations and continued southward, the snowcapped peaks of the Sierra Nevada now towering upon his right. He passed the present sites of Reno and Mammoth, always well received by the natives, trading them tobacco and beads for hospitality and beaver skins, until he carried a tiny fortune on his back which he hoped to exchange with the Spaniards for food and gold when he reached California. But first he must cross the mountain barrier which, the Indians explained, walled him away from their settlements. "Up, up I climbed, making my way through a stony cleft among the clouds where the wind nearly froze me to death and I all but starved, having eaten the last of my pemmican, until finally the clouds parted and I saw far below me a vast valley shining in the sun and knew I was approaching my Promised Land as Moses did!"

As he descended Jenkins came to the shore of a jewel-like lake surrounded by giant trees of reddish wood and, in the hollow of one of those giant sequoias, he found Carlos Dominguez, a deserter from the presidio of Monterey, living an absolute solitude with his Miwok wife and their four children. They welcomed him and gave him food in return for powder and lead and he lived with them all that winter and well on into the following spring, occupying a burnt-out trunk nearby in which he was as snug as in a cabin, restoring his strength, hunting, fishing, and trapping with Dominguez until he accumulated an even larger packet of valuable skins and was ready to travel. Then illness struck him. Another year passed.

Finally, swearing never to reveal the location of his hideaway or the identity of its occupants if Dominguez told him what he must know to reach his promised land in safety, Jenkins said good-bye. Following directions he avoided the marshes and tule thickets of the valley floor and the numerous, not always friendly, tribes living there, and also the hostile stronghold of Tehame, and making his way along the foothills in a southerly direction, he circled the valley's lower end not far from present Bakersfield and entered the coastal mountains without mishap, assured that beyond them lay the missions of the coast and the goals he sought.

Descending a river canyon which led him due westward toward the setting sun, he came to a place where huge sycamores arched white arms over the stream. There was a big pool full of trout and a nice clean sandbar for sleeping and he noticed some deep holes made by Indians for grinding their seeds in the living rock, and many berries in lush patches nearby. It seemed like an ideal campsite as it had seemed to Lospe, Kachuku, and their families nearly half a century before when they traveled to see the Dance of the Condors and the Heart of the World, but as he approached it Jenkins came face to face with a mighty grizzly. "That gentleman rose up to greet me out of that briar patch and I swear I thought he never would stop rising! He was red and ready! Old Rigor Mortis here," patting his gun again, "missed fire. Which left me my knife against his teeth." He indicated the naked blade at his belt. "Took us a little time but we finally did 'er!"

His packet of skins served as a pad to protect him partially from the grizzly's raking claws. But it had been torn to shreds and so had his clothes. The gashes on his arms and face were

This Promised Land

healing. He'd splinted his broken leg with a piece of sycamore wood and lain there by the stream eating berries and dead bear until enough strength returned so he could travel. Father Rafael and his party bearing the pine trunks found him hobbling along looking, as Rafael testified later, like an emaciated ghost.

But now the question was what to do about this remarkable intruder.

"He'd better not remain," Arguello advised, turning to Arrillaga. "Would not Your Excellency agree? Since it would be illegal for a foreigner to linger? But let us offer the poor fellow our hospitality before sending him on his way!"

As commandant at Santa Barbara as well as his old friend, broad-shouldered Arguello was the natural one for Arrillaga to look to for advice in a matter of such importance, and he nodded his graying head. "Yes, if he were to pass through, if like a ship he were merely to pass through after receiving fresh provisions, that would cause no difficulty. I certainly don't want to take him back to Monterey with me and send him to Mexico City in irons."

"But I've just got here!" Jenkins protested when this was communicated to him by Sedley. "You want me to turn around and go back? After I've worked and bled to reach the Garden of Eden?"

To placate him Arrillaga offered him a sweet. With an unabashed grin Jenkins accepted. "Thanks, Your Highness!"

Antonio wrote afterward: "I think we all saw more in him than met the eye, heard more than reached the ear. He was indeed a portentous forerunner! A determined survivor!"

"He can return to Boston with me if he likes," Sedley offered. "I can use an extra hand."

After some difficulty Jenkins was at last persuaded. "Well, let me give the sea a try, Your Honors, for in truth I am a mite tired of footing it across the world by land and homesick for my Missouri bottoms, though I never intended to return there by way of China. But mark my word, Governor," turning to Arrillaga, "I'll be back one of these days! You wait! And I'll bring some kinfolk with me! This is too good a land to miss!"

Juanita and Francisco were among the young people inclined to laugh at this incongruous uncouth figure who seemed to them to have caused an unwarranted interruption in the day's merriment and their lovemaking.

Suddenly irritated, Antonio warned: "Do not laugh!" For he recognized in this indomitable stranger dreams and desires which had once stirred in himself. "You are spoiled rotten by your privileges, having nothing to worry about but your own amusement, while here is a man who has come to us in dire need and has killed his bear with only a knife. And it's not tied to a dead bull either!" This rebuke he instantly recognized as a mistake, for it embarrassed Francisco and Juanita in front of others but his mind had been focused elsewhere as he spoke. He was thinking that if one as determined as Jenkins could come to them in this way, a thousand like him could cross the sierras and pour down upon California like a flood. "And we could no more stop them than we could dam all the streams in those mountains!"

Yet as he looked at Francisco and Juanita he did not feel able to say any of this. What did young love care for such matters?

And this time as he viewed the girl closely he saw something in her dark beauty which disturbed him in a new way. It was an unnatural, almost feverish brightness of eye, flush of cheek, and when he mentioned it later to Clara she replied harshly: "If the girl has an illness, let us hope it takes her out of our son's way!"

All girls were carefully watched by mothers and duennas but toward morning of the third night of the party Juanita managed to escape the vigilance of Ignacia Arguello, and as she lay in Francisco's arms in the warm summer grass in the darkness under the oaks of the hillside, she said: "But you musn't love me. Because I am my father's daughter your parents hate me. And if you love me, they will not let you have this land which otherwise will rightfully be your inheritance!"

"I care not at all for that," he replied, embracing her ardently in his desire, "I'd much rather have you!"

But she was as persistent as he, and more artful. "Is it true that you have an Indian name?"

After a moment he replied reluctantly: "Yes."

"What is it?"

"What does it matter?"

"If you loved me you would tell me!"

"What in Heaven has that got to do with my love for you?" he demanded angrily.

"Everything. If you will deceive me in this, you will deceive me in everything!"

At last against his better judgment, fearing it would bring them bad luck, he told her: "Helek."

"What does it mean?"

"The Hawk."

This Promised Land

"Helek the Hawk," she repeated softly as she gave herself to him. "That is a lovely name! I shall cherish it as long as I live!"

As he and Juanita became one, Francisco realized that here and thus he had found his true identity at last—her mixed blood and rebellious spirit speaking fully to his through her passionate flesh.

Chapter Forty-one

California was not yet ready for independence, as Antonio sensed, but after 1811 the possibility was there and during the next few years it increased as war-torn New Spain was unable to pay much attention to its faraway province, nor was Spain itself, then engaged in throwing off its Napoleonic yoke, in a better position to exercise control. "We're on our own," Antonio told those who like himself sensed independence in the offing, "and time is on our side!" Estenaga and Sedley agreed, and Sedley offered to bring a shipment of arms on his next voyage but before that moment arrived many practical obstacles remained. Loyalty to the crown was deeply engrained among many settlers. Except for Antonio and a few others, most of the wealth and thence the power in the province was in the hands of the missionary fathers, who saw in liberal revolution the loss of all they hoped to accomplish. The military also was at first conservatively inclined, convinced that the upheavals elsewhere of which they heard only vague rumors must fail and the traditional authority of empire prevail. But realities soon began to assert themselves. Supply ships ceased coming altogether and with them the pay of the soldiers ceased too, and bitterness soon arose because of what impoverished privates, corporals, sergeants, and even officers regarded as the wealth and comfort of the missionary fathers compared to their own ragged and penniless state. "They're getting ready to come to our side," Benito Ferrer reported to Antonio "though it's true they have hardly any powder or shot," and in 1815 Sedley again offered to bring a shipment of arms on his next voyage from Boston. But the situation was somewhat alleviated when the friars yielded substantial levies of hemp and tallow, which could be sold or traded, and food stuffs, which could be consumed, to the presidios and mission garrisons in return for drafts on the Spanish treasury which they suspected would never be honored. Nevertheless they knew that without the protection of even a dissatisfied and ill-equipped soldiery, they would be at the mercy of the marauding raids of Asuskwa and his fellow leaders now ranging over a 500-mile front from San Francisco to Los Angeles with independent forays against San Diego by the always bellicose Diegueños, close relatives of the dreaded Yumas.

All of this by necessity opened the doors wider to the officially illegal but openly practiced trade with foreign ships, and these were chiefly American and Russian vessels since those of France and England were otherwise occupied in the Napoleonic struggles. Acting on the advice of Rezanof and Kalenin, the Russians established settlements at Fort Ross and Bodega Bay on the coast not far north of San Francisco, within easy trading and invading distance of that strategic port, and their Aleut otter hunters, carrying lightweight skin boats on their shoulders across country from the coast in order to avoid Spanish eyes and guns at the entrance to the bay, invaded the Great Estuary itself and took hundreds of fine skins there. And as increasingly open dealings with Spanish authorities occurred at every port, further enriching the missions which continued to supply most of the wheat, barley, meat, vegetables, hides, tallow, wool, and furs that made the substance of trade, jealousy and bitterness increased. Nowhere was this more apparent than in the Valley of Santa Lucia which produced the best crops, largest herds and had the finest church in all the province. "All for the padres and their Indians!" people grumbled. Rumors of vast hoards of wealth in Espinosa's secret coffers grew as times became harder for everyone else.

"It's been half a century," Antonio taxed the Father Superior heatedly, "since you friars started to convert the Indians so you could turn over the mission lands to them within ten years—half a century, and you still haven't turned over one acre or freed one Indian to become a citizen of the realm as your original directive required!"

"We are defending them against you predatory ranchers," the friar replied with more than usual warmth, for this touched a sensitive point. "You greedy landlords would seize all their land were we to turn it over to them! Alone against you they would be like defenseless children. With us they have a shield!"

"And so you are extending that shield by establishing new ranches in every empty valley, till you have a network like a spider web extending up and down our entire coast! Why, it was only last week I heard how you people expelled old Reyes and all his animals from that valley now called San Fernando which we discovered in '69 and where Reyes and his people lived for many years! When I hear about your glorious mission chain linking San Diego with San Francisco I know what it truly is: a chain of avarice and bondage!''

The new church was now completed, its lofty nave supported by those logs Rafael brought from the mountains, and the golden cupola atop the central of its five domes could be seen for twenty miles when the sun shone upon it. Captains used it as a landmark when bringing their ships to anchor and most of the Indian converts believed it to be actually the house of God. Espinosa's herds now totaled well over seventy thousand though accurate count was impossible, they ranged so far and wide, and his acreage for grazing and grain production had expanded into six areas or ranches beside the original one now known as Rancho Santa Lucia. He had established an asistencia or branch mission in the large valley to the south. And to maintain all of this expansion he relied on new and increasingly efficient methods of recruiting his labor force. The old voluntarism of Rubio's day when Indian rights were in most cases scrupulously respected and converts came to the mission only by free will had been abandoned as not only quaint but impractical under the new conditions. Birth rates were declining. Death rates were rising as result of the insidious inroads of syphilis and terrible epidemics of measles, smallpox, influenza, and other diseases which carried away hundreds of converts, crowded together as they were in close quarters where infections spread. When replacements were needed Espinosa sent soldiers into the hills and rounded them up at gunpoint. Once at the mission, those who tried to escape were punished severely with floggings, stocks, or leg irons. For other misdemeanors more imaginative chastisement was devised.

An Indian mother who miscarried, as Clara learned on good authority, was accused of infanticide. Her head was shaved and she was flogged daily for fifteen days. She was also required to wear irons on her feet for three months and to appear every Sunday at Mass on the steps leading to the altar where everyone could see her holding a hideously painted wooden child in her arms. Though some gente de razon disapproved, most soldiers and settlers were glad enough to have a continuous supply of Indians to do their work, leasing laborers from Espinosa by day or week, so they did not complain too openly about such mistreatment.

This Promised Land

The friar seemed invincible.

But still runaways continued and the tulares became thronged with refugees while at Tehame, cursed by Espinosa as "a republic of Hell and a diabolical union of apostates," it was said that even women were now riding horses like men, preparing for the general uprising every Spaniard feared. This time it would consist of cavalry as well as infantry and a flaming attack on Mission San Miguel in the upper Salinas Valley in which several were killed on both sides made it a real possibility.

Few whites know that even today there is a clandestine Indian resistance movement in California. Its members are convinced that, as pressures increase in the years ahead, whites will try to push them from the reservation lands they still occupy. A descendant of Clara and Antonio said recently that he and his comrades are buying guns and preparing to defend themselves. "We also are awaiting Our Leader. He hasn't been made known to us yet, but he is there!" pointing into distance. "And when the time comes he will guide us!"

This Messianic belief contains ominous undertones of the Ghost Dance Movement of a century ago which involved many tribes in the conviction that proper dancing combined with proper leadership would magically eliminate the white man and his oppressions. Originating among the Northern Paiute of Nevada, the Ghost Dance spread westward into California where it obtained a strong foothold. Later it expanded eastward and ended in the terrible massacre at Wounded Knee including many innocent women and children.

Thus today as in the time of Espinosa and again later there is increasing resistance.

Feeling against the friar mounted steadily while his income rose likewise, thanks largely to sale of otter skins and resale of goods obtained illicitly from trading vessels. Also he began to accumulate from Indians gold brought secretly from the foothills of the Sierra Nevada. Returning after a sojourn with relatives or from a trading journey into the San Joaquin Valley, an Indian would show him a tiny nugget or pinch of dust, and with a mysterious air say he'd found it while uprooting plants. Espinosa like other padres at other missions would enjoin secrecy. If the Indian were to reveal the source of gold, the wrath of God would fall upon him. But if he were to bring it again to Espinosa, or if his friends and relatives were to do so, God would approve. Thus the crafty father accumulated a substantial supply of the precious metal. To the value of seven thousand dollars it was sent in a fine silk purse made especially for the purpose as a present to the Pope in Rome, and this happened long before the first public discovery of gold in California in San Fernando Valley in 1840, and decades prior to the famous Gold Rush of 1849.

Espinosa did his best to keep his golden secret and succeeded. He knew that if it got out, the land would be flooded by foreigners and many Protestants, and the Catholic faith and his power would likely be submerged.

Antonio and Clara, thanks to their close contacts with Indians, knew something of all this. "But we said nothing," Antonio wrote, "for fear of what might happen to our land and its people. Sometimes Indians would even bring gold to us and we hid it in a hole in the wall behind the crucifix Serra gave us." Antonio thought how ironic it was that he who as conquistador had once sought gold in the mythic land of California should have it come to him in this way!

Meanwhile beneath Mission Santa Lucia's opulent façade, the human matrix on which it rested began to tremble. Yet outwardly Espinosa still seemed unshakable. Periodically, usually on Sunday nights when they were freshly conditioned by the events of the day's worship to his image and authority, he would enter the monjerio after the girls and the maestra retired. As soon as she became aware of his presence—she was a not so elderly widow of a soldier of the garrison—the maestra sat up in bed and began to sing in a special key the grand old hymn:

> "Loving shepherd of your sheep,
> Keep us Lord in Safety keep,
> Nothing can your power withstand,
> None can pluck us from your
> hand!"

The girls would take up the words of this signal and echo it, and as the Father Superior went slowly among them, his dark figure like an apparition from on high, he would select the girl he would have sex with, and have it, while the others kept on singing to mask the proceedings. In this way he enjoyed himself at leisure and on leaving granted the maestra a similar favor. "What a man!" the simple hearted Indians said amongst themselves. "How powerful his God must be!"

This Promised Land

"It is such an easy, easy thing to slip from egotism of spirit to egotism of flesh," Rubio had written with prescient self-criticism in those days when Clara as Lospe first took refuge with him, "to lapse into the delusion of the sanctity of self in all its aspects! Pride is not for nothing the first of the deadly sins!"

"To whom could his victims complain?" Antonio now wrote in impotent outrage. "How effective would the word of an Indian girl be against that of a Father Superior?" As spiritual advisor to the nuns of the convent of Abrojo in Old Castile years before, Espinosa learned not only the aphrodisiacal effects of holy authority upon the feminine sensibility, but also that a woman is reluctant to reveal what she considers her shame in such cases and is intimidated at thought of pitting her word in public forum against her spiritual advisor's. Using the confessional as a means of seduction, Espinosa thus developed an almost foolproof technique. Lately he'd even dared to baptize his bastard son and record the child's name in the mission record. This supreme arrogance came to the attention of church authorities and a letter, which Antonio later learned of, was written to all priests in California stating that better behavior was expected. But so great was Espinosa's power and influence that to avoid a flagrant scandal no direct measures were taken against him. Clara sensed the possibility of all this intuitively at her first meeting with Espinosa.

Now Antonio raged privately to her against what he considered this last heinous vestige of absolutism and despotism.

"I wish there were some way he could be brought to account! Did he ever try anything off color with you?"

"Not while Rubio was alive. He dared not."

"And afterward?"

"He was afraid of you, and your power."

Antonio shook his head. "He must be exposed! But the problem is: an attack on him will be seen as an attack on all the church! He will make it seem so. They will all rally behind him: the whole hierarchy. And they suspect and even hate me, as it is!"

"God will surely punish him. You must not take it upon yourself to do so!"

But Antonio persisted: "Why must we stand by and see innocent people victimized in this way? Are we then to appear to condone a crime?"

"What can we do?"

"Complain to the Governor!"

"Sola? He's a coward, vain, incompetent. Worse than dear old Papa Arrillaga ever was. You'd never get anywhere with him. You'd only make trouble for yourself and me. Be patient. Wait!" She no longer attended Mass but still prayed daily in the room across the hall where the crucifix with the two arms which Serra gave them occupied a niche in the adobe wall. And Antonio knew she was seeing the situation clearly as usual. But still it angered him that Espinosa did what he did without apparent penalty and he hoped God was watching and keeping account. Antonio saw in the new liberalism with its increasing anticlericalism a force which might eventually bring Espinosa to his knees. But this occurred in quite an unexpected way.

Meanwhile Francisco, for reasons of which some were beyond his control, some not, took no part in the rising conflict between ranchers and missionaries or in the independence movement, and this was a new source of concern to his parents who continued to see in him their own expectations.

The year 1823 was memorable in the history of the province of New California for in that year it ceased to exist. The Mexican revolution had at last succeeded. New Spain was no more. Mexico, though rocked by unscrupulous power grabs, was moving toward a system of constitutional government with a congress modeled after that of the United States. In faraway California all this caused hardly a tremor at first and when Luis Arguello, son of his old friend, became California's first native-born governor under the new regime, Antonio felt that a long step toward autonomy had been taken.

Warmed by such pleasant thoughts, he was sitting by the fire one February evening of the following year, reading aloud to Clara from that favorite volume of Rousseau given him by Kalenin in the days when Inquisition and Index Librorum Prohibitorum were still to be feared. Now the volume seemed to glow in his hands like hidden gold revealed at last. "Land is the source of all personal and social strength, and therefore all persons should live upon the land and cultivate it."

At last, long last, those ideas discussed with Costanso as they rode up the trail so long ago, wild imaginings as they seemed, were coming true. It seemed he had lived to witness a miracle. Was it all one quest, this life, all one Sacred Expedition in search of a legendary land? Sometimes it was like a dream in which he saw them, Costanso, Fages, Crespi, Portola, marching in a mist, at others in sunlight that was everlasting. The pain and fear were long forgotten. The glory remained. Only the day before he and Benito Ferrer had discussed it in that very room. "Yes, there's hope," Benito quietly agreed. "Such times as we've emerged from! The power of the mission fathers must inevitably be reduced now. They will be stripped of their vast landholdings and their Indians freed and placed in lawful possession of what has rightfully been theirs from the beginning, and some land may become available to new settlers, old colonists, and to entrepreneurs like ourselves. I think we are continuing a quest begun by Columbus," as they sipped that memorable wine from Antonio's vineyard, from grapes grown from cuttings they'd brought down together from Monterey with the pack train years ago and Rubio had planted. "I'm convinced Columbus was a Jew." Ferrer spoke no longer with an apprehensive glance over his shoulder lest someone be listening.

"Nonsense, he was a Catalan!" Antonio retorted.

"Does that mean he wasn't a Jew?"

"Not necessarily!" Antonio admitted. And Ferrer explained how a branch of his family in the 1400s on Majorca had been cartographers in those days when Majorcan maps were famous as the world's finest and most of their makers Jews. "Columbus, or Colon, came to my family in search of the best maps he could find to guide him on his quest. His wife was a marrano. That is certain. So were his principal backers Jews. There's no doubt in my mind he was a marrano too and I'm convinced that a chief reason for his voyage was to find new homelands for the oppressed, because—mark you this—because at the very moment he sailed—yes, midnight before his departure was the actual deadline—all Jews were either to be converted to Christianity or gone from Spain, and not a few went aboard his ships in the harbor at Palos just before the stroke of twelve!"

"I will not argue with your age-old wisdom!" Antonio replied good-humoredly. "Let us drink to Columbus, and to freedom! If California is to be the westernmost reach in a remarkable gesture which began with the Catalan, Colon, we should feel the more honored to reside here!"

He and Clara were alone tonight because Francisco and Constanza were absent visiting her parents in Santa Barbara. The fever which first had heightened the beauty of Juanita Lopez, as is not uncommon in the early stages of tuberculosis, quickly consumed it. After the death of what was to be his one passionate and total love, killed, or so he believed for the rest of his life, by his own mistake in revealing to her his Indian name, Francisco with characteristic determination threw himself wholly into a new and different quest, this one for self-indulgence and forgetfulness. "At least it will be something new and untried!" he retorted when his parents remonstrated. And in later years, remembering Juanita, in anguish and bitterness he would fling out at them sarcastically: "Yes, I am the man of the Promised Land! I am your damned mestizo halfbreed!" And in this context defiantly shutting away his old life and its painful memories, he married wealthy Constanza Estenaga and embarked with her upon a new one.

For Antonio it had been a good day. Rising as usual at dawn he'd ridden with Pablo and his four sons to hunt wild cattle as was customary in February when the watery young grass provided less strength for the wily outlaws that ranged the backcountry, and a well fed horse with a good man on its back stood a better chance of success against them. Pablo still rode a white mule as in the beginning, his original Moses being followed by a long line of that name, all with the distinctive dark rings painted around their eyes ostensibly to keep out the glare of the sun, but in part to establish Pablo's uniqueness; for still wherever he went his history had gone before him, as his black dog had once gone. His sons rode the dappled grays and chestnut sorrels which had become the established breed of Rancho Olomosoug, the grays descended from the stallion Portola rode and bequeathed to Fages and he to Antonio, the sorrels from Antonio's own Babieca, and so the horses of the Conquest, his brand upon their hips, were still alive under Antonio and his men.

His gray bore him strongly up the trail as they climbed to the highlands. The day was unseasonably warm, the first wildflowers, the graceful white milkmaids and blue brodiaea, in bloom, and the wild lilac, blue and white, making the chaparral a matrix of colorful perfume. And its fragrance seemed to pass into Antonio with new meaning. As they climbed the winding trail, Pablo whispered: "Look!" and there miraculously was a young fawn wobbling after its mother on legs that could barely carry it.

Pablo's own legs were none too good and he rode stiffly if gamely, while Antonio sensed in himself that renewed vigor which always seemed to flow into him from the wild country, and so they climbed through oak woodland and chaparral and came to the high clear pines where the outlaw cattle roamed.

This Promised Land

It had been a long ride and the day was passing into afternoon as they found position so that the westerly sea wind would be in their faces and not betray them as they approached the wild band. The two oldtimers let the youngsters lead. But when they saw Isidro, Pablo's oldest, draw rein and raise his hand, they spurred forward. Isidro held a finger to his lips and pointed. There in the next hollow a dozen wild ones, blacks, reds, and a dun or two were feeding, secure in what they thought their perfect isolation.

Antonio motioned left and right deploying his men in traditional fashion, they now turning watching eyes to him, and as he raised his hand, spurs were set, and at dead run, reatas whirling, the riders charged.

The startled cattle broke away like deer but the momentum of the men was too strong to be escaped and quickly brought them alongside. And as Antonio, racing at full speed, came abreast of a huge black bull which seemed to contain the very spirit of wildness, instead of putting his reata over its horns and forelegs as he could easily have done, on sudden impulse he reached out and touched its warm body as he had done that great steer of the first trail drive so long ago, and he felt something marvelous pass into him from the animal, and it seemed he had touched the mystery of life and death and was at the very heart of existence. A new sense reached him of the interrelationship of all living things in the world of which he was a part and their mutual interdependency—as his hand had depended upon the warm back of the great bull.

Each of the boys roped and tied his outlaw masterfully and they looked up in surprise when they realized that Antonio for the first time had let his go, but Pablo who'd seen and understood said simply: "Well done, Compadre!" For it was like the old whimsical days of their youth when they had done those strange creative things together.

Antonio was late getting home and Clara felt anxious. She always secretly worried when he went into the hills, wondering if he would return alive or would meet the fate which Nunez the deserter had met: a red arrow between his shoulder blades. And yet the days had flowed into years and still it hadn't happened. But she never was sure. She brightened when she saw how happy and satisfied he was as he entered the room with his usual shout, and _he_ tried to tell her something of what occurred during the hunt and what he'd thought. The idea of a compact between man and land, an implicit agreement between the earth and all its living things, its grass, its animals, its people, its beauty, had entered his mind as result of the day's experience, but he was unable to articulate much of this beyond telling her he'd had a wonderful time. Later he scratched a few notes which she cherished. "Under the terms of the social contract all citizens are equals, says Rousseau. Why not a larger contract which will encompass all living things? For is there not an indissoluble compact between the earth and its creatures, to which we are all involuntary signatories and which we violate at our peril?"

He ate ravenously of beefsteak, rich gravy and onions, eggs fried into an omelette, red beans, tortillas, bread, coffee, and of course the red wine from those ancient Mediterranean grapes, originating perhaps in Egypt, which followed conquistadors and padres to the ends of the earth, and likewise the olive and its oil harvested from his own trees and compressed in his own press.

A wind was rising around the eaves of the house. When it suddenly turned from cool to hot and began with what seemed deliberate malice to curl around corners and enter the room from unexpected angles, Antonio and Clara avoided looking at each other. Whenever the hot wind, the Breath of the Torch of the Sun, which in later days would be called the Santa Ana Wind and would push flames into cities and devour houses, began to blow they could not help but remember that terrible night when it seemed a supernatural force helping Asuskwa destroy the mission, bringing fire, blood and death, Rubio's martyrdom, anguish, and sorrow with it, igniting a sequence of discord and pain which had continued down to this moment. Clara was particularly uneasy because she was reminded of what she dreaded most: a confrontation between her husband and brother which would embody the conflict within herself between white and Indian ways.

Sensing what she was thinking, Antonio lowered his book and said reassuringly: "This is February. The grass is green. The brush is damp. Our roof is tile. There's little danger of fire!" But he too was remembering the days of the red arrow placed upon the Sacred Stone at the center of the courtyard and was forced to restrain himself from getting up and going to see if the gates were securely locked and the dogs alert and if old Pablo and Kachuku and their sons and families who now occupied the other broad wing of the hacienda were feeling as he did. He guessed that they were.

Keeping his seat by the fireplace, he resumed reading aloud,

This Promised Land

raising his voice to make himself heard above the rising wind and to hearten Clara who sat opposite. He had come, eerily as it would seem later, to the passage which declares that "each man having been born free, no other man can bind him, on any pretext whatever, without his consent," when suddenly there was a violent gust and the door flew open, letting in a blast which almost extinguished the candles on the tables beside them, and in the doorway stood a naked Indian. Clara did not recognize him at first. His hair was white. The skin of his arms and neck hung loose. But the hatred in his eyes was undimmed. She cried out: "My brother!" And Antonio laid down his book again and sat perfectly still holding it on his lap in both hands.

Asuskwa held a half drawn bow in his with an arrow fixed to fly. "Like the condor of dreams," as Clara said afterward, "he had come to us through the night." Like the condor he was painted black and red, hair up in a topknot as of old time with his black obsidian knife thrust through it. The arrow at his string did not tremble. It was aimed straight at Antonio. "The moment is now!" he said quietly. "I have given you warning. Yes, I have given you a lifetime. Now the red arrow must find its home."

"Put down your bow," said Clara, and her voice was fully as commanding as his, as she took the pistol from the drawer of the table beside her and leveled it at him. It was the rifled one Sedley had given her. Its wooden stock ran the full length of its barrel and it was of .50 caliber made by an expert Pennsylvania craftsman in the model known as Kentucky. She could hit an oak knot with it at thirty yards and kill a deer at sixty. "Go while you are still alive," she said.

"I do not think you will kill your brother for the sake of a robber who has taken our land and destroyed our home and the life of our people," Asuskwa replied after a moment. "What good would it do you? Because after tonight his race will be powerful no longer. Tonight is the night. All along the coast the People of the Land and the Sea are rising against the white usurpers, and tomorrow there will be no more A-alowow, only ourselves!" She saw the gleam of madness in his eyes. "Look at your skin, Sister" he continued. "Listen to your blood. Do your hear the wind? It is the breath of the Sun our Ruler telling us what we must do."

A tremor ran through her but her hand with the gun did not waver, and she placed her other upon it too so that it would not, and so that he would see her determination.

"Go!" she said.

"I will not go. Tonight the time for payment has come. Tonight his blood will be added to all that which will compensate for our mother's, our uncle's, our aunt's, and countless others. Tonight the missions are being surrounded. Not only yours but all the others that are central. With them in our hands, we shall have broken the grasp of Sutupaps here where it was always weakest, at our own coast, and those north and south will surely wither and perish."

She felt then he was talking of mad dreams but still she could not be sure. Was there indeed an army of thousands at his back? "Continue to talk!" Antonio said quietly in Catalan.

"You are mad!" she said. "Long hatred has deranged your mind!"

"I am not mad," he said, "but I am ashamed that I ever wavered. Because I loved you, I gave you warning. And again warning. And again and again, so that even your son came to me. But still you would not heed. Now the moment has come!" And he drove the arrow into Antonio's body. Her pistol spoke. Both men fell forward.

As Clara bent over Antonio she saw with agonized relief that his eyes met hers with recognition. The arrow had gone through the middle of his body. Blood poured from him. But he was alive and conscious. He motioned toward her brother. "I did as he bade me," she said afterward. "My brother was dying. My shot had gone straight to his heart. And as his eyes glazed in faraway look, I knew he was seeing for the last time that secret place where condors dance in the sun. With a tremor his soul departed. I could imagine it winging from Tolakwe far out over the sea toward the Land of the Dead. I did not cry. There was no time. An arrow whizzed through the window, just missing me. Outside I could hear gunshots, see fire, hear the terrible wind."

The raiders had rushed into the courtyard bearing firebrands. Pablo and the boys were engaging them. Reenforcements were coming from the Indianada. As she crouched again over Antonio, his head in her lap, trying to staunch his blood, she heard the wild cries. More arrows whizzed through the room. She put down his head on a cushion, seized a gun from the rack in the corner, ran to the window and fired back at them.

But this time the wind dropped as suddenly as it had begun. As if deliberately leaving the attackers without support, it died away, and without their leader they receded with it, raiding storerooms and corrals, setting fire to a shed, carrying off some cheeses, driving away some horses and cattle, never attacking the mission at all but retiring with their loot toward the tulares, reenacting their perennial failure to unite and persist. Indian resistance was to smoulder on but only in isolated instances, never on such a wide front or with concerted purpose. There had been no army, merely a handful. Simultaneous attacks or uprisings at La Purisima, Santa Ynez, Santa Barbara, San Luis Obispo proved similarly abortive. Thus Asuskwa's dream ended in delusion. And yet Clara's heart ached with admiration as with sorrow.

The dilemma of her conflict had been resolved at last. She had resolved it. The blood of her brother and of her husband was on her hands. She had been baptized into a new reality, and there she felt herself utterly alone, in a new way where she was the only traveler.

Antonio lived two days. He never spoke again. Motioning feebly toward the last, he indicated he wanted pen and paper. "To our hilltop," he scrawled faintly. Pablo and the boys made a litter and carried him across the river, past the green momoy bush and up the hill to the spot where she had first seen him in her dream, where he had first entered her world. At the end they were alone on the summit.

Epilogue:
SEÑORA BONEU

Clara was alone when young Father O'Hara found her in the summer of 1852, seated on the shady verandah up whose columns honeysuckle and wisteria climbed toward the sun.

O'Hara was the last of the old, first of the new. Son of an Irish soldier of fortune who fought in the peninsular campaigns of Wellington against Napoleon's forces and afterward became a general in the Spanish army, he had red hair, and he like her was a rebellious adventurous spirit who'd turned his back on quiet ways and come with missionary zeal to the new state of California where there were no longer any missions, only ruins. Expropriation in late Mexican times stripped the padres of their lands, dispersed their converts, left their churches in decay. In what remained of Mission Santa Lucia, Michael O'Hara would like his father seek his fortune in devastation and chaos, for those terms accurately described what was left of the dreams of Serra and Rubio, and of Espinosa.

She was so old she seemed to him to have passed beyond time. Yet her spirit was youthful, her mind alert, and though she wore the Mother Hubbard, the drab overall garment of a Christianized Indian woman, her manner said unmistakably that she was Señora Boneu, mistress of 48,000 acres, widow of a conquistador, daughter of a legendary chieftainess. O'Hara knew the respect and affection with which she was regarded by the people of the valley, to whom she seemed a mythic figure.

"Whatever happened to Father Espinosa? There seems to be some mystery. A total blank. Nothing in the record." O'Hara was eager for every drop of information he could extract about those who had gone before, in whose footsteps he followed.

"Then I shall tell you. That Sunday morning was sultry, the kind of weather we call earthquake weather. He was conducting Mass in the grand new church. It was the grandest in all the province. Its five domes lifted like five mountain peaks toward the sky and the golden cupola atop the highest could be seen for twenty miles when the sun struck it. He was consecrating the Host, holding it up to Heaven with both hands when the earth under his feet began to tremble. I knew God would punish him for his wrongdoing but I did not know how. A crack appeared in the blue dome of the roof over his head. He was knocked to his knees. Pieces of the sky he had created with so much arrogance at the cost of so much suffering on the part of my gulled and exploited people began to fall down upon him. He gave a great cry. Then the whole sky fell upon him and he was crushed."

"Where was Father Rafael?"

"He had gone to the asistencia in South Valley to conduct services. All that remains of the Mission Santa Lucia today is Rafael's work."

"But I see no great domes or cupolas!" It was Michael O'Hara's dream not only to follow in the footsteps of the apostolic fathers but to recreate and revitalize their churches.

"After Espinosa was dead, Rafael was free to carry out what Rubio had in mind. Somehow he knew. Somehow God told him. Because those proud walls Rubio abhorred had come down once and for all. In their stead rose the simple beautiful building you see, with its modest belfry and long arched portico which greet the sunrise as Rubio and I used to do."

During a similar conversation O'Hara asked her about the abortive revolution of independence and Clara responded with usual frankness: "That was a moment when my son became for a time the man his father wanted him to be. My husband, you see, was a very great man. He had a vision of this land as a place of liberty and justice, a place where people could live in their own ways without interference from others. And as his son and mine, our Francisco, and Pablo's sons, and all my able-bodied men rode north to Monterey at the moment of revolution to join the uprising against Mexican rule, people ran out to cheer. For the moment had come at last. 'We shall rid our land of the Mexican intruders!' everyone cried. 'At last we shall be free!' It was the moment of which my husband dreamed. . . . It was 1836, the year in which there was a revolution in Texas too and there was talk of it and people argued: 'If Texas can be free, why cannot we?' Nobody supported Governor Gutierrez and his cholos* whom Mexico City had sent us. We wanted to govern ourselves. Alvarado and Vallejo, sons of my husband's old friends, who visited here as boys at Francisco's birthday celebration, were the ringleaders. They and their men besieged Gutierrez inside the presidio walls. Captain Sedley and his ship were hovering offshore with arms. It was just as he and Antonio had planned. And Francisco behaved like the son of his father. You see, for the moment it took his fancy! Captivated all his obstinacy! He supervised the ferrying of the guns and ammunition ashore, and he directed the fire of the one cannon the insurrectionists possessed so accurately that its one shot landed right on the governor's house inside the presidio walls! The very same house I once slept in and danced in in the days of Don Pedro Fages!'' Father O'Hara, listening intently, transported by her powerful words, recreated in his imagination the crumbled edifice of his promised land in its original glory.

"Gutierrez, mighty warrior," Clara went on derisively, "immediately surrendered! Francisco arranged the terms whereby Sedley carried him and his men back to Mexico. Next Francisco helped write the declaration which declared us to be a 'free and sovereign state' with a constitution regulating all branches of the government, and thus like rain which falls upon our back country and travels underground in secret veins to emerge in that spring on the hillside you see there, ideas pass quietly from one generation and emerge in another. But Francisco's dashing success made others jealous. Alvarado particularly. He was ambitious, unscrupulous. A dispute about the flag arose. Should it have a large red star on a white field like Texas' or should it not? 'Why should we mimic Texas?' Francisco argued. 'Let us have a grizzly bear instead which represents our courage and strength?' But the others hooted at this, egged on by Alvarado, and taking affront Francisco turned his back on them and rode away. After which Alvarado betrayed everything. 'You see, Mamacita, what comes of getting yourself involved in the affairs of others?' my son told me when he returned here. And from that moment he has devoted himself entirely to his own interests," she grew thoughtful in an unhappy way, "until now they call him in his lavishness 'Francisco El Magnifico,' these Yankees do, flattering him shamelessly because he spends so much money with them. I tell him the Gold

---

*contemptible scum

Rush is like a bad dream. It will go away. So will the high prices of our cattle. Seventy-five dollars for one animal. Can you imagine? Only the land will remain, I tell him. But he will not listen. He laughs and says I am old-fashioned. But if I were he I'd apprentice my grandson to Santiago Ferrer who runs the store in town as you well know. Santiago is Jewish like his father, my husband's close friend. He knows how to survive. He will surpass these Yankees in this new commercial world they have thrust upon us, or I miss my guess."

O'Hara did not ask further about Francisco. He'd heard how that tragic figure of a man, sometimes sarcastically styling himself The Magnificent Halfbreed, sometimes screaming the epithet at his mother, spent and womanized, drank and seemed bent on destroying the heritage his parents had given him. Instead O'Hara said: "Tell me about the time you were visited by the American author Richard Henry Dana?" O'Hara was a reader and his copy of *Two Years Before the Mast* was well thumbed.

"Dana? His firm bought many of our hides in those days. Tallow too, packed in bags weighing half a ton for making soap and candles, and he took horns for buttons for the New England ladies' shoes and dresses. He was a good lad, if naïve. 'Well out of that place they call Harvard!' he told me. Too much study had nearly blinded his eyes! Here we showed him what real life could be. And he went home and wrote a book about it. My husband was a friend of many writers. Did you ever read Fages' *A Historical, Political and Natural Description of California* or Costanso's diary of the Sacred Expedition or textbook on Geometry? You must. They are great works. Dana's is juvenile by comparison."

"And later did not the famous explorer John C. Fremont come to see you?"

"He sat in that very chair you are sitting in, a surprisingly sensitive dark little man. Moody eyes. Very attractive to women, I should think. And do you know who was among the soldiers accompanying him that day? Who actually led him here? That incredible galoot Jenkins, the one I told you about who came to us so surprisingly the day of my son's birthday celebration. 'Told you I'd be back, lady!' he said in his insufferable way. A battalion of those gabby Missourians was with them. It was in '46 at the time of the American takeover which my husband had always hoped might happen. So I told them how to get through the mountains by secret ways and sent Isidro, Pablo's oldest, my mayordomo now, to guide them, and they fell upon Santa Barbara by surprise and captured it without a shot . . . And now, if you please, right now this week, that old scarecrow Jenkins has come back and camped upon my land, as you see," she pointed to the whitehooded wagons in the oaks of the grove at no great distance down the valley. "He claims this is his land. He says the Americans won their war against Mexico and my land is his reward. What am I to do? That is why I am so dependent on Eliot Sedley. For nearly a decade that fine young man has been upon our coast as representative of his father's firm. He is very knowledgeable about business matters. He tells me that to establish title to my ranch—this place where I was born and have occupied all my life—to do such an incredible thing I must appear before what is called the Land Commission so that they may confirm to me what is already mine! It's costing me a pretty penny! But where else can I turn? So I'm leaving it entirely in Eliot's hands. I trust him completely. And every time I think of him I think how his father's ship was lost off Cape Horn, and all those brave men drowned, which in turn reminds me how the Comte de La Perouse, with whom I danced at Monterey, also disappeared without a trace with both his ships. Alas!" It was a rare moment of sadness that O'Hara saw cross her face, rather like a cloud shadow upon a piece of weathered hillside than despair or gloom.

"And what is this about your attendance as representative of your people at the conference called by the Commissioner of Indian Affairs regarding the formation of reservations?" he prompted.

This time her eyes flashed as she responded: "Never shall I sign such a document which gives away our ancestral lands. Already hasn't there been enough? Why, even the grass which grew here when I was a child has been choked by the weeds brought by the white man, escaped from his fields and advancing voraciously into our countryside, yes, the wild oats and the clover and the mustard and radish, displacing our sweet grasses. They are like the white man himself. They take over everything."

On her way to that famous conference at the foot of Tejon Pass overlooking the Great Valley into which Antonio and Fages had ridden in the fall of 1772, to find the Tulamni and later the Painted Rock in the Plain of the Carrizo Grass, she had ridden through the mountains and stopped at the Cave of the Condors to worship once more, and there before the sacred painting on the interior

This Promised Land

wall she saw the gun of Nunez, still untouched, as it would remain for another hundred years and more, and outside on the cave's lip the painting of Owotoponus still blazed brightly, waiting like the gun to be "discovered" as it would in the 1980s. Then it would be much discussed and analyzed, some experts declaring it a masterpiece, others a masterful hoax perpetrated by some gifted modern. After a fragment was radiocarbon dated to 1750 plus or minus twenty years, the painting was photographed in finest Kodocolor and appeared in glossy magazines and books which carried those brush strokes of Owotoponus to many parts of the world, strokes made that summer before the white man came, as Clara remembered. As she bowed her head in silence, it seemed as if the Great Spirit of the Canyons which spoke to her and her father that day upon the summit of Iwihinmu was listening and understanding, knowing of everything that had happened to her since, knowing of the aching hollow left by the loss of Antonio, knowing of the terrible anguish caused by the behavior of Francisco. Sometimes it seemed as if all of herself, all her life, had been a projection of her dream, as insubstantial as thought or cloud, as beautiful, and as terrible. It seemed she was receiving her allotted portion as Antonio had received his, he often telling her of his thoughts that day in August on the banks of the Porciuncula with Portola when he had listened to Father Gomez and wondered what his own little portion might be. Looking at the Eastern Window, the tiny hole bored in the cave wall so long ago, Clara wondered if it would ever again let in light upon her world.

The gun of Nunez, the bell-mouthed trabuco of .56 caliber with the once shiny brass fittings, also came to public attention and is now on display at the historical museum in Santa Lucia.

"It is time for me to go," she said to O'Hara, "and take my daily swim in the water we call the Tears of the Sun, which flows from the Heart of the World." And he understood if but dimly something of what was passing in her mind.

Calling to Kachuku who since Pablo's death had been closer than ever before, closer even than when they were girls because so much had happened since to bind them, Clara started slowly toward the river, and watching the two old women, O'Hara gave a shake of his head in wonder. The dreams which had led him to his promised land were taking on greater dimensions.

As the two old friends moved slowly toward the stream Clara

said: "Do you remember that day we went together to meet the white men for the first time?"

"I remember it well," Kachuku replied.

"And do you remember the song that we sang?"

"Not so clearly."

And Clara began to sing:

> We are the People of the Land and the Sea,
> We bathe in the River of Dawn,
> We bathe in the River of Dawn!

After they had bathed in the water that ran from the side of Iwihinmu, down over the waterfall cliff where the condors dance in the sun, they slipped back into their Mother Hubbards, lit their cane cigarettes and were starting back up the path toward the hacienda when they saw a slim blond figure approaching.

"Who is it?" for though Clara's mind was sharp her eyes were not what they used to be.

"It is your grandson Pacifico."

"Ah," her face brightened because the boy was her special pleasure. "And what is that shining at his belt?"

"Why, that is the silver buckle!" Kachuku prompted. "Surely you remember!"

"Yes," said Clara thoughtfully after a moment of reflection, blowing a puff of smoke, "yes, I remember."

Robert Easton was born in San Francisco, California. In one way or another all of his work has been centered on the history and people of the American West. His first great critical and popular success was *The Happy Man* (1943), a portrait of California ranch life in the late 1930s. *The New York Times Book Review* said of it, "Good writing of a kind that is difficult and rare." And *The New Yorker* stated that it has "a clear narrative style and a sure sense of authenticity." Easton went on to write *Max Brand: The Big "Westerner"* (1970), a biography of Frederick Faust, and recently with his wife, Jane Faust Easton, edited *The Collected Stories Of Max Brand* (1994). After three decades of research, his epic Saga of California began with *This Promised Land* (1982), spanning the years 1769-1850, and is continued in *Power And Glory* (1989). He is currently at work on the third volume of this saga, *Blood And Money*, providing a panoramic view of California during the Civil War. Since *The Happy Man* there can be no doubt of Robert Easton's commitment to the American West as both an idea and as a definite and distinct place. Beyond this, in all of his work he has been guided by his belief in what he once described as a writer's concern for "the living word—the one that captures the essential truth of what he is trying to say—and that is what I have tried to put down."

DON'T MISS THIS UNFORGETTABLE SAGA OF THE OLD WEST!

KANSAS BLUE

Dylan Harson

By journeying to Kansas, Danni Coopersand hopes to start a new life. But she soon loses her dream in the nightmare of the untamed land. As the way west turns into a relentless struggle against storms, floods, outlaws, and Indians, she seeks comfort and courage from three brave men:

JACK COOPERSAND: His body and mind broken by the Civil War, he can only pray for the strength he needs to protect Danni on the open prairie.

KIOWA: Little more than a boy, he has seen horrors few adults could bear, and he vows to save Danni such a fate.

AUSTIN BOURKE: A former Union soldier, he has the resolve to survive the harshest ordeal, but he can't resist the temptations offered by one married woman.

On the Smoky Hill Road from Fort Leavenworth to Fort Wallace, Danni ventures her heart and soul to meet the challenges of the trail, shelter her loved ones, and stake a claim on the brutal frontier.

_3896-X $4.50 US/$5.50 CAN

Dorchester Publishing Co., Inc.
65 Commerce Road
Stamford, CT 06902

Please add $1.75 for shipping and handling for the first book and $.50 for each book thereafter. NY, NYC, PA and CT residents, please add appropriate sales tax. No cash, stamps, or C.O.D.s. All orders shipped within 6 weeks via postal service book rate. Canadian orders require $2.00 extra postage and must be paid in U.S. dollars through a U.S. banking facility.

Name_____
Address_____
City _____ State_____ Zip_____
I have enclosed $_____in payment for the checked book(s).
Payment <u>must</u> accompany all orders. ☐ Please send a free catalog.

ELIZABETH, BY NAME
WILL COOK

Bestselling Author Of *Sabrina Kane*

IN THE EARLY DAYS OF THE TEXAS TERRITORY, ONLY THOSE WITH COURAGE AND STRENGTH CAN SURVIVE....

There is a cattle crossing at Mustang Creek. It is miles from anywhere, and no one has ever lived there—until Elizabeth Rettig comes. Since she knows the Texans will be driving their great herds of longhorns by on the way to Dodge, she sets up a trading post.

The territory is plagued by deadly tornadoes, burning summers, and freezing winters. Indians and trail hands and vicious, lawless men ride past on their way to fame or infamy. And because Elizabeth is young and spirited, suitors come too. But only the man with the strength to tame the wild land—and the patience to outlast Elizabeth's stubbornness—will win her heart.

_3868-4 $4.99 US/$6.99 CAN

Dorchester Publishing Co., Inc.
65 Commerce Road
Stamford, CT 06902

Please add $1.75 for shipping and handling for the first book and $.50 for each book thereafter. NY, NYC, PA and CT residents, please add appropriate sales tax. No cash, stamps, or C.O.D.s. All orders shipped within 6 weeks via postal service book rate. Canadian orders require $2.00 extra postage and must be paid in U.S. dollars through a U.S. banking facility.

Name_____
Address_____
City _____ State_____Zip_____
I have enclosed $_____in payment for the checked book(s).
Payment <u>must</u> accompany all orders.☐ Please send a free catalog.

THE UNFORGETTABLE LIVES AND LOVES OF
SABRINA KANE
WILL COOK

"A lot of good fun. Yes, there is romance—hell-raising romance!"

—*Oakland Tribune*

Hardly taller than a long rifle and lighter than a barrel of rum, Sabrina Kane is more than a match for the raw and rugged world of a pioneer woman. The young widow is a woman alone, but she is not without men:

PRIAM THOMAS: Sabrina's father has lost all hope for the future, and it is up to her to teach him to live again.

BENJAMIN TRAVIS: He is more man than Sabrina has ever known, but she is more woman than he can handle.

ABLE KANE: He loves Sabrina more than life itself, but does she dare give herself to her dead husband's kin?

A trailblazer, a healing angel, a passionate lover—Sabrina Kane is all that and more. With courage and determination, she will conquer the virgin land and win the hearts of her men.

_3827-7 $4.50 US/$5.50 CAN

Dorchester Publishing Co., Inc.
65 Commerce Road
Stamford, CT 06902

Please add $1.75 for shipping and handling for the first book and $.50 for each book thereafter. NY, NYC, PA and CT residents, please add appropriate sales tax. No cash, stamps, or C.O.D.s. All orders shipped within 6 weeks via postal service book rate. Canadian orders require $2.00 extra postage and must be paid in U.S. dollars through a U.S. banking facility.

Name_____
Address_____
City _____ State_____ Zip_____
I have enclosed $_____ in payment for the checked book(s). Payment <u>must</u> accompany all orders. ☐ Please send a free catalog.

SILVER STREET WOMAN
LES SAVAGE JR.
THE SWEEPING SAGA OF THE FEARLESS PIONEERS WHO RISKED THEIR LIVES AND LOVE ON THE MIGHTY MISSISSIPPI.

Few settlers have the nerve to challenge the raging torrents of the unstoppable Mississippi. But riverman Owen Naylor has courage enough to forge his own destiny—a destiny that is bound to the glory he craves, the woman he desires, and the men he defies:

CHARLOTTE DUMAIN: The untouched beauty tests Naylor beyond all endurance, but he will give all he has to possess her.

LOUIS REYNAUD: The wealthy Creole stands between Naylor and his heart's desire, but he won't surrender Charlotte without a fight to the death.

KENNETH SWAIN: The brawny keeler wants to rule the river, but as long as Naylor lives, he will never have a chance.

Naylor will need a soldier's strength, a shootist's skill, and a gambler's luck to realize his dreams. If he fails, he'll be forever forgotten. If he succeeds, he'll change history.

_3854-4 $4.99 US/$5.99 CAN

Dorchester Publishing Co., Inc.
65 Commerce Road
Stamford, CT 06902

Please add $1.75 for shipping and handling for the first book and $.50 for each book thereafter. NY, NYC, PA and CT residents, please add appropriate sales tax. No cash, stamps, or C.O.D.s. All orders shipped within 6 weeks via postal service book rate. Canadian orders require $2.00 extra postage and must be paid in U.S. dollars through a U.S. banking facility.

Name_____
Address_____
City _____ State_____ Zip_____
I have enclosed $_____in payment for the checked book(s).
Payment <u>must</u> accompany all orders.☐ Please send a free catalog.

Incident At Sun Mountain

TODHUNTER BALLARD

Winner Of The Golden Spur Award For Best Historical Novel

The fabulous Comstock lode—the silver strike that made the California Gold Rush look like a Sunday social—grips every able-bodied man with a frenzy for wealth. The ore dug up near boomtowns like Virginia City, Gold Hill, and Silver City is enough to finance any foolhardy notion or traitorous scheme, even a civil war that will rip the young nation asunder.

Sent to Nevada to investigate reports of Rebel activities, Ken English is thrust into a region full of miners and gamblers, heroes and killers, Union supporters and Southern sympathizers. As the threat of bloody conflict looms over the country, English and scores of brave men and women will risk their fortunes, their loves, and their very lives to quell the revolt—and save the land they helped to build.

_3935-4 $4.99 US/$6.99 CAN

Dorchester Publishing Co., Inc.
65 Commerce Road
Stamford, CT 06902

Please add $1.75 for shipping and handling for the first book and $.50 for each book thereafter. NY, NYC, PA and CT residents, please add appropriate sales tax. No cash, stamps, or C.O.D.s. All orders shipped within 6 weeks via postal service book rate. Canadian orders require $2.00 extra postage and must be paid in U.S. dollars through a U.S. banking facility.

Name_____
Address_____
City _____ State_____Zip_____
I have enclosed $_____in payment for the checked book(s).
Payment <u>must</u> accompany all orders.☐ Please send a free catalog.

Gold In California!
TODHUNTER BALLARD

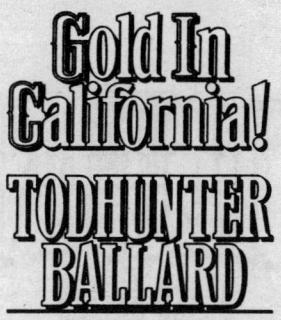

Winner Of The Golden Spur Award

Gold Fever! Some call it madness, some a fantasy. Yet the promise of untold wealth draws people west like bees to honey.

Determined to strike the mother lode, young Austin Garner and his family set out to cross the untamed American continent. The going is brutal—nearly three thousand miles of desert, disease, and death—and without extraordinary strength and courage, the pioneers will surely perish.

But California is the greatest challenge of all: a sprawling, unforgiving land full of scoundrels and scalawags, claim jumpers and con men, failures and fortunes. Yet Garner and his kin are ready to sacrifice life and love to realize their dream of gold in California!

_3888-9 $4.99 US/$6.99 CAN

Dorchester Publishing Co., Inc.
65 Commerce Road
Stamford, CT 06902

Please add $1.75 for shipping and handling for the first book and $.50 for each book thereafter. NY, NYC, PA and CT residents, please add appropriate sales tax. No cash, stamps, or C.O.D.s. All orders shipped within 6 weeks via postal service book rate. Canadian orders require $2.00 extra postage and must be paid in U.S. dollars through a U.S. banking facility.

Name_____
Address_____
City _____ State_____Zip_____
I have enclosed $_____in payment for the checked book(s).
Payment <u>must</u> accompany all orders.☐ Please send a free catalog.

WILL HENRY
JESSE JAMES
DEATH OF A LEGEND

Beneath the bandanna, underneath the legend, Jesse James was a wild and wicked man: a sinister and brutal outlaw who blazed a trail of crime and violence through the lawless West. Ripping the mask off the mysterious Jesse James, Will Henry's *Death Of A Legend* is a novel as tough and savage as the man himself. Only a great Western writer like Henry could tell the real story of the infamous bandit Jesse James.
_3990-7 $4.99 US/$6.99 CAN

Dorchester Publishing Co., Inc.
65 Commerce Road
Stamford, CT 06902

Please add $1.75 for shipping and handling for the first book and $.50 for each book thereafter. NY, NYC, PA and CT residents, please add appropriate sales tax. No cash, stamps, or C.O.D.s. All orders shipped within 6 weeks via postal service book rate. Canadian orders require $2.00 extra postage and must be paid in U.S. dollars through a U.S. banking facility.

Name _____
Address _____
City _____ State _____ Zip _____
I have enclosed $_____in payment for the checked book(s). Payment <u>must</u> accompany all orders.☐ Please send a free catalog.

ARROW IN THE SUN
T. V. OLSEN

Bestselling Author Of *Red Is The River*

The wagon train has only two survivors, the young soldier Honus Gant and beautiful, willful Cresta Lee. And they both know that the legendary Cheyenne chieftain Spotted Wolf will not rest until he catches them.

Gant is no one's idea of a hero—he is the first to admit that. He made a mistake joining the cavalry, and he's counting the days until he is a civilian and back east where he belongs. He doesn't want to protect Cresta Lee. He doesn't even like her. In fact, he's come to hate her guts.

The trouble is, Cresta is no ordinary girl. Once she was an Indian captive. Once she was Spotted Wolf's wife. Gant knows what will happen to Cresta if the bloodthirsty warrior captures her again, and he can't let that happen—even if it means risking his life to save her.

_3948-6 $4.50 US/$5.50 CAN

Dorchester Publishing Co., Inc.
65 Commerce Road
Stamford, CT 06902

Please add $1.75 for shipping and handling for the first book and $.50 for each book thereafter. NY, NYC, PA and CT residents, please add appropriate sales tax. No cash, stamps, or C.O.D.s. All orders shipped within 6 weeks via postal service book rate. Canadian orders require $2.00 extra postage and must be paid in U.S. dollars through a U.S. banking facility.

Name_____
Address _____
City _____ State_____Zip_____
I have enclosed $_____in payment for the checked book(s).
Payment <u>must</u> accompany all orders.☐ Please send a free catalog.

ATTENTION PREFERRED CUSTOMERS!

SPECIAL TOLL-FREE NUMBER
1-800-481-9191

Call Monday through Friday
**12 noon to 10 p.m.
Eastern Time**
*Get a free catalogue
and order books using your
Visa, MasterCard,
or Discover®*

Leisure Books

Love Spell

THIS PROMISED LAND

For Lospe, the gold rush of California brought only an onslaught of yellow-bellied greed to her peaceful native settlement. Spirited pioneers came from faraway cities recklessly staking their claim, only to discover unparalleled struggles. And with the arrival of foreign explorers, Lospe's people prayed they would survive the bloody battle that overshadowed the mother lode's glittering fortune.

Praise for Robert Easton

"I know of no author who has so successfully superimposed a modern consciousness on an ancient Indian one."
—Ruth Beebe Hill, author of
Hanta Yo

"Good writing of a kind that is difficult and rare."
—*New York Times*

"Drama in plenty."
—*San Francisco Chronicle*

"A clear narrative style and a sure sense of authenticity."
—*The New Yorker*

"Always engrossing." —*Chicago Tribune*